AN ARRANGED AFFAIR

She found him sitting in the shade of a cerasa fruit tree, munching on one of the crisp, sweet fruits. As she drew near, the breeder rose to his feet and rendered her a small bow. "Domina."

Shyly, she glanced up at him through her lashes. "And may I know *your* name?"

He scowled. "And what does it matter? I am not a person to you. I'm an object to use. You'd be wise to keep it impersonal. Makes for fewer pangs of conscience."

Meriel's head snapped up. She jerked her hand away. "You sound like you speak from experience. Is that how you plan to deal with me?"

"I will enjoy you," he growled, his glance raking her slender form. "It's difficult to mate without first doing so. But I don't delude myself there will be anything more than a physical release for me—and an impregnation for you."

D0499126

Firestar

KATHLEEN MORGAN

LOVE SPELL NEW YORK CITY

LOVE SPELL®

October 1993

Published by

Dorchester Publishing Co., Inc.
276 Fifth Avenue
New York, NY 10001

The name "Love Spell" and its logo are trademarks of Dorchester Publishing Co., Inc.

Printed in the United States of America.

To Patricia Coleman,
a dear friend and fellow writer
who has always been there for me.

Firestar

Prologue

The room looked like a battle station, the air tense with anticipation, a myriad of military documents strewn haphazardly about the huge, carved monstrosity of a table, the static of distant communications from the comvid crackling in the background. The room's three occupants, however, seemed oblivious to anything but the message spread out before them on the table.

"It's worse than I imagined," Teran Ardane muttered. "The rumors are fast becoming fact, and those facts place the Imperium in the gravest danger."

"By the five moons!" Brace Ardane slammed his fist on the table. "What else could I have done, Teran?"

His gaze lifted and locked with his older brother's. "Yet now, the destruction of the Knowing Crystal has exposed us to even greater threats

9

from abroad." He shook his head, his brow furrowed in thought. "The stone of power must have been the sole deterrent to the Volans all these hundreds of cycles. And now, in the Crystal's absence . . ."

Teran clasped him by the shoulder, his gray eyes warm with compassion. "You could do no less, Brace. No man of honor could. We'll just have to deal with the Volans as we did the Crystal—with all the power of our hearts and minds. But first, we must gather further information."

"And how do you propose we do that, Nephew?" King Falkan, ruler of the system of planets known as the Imperium, demanded, clamping down on his surge of frustration. "Though your and Brace's particular gifts with the Knowing Crystal stood you in good stead in the past, both in its rescue and eventual defeat, they'll be of little use against the Volans. We've yet to find a way to counteract their evil ability to take possession of unsuspecting beings and enslave their minds. It could be very dangerous, if not fatal, for anyone who got too inquisitive or too close to one of those aliens."

Teran turned. "I've sent for a friend, Uncle. A man who will bring back the answers we need. His name is Gage Bardwin."

"Bardwin!" The King scowled. "Of all the men to choose for the job! I don't understand him. Why would anyone in his right mind turn his back on a kingdom to take up the life of a bounty-hunting tracker? He's nothing more than an unprincipled renegade who lives on the edge of the law. I don't like the man—and never will!"

"But Gage is renowned for his special abilities," Teran calmly reminded him. "Abilities we desperately need. And, as far as his principles go, he'll give his loyalty to me. Trust that, if you trust nothing else."

Falkan sighed. Teran was right. They *were* getting desperate. "When will Bardwin arrive?"

"Soon, m'lord. Gage is transporting even now from an assignment on Cygnus. He should be here—"

A small tone sounded. King Falkan turned to the door. "Enter," he commanded, his broad shoulders squaring beneath his tunic of shimmering royal purple serica cloth.

The portal slid open soundlessly. A tall, powerfully built, dark blond man strode through. His piercing gaze scanned the room, halting when it alighted on Teran. The man's ruggedly handsome face creased in a broad grin.

"Well, what's it now, Ardane?" Gage Bardwin growled. "Each time you call on me the missions get a little more complicated, and a lot more dangerous. My usual fee won't do anymore. Whatever it is you want, it'll cost double."

Teran chuckled. "A fair enough price, my friend. Double of nothing is still . . . nothing." He strode over and extended his hand. They clasped, arm to arm, in the traditional Imperial greeting. "It's good to see you. The past months have set well with you."

Gage's mouth twisted wryly. "Have they now? Comes from living with a clean conscience, I'd wager. Keeps things simple for all concerned."

"Nothing's simple anymore, Bardwin," Brace said, stepping forward to clasp Gage's arm in greeting. "The Volans are on the move again, infiltrating the Imperium."

"Volans? Be damned!" The tracker's dark brown eyes riveted on the King. "When did this happen?"

"About three or four months ago," Falkan grimly replied. "As soon as the Knowing Crystal disappeared in the pools of Cambrai, whatever power that had kept the Volans at bay disappeared as well. The Crystal must have exerted some form of psychic influence over them, an influence obviously no longer in effect."

"What do you want from me?"

The King tensed at the blunt demand. Bardwin was far too imperious for his tastes, even if the man did come from stock as noble as his own house. He choked back a royal reprimand, reminding himself, once more, of the seriousness of their cause.

"We need a secret operative, someone capable of discovering their plans." Falkan indicated the documents scattered upon the table. "There have been reports they're already on Tenua."

"Tenua?" Gage frowned. "Yes, it *would* be the most logical place to infiltrate first. And a perfect way station between the Volans' galaxy and ours."

"You'll go to Tenua, then?" Falkan asked. "For the sake of the Imperium?"

Bardwin's roughly chiseled features hardened. "No. I won't do it for the Imperium. No amount of money is worth risking a Volan mind enslavement."

"I thought as much." Falkan's voice tautened with mounting anger. "Then why? Why did you bother to come?"

Brown eyes swung to meet those of gray. "I came because the only man I call friend asked me." Gage's glance locked with Teran's. "And, because *he* asked me, I'll go to Tenua and bring back the truth."

A slow grin of relief spread across the King's face. "Good. Then it's settled. And when you return from this mission, perhaps you'll at last claim your rightful place in House Bardwin. It's long past time . . ."

House Bardwin. A sudden wave of memories flooded Gage.

How long had it been since he'd thought about his boyhood home? Longing—unbidden, unwanted—welled in Gage's heart. Then the face of his mother intruded in his poignant musings. His beautiful mother, angry, disbelieving, screaming at him.

"You're a fool! A fool and a coward if you don't take what's rightfully yours!"

Gage shook the painful memories aside, the barriers rising once more about his heart. He had no home—not then, nor now.

He gestured toward the table. "Come, let's sit and map out a plan. The more time I waste here, the more difficult the mission becomes." He shot Falkan a meaningful glance. "And I've several far more lucrative offers going begging in the meanwhile."

Chapter One

"Strip him! Strip him naked! Let's have a look at what we're bidding on."

The strident female voice rose on the sweltering air, stirring a ripple of movement in the sullen, sweating crowd. All glanced in the woman's direction. Then, with a collective sigh, the people turned back to the huge raised platform in the city square.

"She's right," another female cried. "These males come too highly priced as it is. He's pretty enough, but we're not buying his looks. We're buying his breeding abilities. Strip him, I say!"

The auctioneer, a huge, hairy bear of a fellow, grumbled and mumbled to himself as he strode over to the bare-chested blond man pinned between two guards. "Damn them," he growled. "I'm a busy man and haven't the time to display each slave that passes through here."

He halted before the prisoner. Hard, dark brown eyes slammed into his. The auctioneer paused, startled by the savage look of warning. Then he grinned, his aterroot-stained teeth gleaming in the midday sun.

"You've only yourself to blame, you high-and-mighty off-worlder," he said to the man. "Strutting out here as cocky as you please, flaunting yourself before these women. You're lucky they don't swarm up here and tear you to pieces." His smile widened. "We had that happen once, you know."

The auctioneer's hands moved toward the prisoner's breeches. "Now, be sensible and don't give me any—"

A booted foot snapped out and upward, catching the auctioneer squarely in the groin. "Be damned!" Gage Bardwin snarled. "I'll not add to anyone's entertainment!"

With a whoosh of exhaled air, the big man clutched himself and sank to his knees. His face twisted in agony. For long seconds he knelt before Gage, breathing heavily. A stream of aterroot juice trickled down his chin to drip onto his shabby tunic.

Behind him, female voices rose to a wild shriek, a cacophony of primal excitement mixed with a growing bloodlust. "Strip him! Strip him! Teach the arrogant male a lesson!"

A small, scrawny man hurried over, nervous and perspiring profusely. He mopped his brow with the back of his sleeve, then grabbed at the auctioneer's arm, tugging him to his feet. "Get up, you fool! You should know better than to stand too close to a breeder."

He pulled the auctioneer out of harm's way, then motioned over four more guards. "Do whatever is necessary." He indicated the prisoner. "Just give the women what they ask. I want this one sold and out of here before he starts further trouble."

The guards advanced on Gage, all eyes riveted warily on his legs. He fought against the two men who held him, struggling to break free.

Helpless frustration welled up in Gage. Gods, what else could go wrong? Beryllium shackles bound his wrists and arms, he faced four men, and he was trapped on an unfriendly planet with no weapons or money.

Curse his lapse of vigilance in that tavern on Locare, the final transport station before Tenua! If he hadn't been so exhausted from a particularly long and difficult transport process, if he hadn't.imbibed one mug of Moracan ale too many or been so overly attentive to that seductive little barmaid, he'd have seen those off-world bounty hunters coming. But none of that mattered now. He'd been careless. He must extricate himself as best he could.

There was only one consolation. He *had* arrived at his destination, the capital of Eremita on the planet Tenua. He just wasn't in any position to do anything about it right—

With a shout, the extra guards rushed Gage en masse. Two leaped simultaneously for a leg. Another slipped behind to snake an arm about his neck and throttle him.

Gage fought wildly. He threw the full weight of his heavily muscled body first into one guard, then another. He managed to fling one man free of his right leg, then lashed out, kicking him full in the chest. The guard snapped backward, the wind knocked out of him.

Pivoting on his still encumbered leg, Gage kicked at the other man. Something flashed in his peripheral vision. A fist slammed into his jaw, then his gut.

The fourth guard.

Gage staggered backward, his knees buckling. Bright light exploded in his skull. Pain engulfed him. He battled past the agony, shaking his head to scatter the stars dancing before his eyes.

It was too late. The six men wrestled Gage to the platform, encasing him in a body lock he could only jerk against in impotent fury. His upper torso pinned, his legs held down in a spread-eagled position, Gage fought with all the strength left in him. Finally, as oxygen-starved limbs weakened, his powerful body could give no more. He lay there, panting in exhaustion, his face and chest sheened with sweat.

The sun beat down, its radiance blinding him. Gods, but it was hot on this hellish planet. So very hot. So draining . . . desolate.

A huge form moved to stand over him. "Proud, stupid off-worlder," the auctioneer snarled. "You'll pay dearly for your defiance before I'm done and satisfied, but first we'll give the women what they want."

He knelt between his prisoner's outspread legs. With a smirking grin, the man grasped the front of Gage's breeches and ripped them apart.

"No, damn you!" Gage roared. With a superhuman effort he reared up, sinews taut, muscles straining.

The guards' grips tightened, strangling the life from him. A swirling gray mist swallowed Gage. He fell back. At the sudden lack of resistance the guards' holds loosened.

Gage dragged in great gulps of air, fighting past the loss of consciousness, sick to the very marrow of his bones. Sick with his sense of helplessness, of defeat.

It didn't matter that they'd bared his body. What mattered was the implied submission of the act—the utter *subservience*. And he'd never, ever allowed another to use him without his express consent. Never, since that day he'd confronted his mother . . .

Rage swelled, white hot and searing. In a sudden, unexpected movement, Gage twisted to the side, dragging all six guards with him.

"Let . . . me . . . go!"

The endeavor took all he had. They quickly wrestled him back to the floor, slamming him down, crushing his head into the rough, splintered wood. Gage tasted his own blood, then his despair, bitter as gall.

"Damn you all! Let me go!" he cried again, choking the words past his sudden surge of nausea.

"Do as he says," a new voice, rich with authority, commanded. "Free him. Now."

The guards paused, looking up in surprise. The auctioneer glanced over his shoulder. With a strangled sound he released Gage, then climbed to his feet.

"Domina Magna," the man murmured, bowing

low to the woman who was Queen and ruler of the planet. "I—I am honored that the royal family chose to attend my humble sale."

"And why not?" the Queen's voice came again. "Haven't you some of the finest breeders in the Imperium? Now, get out of my way. Let us have a closer look at the male."

"As you wish, Domina Magna." The auctioneer stepped aside.

For a moment all Gage saw was color, a bright, vibrant swirl of crimsons, blues, and greens. Then the hues solidified into folds of shimmering, ultralight fabric, and the fabric into gowns. Gage levered himself to one elbow and glared up at the two women.

One was young, with glossy black hair tucked under a sheer veil and striking, deep violet eyes. She was dressed in a loose, bulky gown that completely disguised whatever figure she might have. At his direct scrutiny her lashes lowered. A becoming flush darkened her cheeks.

A maiden, Gage thought wryly, and as shy as they came.

He shifted to the other woman. She was equally striking—her ripe femininity blatantly accentuated by the voluptuous bosom thrusting from her low-cut, snugly molded dress. There was no doubt as to the quality of her figure.

She met his hard-eyed gaze and held it for a long moment before turning to her younger companion.

"Well, Daughter? Are you certain he's the one for you?" Her bold glance lowered to Gage's groin. "Your maiden's flesh will be sorely tried by a man such as he. And he strikes me as none too gentle, if his antics a few seconds ago are any indication."

"Mother, please." The girl bit her lip, turning nearly as crimson as her gown. Her hesitant gaze lifted, meeting Gage's for an instant before skittering away to slide down the tautly sculpted, hair-roughened planes of his body.

The girl's eyes halted at the gaping vee of his breeches. A river of dark hair arrowed straight down from his flat belly to a much denser nest and the hint of a large, thick organ before disappearing beneath the torn cloth. She swallowed hard, dragging her gaze back to her mother's.

"H-he couldn't help it. His pride was at stake. He had to fight them."

A slender brow arched in amusement. "Did he now? I think the sisters at our royal nunnery filled your head with too many tales of days long past. Days when men still possessed some shred of gentleness and integrity. And I think," the Queen said as she took her daughter's arm and began to lead her away, "that I called you back to your royal duties none too soon."

"Mother. Wait." The girl dug in her heels.

"Yes, child?"

"May I have him or not? You said it was my choice."

The Queen eyed her daughter, then sighed. "Yes, you may have him if your heart is set. The law dictates that you take a breeder before commencing a royal life mating. But heed my words. You'll regret it. He's not the male for you."

She glanced at the auctioneer. "We'll take him,"

she said, indicating Gage. "Have him sent to the palace immediately."

"Er, pardon, Domina Magna." The small, scrawny man stepped forward.

"Yes?"

"This is an especially high-quality breeder. He'll cost extra."

The Queen's lips tightened. "How much extra?"

"Five thousand imperials."

Her nostrils flared. "No breeder, not even one for a Royal Princess of Corba, is worth that much! I'll give you two thousand and not an imperial more!"

"But, Domina Magna—"

"Enough!" The woman held up a silencing hand. "Another word and I'll forget I'm your queen and simply confiscate the male." She smiled thinly. "And everything else you possess as well."

"As you wish, Domina Magna," the little man croaked, bowing and backing away. "The breeder will be delivered immediately."

Triumph gleamed in the Queen's eyes. "Good. See that he is."

"You will mate with my daughter and impregnate her. An easy task, I'm sure, for a breeder of your quality," Queen Kadra proclaimed, leaning back with an air of finality in her ornately gilded throne.

"Indeed?" Gage Bardwin drawled.

The woman glared down at the prisoner, her patience at an end. Though still bound and ensconced between two burly guards, the man was as defiant as he'd been on the auctioneer's platform.

Obviously, more drastic measures were needed to ensure his cooperation.

She motioned to the guards. "Leave us."

At the order, Gage arched a dark brow. His lips twisted in cynical amusement.

Kadra waited until they were alone. "Have you had an opportunity to observe my palace?" She indicated the room with a regal sweep of her bejeweled hand.

Gage shrugged. "It appears adequate."

"*Adequate?*" Kadra nearly choked on the word. "It's *impregnable*, both from within and from without." Her smoldering gaze met his. "There is no hope of escape."

He eyed her, knowing there was more to come.

"You will service my daughter and impregnate her, or you will die. It's that simple."

"Is it now?"

Gage slowly surveyed the room. She was right. This chamber was just as heavily fortified as the rest of the palace. The doors and windows were barricaded by a sturdy grillwork of what looked to be a beryllium-impregnated alloy. Not even a laser gun could cut through that metal. The exterior walls were of solid rock and several feet thick. Add to that the highly complex video monitoring system Gage had noticed in his journey through the palace, and escape seemed a near impossibility.

He clamped down on a surge of angry frustration and turned back to the Queen. "And what's wrong with your own men, that you must turn to an off-worlder for breeding purposes? Especially for your own daughter?"

The Queen's grip on her chair tightened. "Tenuan men are not the issue here. I have given you a command. The consequences are clear. What is your decision?"

Gage's eyes narrowed. Damn her. She held the advantage—at least for now—and she knew it.

He was on a mission of vital importance. The issue of his pride, no matter how dearly cherished, paled in light of the threat of Volan infiltration. And there *were* potential benefits to stalling for time, for being in the Tenuan royal palace. Information could be gleaned, conversations overheard . . .

"She's a pretty one, your daughter," Gage said, conceding the Queen a temporary victory. "What's her name?"

A smile glimmered on Kadra's lips. "Meriel. Do I take this to mean you accept my terms?"

"A mating with your lovely daughter in exchange for my freedom?" Gage nodded. "In reality, I win all the way around. How soon do you require my services?"

"My daughter's fertile time spans this very day. You will be bathed, dressed more appropriately, then taken to her. I expect several matings to assure your seed is properly planted. Do you understand me?"

Gods, there went his opportunity for leisure to explore the palace. Well, the girl herself might be the best source of information anyway. He nodded. "Yes. And on the morrow I am free to go?"

"But of course. There will be no further need for you."

"No, I'd imagine not." Gage paused. "Is there

anything I need to know about your daughter? To ease the 'wooing,' as it were?"

Kadra bristled at the barely veiled sarcasm. The insolent bastard! But why should she be surprised? Bellatorians were all alike—arrogant, unfeeling, and endlessly belittling of Tenua and all things Tenuan. It was exactly that attitude that had finally prodded her to cut her planet off from the rest of the Imperium. She'd be damned if she'd grovel and beg for the few crumbs of support that the Bellatorian-led, exalted organization of planets deigned to toss her way.

Meanwhile, she'd deal with this particular Bellatorian as she saw fit, the only possible outcome his death. Kadra smiled grimly. She'd take great pleasure in seeing this breeder die as painfully as possible. She had enough problems without being forced to tolerate his arrogance.

"Meriel is gently reared, having just completed her girlhood training at the royal nunnery. She knows little of men. You will treat her with care and not subject her to any crudities. And you will be constantly monitored, so don't think I won't know what you do or say."

"Even our mating?" Gage inquired dryly. "Will you be privy to that as well?"

The Queen's eyes narrowed. "I owe you no explanation of what I will or will not do. You're a breeder, not a compatriot. Use your body and use it well. That's what I bought you for."

Her hand moved to a small button inset in the arm of her chair. Two guards stepped through the door and strode over to stand on either side of Gage.

"Go with them," Kadra ordered. "Our audience is over until I wish it again. They will prepare you, then take you to my daughter."

Gage turned to leave when the Queen once more halted him.

"Breeder."

He stiffened, then slowly glanced back.

"Heed me and heed me well. Shame my daughter, and you shame me. Hurt her, and you hurt me. And I don't suffer arrogance or cruelty well. The Imperium learned that long ago." She smiled, a hard, bitter look gleaming in her eyes. "Remember that, breeder."

"It is time, Meriel. He awaits you."

The softly spoken words penetrated Meriel's dejected survey of the palace gardens. With a small sigh, the girl turned from her bedchamber window to face her maidservant and friend. "I know, Dian. But now that the moment is upon me, I'm so afraid. I don't know how to act, what to do. How *does* one compel a male to mate?"

The other girl's lips tightened and a look of intense concentration furrowed her brow. "It's said a male enjoys the sight of a female's naked body. You could disrobe before him. From what you've told me, this breeder will know what to do from there."

"Right out in the middle of the garden? Oh, I'd die of the shame!"

"Silly little cerva!" Dian strode over to grasp Meriel by the shoulders. "Of course not right in the middle of the garden. Find some secluded spot, like the water grotto. The moss flowers are thick and soft beside the pool. Or bring him up here, to your bed."

Meriel forced a wan, trembling little smile. "I'm sorry if I seem such a fool. But so much has happened in this past month since we left the nunnery. My formal betrothal to Prince Pelum, the commencement of my royal duties, and now . . . this."

"The Queen never said you needed to breed a child the first month you returned home, Meriel. You could still change your mind, ask for more time before taking a breeder. Surely your mother would understand."

"Yes, I suppose she would, but what would be the sense of waiting? Times are hard. My mother needs a daughter who knows her duty and does it, not some weak little coward afraid of her own shadow. No good will come of delaying the inevitable."

"You aren't a weak little coward, Meriel Corba!" her friend cried. "I've grown up with you all these cycles, seen your goodness and courage, day after day. But this loveless mating with a stranger! It would sicken anyone!"

"It's my duty, Dian. I must carry a child before I can ever hope to take a royal husband. And I cannot become queen until I have borne that child." Meriel's eyes lowered. "Some good will come of it. I will have earned the right to wed Pelum. I will have a babe."

"Indeed you will. And I confess to a great anticipation of holding the little one, of helping you care for it. We will have such fun, won't we?"

"Yes, we will." Meriel smiled, a soft light glowing in her eyes. "To have such joy is well worth the purchase price." She paused. "The breeder. Do you think he'll find me desirable? That he'll mate with me?"

Dian's glance swept over her friend and she shook her head in loving exasperation. What male wouldn't find Meriel desirable? Even her betrothed, though as impotent as all other Tenuan males, still looked at her friend with hungry, tormented eyes. Meriel was exquisite, from her flawless skin and violet eyes to her shimmering long black hair, thick lashes, and full, rosy lips. And her slender form, though still lacking the ripe curves of mature womanhood, promised a figure as provocative as her mother's in but a few more cycles.

Yet as physically lovely as Meriel was, it was her goodness, her innocence, her exuberant love of life that added the final, irresistible touch to her vibrant beauty. There was a fire in Meriel, a certain strength not yet fully tapped, that promised the woman she would soon become. A woman twice the person her mother was—and, someday, twice the queen.

Dian released Meriel's shoulders and took her hand. "Come, my friend. By the next sunrise it will all be over. You'll have fulfilled your duty and need never see this breeder again. You can turn away forever from the memories of what he does to you, forget he ever existed, and face the future, a future bright with promise, with the man you love."

"A future with the dearest friend a girl could ever hope to have," Meriel whispered, squeezing

Dian's hand. "Come, walk with me till we reach the garden."

Hand in hand, the two girls turned and left the room.

She found him sitting in the shade of a cerasa fruit tree, munching on one of the crisp, sweet fruits. As she drew near, he rose to his feet.

The breeder swallowed one last bite when Meriel halted before him, then tossed the half-eaten fruit aside. He rendered her a small bow. "Domina."

Meriel inhaled a deep breath and extended her hand. "Please, you may call me Meriel. It hardly seems appropriate to be so formal, considering. . . ." Her voice faded and she blushed.

The breeder cocked a dark brow, then accepted her hand. "Considering the intimacies we'll share? Is that what you meant to say, Meriel?"

Meriel's blush deepened. She dipped her head. "Yes. I suppose so."

Shyly, she glanced up at him through her lashes. "And may I know *your* name?"

He scowled. "And what does it matter? I'm not a person to you. I'm an object to use. You'd be wise to keep it impersonal. Makes for fewer pangs of conscience."

Meriel's head snapped up. She jerked her hand away. "You sound like you speak from experience. Is that how you plan to deal with me?"

"I will enjoy you," he growled, his glance raking her slender form. "It's difficult to mate without first doing so. But I don't delude myself there will be anything more than a physical release for me—and an impregnation for you."

She forced herself to return his steely gaze. "Nonetheless, you're a human being. I would still like to know your name."

"Little fool." He pulled her to him, twisting her arm to pin it behind her back. Angry eyes, darkened to blackest onyx, glared down at her. "My name is Gage."

For a fleeting moment, pressed into the hard planes of his body, all thought fled. Meriel gazed up at him, mesmerized by his maleness, his musky scent, the sudden heat that flared between them. He was tall, towering over her by at least a full head, his broad shoulders straining the dark green fabric of the sleeveless tunic he now wore. The tunic's vee neckline dipped low in front, halfway down his abdomen, revealing his hair-whorled, deeply bronzed skin and bulge of muscle.

As Meriel watched the rise and fall of his chest, his breathing accelerated. Something hard swelled against her, pressing where the juncture of his thighs met her belly. Startled, Meriel lifted her gaze to his.

Gage's eyes scorched through her, hot, hungry and dangerous. A slight flush colored his tanned skin. His mouth was set in a grim smile that hinted of bitter secrets, tightly guarded emotions.

Unnerved, Meriel scanned the rest of his face, hoping the distraction might calm the sudden pounding of her heart. His dark blond hair was thick, dipping forward onto his broad forehead, curling downward to the back of his neck. His features were roughly chiseled, his jaw shadowed with the stubble of a beard. Yet, as bruised and abraded as he still was from his earlier scuffle with the auction guards, Meriel found him handsome.

As she stared up at Gage, a strange new emotion shivered through her. A feeling of . . . attraction. A desire to touch him, to give him solace. To make him laugh, to share with him the wonder and the joy of life.

Yet it could never be. Though she now knew his name, he was still nothing more than a breeder. No matter what she might wish to the contrary, he could serve no other purpose.

Suddenly the air around Meriel seemed too heavy and close. A lightheaded sensation engulfed her. She could barely breathe. "Please," she gasped, shoving at his chest to put some distance between them. "I-I . . . let me go!"

He loosened his hold only slightly. "What's wrong, sweet femina? Am I too crude for your delicate sensibilities? Do you require a courtship of flowers and eloquent words to stir your desires? Tell me what you need. I am but a simple breeder, after all, and only seek to please."

"Stop it!" Meriel twisted free and took several steps back. "You make a mockery of this—and of us—with your sarcasm!"

"Do I now?"

"Y-yes!" she replied, tears welling in her eyes. "You do. And I-I don't like it!"

Gage scowled. Gods, what else could go wrong? In another second the girl would begin to wail and surely bring her irate mother down on his head. She must indeed desire the semblance of a courtship. Gage swallowed a frustrated curse. Maidens!

"I beg pardon for my crudeness," he said, running a hand through his hair with a quick, frustrated motion. "I meant no harm. I assumed you found our mating offensive and wanted this over quickly."

"I *do* find this offensive and want it over quickly," Meriel gulped, swiping away a traitorous tear.

"Then why did you choose me, if you find me so repulsive?"

She paused, confused by his question. "Repulsive? I don't find you repulsive. And as far as why I chose you, it's too complicated to explain."

Gage motioned to the ground beneath the tree. "Sit. We have time. Complicated or no, I'd like to hear your reason."

Meriel hesitated. "I don't understand. How would that help?"

He grasped her arm, gently tugging her down with him. "You need time to feel comfortable with me. Talking will help."

They sat beside each other for a long while, neither speaking. Meriel plucked an arosa flower from a low-growing bush and lifted it to her nose. She inhaled deeply of its delicate perfume, allowing the fragrance to inundate her and soothe her ragged nerves.

Long, strong fingers captured hers, seizing the arosa and drawing it away. In the next instant Gage touched its silken petals to Meriel's face, stroking the flower down from temple to jaw with a light, featherlike motion. The sensation tickled, yet stirred her all the same. Meriel's heart fluttered beneath her breast. Her mouth went dry.

She turned, her luminous eyes wide with surprise. Her lips parted, full and soft and sweet.

Gage's heart skipped a beat. A familiar sensation tightened his groin and, once again, he grew hard.

Gods, what was this girl doing to him, with her maiden's innocence, her need to find a dignity, a humanity in this forced mating? Or was it instead some sort of act, a seductive game? He had to know.

Gage trailed the arosa across her face, grazing her mouth, then encircled its rosy, pouting curves. He lowered his head, intent on replacing the flower with his lips.

Meriel stiffened. She drew away. "Don't."

He sighed and leaned back. "If you loathe everything I do, even to touching you with a flower and attempting a simple kiss, how are we ever to mate? The act requires—"

"I know what the act requires!" Meriel snapped, stung by·his tone of weary frustration. "You needn't lecture me as if I were some ignorant child."

"Then what would you have me do, Meriel? If this is to succeed, you must meet me halfway."

"I know." Her head dipped and her dark hair cascaded down to hide her face. "It wasn't because I loathe you that I asked you to stop."

"Then why?" He crooked a finger under her chin and lifted her gaze to his. "Why, Meriel?"

She jerked her head away, her lips tightening. "It doesn't matter. It has no bearing on why we're here."

Gage's features hardened. "No, I suppose it doesn't."

Damn her. There she went again with her little games. He hadn't the time or patience for seducing a maiden intent on plying her new-found feminine wiles. Why couldn't she lie back and just let him take her, get this over with?

He tossed the flower into her lap. "I ask you again, Meriel. Why did you choose me?"

Meriel tensed at the sudden harshness in his voice. What was he so angry about?

She picked up the arosa flower and sniffed it again, not meeting his gaze. "I had to choose someone. When I saw you fighting the guards, them beating you, and knew they meant to strip you naked, it seemed so cruel, so unfair. You were a human being, after all, and deserved better than that. And . . . and you fought so hard, as if something would die in you if they succeeded."

Her eyes met his. "My heart went out to you. In a way, your plight was like mine—forced into something you didn't want. I suppose I thought to at least spare you the pain . . . the shame."

He studied her intently, his eyes capturing and holding hers. For the first time, Meriel noted the golden lights that danced there. For the first time, she saw something else in their dark, mesmerizing depths—something besides the hard, guarded bitterness. Her mouth went dry.

"Why, Meriel?" his deep voice rasped. "Why are you being forced to mate with me? You're a royal princess. You, above all others, should be permitted to take a husband, not some off-world breeder, to give you a child."

She blinked once, twice, calling herself back to the reality that Gage's question demanded. Her smooth brow furrowed in puzzlement. "You don't know? My mother didn't explain?"

"No."

Uncertainty clouded her eyes. "Then perhaps I shouldn't say . . ."

Gage took her hand, pulling her to him. "Meriel, it won't change what I must do, but it would help me understand the reason why. And perhaps bring a little honor to this mating—for both of us."

A sad smile curved her lips. "Honor," she murmured. "There's been little of that for a long while now. And most especially for our men . . ."

"What's wrong with your men, Meriel?"

She sighed, then squarely met his gaze. "They're impotent, all of our high-born males for the past seventy or eighty cycles, and now, gradually, the affliction is beginning to affect them all."

"Why? What's happening?"

Meriel's gaze lifted to the sky, to the giant red orb blazing overhead. "Firestar. Our sun is dying. And, somehow, the plight of our men is tied to its death."

Chapter Two

Puzzlement furrowed Gage's brow. "Your dying star has made your men sterile?"

Meriel sighed. "We're not certain how it all came about. Our scientists are still working on the problem. Somehow, though, the gradual dimming of Firestar's brightness has affected our males, lowering their reproductive potency."

"And that is why you've turned to 'importing' off-world males to service your women," Gage drawled, finishing for her. "To keep the planet alive, as it were."

A pair of penetrating eyes ensnared hers. "Though I find it hard to appreciate this enforced servitude," he continued, "I can understand the motives behind it. Desperate people resort to desperate measures."

Uneasiness skittered through Meriel. Suddenly she didn't like the course of the conversation. And didn't like, as well, the burgeoning emotions the

handsome breeder stirred in her. Emotions her
mother had warned should never be allowed into
this necessary but crude mating to procreate the
race. But Gage's willingness to go slowly with her,
his compassionate insight into the plight of her
people, touched something deep within Meriel.

Touched her so deeply, so unexpectedly, so shat-
teringly that she knew, with a certainty sprung
from some secret innermost part of her, that
she would never, ever forget him. At the realization, a savage pain slashed through her. It
wasn't fair! Beneath that gruff, hardened exterior, Meriel knew Gage was a good, decent man.
He didn't deserve to be treated like this. And neither did she.

Yet there was no other recourse. For the sake
of her people, she must produce an heir. For the
sake of her people, she must wed a royal prince
and uphold tradition. For the sake of her people,
she must use this man like some breeding animal, his seed, not his heart, the only thing of
consequence.

The pangs of her conscience, the ache in her
heart over her coldly calculated use of him,
had never been the issue, either. In times such
as these, devotion to the law was all that
mattered, unquestioning obedience vital to her
peoples' sense of continuity and stability. There
was so little else that could be counted on
these days.

Yet, it was still so unfair . . .

A painful lump of desolation swelled in Meriel's
throat. She swallowed hard, shoving it down. With
a deep breath, she reached for her resolve, drawing

it about her like a garment . . . like a coat of armor
to gird her for what was to come. She tossed the
arosa flower away.

Meriel squarely met his gaze. "Come. You've
courted me long enough. It's time we see this
mating done."

Gage's lips twisted in amusement. "Indeed?
And to what do I owe this sudden burst of
passion?"

"Does it matter?" She rose and extended her
hand. "You *are* ready, aren't you?"

He chuckled. Refusing her hand, Gage climbed
to his feet. His gaze dipped to the rounded full-
ness of her breasts, lingering there until a curious
excitement strummed through her.

"More than ready, sweet femina," he finally
replied, his deep voice rich with meaning. "I but
await your pleasure."

Meriel flushed angrily. Curse the man. As hard
as she tried to keep a cool distance, to maintain
control of the situation, he invariably found some
way to unnerve her.

"Fine." She gestured toward the far end of the
garden. "There's a grotto with a hot spring. We'll
go there."

As they made their way across the garden, Gage
eyed her closely. Meriel's lips were clamped in
a determined line, her shoulders squared, her
stride resolute. If not for the flush that washed
her creamy skin in pale strokes of rose, if not
for the rapid flutter of the pulse in the hollow
of her throat, he'd have thought her a regal ice
maiden. But Gage's skills of observation were far
too acute, too well-honed by cycles of tracking,

not to realize the significance of such signs.

Meriel was clearly upset, and, one way or another, he was the cause. For a crazy, irrational moment, the thought gladdened him. She wasn't indifferent. Far from it.

Quickly, almost violently, Gage shoved aside the pleasant speculations that that realization stirred up. He was here on a mission and, ultimately, it wasn't one of seduction. He must remember that and keep his head about him at all costs.

Meriel halted at a small stone cave. Set in a low rise of land, its opening was small for a man of Gage's size. To enter, he was forced to duck his head. Only as the path began to lead downward was he finally able to straighten to his full height.

The narrow passage gradually widened, opening into a long, high-ceilinged room hewn out of solid rock. Artfully recessed perpetual lights illuminated the grotto, bathing the chamber with a soft, muted glow. A small pool, enveloped in steam, lay at the back of the room, its center bubbling with an erupting jet of superheated water. Wide expanses of rich, grasslike vegetation interspersed with thick cushions of fragrant moss flowers lined the pool on three sides. Moisture coated the walls, dripping off the ceiling to splatter soundlessly back into the gently agitated waters.

Gage grinned. "A perfect place for a romantic interlude." A speculative look gleamed in his eyes. "Have you perhaps shared it with some other lover?"

Meriel nearly choked in her outrage. What did he think she was, to have purposely brought him here like some . . . some alley walker! Ah, the insult, the shame!

Her hands clenched at her sides, and an urge to slap that knowing smirk off his face flooded her. Her hand lifted before Meriel caught herself. She stared at the open palm, amazed at her intent. She had never, *ever* raised her voice to another, much less wanted to strike someone! By all that was sacred, what was this man doing to her?

"Think what you want of me," she muttered, refusing to meet his gaze until she'd once more mastered herself. "If the grotto pleases you, it has served its purpose."

Gage pulled her to him. "And will it please you as well, sweet femina?"

With a frantic motion, Meriel jerked away. "What will please me is an end to this charade of tender words and false concern for my feelings. You don't care one way or another, so stop pretending you do!"

A fierce-burning fire flared in his eyes. "And how can you say that, *sweet* femina? Why, I care as much as you. Surely that's enough."

She stared up at him for a long, anguished moment. "I-I beg pardon," Meriel forced herself to reply. "There was no reason for my cruel outburst, save my maiden's nervousness. And, in answer to your original question, no, I've never shared this pool with any other man."

Her lashes dipped to settle against her high cheekbones in a seductive, ebony fan. "You are the first, the only lover I will ever have."

Gage's heart pounded a staccato rhythm. He stepped close until they stood a hairsbreadth apart, wanting yet suddenly afraid to touch her. Knowing that if he did, he risked total loss of control—and the loss of a part of him even more precious and fiercely guarded.

He struggled for something, anything, to say that would divert the course of the conversation and distract him from the heady effect Meriel was having upon him. The recollection of his mission flashed across his mind. Gage grasped at it like a drowning man.

"Why didn't you ask the Imperium for aid?" he blurted, desperately turning the conversation back to the safer topic of Tenua. "There are men aplenty who'd offer their assistance in such an exalted undertaking as providing stud services."

Meriel frowned. What in the world was the man talking about? She shrugged. Whatever his motives, better to humor him and then get on with the real issues at hand.

She smiled bitterly. "Ah, yes. The Imperium. And when has that union of planets ever shown interest, or even one shred of concern, for Tenua's welfare? We long ago ceased to hope for anything from them."

"The Imperium was once a tightly united entity," Gage was quick to offer, relieved that Meriel had so cooperatively entered into the conversation, "where one planet's problems were the problem of all. But that was before the Knowing Crystal."

Meriel's lips pursed in exasperation. "It matters not what caused the disunity. What matters is that Firestar is dying. It will go supernova in the not too distant future. In the meanwhile, its death throes affect more than the fertility of our race. Firestar's rising heat will soon make life here untenable."

The memory of the Tenuan sun burned brightly in Gage's mind. Though considerably dimmer than the yellow or blue-white stars of most other Imperial planets, a red sun was still capable of sustaining life for thousands of cycles. But now, with Firestar on an inevitable course of internal collapse and catastrophic destruction, the danger to the inhabitants of Tenua grew with each passing day. A planet-wide evacuation was imperative. Why hadn't King Falkan mentioned this in his pre-mission briefing? Was the planet's death incidental to the Imperium-wide Volan threat?

A sudden thought struck Gage. Was this why the Volans had chosen Tenua for its initial infiltration point? It was well known that the alien mind slavers vastly preferred a planet similar to their own fiery home environment. Tenua would soon be theirs—either with the evacuation of the original inhabitants or from their death as the sun's rising heat slowly sucked the planet dry of life. Until Firestar finally exploded, the planet was the perfect way station into the rest of the Imperium.

The Tenuans, distracted with their own mounting concerns, would be easy prey for the Volans. Though no one was as yet certain how the aliens entered a host—or, more importantly, how to ascertain when a being was possessed by a mind slaver—the growing danger could not be ignored. Any day now, the Imperium would have the answers. In the meanwhile, some sort of plan to combat the Volans must be implemented. And now there was the added problem of what to do about the Tenuans.

Gage sighed. The Ardanes wouldn't be pleased with the information he'd be bringing back. Not pleased at all.

He forced his attention back to Meriel. "And what plans has your mother made regarding the evacuation of Tenua? Moving an entire planet's population is a monumental undertaking."

She couldn't quite meet his gaze. She had already revealed too much. "The Queen is considering her options. But that hardly concerns us, does it?" Her deep violet eyes lifted. "Does it?"

At the husky purr in her voice, Gage smiled. It was a typical female ploy to turn a male back to the true purpose at hand. But it no longer bothered him. He was calm once more, totally in control, and he'd discovered quite enough for the moment.

"No, femina," he replied huskily. "It doesn't really concern us."

Taking her hand, Gage turned it over and slowly, sensuously, kissed her palm. At his touch, Meriel started. She tried to pull away.

Gage glanced up, his look smoldering, languorous. "Don't, sweet femina. You are right. It's past time we embark on what we came together for. You know that as well as I."

His tongue emerged to caress the gentle swells and hollows of her palm. "Don't you, Meriel?"

"Y-yes," she whispered.

A tremor coursed through her as his soft, warm lips trailed past her wrist to the creamy smooth skin of her forearm. The brush of his mouth tickled, stimulating strange new sensations all the while. Sensations that stirred something hot and aching. She inhaled a shuddering breath.

"P-please, Gage. I . . . I . . ."

His head lifted. "What is it, Meriel? The time is past for talk."

The deep rasp of his voice prickled down her spine. Meriel swallowed hard. By all that was sacred, but she wanted him!

The realization startled her. He was a breeder, a stranger. She knew nothing about him. Yet in the short span they'd been together in the garden, her feelings for the handsome prisoner had encompassed the gamut of fear, frustration, compassion, then attraction—and now, a fevered desire. Was this a typical feminine response to a male? If so, why had she never experienced such feelings for Pelum?

Meriel shook the traitorous thought away. It was the mating urge, nothing more, an emotion that poor, dear Pelum, through no fault of his own, would never be able to stir.

And it didn't matter. He was her betrothed, would someday rule at her side. He was a good, gentle, loving man. A man who'd been raised as exactingly as she to devote his life to Tenua's welfare.

Pelum was the man of her heart and soul. As coldly calculating as it might be, she must allow this breeder named Gage to touch only her body, and that just for the briefest moment in time.

"What would you have me do?" Meriel said, forcing the words through a tightly constricted throat. "Just tell me and I will do it."

He gestured toward the pool. "Though I've had a bath, suddenly I find I want another. Would you care to join me?"

Meriel stood there, frozen in indecision, as Gage proceeded to strip off his tunic and boots. Only the movement of his hands toward the waistband of his breeches was enough to finally stir her to action. She stopped him.

"I don't understand. Why do you desire another bath? I thought we were here—"

He moved to stand before her, his smile gentle. "Trust me, Meriel. This is all part of the seduction."

She gave a nervous, strident laugh. "The seduction? But shouldn't I be the one seducing you?"

"Ah, but you *are* seducing me, sweet femina. Have no fear of that."

"Oh," was all she breathed as his hands lifted to the neck of her gown.

Her heart pounding beneath her breast, Meriel allowed Gage to unfasten the front of the garment, stood there as he slipped it from her shoulders, though she clenched her hands into tight little fists at her side. A moment later Meriel was all but naked in her sheer undershift. She glanced down at herself and blushed. Her fingers moved to tug frantically at the low neckline that generously exposed her firm, jutting breasts.

"Meriel, sweet femina," Gage said, capturing her hands. "It's past time for modesty between us. You are beautiful. Let me look at you."

He held her hands far out at her sides, his glance raking her body. Fire, then ice, then fire surged through her. She couldn't bear to meet his gaze. She couldn't breathe. She thought she'd die right there from the shame.

"Look at me, Meriel," he commanded, his deep voice thick with some strange new emotion. "Look at me."

Her eyes lifted in wary hesitation. Lifted, and were snared by hard, hot ones of deepest brown. Hungry eyes, full of a mesmerizing desire that sparked an answering response in Meriel.

He wanted her! Not because it was his duty as a breeder. Not because she was an available female or a royal princess. He wanted *her*, Meriel Corba, maiden though she was.

The realization thrilled her, flooding Meriel with a curious sense of elation and anticipation. He would be careful with her, kind, that she now knew. And how she wanted him, wanted to know the ecstasy between a man and a woman, for one single, precious day in her life.

She moved until her body touched his. Her mouth lifted, offering lips full and ripe and eager. She tried to free her hands, intending to entwine them about Gage's neck.

He wouldn't release her. Instead, he pulled her arms around to her back, capturing her in the embrace of his arms.

"So you want to be kissed, do you?" he rasped, pressing the full length of his hard-muscled body into hers. Her soft breasts were crushed against his hair-roughened chest. Heat flared between them.

"Yes," Meriel said, mortified at her boldness, yet proud as well. "I want that, and so much more."

"Then open for me," Gage ordered in a raw, savage whisper. "Open, and I'll give you more than you could ever dream of."

His head bent. His lips devoured hers in a fierce, hard, utterly uncompromising kiss. For the briefest moment, panic engulfed Meriel. He was too much, too big, too aggressive for her. She *had* to get away!

Then reason—or was it something else?—returned. Meriel lifted on tiptoe, meeting and equaling his hungry, aching attack. His mouth slammed down on hers, grinding her lips against her teeth. His tongue prodded for entry.

"Open for me, Meriel," Gage growled. "Give it all to me. Your mouth, your body, your passion."

"Y-yes! Please!" she gasped, the sound a startled entreaty.

He plunged in then, taking possession, thrusting, licking, sucking her tongue, then moving to delve even more deeply into her sweet, secret recesses. A mounting passion rose in Gage. Gods, but he couldn't seem to get enough of this delectable girl!

He jerked her more tightly to him, grinding his engorged shaft against her. She tensed at the strange new feel of him, a maiden's seeming instinctual response, then pressed against his full length in unabashed delight.

Once again, Gage thought he would lose control. Never had a female affected him so strongly, so potently, as this sweet, innocently passionate girl! He shoved Meriel back, fighting to master himself.

"Gage?" she murmured, her soft voice piercing the heavy mists of his desire. "What's wrong? Did I . . . did I do something to offend you?"

He raised passion-drugged eyes. "No, sweet femina. On the contrary, you've done everything right. But I want this to be as pleasurable for you as it is for me. And this is suddenly going far too fast for the both of us."

In a quick movement of hands, Gage divested himself of his breeches to stand before her, magnificent in his nakedness. Meriel's eyes lowered for a brief moment to the huge, thick organ jutting from his body, then jerked up to meet his. She blushed again. "Did I . . . ? Am I . . . responsible . . . ?"

"For my hardened body?" Gage couldn't help but smile. "Yes, femina. You most certainly are. Does that please you?"

She hesitated, then squared her shoulders, faced him—and the truth. "Yes, it does. Your need for me is the final confirmation of my womanhood."

Gage took her hand and drew her across the grass to the pool. "No, sweet Meriel. Your body's acceptance of mine when we finally join is the confirmation. Your cry of ecstasy when you find your release will be the confirmation. Then, and only then, are you at last a woman."

Meriel drew back at the water's edge. An impish smile glimmered on her lips. "And when is your manhood at last confirmed?"

He stepped down into the pool, then turned, reaching up for her. "Mine? Why, I confirm it each time I bring a woman to her release, each time I share her pleasure."

Her hands stayed his attempt to pull her into the water. "And have there been many women in your life? Many who have assisted in the confirmation of your wondrous manhood?"

For an instant something dark and memory-laden flashed across his face. "Many, sweet Meriel, but never one like you."

She smiled archly, enjoying what she imagined as their little game. "You mouth such clever, honeyed words. I see why you've been so successful in the past."

Anger flushed his roughly chiseled features, then was gone. Grasping her about the waist, Gage pulled Meriel down into the pool and jerked her to him. Before she could do more than gasp in surprise his mouth covered hers, slanting brutally.

She fought back against him, her small fists pounding at his head, then slipping between their bodies to scratch and push at his broad chest. But it was all for naught. Meriel's strength waned rapidly, subdued by the immense power of the man who held her. Finally, she sighed in defeat and slumped against him, allowing Gage to kiss her as he would.

Her fists opened, her fingers splaying out through the dense sea of hair that swirled across his chest. Her hands trailed up to clutch at his broad, sinew-threaded shoulders, then moved to entwine behind his neck. Her slender body pressed into his.

"Gage," she moaned when he drew back momentarily for breath. "Please. I don't understand. Why are you angry at me?"

"Angry with such a delicious morsel as you in my arms? How is that possible?" His dark eyes, glittering down at her, belied his words. "Do you take me for a fool?"

"No, never a fool," she whispered achingly. "Then have I hurt you instead?"

"Hurt me?" Gage's brittle laugh cut through the air, its echo a hollow sound off the moisture-laden walls. "There's no woman alive who can hurt me."

Even as he spoke, Meriel saw the barriers fall back in place, barriers that had briefly lifted in the moments when their passion burned brightest. Once again Gage was a bitter, guarded man. The man she had first met.

Confusion swelled in her. What had happened? What had she done or said to change things between them?

Her mind raced. Was it her tiny jest about his clever words with women? The implication that he didn't take his relationships seriously? Meriel searched his face, a face once more implacably set in stone. A face that she now found devastatingly, heartbreakingly handsome. A face that was rapidly growing very dear.

Remorse flooded Meriel. She had indeed offended Gage in her foolish attempt to extract assurance of a similar measure of affection from him. She had been selfish and unwittingly cruel, indulging in a game neither had any hope of winning. A game she possessed neither the experience nor the cold manipulativeness to play.

Meriel sighed. When it came to males, she would never equal her mother. And never hoped to, if the truth be known.

"I . . . I am sorry if I belittled your earlier comments," she began, blinking back the tears.

Gage's mouth quirked wryly, but the guarded look remained. "And what comments were those?"

"You said there was no woman ever like me." Meriel swallowed hard, then forced herself to go on. "You meant it as a compliment, didn't you?"

He shrugged. "Did I? Truly, femina, you shouldn't take everything a male says so seriously. When it comes to procuring a mating partner, a man will tell a woman almost anything."

"And is that what you did? Told me what I wanted to hear?"

Piercing brown eyes leveled on her. "It was evident from the start that you desired a period of courtship."

"So this was all an act—your kindness, your patience, your passion?" Meriel struggled to fathom this new turn of events. "But why? You have my body whether you woo me or not. I need your seed; I need your babe. If anyone should have lied in the cause of seduction, it should have been me!"

"But it was you who needed the sweet words, not I," Gage replied softly, wiping away a tear that had escaped to trickle down her cheek. "I meant nothing cruel by it."

She jerked her head away. "Well, spare me more of your untruths. I-I can't bear them!"

"I've never lied to you, Meriel."

"Never lied—!" Meriel choked back further words, her pain and anger suddenly encompassed, muted, by the deep, rich timbre of his voice. A wary surprise narrowed her eyes. "You've always told me the truth? Then, that means—"

Gage silenced her with a gentle finger. "Enough, femina. You maidens all talk too much. Not a word more."

As he spoke, he slid a water-slick hand up Meriel's waist, capturing a softly rounded breast. With expert fingers, he massaged the nipple until it firmed to a pouting little nub. Meriel's eyelids lowered in pleasure. She pressed into him, her head dipping to lie upon his chest.

"Do you like this?" Gage demanded huskily. "Do you like what I do to you?"

"Y-yes. Oh, yes!"

"Then kiss me. Show me how much you like it."

She raised her head then, capturing his face between her hands to pull his mouth to hers. With a fierce, wild abandon, Meriel did as she was told. Her lips settled over his, her tongue delicately prodding for entrance. When Gage opened to her, she thrust inside, meeting his tongue in a hot, ardent dance. With a growl, Gage crushed her to him, pulling her with him to their knees.

The warm waters swirled around them, lapping gently at Meriel's shoulders. The steam enveloped them, swallowing Gage and Meriel in a thick, soothing mist. Everything narrowed to a ghostly world of steaming vapors and whiteness—the only reality the heated imprint of greedy, straining bodies.

It felt good, right. Meriel sank still lower. Her thick black hair fanned out in the agitated water until it covered her in a cloak of rich ebony.

Gage stroked her hair aside, lifted her half-way out of the pool, and lowered his head to her breast. His mouth moved voraciously over her nipple, suckling it, then laving it with his tongue.

Meriel moaned and writhed against him. "Gage! Please!"

"Soon, femina. Soon," he growled, then moved to attack her breast's twin just as savagely as the other.

Gods, Gage thought through a rising haze of desire. He was so hot, so uncomfortable, his groin swollen and throbbing. If he didn't find release soon . . .

Yet, for some unaccountable reason—a reason he didn't dare examine—he wanted more than just a physical easing. He wanted to imprint him-self in Meriel's memory, sear his image, the touch of his mouth, his hands, his body, so indelibly that she would never, ever forget him. He wanted to matter to her—just as she had come, in this short passage of time, to matter to him.

A small voice in the back of his mind whis-pered to beware. Whispered it was never wise to let anyone get too close—and especially not a woman.

But for once Gage knew it was safe. He would never see Meriel after this day, and she was so young, so sweet and pure and good. Eventually life would taint her, twist her heart into a cold, hard little knot, but that would come long after he was gone. Long after this wondrous, loving moment.

"Meriel!" The cry escaped from a throat raw with pain and longing. "Gods, Meriel!"

Gage pulled her to her feet and swung her up into his arms. He carried her to the pool's edge, where he laid Meriel on a thick cushion of moss flowers. He moved to lie beside her, his hot, hungry gaze raking her slender form again and again.

She lay there, the sheer gown plastered to her body, glistening with a damp, seductive sheen. Her dark rose nipples thrust against the fabric, the excitement-hardened nubs tantalizingly impudent. Folds of wet cloth wreathed her softly rounded belly, the sight as equal a distraction as her breasts. But it was her dark nest of curls, the merest hint of an alluring black shadow beneath the gown bunched up around her sleek thighs, that nearly sent him over the edge.

He swallowed a savage curse and ripped the undershift from her, tearing it from top to bottom. Meriel gasped, startled at her sudden nakedness as much as from the surprising roughness of the act.

She rose on her elbows, intent on scooting away. Gage was upon her before she could do more. He pulled her to him, his body hard, trembling with its own uniquely male need. He rocked his thick erection against her.

"Meriel," Gage groaned, his head buried in the fragrant curve of her neck. Gods, he couldn't think. He didn't care about anything but this moment and the next to come. "Forgive me. I-I want you so badly! I *have* to have you!"

At the sound of his deep voice, filled with equal portions of pain and longing, her last reserves melted. She clutched him to her, stroking his damp blond curls, a fierce female exultation welling inside.

Gage had been wrong when he'd claimed that the act of mating would confirm her womanhood. His need for her, his vulnerability in her arms—something she sensed he rarely allowed himself to experience, much less reveal—was what made her a woman. And the emotions *she* experienced with this magnificent, savagely passionate man confirmed her womanhood as well.

"It's all right," she soothed, her voice quavering with its own mixture of torment and desire. "I need you just as badly. Give yourself to me. Give me your child."

With a growl of pure desperation, Gage pulled her to him. His hand slipped intimately between her thighs, to the velvet-smooth inner recesses of her body. She was hot, wet, ready for him. Gage waited no longer.

He spread her wide, then positioned himself between her legs. Grasping her hips between his two large hands, Gage poised over her for one last delicious instant, savoring the moment to come.

Meriel glanced up at him, at his glistening, thickly muscled body, then down to his organ, huge and red and slick. An ache throbbed deep within her, a burgeoning, bittersweet pain. She wanted him so badly she thought her heart would burst. Her hands moved, encompassing his own narrow hips. Her nails dug into the tautly drawn flesh.

"Now!" Her voice trembled with a wild excitement. "Please, Gage. Now!"

With a hoarse, husky sound, Gage lifted Meriel completely against his erection, his big, wet shaft a hairsbreath from the moist heat of her. In the next instant he thrust into Meriel, sheathing himself to his full length.

She tensed, a strangled cry on her lips, arching up to meet him. "G-Gage!"

"Hush, sweet femina," he soothed, his own voice ragged, unsteady. "Lie still and the pain will ease."

"W-will it?" she whispered. "Will it really?"

He stroked the damp, tangled hair from her face. "Yes. And it will never, ever hurt again. I promise."

She smiled, then with a contented sigh nestled her face against his chest. "I believe you, Gage. I believe, because I love you."

Meriel's words, and the gentle, trusting look shining in her eyes, sent a sharp pain stabbing through Gage. By all that was sacred, he wasn't worthy of her! He'd never be worthy of a good, decent woman, if more than one still truly existed in the universe. And yet, to turn away, to leave the tight, moistly delicious heat of her body, would require more strength than he possessed.

No, he didn't deserve Meriel, nor the adoring, girlish love she offered. Yet he was still selfish enough to crave this single moment in time. And have her he would.

She felt him throbbing within her, fighting back his need, awaiting her sensual response. Meriel's own need grew. An instinctive urge rose within.

She began to move beneath him, a gentle, rhythmic undulation of her hips. It felt surprisingly good, that delicious tug of his big shaft. She quickened her pace.

"Meriel! Gods!" Gage nearly shouted the words. The last of his control shattered, shredding, disintegrating into the rising, swirling tumult of his passion. He plunged into her, driving himself roughly, deeply. He laughed, the hoarse sound full of fierce male triumph.

And Meriel met him, thrust for thrust. Her own excitement spiraled higher and higher, toward what she didn't know save for the conviction it promised an exquisite ecstasy she would never experience the like of again. She pulled his head down to her, her mouth taking his in a greedy, ardent kiss. She kissed him, she licked him, she drew his tongue into her mouth to suck it wildly.

Then everything went dark. From the depths of the blackness something exploded into a myriad of dazzling, sparkling lights. Simultaneously, from deep within her body thick, heavy pulsations began, spreading ever outward in wave upon wave of physical delight. Meriel tensed, arching up against Gage. Her fingers dug into his heavily muscled buttocks.

He smothered her cry with his mouth, drawing it into him as if to hold, to cherish it for all the long, lonely days and nights to come. Then, with a final violent thrust and guttural sound, his own release came. In a series of gasping spasms, Gage spewed out his seed, filling Meriel with his gift of life.

She held him to her until he finally quieted, stroking his hair, murmuring soothing words, so happy yet so infinitely sad. Held him until, lulled by the hypnotic sound of the churning waters and blanketed by the warm mist, they fell asleep.

"Where is Meriel?" Gage snarled. "I demand to know!"

Kadra turned from the open balcony door. The early morning sun already drenched her bedchamber in brightness and warmth. A sultry breeze ruffled the hem of her emerald-hued gown and delicately brocaded over-robe.

"You *demand?*" She arched an amused brow at the man who stood before her. "And why would you care, one way or another, where Meriel is? You've done your duty as breeder; you've had your pleasure with her time and again in the past many hours. How is it possible you're still hot for my daughter?"

"What I feel for Meriel is no concern of yours," he snapped. "I'm quite aware our time is over. I only wished to say good-bye."

"Did you now?" She moved across the room in a swirl of lustrous fabric to stand before him. Her thick black hair was dressed in an elaborate coil, huge earrings dangled from her ears, and her hands were laden with a dazzling assortment of rings.

"Well, my handsome breeder," Kadra purred, gracing him with an appraising stare, "it is too late. Meriel left for our summer palace an hour ago. She's to meet with her betrothed and prepare for their impending wedding."

"Her betrothed?"

"Why, yes." Kadra smiled pityingly. "Didn't she tell you? About Prince Pelum of Aristan, her life-long love? She couldn't wait to share the news of her conception after last night."

"She knew already?" Anger surged through Gage. "It's not possible. You're lying!"

"Impregnation for a Tenuan female can be determined quite easily and quickly by a knowledgeable physician. You've done well, my virile breeder. She carries your son. After all these cycles we will finally have a prince."

"I'm honored to have served you so handily," Gage muttered. A confusion of emotions roiled within. He fought through them, forcing all but a calm, cold logic to the back of his mind.

Was it possible that Meriel had cared so little for what had transpired between them that she had raced to her prince's side the moment she'd gotten what she wanted? Try as he might, Gage couldn't believe it. She'd been too responsive, too tenderly passionate, too emotionally touched by their matings to have so easily discarded him. Meriel, if she'd been permitted, would have lingered at least to say good-bye. Someone had forced her to leave.

Kadra saw the conflict play across Gage's face and knew he doubted her words. It was past mattering, though. She had already used the knowledge she'd gained from viewing the matings on the video monitor. Combining it with the fabricated tale of how Gage had come to her earlier in the morning and demanded that he now be permitted to bed the Queen—a real woman—in payment for servicing Meriel, it had been an easy task to convince her daughter that the breeder cared nothing for her. All cruel lies, but Kadra would do anything to protect the innocent girl from further pain. The Queen had seen the intense bonding that had so quickly flared between Meriel and the breeder, a bonding that would only serve to distract her idealistic daughter with memories and dreams that could never be. And distract her as well from the harsh destiny that lay ahead, a destiny from which Kadra was determined to spare Meriel for as long as possible. The mating with this breeder had been an unfortunate necessity, a matter of survival for their race and royal line. Even as Queen, Kadra couldn't protect Meriel from that.

But as Queen she was also a woman in the prime of life, healthy, vibrant, vital, and would be for a long time to come. There was no need to force the heavy responsibilities and burdens of office upon her daughter's slender shoulders prematurely. That could all wait for a time. There wasn't any hurry. She could at least give her daughter that.

As for the lie that she'd been forced to tell Meriel a short while ago, well, it was so very little when placed in perspective of the rest of her daughter's life. Such a little lie, and for such a good cause. . . .

The act of deceiving the arrogant breeder, on the other hand, would be a distinct pleasure. Males had their place, and when they dared step out of it, Kadra's patience quickly wore thin. She had vowed to teach this one a lesson—and teach him she would. Then, when she was done, she would salve his injured feelings by offering him the supreme honor of becoming her lover. His death could wait a time, until she'd had her own fill of him.

Kadra's glance moved down Gage's powerful frame. He was magnificent, in body and performance, a tautly muscled, superbly conditioned animal. Though a skilled, gentle lover, the breeder could turn hotly, savagely passionate when the occasion called for it.

His stamina was unrivaled as well, Kadra mused with a tremor of delicious anticipation, recalling the many times he'd roused to mate with her daughter in the past night. Yes, this breeder promised to be one of her finest, if not *the* finest lover she'd ever taken. And if he'd found Meriel exciting, he was certain to be intensely gratified with her. . . .

"You are hurt that my daughter failed to thank you, aren't you?" Kadra began, soothing her tone to one of gentle concern. "That she didn't linger to say good-bye?"

"You forced her to leave, didn't you?"

"No. On the contrary, it was Meriel's choice." And it had been, once the girl was convinced of Kadra's tale. Deeply hurt and weeping as if her heart would break, Meriel had begged to leave, to be allowed to seek out Pelum for comfort. Her daughter's distress had pained Kadra, but it had been necessary. She had sent Meriel away within the hour, then turned to the more pleasant task of dealing with the breeder.

"Her choice?" Gage gave a mocking laugh. "I don't believe that."

Kadra smiled. "Don't you? Well, I'd meant to spare you the pain of my daughter's rejection, but since you seem so intent on calling me a liar . . ."

She paused. "Meriel came to me early this morning, quite pleased with herself. She told me everything about your matings. How she played the shy innocent and lured you to the pool, how she gained your trust, stirred your desire. She said she thought you were even beginning to fall in love with her. She was particularly pleased with that. You were her first conquest, you know."

At Kadra's words, something snapped within Gage, shattering the last of his trust in Meriel. The memory of the girl, her innocence, her sweet concern, disintegrated in this final, bitter realization of her betrayal. Nothing remained but a seething, icy rage.

She was no different from the rest.

"Lying, scheming little bitch!" Gage snarled through gritted teeth.

"And is her conduct any worse than your lust-crazed arrogance?" Kadra prodded coolly. "You were bought as a breeder. When, in all of this, were you ever led to believe otherwise? Is it Meriel's fault you chose to think you could ever matter to a royal princess—you, a lowly slave, an off-world stud? When did you ever imagine you were worthy of her?"

"Never. I never imagined any such thing." He ground out the admission even as the truth of Kadra's words seared a fiery path to the depths of his soul. "But she played me for a fool." A cold, ruthless light flared in Gage's eyes. "Worthy or not, I don't suffer that well."

The Queen shrugged. "Be that as it may, it was Meriel's decision. And you *were* so very gullible. She said she told you she loved you, said you believed it. That each time she repeated the words throughout the night, it stirred you to even greater efforts." She smiled. "You truly were a fool, my handsome, virile breeder."

Anger burgeoned within him. His fists clenched at his sides. Damn Meriel! Damn her mother for grinding his pride in the shame of her daughter's betrayal!

The sudden realization of Kadra's motives flooded him. Gage bit back a savage curse. The woman was baiting him—and enjoying it in the bargain. He forced his features into an implacable mask.

Almost as if sensing his change of mood, Kadra sighed, her approach now sympathetic, soothing. "You must forgive her. Meriel is so young, so overcome with the realization of her exquisite beauty and its effect on males. This newly discovered power went to her head. I think in a way she did love you, or at least loved being with you. Any woman would."

The seductive tone in the Queen's voice wrenched Gage from his battle to contain his fury. He immediately recognized it for what it was—her own interest in him as a breeder. Not that her intentions included the conception of a child. Far from it.

Gage's eyes narrowed as he met her gaze. His jaw clenched. Gods, was that all he would become on this planet? Was that all his life would finally amount to? A piece of meat to be passed from woman to woman, until he'd lived out his only purpose?

He was well aware what would happen once Kadra tired of him. He had known women like her before, hard-eyed, insatiable predators. Women who hated men as much as they desired them. His death was a foregone conclusion if he lingered too long in her clutches.

Well, he hadn't survived all these cycles as a tracker, a bounty hunter of man and alien alike, without learning a few tricks. If playing the rutting male would gain him his life—and freedom— Gage would give the Queen just what she asked for. He'd done as much for her daughter. The Queen, at least, was honest about the stakes.

"I don't care what *any* woman would think," he growled, his voice silky, laden with meaning. "What does a Queen think? Would she perhaps find me attractive?"

Kadra smiled. "Quite possibly." She moved to stand before him, her hands lifting to massage his thick chest muscles. "But why not first determine what you have to offer?"

"You didn't see enough on the video monitor?" Gage drawled suggestively.

She smiled in remembrance of his deliciously naked body, of his powerful thrusts, his groans of pleasure as he mated with her daughter. "Oh, I saw quite a lot, but it wasn't close enough. This is *much* better."

With that Kadra's nails dug into Gage's chest, bunching the thin fabric of his tunic beneath her fingers. In the next instant she ripped the garment apart, baring his chest.

She slipped the torn tunic from his shoulders, her hands lingering over the broad expanse of muscle before tugging the garment completely away. With a hungry smile, she ran her hands back up his body, lightly stroking the rippling ridges of his abdomen, then moving to outline his flat male nipples before finally threading her fingers through the tangle of dark chest hair to clutch the firm swell of his pectoral muscles. Her nails dug into him, scoring his flesh, then gouged even deeper.

Gage tensed, biting back a gasp of pain.

"Do you enjoy it rough, my handsome breeder?" Kadra whispered. "I do."

He grasped her arms, pulling her hands away to pin them behind her back. "If the woman stirs me enough, I enjoy it as rough as she can bear it." He paused, glancing up at the video monitor positioned on the wall across from the bed. "Do you have your own matings viewed as well?"

She shrugged. "You could be dangerous. Intent on harming me."

"You promised me freedom. It would be foolish for me to risk losing that. And besides," Gage added, a wolfish smile curling his lips, "why would I toss aside the offering you've made of yourself? If I found your daughter appealing, why wouldn't I find an experienced, deliciously voluptuous woman like you even more so?"

"But you don't like to share our lovemaking with others, is that it?"

"It's not one of my fonder fantasies."

"Nor mine," Kadra purred. "Nor mine." Her hands entwined about Gage's neck. "Take me to the bed. The video controls are there."

With a low growl, Gage swung her up into his arms and strode over to the bed. Kneeling on the edge of its massive expanse, he laid the Queen down. He towered over her like some huge beast of prey, meeting her hot gaze with an equally smoldering one of his own. His hands moved to the waistband of his breeches, unfastened it, and began to spread the fabric apart. Then he hesitated.

Kadra rose to her elbows, her eyes glittering with anticipation. "Well, what are you waiting for? I don't like games. Strip yourself!"

"The video monitor," Gage rasped. "You said you'd turn it off."

She gave a low, throaty laugh. "Ah, yes. My handsome stud turns suddenly shy in the presence of too large an audience." Kadra leaned over and flipped up the lid of an intricately carved wooden box that lay on the bedside table. Inside was a set of buttons. She keyed in a series of commands. Behind them, the video monitor clicked off.

The Queen glanced up. "Satisfied?"

"Yes." Gage climbed onto the bed to lie beside her. With one savage sweep of his hand, he ripped the Queen's gown apart, exposing her ripe, smooth-skinned body. From the ruined fabric he tore a long piece away, then grasped first one, then her other hand and pulled them above her head.

"What are you doing?" Kadra cried.

"Calm yourself," Gage murmured huskily. "You said you liked it rough. And I like my women bound."

There was something in the tone of his voice, something that flickered in the depths of his dark eyes, that gave Kadra warning. With a wild twist, she managed to free a hand. In the next instant an earring was in her grip and pointed at Gage.

He flung himself aside, barely evading the laser beam from the minature weapon aimed at his head. It caught the side of his face instead, slicing him from temple to jaw. With an angry grunt, Gage grabbed Kadra's wrist, pinning it once more above her head. His mouth covered hers, smothering her cry of alarm until he was able to gag her.

She fought like some wild animal, bucking and twisting beneath him, but Gage's greater bulk and strength soon wore her down. The laser dropped from Kadra's fingers. She lay there, panting in terror. With a few deft movements, Gage soon had her hands tied above her head.

Though his facial wound oozed blood that trickled from his jaw onto his bare chest, a triumphant expression gleamed in Gage's eyes. He climbed off the bed. Leaning down, Gage pulled off Kadra's other earring and examined it. He grinned.

"Very clever. One earring's a minature stunner, the other a hand laser. You come very well armed."

He retrieved the other weapon from the bed. "I wondered what surprise you had in store for me. I knew you weren't foolish enough to turn off the video monitor without some other form of defense. I never imagined it would be in your jewelry, though."

Gage pocketed the weapons. "Thank you. These will greatly aid in my escape."

Her wide, frightened eyes stared back at him, gleaming with a silent question.

"What am I going to do with you?" Gage put words to her unspoken query. "I should kill you, for all the pain and inconvenience you've caused me. Or," he said, his gaze raking her tantalizing nakedness, "I could still take my pleasure with you. You'd like that too much, though, wouldn't you?"

He shook his head, the motion wry, resigned. "Have no fear, Queen of Tenua. I'll do neither. I find the murder of women distasteful and I'll certainly not give you what you want. But heed my words and heed them well. If our paths ever cross again, beware. You and your conniving little daughter have angered me like few others. Next time, if there ever is one, I'll be far less generous with the both of you."

With one last, mocking glance at Kadra's bound and gagged form, Gage turned and slipped out the balcony door.

Chapter Three

Three cycles later

"No." Gage Bardwin adamantly shook his head. "No concessions. They had their chance. This time the Tenuan surrender will be unconditional."

"And I say you are wrong in this." Teran Ardane moved to stand beside him at the helm of the small transport craft that carried them to the military landing port set up a few kilometers outside the Tenuan capital. "What are a few concessions to salve wounded pride? We need to welcome these people back into the Imperium, not drive them further away. Put the past, whatever it may be, behind you."

"Time enough to do that once I've dealt with Queen Kadra and her daughter!" Gage turned to Teran. "I never wanted the position of battle commander and leader of this war against Tenua. But you, as always since our days at the Imperial Academy, have once again managed to talk me into something against my desires. Will you go against me in this as well?"

Teran sighed and shook his head. "You know I won't. You are now Lord Commander. Your control of this planet is total, as well it should be for the undertaking ahead. I'm only here as King Falkan's representative to advise, to ease the transition of power."

"And your advice has been heard and noted."

His jaw set in grim determination, Gage turned to gaze out the window. Behind him, Teran moved to take a seat in one of the high-backed passenger chairs. Guilt plucked at Gage. He shouldn't have been so abrupt in dismissing his friend's counsel. But Teran didn't understand . . . couldn't understand. And, curse it all, neither did he.

Gage clamped down on a brief surge of remorse. It was a fruitless emotion at any rate. Feelings solved nothing. Action, coolly reasoned and planned, was the only recourse to the horrendous problems that lay ahead. Yet each time he recalled those days in the Tenuan royal palace . . .

As the craft began its downward descent in preparation for docking, his gaze scanned the scene of devastation that lay beyond the window. Little remained standing of the city of Eremita save its imposing, high-walled palace. The surrounding countryside was pockmarked and scorched by war. The fields were ravaged, the rivers fouled by animal carcasses and dead bodies.

"We had no choice, Gage." Teran's deep voice

rose from behind him. "Queen Kadra wouldn't listen, refused to accept our offer to assist in the evacuation of her people to an Imperium planet. Her single-minded obsession with moving the Tenuans to the Abessian galaxy was insane. For us as well as for Tenua. We had to go to war to stop her."

"But the extent of the ruin!" Gage's hands gripped the top of the co-pilot's chair that stood before him. "By all that is sacred! The destruction!" He wheeled about to confront Teran, his features twisted in anguish. "Was I too harsh, too driven in my quest for vengeance?"

Teran's glance mirrored the pain Gage felt. "We offered the Tenuans the opportunity for surrender at each step of the takeover. And each time the Queen threw our offer back in our face. *She* is the one responsible. *She* allowed this to go on far past the point of any hope of victory."

"But there was no logical reason for her to continue!" Gage protested. "It was almost as if she no longer cared what happened to Tenua. As if she fought on for some reason totally separate from the welfare of her people." He sighed and shook his head. "As if she herself were Volan enslaved . . ."

"Starboard thruster firing. First-stage landing pattern commenced," the pilot at the nearby console announced.

Gage glanced briefly in the man's direction, then squared his shoulders. He turned back to the window. They'd be landing soon and there was nothing more he could do about what the war had wrought. The future lay in resolving the still existing problems. And the first of those was dealing with the Queen and her manipulative daughter.

It wouldn't be long now, he thought, before their arrival at the palace—and the final, soul-satisfying confrontation with the two women. He planned on stripping them of their royal standing, transporting them back to Bellator and allowing King Falkan and his High Council to determine their eventual fates. Fates that would never allow for a position of power again.

Gage scowled at the memory of those two days in the royal palace, distant as they now were. The time spent there had been nothing more than a temporary detour from his true purpose on Tenua, he reminded himself for the hundredth time. After his escape, he had quickly put the unpleasant experience behind him and efficiently completed his undercover mission. Though rumors abounded of mysterious deaths, all of them similar in the abrupt, total collapse of the victim, he had been unable to ascertain the cause. The deaths—almost universally of healthy young adults—were unsettling enough to warrant further suspicion of Volan involvement, however.

"Port thruster firing. Second-stage landing pattern commenced."

This time, Gage didn't spare the pilot a glance. His gaze was riveted on the palace, a distant specter of tall white turrets, spires, and walls that shimmered through the haze that rose from the overheated land after a recent rainstorm. On the horizon, the Tenuan red sun was setting, bathing everything in an eerie, mist-muted light.

Tenua, Gage mused, a bitter melancholy settling over him. Planet of doom, filled with haunting, emotion-fraught memories . . .

Memories he would purge, from his heart as well as mind, just as soon as he faced the Queen and her daughter. He'd yet have his victory. Even after three cycles, the rage burned hotly.

He was fortunate for the presence of Teran Ardane at his side. His friend had always been a steadying counterpart to Gage's more volatile nature. Indeed, Gage feared what he might do if he attempted to deal with the two women himself. And feared as well delving too deeply into the source of that rage—a rage that burned brightest of all for the young, beauteous Meriel.

The Queen's motives he understood. She'd made her choice long ago to rule with a heavy hand, to use others to her own purposes. She was a cruel but predictable woman. Gage had always known how to deal with her.

But Meriel. Meriel had somehow managed to slip past his defenses, to touch that tiny part of him that still hoped there were a few good people left in the universe who acted from purely altruistic motives. He'd thought her youth, her sheltered upbringing, had protected her, kept her innocent and good. Yet she'd been even more brutal, more insidiously crippling, for she'd never been what he'd imagined her to be.

Gage shook his head, his laugh low and bitter. Gods, but he'd been the most ignorant of fools! Perhaps that was what angered him most. He knew better, had been taught time and again about the self-serving cruelties of others. And yet a particularly pretty face and wide, violet eyes had lured him as easily as any hormone-driven lad, laying siege to vulnerabilities he'd thought long dead. But no more, he reiterated in a sudden savage turn of emotions. Never, *ever* again!

"What's so amusing?" Teran's deep voice intruded. "It's a rare occurrence to hear you laugh."

Gage glanced around, brown eyes slicing into those of gray. "Nothing special. Just a memory to fortify me for the confrontation to come."

Teran smiled. "They are women, the Queen and her daughter. No matter how bitter the memories, no matter how hard-fought the battle, remember that. There's no honor—"

"Honor's an easy word to throw about," Gage snapped savagely, "when one hasn't been personally involved with these two women! So don't speak to me of empty concepts like honor, Ardane, nor expect mercy from me because of their sex. Not where these two are concerned!"

Teran frowned. "Your emotions aren't those of a battle commander. What exactly did Queen Kadra and her daughter do to you?"

"Enough to teach me, and teach me well, of their own special kind of treachery!" Gage turned back to the helm as they hovered in for the docking. "Now, no more of it. Do I pry into your secrets?"

"No," Teran replied softly.

"Then stay out of mine."

"As you wish, *Lord Commander*." With a wry shake of his head Teran settled back in his chair.

Renewed anger roiled within Gage. Gods, had it come to this then, that he couldn't even con-

tain his fury and frustration with his best friend?
What in the heavens was the matter with him?

A tiny voice whispered in the back of Gage's
mind, easing the niggling realization to the
forefront of his consciousness. Meriel's deception touched a similar chord, was too acutely
reminiscent of another woman's—his mother's—
betrayal. Both had tantalized him with the promise of unconditional love and acceptance, and both
had never had any intention of granting it. Both
had used him for their own means, then cast him
aside when he was no longer of value.

The realization was like a knife gutting his
insides, slashing and tearing until there was
nothing left but a bitter, hollow core. A core
that had to be filled with something. And that
something was a lifelong, smoldering, barely contained rage.

There was only one solution. He must deal with
the women as quickly as possible, then banish
them. It was the only way to regain control.
He hadn't time to waste wallowing in fruitless
emotions. There was too much work—work of
Imperium magnitude—to be done.

With a low growl, Gage flung the memories
aside. Memories of Meriel and a few cycles past.
Memories of even further back, when he was
a young man, jubilantly graduating with Teran
from the Imperial Academy.

A promising future had lain before him. Then
his father died of mysterious circumstances. A
covert investigation eventually revealed a horrible
secret that his mother had hidden all the cycles of
Gage's youth. From that day forward his life had

changed—and he'd never trusted another woman again.

No woman, that was, until Meriel.

The transport craft landed with a soft bump. The low whir of engines faded. With a buzz of well-lubricated gears, the exit portal opened. Gage dragged in a deep breath and turned to his friend.

"Come. It's time to complete the takeover of Tenua and set the evacuation into motion. And time, as well, to at last confront the Queen."

Teran nodded, then rose and followed Gage from the transport craft.

Queen Meriel Corba restlessly paced the length of the throne platform. The Bellatorian-led conquerors' arrival was eminent and she didn't know what she would say or how to deal with them. Even worse, she didn't know what *they* would do—to her or her people.

"What will become of us, Meriel?" a fretful voice intruded on her thoughts. She turned to the twin throne chair where her husband sat.

"I-I don't know, Pelum." She forced a wan smile. "There is only one certainty. I am now Queen and must accept the consequences."

"But it's so unfair!" her husband cried. "Kadra's death was so sudden, so mysterious! And she never prepared you to rule, never allowed you any responsibilities. This senseless war was all her fault, yet now you must pay the price!"

Meriel sighed. It *had* been such a short reign, in a time fraught with death and destruction. And it *wasn't* fair. She would never have a chance to make her own mark as a ruler. Even as she took the throne, Tenuan forces had been on the verge of defeat.

One thing was certain. She knew *she'd* never have sanctioned a war. Though the Bellatorian High King's proposal of the prison planet of Carcer as sanctuary was hardly the most palatable of offers, it was still shelter on a safe planet. With the Imperium's additional promise of aid in reclaiming the land of that essentially barren planet and the recapture and imprisonment of all the criminals still roaming it, in time Carcer could have been restored to its former lushness.

Yet, for some reason, Meriel's mother had been adamantly against the Imperial plan. For some unknown reason, the Queen had unswervingly committed Tenua to evacuation to the Abesse. And nothing, absolutely nothing Meriel had said could sway her.

"Fair or not, it doesn't matter," she replied sadly. "What matters is what will happen next. What will become of our people, of you and our son?"

Her gaze locked with her husband's. He sat there, pale and haggard, his knuckles white on the chair arms. His breath came in ragged little gasps. A fine sheen of sweat dampened his brow.

Meriel sighed and stepped forward to kneel before him. Her small hands covered his. "Pelum, my love. Don't fret so. It'll be all right. The war is over. The Imperium has won. There's nothing more they can do."

"N-nothing more?" Pelum's fingers slipped from beneath her grip. He buried his face in his hands. "G-Gods, Meriel! They can still murder us all! The royal family is always a threat. Always possesses the potential to inspire the people to revolt. And what use are we to their ultimate plans? All Falkan has ever wanted was to maintain his control of the Imperium—and that includes keeping Tenua in its subservient place!"

"Hush. Hush, my love," Meriel soothed, tenderly stroking his head. "It'll be all right. If there is punishment required, I will bear it, not you. It's my duty."

"But I don't want anything to happen to you!" Pelum lifted his head, his delicately chiseled features twisted in anguish. "I-I have never been much of a husband to you, but it's never lessened the depth of my love. What will I do if I lose you?"

"You will go on, as any of us would. Our people need you. You must always be there for them. You must!"

A shy, hesitant smile brightened his face. "I'll try, Meriel. Truly, I will."

Meriel forced her own brave smile. "I know you will, my love. And you'll take care of Kieran for me, too. Won't you?"

Pelum nodded. "I love the lad as if he were my own. I'll guard him with my life."

"Good." Meriel rose. "Then my heart is at peace. I can face our enemies—"

A pounding on the great doors drew her up short. Meriel signaled to her men-at-arms to allow the visitor in. When the door was thrown open, Torman, her captain of the guard, immediately strode in and across the huge, mosaic-tiled hall. The broad-shouldered, huskily built man dropped to one knee before her.

"Majesty," his sonorous voice boomed. "The conquerors have arrived."

"Rise, my faithful Torman," Meriel commanded, struggling to keep the tremor from her voice. "Treat them with all courtesy and bring them to me immediately."

The captain straightened. For a fleeting instant his glance lighted on the trembling form of his queen's consort. Something flickered in his piercing blue eyes. Then he turned, to meet Meriel's steady gaze. "As you command, Majesty."

With that he bowed, then strode away, the thud of his heavy, booted feet echoing loudly in the nearly deserted hall. Echoing as loudly as the sudden hammering of Meriel's heart.

She shot Pelum a quick glance. He'd gone white and was close to fainting. He would be no help in the ordeal to come.

Meriel moved to claim her own chair. There was nothing more to be done but face the inevitable. As long as she ensured the welfare of her people, the safety of her family, it would be worth it. And she'd do *anything* to achieve that. The Bellatorian conquerors were sadly mistaken if they thought the war was over. The battle that really counted had just begun.

With a resolute squaring of her slender shoulders and proud lift of her chin, she awaited the arrival of her conquerors.

"Be damned!" Gage cursed savagely as they paused in the open doorway to the large throne room.

A cohort of heavily armed Bellatorian Imperial troopers pulled up behind them. The thud of booted feet, mingling with the shouts of hoarse male voices, reverberated throughout the palace as each room was systematically searched by the invading army and any remnants of resistance subdued.

Teran shot Gage a quick glance. "What's wrong? The palace is even now being secured. There's no danger—"

"Meriel," his companion ground out. "She sits on the Tenuan throne of power. But why? Where is her mother? Damn her conniving little soul! Damn her mother!"

"Calm yourself." Teran gripped Gage's arm. "And remember. There is still much to be gained with but a small show of diplomacy."

Blazing brown eyes riveted on Teran. "Enough, Ardane! I don't need some schoolboy lecture. I need my rage to gird me for what I must do!"

"This is a sensitive mission—"

"And do you take me for a fool, not to know how to handle it? Do you think me a man governed by my emotions?"

The other man's lips quirked in amusement. "Not normally, but in this case—"

"Not ever! Now, no more of it." Gage motioned his friend forward. "I've a Queen, one way or another, to deal with."

As he headed toward the dais, his men following behind, the face of Meriel sharpened, every detail of her countenance coming into striking relief. A faint flush shaded her high cheekbones. It was the only color in her otherwise pale, tautly drawn face. A face that had matured in the past three cycles, softening into deliciously tender curves, a full, sensuously molded mouth that all but begged for a man's kisses, and wide, darkly expressive eyes. Eyes that now glared down at him in wary defiance.

For a fleeting moment Gage was overcome with a strange, long-suppressed emotion. An emotion of hot, primal desire—and curious, aching need. He caught himself, choking back another curse. Be damned, but he was reacting like some loins-crazed fool! And for a woman who was now his bitterest enemy!

His jaw hardened, his fists clenched. A cold, controlled fury quickly cooled his heated lust, freezing it into an icy little lump that throbbed with each beat of his heart. Suddenly Gage felt nothing save a fierce resolve to see the long-anticipated and now dreaded confrontation over and done with.

With long, resolute strides he and Teran crossed the hall, their steps reverberating throughout the room in a rhythmic cadence. Meriel watched as the tall, powerfully built men approached. One was black-haired and bearded, garbed in the aureum-shot robes and bejeweled belt of the High King's royal emissary. The other, with dark blond hair that curled down the back of his neck, was clothed in warrior's dress of beryllium-impregnated chest armor worn over his black tunic and breeches, a wide pouch belt cinching his narrow waist and a blaster gun slung over his shoulder.

The blond warrior was a far more formidable-looking adversary than the calm, stern-featured diplomat. His handsome jaw was taut with rage, his mouth was drawn into a ruthless, forbidding line, and his eyes were filled with cold loathing. Eyes, suddenly familiar, that slammed into Meriel's.

Her hand rose to her throat, a throat suddenly gone tight and dry. "No," she whispered. "It can't be!"

"W-what's wrong, Meriel?" Pelum quavered beside her.

"Run, Pelum. Hide," she cried. "I-I must face him alone!"

Her husband rose from his chair, hesitated, then scooted around to cower behind Meriel's throne. "What's wrong, Meriel? Tell me! I don't know what to do!"

She opened her mouth to reply, then clamped it shut as the two men drew up before her. With heart pounding so loudly she thought she'd drown in its deafening sound, Meriel forced herself to nod her recognition.

"Welcome to Tenua." She rose in a rustle of shimmering gown and stiff, ceremonial underskirts. "The hospitality of my land is yours."

"As is its total ownership," Gage Bardwin snapped. "As are you and your people."

He glanced about the hall. "And where is your mother? Too afraid? Too ashamed to face us after all she's done?"

"My mother is dead."

The flat, emotionless announcement only angered Gage further. It seemed that one woman had managed to escape his vengeance. But there was still the other . . .

He swung back to face her. "Dead is she? Then that makes you Queen. Step down from there. As conqueror of your planet, I hereby claim you as slave and spoils of war."

Heavy silence settled over the room. Meriel stared down at Gage, momentarily wide-eyed and speechless. His steely gaze never wavered, capturing and holding hers in a grip of implacable anger.

For an instant his image swam before her, a shimmering focal point in a room of whirling colors. Her stomach churned with a sudden surge of nausea. Then dizziness engulfed Meriel and she thought she'd faint.

With a superhuman effort she fought past the lightheaded sensation. By all that was sacred, but she'd not shame herself or her people before *him!* She swallowed hard, clenched her hands into fists, and shot him a resolute glance.

"You are conqueror," she began, forcing a tone of regal calmness. "You may do what you wish with me. But I beg you treat my family, my people, with mercy. They have suffered greatly—"

"They have suffered because of *your* ambition and self-serving arrogance! This war should never have been. But have no fear. I'll not inflict further suffering on the Tenuans. I, at least, have some compassion. "As for your family . . ." His glance shifted to the man cowering behind her chair. His lips curled in disgust. "Who is he?"

Meriel's eyes widened. "He is Pelum, my consort. He is innocent—"

"He is as guilty as you!" Gage's eyes narrowed in cold, savage contempt. "Is this what you preferred to me?" he demanded hoarsely, his voice dropping so it could not be heard beyond the immediate vicinity of the throne.

Teran stepped up beside him to grip his arm in a warning gesture. Gage shrugged aside his hand. At that moment, nothing existed, nothing mattered but Meriel—and what lay between them.

"Not only is he impotent as a lover," he continued in a low, ruthless voice, "but as a man as well. If this consort of yours is any example of Tenuan manhood, it's no wonder you were defeated."

"Save your cruel tongue for where it belongs!" In an instinctive attempt to block Gage's view, Meriel moved to stand before Pelum. "I surrender to you. What more do you want?"

In two quick strides Gage mounted the platform. He grabbed Meriel by the arm and jerked her to him. "You have only *begun* your surrender to me, my sweet little femina. And before I'm finished, you'll beg for more than mercy."

"Then kill me now and be done with it," Meriel whispered, devastated by his cruel, sordid implications. She had done nothing to deserve the hatred, the utter loathing burning for her in his eyes. Yet, what had she expected? He was little more than a base, lust-crazed animal. There had never been even the tiniest bit of compassion or concern for her in his heart.

Summoning all the strength within her, Meriel met him eye to eye. "I am Queen. I demand the right to choose my fate, and I'd rather die than be subjected to a moment more in your loathsome presence!"

"Would you indeed?" Gage snarled. "But you're a slave now—my slave—not a queen. And a slave has no rights at all." He gave her a hard shake. "No rights at all, save what her master grants her."

"Vile, soul-rotted slime worm!"

"Er . . . pardon, if you will." Teran's words pierced the red hot mists of Gage's anger. "This is neither the time nor place for a public discussion of the Queen's punishment. Why not confine her to her chambers while the palace is secured? Then, at your leisure, deal with her later?"

Gage whirled around, dragging Meriel with him. His gaze slammed into that of his friend. A warning light gleamed in Teran's eyes. Gage knew the look well. He inhaled a deep, steadying breath and loosened his tight grip on Meriel.

"Your plan is wise, Lord Ardane. There's time enough to deal with her later." He motioned toward the troopers who had followed them into the room. "Seize the man hiding behind the chair and take him to the palace's holding cells. Place a guard on him at all times. And kill him if he tries to escape."

Meriel watched in helpless anguish as Pelum was roughly jerked from behind her throne chair and all but carried out of the room, piteously calling her name. Hot tears stung her eyes as she followed his progress.

"Your tears are wasted on him." Gage's deep voice dripped with sarcasm. "As is your life as well."

Her head snapped back, her eyes pools of blazing anger. "And what would you know of kindness, of compassion—of love?"

"I know enough not to use someone, then callously toss him aside. I know enough to be honest with another person!"

Meriel gave an unsteady laugh. "Do you now? I'd have thought differently. Have you changed then, since we last met?"

"Enough to know a heartless bitch when I see one."

"Gage, that's enough," Teran commanded. "Take the femina to her room, or allow me to do it. But, one way or another, put an end to this immediately."

Once more Gage fought past his fury, shaking it off with only the greatest of difficulty. He stood there for a long moment, staring down at Meriel, struggling to fathom the anger that threatened such a total loss of control. Gods, what *was* the matter with him?

She was still in his blood, he realized in a flash of insight. Unlike his experiences with other women, he'd never had the opportunity to take his fill of her, to tire of the whining and inopportune demands all females eventually placed on a man.

Relief flooded him. That was all it was, Gage thought, and so very simple to solve. He'd take her to his bed, savor the pleasures of her lush body until he was sated, then toss her aside— from his heart as well as mind. Toss her aside as another woman, more dear than all the rest, had once done to him.

The tension eased in a dizzying rush. He smiled, a grim, wolfish curl of lips baring his teeth. "You are correct as always, my friend," Gage said, never taking his eyes from Meriel's. "Time enough to settle this issue between us later." He began to pull her forward. "Time enough indeed, this very night, in the only way this woman understands."

Meriel dug in her heels. Her eyes flashed violet fire. "And what way is that, *Lord Commander?*"

The dark brown eyes staring down at her glittered dangerously. "Why, how else but with a man between your legs, sweet femina? Three cycles is a very long time between matings, wouldn't you say? And I'd wager a woman as hot-blooded as I recall you to be would gladly take any male she could get who was capable of performing.

"Even," he ground out as he once more dragged her along, "a vile, soul-rotted slime worm like me!"

Kathleen Morgan

Chapter Four

The journey through the palace's long stone corridors seemed interminable. All the while, Meriel waged battle between her pride and the impulse to beg her captor to have mercy on Tenua. But one surreptitious glance at the hard set of his features quashed her hopes that he'd listen, much less grant her request. There *had* to be another way to save her people. She just needed time to discover what it was.

Gage pulled her to a halt just outside her private quarters. Two armed guards drew up a few steps behind them. Slowly, reluctantly, Meriel's eyes lifted to his.

"You'll await me here until I ensure the security of the palace," Gage growled. "Then I'll return and deal with you."

"My soldiers," Meriel haltingly began. "There's no need to harm them. I've given orders for all to surrender."

"If they throw down their weapons, there'll be no fight. I'm not totally without mercy."

Perhaps not for my men, Meriel thought, *but what kind of mercy is it to threaten to ravish me?* Yet that was the way of war, she reminded herself bitterly. When the fighting was done, men, with their twisted sense of honor, quickly forgave and forgot, while the women continued to suffer for a long time thereafter. Anger at the unfairness of it all surged through her. A stinging retort rose to her lips, and only with the greatest of difficulty did Meriel call it back. For the sake of her people . . .

"I-I thank you for that kindness, Lord Commander," she murmured.

His contemptuous gaze raked over her. "Don't delude yourself, femina. My mercy will never extend to you."

She started, then clamped her lips shut. A spark of defiance glimmered in her striking eyes. "I never presumed your feelings for me had changed. Not that it matters, one way or another."

"Indeed?" Gage's mouth quirked in wry amusement. He motioned for Meriel to use her hand imprint to open her door, then escorted her in. "Well, time will tell how much it really matters, won't it?"

Meriel wrenched her arm free, then whirled around to confront him, mutiny trembling on her lips and flashing in her eyes. "Yes, I suppose it will, Lord Commander. But it remains to be seen how much and to whom."

His only reply was the quiet closing of the door as he departed.

For a long moment Meriel just stood there, her seething, impotent rage rendering her immobile. By all that was sacred, what a vile, crude, ignorant man! How was it possible she'd ever considered him attractive, or kind, or even human?

Meriel turned. The room once more came into focus, a haven of soothing teals, mauves, and lavenders. Floor-to-ceiling windows spanned the far wall, their length hung with long, gauzy curtains that billowed in the warm evening breeze. A big bed lay nearby, invitingly plump with cushions. On the opposite wall was the long-unused hearth, the overstuffed, low-backed lounge chairs set before it beckoning her with their soft promise of restful comfort.

From across the room came the low rumble of the mineral baths in the bathing room. The sound mingled with the chirps of the tiny birds flitting through the foliage in the adjacent herbivorium. Normally, Meriel would have instantly relaxed in this special world within a world, the cares and responsibilities slipping from her shoulders as easily as she shed her royal robes.

But there was no time for leisure just now. Not with the specter of what the Bellatorian breeder had planned hanging over her head.

On the other side of the huge bedchamber stood Dian, Kieran in her arms. At the sight of her son, Meriel's anger faded. She gathered her skirts and hurried across the room.

Taking the child from her friend, she clutched him to her, burying her face in his soft, fragrant blond curls. "How's my sweet lad?" she asked softly. "Mama missed you so."

Independent two-year-old that he was, Kieran squirmed in her too-tight grasp. "Mama. Down. Let me down."

With a sigh and a loving shake of her head, Meriel released her son. He toddled out toward the balcony where several of his toys lay. Meriel turned to Dian.

"You must keep him hidden from now on. His father—the breeder—is now Lord Commander, and I don't know what he'd do if he found Kieran."

The maidservant's eyes went wide with shock. "Th-the breeder? How is that possible? And surely he'd not harm his own son!"

Meriel grasped her friend's arms. "I don't know how it all came about—that he's now conqueror of Tenua—but it doesn't really matter. He *hates* me, Dian! Son or no, he might decide to use Kieran against me. We must not allow him to find the lad. And we must discover some way to smuggle Kieran from the palace to a safe hiding place."

"There are the passages that wind through the bowels of the palace," Dian offered hesitantly. "They haven't been used in hundreds of cycles, but some lead to the holding cells and others to places outside the palace."

"Then it is past time to use them. Torman carries all the palace key controls. You must find some way to get to him."

Dian frowned. "That might be difficult. I have no idea where Torman is, or what happened to him."

"Then you must find an excuse to search the pal-

ace for him—and as quickly as possible." Meriel
paused, releasing her friend's arms. "The hardest part will be getting the breeder to allow
you free access to the palace. He has set a
guard outside my quarters to ensure I don't
escape."

"What does he plan to do to our people?"

"He claims he'll have mercy on our soldiers—
so your Torman should be safe—and I presume
that mercy extends to our people as well. As for
Pelum, the breeder has sent him to the holding
cells."

"Poor Pelum." Dian paused, a flush spreading
up her face. "And he's not *my* Torman. At least
not yet. Besides, what really matters is you. What
will the breeder do with you?"

Meriel couldn't quite meet her gaze. "I-I'm not
certain."

"Meriel!" Dian captured her chin and turned
her face to meet her eye to eye. "Don't play the
evasive little cerva with me. I know you too well
for that. I ask again. What will he do with you?"

"He means to force himself on me, to teach me
a lesson."

"A lesson? But what did you ever do to him?
Surely he doesn't hold you responsible for this
ill-fated war?"

"I don't know what he holds me responsible
for." Meriel shook her head, misery flooding her
in a heavy, exhausting wave. "Indeed, he may well
hold me responsible for the war. Few knew that
Mother had died. He may have thought I was just
as involved in the plan to evacuate our people to
the Abesse as Mother was. In the end, it doesn't

really matter. I am Queen now. I am the one responsible."

"But it isn't fair!"

A sad, resigned smile touched Meriel's lips. "No, it isn't, but it's reality nonetheless. And that is all we have left." She made a small, impatient motion with her hand. "Now, no more of it. I'll deal with my fate when the time comes. In the meanwhile, we must have a plan."

"What would you have me do?" Dian asked, her pretty face hardening with resolve. "You know I'll do anything for you and Kieran, to the giving of my life if you ask it."

"And *you* know I'd never ask such a thing." Meriel's brow furrowed in thought. "The breeder said he would come for me once the palace is secured. Considering the purpose of his visit, it should be easy to convince him to send you away. We'll hide Kieran while you search out Torman."

Dian immediately protested. "I won't leave you alone with that man! If he means to harm you, he'll have two women to deal with instead of one."

"One or two, he could handle us both." Tenderly she stroked her friend's cheek. "No, whatever is between the breeder and me must be faced alone. This chance for you to look for Torman might not come again. Your mission is of greater import than what I do by staying behind. And we must all be willing to sacrifice—in whatever way is demanded."

Tears flooded the maidservant's eyes. "B-but he means to ravish you!"

"I've lain with him before and can survive it again. Perhaps if I don't fight him it will be over quickly. I can bear it, Dian. I have to. Kieran and Pelum, and our people, are what matter."

Dian wiped her tears away. "It will be difficult to hide the lad. He's not known for keeping quiet."

"We'll give him a mild narcotic," Meriel said, making a quick decision. "He'll sleep for hours."

Her friend nodded slowly. "Yes, that might work. Just as long as the breeder doesn't decide to spend the night."

Meriel gave a bitter laugh. "I hardly think that's a worry. What man would dare fall asleep with a woman he not only despises but mistrusts as well?" She shook her head. "No, I doubt he'll stay a moment longer once he's done with me. Our plan for Kieran is sound."

Her gaze shifted to the balcony where her son played in happy, if vocal, contentment. "The only thing left to chance is the timing . . ."

"What do you plan to do?" Teran asked as he strode down the palace corridor with Gage several hours later. "About the Tenuan Queen, I mean."

Gage shot him a narrow glance. "I haven't decided."

"I assume that rape is no longer an option."

"By the five moons!" Gage slid to a halt, then swung around to confront his friend. "Don't interfere in this, Teran. She needs to be taught a lesson she won't soon forget!"

"And you're the man to teach her, are you?"

"Yes, damn it all!"

Teran grasped Gage by the arm. "I don't believe for one second, despite your threats to the contrary, that you intend to rape Queen Meriel. If I did, you know I'd stop you."

Gage's jaw went hard. "And I'll damn well . . ."

He paused, battling the rage that snaked through his body, tightening his muscles to whipcord tautness. Then reason returned. Gage dragged in a shuddering breath. "You know I won't harm her. I give you my word on that. Though I hate her more than I've ever hated another being, I'll never harm a woman." He shot Teran a piercing glance. "But I do mean to gain Meriel's total cooperation. My original plan to banish her may not have been the wisest. We'll most likely need her help if we're to successfully evacuate this planet."

Teran glanced around, then pulled him into a small alcove. "Your change of heart is wise. Time is of the essence," he said, his voice lowering. "Our jamming signals will block the Volans' interplanetary transmissions only so long. Sooner or later, their mother ship will find a way to circumvent us and resume communications with the infiltrators here. You can be sure the Volans don't want to lose Tenua and its source of fresh bodies to enslave."

He released Gage's arm. "Go. Do what you must to ensure the Queen's cooperation, but beware the source of your anger toward her. Deep pain can incite such feelings. And there are few ways a woman stirs a man to strong emotions other than by touching his heart." A sad, knowing expression glimmered on Teran's lips. "Admit it, my friend. You let yourself care for her and she betrayed you. That hurts."

A dark flush crept up Gage's neck and face. "And I say you couldn't be more wrong. It's much simpler than that. She lied to me, manipulated me—and you know how I feel about people who do that."

"And *I* say, give it time. Whatever happened, putting the past behind you—forgiving—has a certain honor and healing." Teran paused, carefully framing his next words. "If you can learn that from this experience with Meriel, the same ability might well carry over to another woman . . . an even more distant betrayal."

"No. Never. Never with her."

Teran studied his friend. A bleak, haunted expression dulled the light in Gage's eyes.

"Be that as it may," Teran said, "you must come to some sort of peace with the Tenuan Queen—and soon."

"I know that," Gage growled. He stepped back. "By your leave, I'll embark upon that unpleasant task right now."

Teran grinned. "Yes, do that. And let me know how it goes."

"As you wish, Lord Ardane," Gage replied with a wry twist of his mouth. "You are, after all, the King's emissary, and privy to everything that transpires. Everything, that is, pertinent to the mission."

"But, of course, Lord Commander."

"Why am I rapidly becoming sick to death of that title?" Gage muttered as he turned and headed back down the hall.

"Perhaps because it's always used to remind you of the magnitude of your responsibility," Teran's reply followed him, "and the faith I have that you'll always choose the better course."

A half hour later, after a purposefully circuitous route through the palace, Gage paused outside Meriel's door. His fist lifted, then hesitated before the imprint entry panel he'd earlier had reprogrammed to only his and the guard's hands.

Frustration lanced through him. Despite Teran's assurances to the contrary, time had done little to ease the anger—and the groin-hardening need—that filled him every time his thoughts turned to Meriel.

Perhaps it *was* wiser to allow more time for his feelings to cool, to walk away before he did something he'd regret. Perhaps now *wasn't* the moment to confront old conflicts, nor look too closely at poorly healed wounds.

But a mating with Meriel would solve a myriad of problems. He'd release his anger and frustration as well as ease the tensions of the past six months of battle. Taking a comely female to bed had always soothed him in the past. And, like it or not, Meriel had flowered from a sweetly beguiling girl into a tantalizingly seductive woman.

But to force himself upon her . . .

He had promised Teran he'd not harm Meriel. He had given his word. Yet the anger—and the surprising intensity of his need—were potent, mind-numbing, honor-draining forces. Suddenly there was nothing that mattered more than easing the agonizing emotions that overpowered all rational thought. Short of rape itself, he *must* find some release!

Swallowing a savage curse, Gage strode in unannounced to imperiously survey the room. He found Meriel seated in a chair before the hearth. At his entry she rose, smoothed the thin, airy gown she now wore. Briefly, her glance met that of the room's other occupant, a young woman who appeared close to her age.

Gage noted the quick, encouraging smiles that arced between them. He frowned. Something was amiss here . . .

He strode over to Meriel. "Who is this?" he demanded, motioning toward the other woman.

His gaze skimmed the slender, brown-haired female with the soft brown eyes. Pretty enough, Gage thought, in a shy, gentle sort of way. And, most likely, a far more pleasant bed mate than the treacherous Queen of Tenua would ever be.

A memory of warm bubbling water and gentle mists, of a sleek female body joined with his in a heated embrace, eased into Gage's mind. For a brief, passionate moment, Meriel *had* been more than just a pleasant bed mate. She'd been everything he'd ever dreamed of in a woman.

The realization of where his train of thought was leading brought Gage up cold. *Fool!* he berated himself. That time in the garden grotto was long past. He must deal with the present—and the reality of what the lovely, innocent girl had become.

Standing there, gazing up at him, Meriel felt encompassed by his presence. Panic fluttered beneath her breast, her mind went blank, and her world suddenly narrowed to just the powerful man glaring down at her. She took a step back.

He smiled, a movement of his mouth that never quite reached his eyes. "Well, femina? I await your answer. Who is this woman?"

Meriel blinked in confusion, then her awareness returned. Awareness of his purpose here—and her plan to ultimately thwart that purpose. Unflinchingly she returned his gaze.

"She is my friend and maidservant. Her name is Dian."

Gage's glance shifted to Dian. "Get out."

The maidservant swallowed convulsively, then looked to her mistress. "Meriel?"

"Go." Meriel indicated the door. "I'll send for you later."

In a flurry of diaphanous fabric, Dian fled the room.

Meriel turned back to Gage to find him studying her with speculative eyes. "Is there something wrong, Lord Commander?"

"You allow your servant undue familiarity in the use of your first name."

"We are lifelong friends, having been raised together since childhood. I love and respect Dian."

"Then she must be cut from the same cloth as you. I'll have to have her watched."

"I'd imagine so," Meriel muttered, "if you judge everyone by such low standards."

A dark brow arched. "My standards may be low, but I'm rarely disappointed. Would you care to try?"

She shot him a look of withering scorn. "Hardly. It's no concern of mine what code you choose to live by, as embittered and cold-hearted as it must be. I only care what becomes of my people."

White teeth flashed in a lazy grin. "The issue of your people can be dealt with later, after we settle what's between us." Gage's glance moved slowly, languidly down her body. He stepped closer. "I did promise you a mating, didn't I? And, after all this time—"

"I want nothing from you!" Meriel cried, unnerved by the nearness of him. "Nothing, save the promise you'll help my people and let my husband go!"

A long, strong finger moved to trace a sinuous line down the side of her face. "Indeed? I'm a reasonable man. Perhaps there's some way to persuade me to give you what you want."

Nausea churned in the pit of Meriel's stomach, then surged up to swell in her throat. She swallowed hard, inhaled a shuddering breath, and willed all the strength of her resolve into her next words. "And mating with me will ensure these things? You'll help my people, free Pelum?"

At the reminder of the man whom Meriel had run to after discarding him, something inside Gage snapped. With a low growl, he grasped Meriel about the waist and pulled her hard up against him. "You value yourself too highly to ask so much. I'll help your people, but your husband stays right where he is until *I* decide what *I* want to do with him. Agreed?"

The feel of his body through the thin fabric of her gown, the hard play of muscle and sinew—and something even harder—wreaked havoc with Meriel's senses. Suddenly she couldn't think, couldn't breathe. Desire—shameful, despised—shot through her in a smothering, mind-numbing wave.

Gage gave her a fierce shake. "Well, femina? Tell me now before you lose the favor of even having a say in this. Will you mate with me if I swear to help your people?"

"Yes!" she gasped, her hands rising to press between them. It did little good. The solid wall of Gage's chest was more than Meriel's strength could prevail against. Her hands fell back to her sides. Her head lowered. "Yes, I'll mate with you if that's what it takes."

He crooked a finger under Meriel's chin and lifted her gaze to his, regarding her dispassionately. "That's probably the wisest decision you've made in your entire reign. Or at least," he added, "as far as your people are concerned." Dark brown eyes stared down at her, bold and disturbingly sensual. "I've never bedded a queen before. And certainly not one so well-curved and provocatively rounded. This bargain may well be one of the more pleasant ones I've made."

Meriel jerked her head away. "Spare me your false compliments! This is business and nothing more. What are the terms of this agreement?"

The look in Gage's eyes turned cold. "A business agreement, is it?" he asked softly. "Well, have it your way. I'll arrange for the evacuation of your people to Carcer, and Imperial assistance with the settlement into a new life there, in exchange for unlimited use of your body."

"U-unlimited use?" Meriel nearly choked on the words.

"Well, at least until I tire of you. I'll be sure to let you know when that happens." His mouth curved up into a slow, mocking grin. "Of course, depending on your needs, there is much that can be done to prolong my lust for you. A warm, willing woman can be assured of my extended attentions."

"Why, you vile, loathsome—"

He silenced her with a firm finger upon her lips. "Enough, femina. Is it a bargain or not?"

Awash in a sudden sea of misery, Meriel squeezed her eyes shut and nodded. He had all the power, she reminded herself, and her people were what mattered. Better to get this first mating over and done with, and hope Dian discovered the whereabouts of Torman and the key controls. If luck was with her, Meriel might then be able to free Pelum and send Kieran and her husband to safety. There was no hope for her, not while the plight of her people remained so precarious, but if her family were free of this breeder's cruel clutches . . .

Gage released her and stepped back. Taken off guard, Meriel nearly stumbled in her attempt to regain her balance. Her eyes snapped open and she stared up at him, confused, wary.

Frigid eyes glared back at her. "I have a need to consummate our agreement. Strip yourself and climb into bed."

"N-now?"

"Yes. Now."

The blood drained from Meriel's face. She

swallowed hard, willing herself to fight past the dizzying mists, the blessed oblivion, that beckoned at the edge of her consciousness.

She'd made a bargain and meant to see it through. If this disgusting, leering male thought to intimidate her, he was sadly mistaken. She was Queen. She could face anything—even the humiliation of stripping naked—with the dignity and pride of generations of Corbas before her.

"As you wish, Lord Commander."

With a mocking smile, Meriel unfastened the jeweled belt that cinched her waist. She dropped it to the floor, then moved to the clasps that bound the shoulders of her gown.

With a grace that belied an act that Gage suspected had never been performed for another man, Meriel released first one, then the other shoulder clasp. The gown fell in a rush of shimmering fabric to pool at her feet. Meriel immediately stepped out of it and turned toward the bed.

"Wait."

The hoarse command gave her pause. She glanced over her shoulder.

"Turn back to me," Gage rasped. "I . . . I want to look at you."

If it were possible to layer blush upon blush, Meriel thought she must certainly be doing so. But she turned nonetheless and faced him squarely.

Blood pounded through Gage as his eyes devoured her, racing through a rapidly beating heart and fever-hot body to pool in his groin.

His sex filled, thickened, pressing tautly against his breeches. Desire, scalding and overwhelming in its intensity, engulfed him.

She was exquisite, her slender but ripely curved young body perfection itself. Her breasts were full and pouting, tipped by soft, impudent, rose-colored nipples. Her waist was impossibly narrow, her hips womanly full. Her legs were long and well shaped. Her stomach was softly rounded, and the dark triangle of curls at the apex of her thighs were lush with a woman's mystery.

It isn't rape, Gage assured himself as he moved toward Meriel. He had kept his word to Teran. She wouldn't fight him; there'd be no need to risk harming her. She'd made a bargain and her body was payment. In the end, they'd both get what they wanted—Meriel, the evacuation of her people to safety, he, an easing of the seething anger and need for vengeance.

Yes, that's all it was for either of them. A business agreement.

In one sweep of his arm Gage jerked Meriel to him, pulling her stiff, unyielding body against his. He grasped her head in his other hand and bent to cover her mouth, slanting fiercely over Meriel in a savage, greedy kiss.

Her mouth remained closed, lips clamped shut over a barrier of teeth. Frustration flooded Gage. Damn her, must he lead her every step of the way?

"Open your mouth," he growled. "You know what I want. Give it to me!"

With a shuddering sigh, Meriel complied. He

plunged into her then, his tongue bold and probing. His hand closed on a breast, squeezing, then kneading, rousing the nipple to a firm, taut bud.

Strange, long-repressed sensations rippled through Meriel. A need to press into Gage, to touch his body, to meld mouth and tongue and mind. She moaned, a tiny sound that rose unbidden from deep in her throat. Her knees went weak. She sank against him.

At the sound, Gage nearly lost control. He didn't care if his desire drove him, blinding him to the woman Meriel truly was. All he wanted, all he could envision, was to drive his shaft into her, sink into Meriel's warm, tight, woman's sheath, and spew himself into her. Shuddering his release, groaning her name . . .

A cry, startled and frightened, pierced the mists of his passion. It came from somewhere beyond the hot, damp circle of their embrace—another world, another reality. Gage shrugged off the intrusion. His kiss deepened, his lust rose to soul-grabbing heights.

The cry came again, a child's plaintive wail of terror. Meriel stiffened in his arms, then struggled, pushing against him.

Kieran. Kieran had awakened.

The heated pleasure she'd so mindlessly allowed herself to indulge in dissipated in a rush. In its place flowed panic. She had to get the breeder out of here!

"P-please!" Meriel breathed. "I-I can't go through with this. Leave me!"

Gage released her, his features tightening with

suspicion. "What's going on? If you play some game . . ."

"No!" Meriel hastened to say. "I meant no game. I-I just need some time alone. This . . . this is all going too fast." She shoved at him, motioning toward the door. "Please leave. I'll send for you in a short while."

Gage scowled. "No, I think not. You're no longer in any position to order me—"

"Mama! Mama! Scared!"

The tracker wheeled about. A child's voice emanated from a large, intricately inlaid wood wardrobe. The delicate blend of rich, dark robur wood and paler sempervivus formed a scene that filled both panels of the front doors. A scene of a garden and grotto—a grotto wherein lay a mist-shrouded pool.

Gage choked back a brutal curse. Before he could take a step forward, Meriel was beside him. Her hand stayed him.

"Please," she whispered, her voice strained and trembling. "It's nothing, really. I'll take care of the lad."

Something in her manner, in the fear that vibrated through her words, gave Gage pause. All his tracker's instincts rose to the forefront. Meriel was trying to hide something. But what?

He had to know.

He shrugged her hand from his arm and strode over to the wardrobe. Flinging it open, Gage gazed down on a makeshift bed of several pillows and a lightweight, multicolored blanket. Within that bed sat a small boy, blond-haired and brown-eyed. At the sudden glare from the perpetual lights overhead, the lad blinked sleepily. Then he smiled, a toothy, face-widening little grin, and awkwardly climbed to his feet.

Chapter Five

Before Gage could reach down to assist the boy, Meriel was scooting between them to gather the child into her arms. She'd donned a crimson, silky serica cloth bedrobe, and her ebony-colored hair tumbled in wild disarray down her back. She clasped the lad to her bosom, her head bent protectively over him as she murmured soothing words.

Meriel, in the full, radiant flower of womanhood, knelt there, totally oblivious to Gage as she stroked and petted the chubby, tousle-haired, squirming little boy. There was no doubt in Gage's mind that she held her son—a son who was also his.

Tenderness, a protectiveness that both surprised and disturbed him, flooded Gage. A distant memory flickered in the furthest corner of his mind—of his own mother cuddling him close, crooning an ancient lullaby while his father hovered nearby, carving a wooden equs for a toy.

Pain, sharp and searing, lanced through him. With a hoarsely whispered curse, Gage clamped down on the memory, shoving it once more into his subconscious. There was work to be done here, he reminded himself grimly, and, tender scene or no, Meriel was still a conniving, treacherous little bitch.

He leaned down and pulled her to her feet. She rose awkwardly, lifting the boy with her. Violet eyes, wary with apprehension, met his.

"The lad," Gage spat out the words. "He's mine, isn't he?"

What could she say to ease the anger burning in his eyes? Meriel thought wildly. And indeed, why *was* he so angry? Most men would be happy to learn their seed had borne fruit. Yet the breeder looked even more upset than before, almost disgusted by the discovery.

She considered her options, then carefully wet her lips. "Yes, he's yours," Meriel said, deciding that anything but the truth would be pointless. "Who else's could he be?"

"Knowing the female propensity for lies and tricks, anyone's, I'd imagine," Gage snarled. "Let me see him."

Meriel hesitated, uncertain what he'd do with Kieran. "If you don't believe me, then it really doesn't matter, does it? Allow me to summon Dian. She'll take him away."

"Let me see him!"

At the soft, deadly tone, fear rippled through her. Meriel handed Kieran to Gage.

He took the boy from her awkwardly, uncertain quite how to handle the child. Kieran turned, clasping Gage about the neck and snuggling close, still intermittently drowsy from the effects of the narcotic. Gage's arms curled about him then, finding a secure hold.

The small boy's utter trust and unconditional acceptance plucked at Gage's heart. Tentatively he stroked the curly head that lay upon his chest, marveling at the hair color. His own hair had once been such a light golden hue, he mused, recalling the lock his mother had saved from his first haircut, and the big brown eyes that had briefly lifted to his before closing in sleep were his exact shade, down to the dancing golden flecks.

No, there wasn't any question the boy was his. Somehow, though, the realization did little to ease the turmoil in his heart. A child only complicated things. It was harder to hate a woman who had borne him a son—and far more difficult to treat her cruelly.

He inhaled a ragged breath. "The lad. What's his name?"

Relief shivered through Meriel. The breeder appeared moved by his son. He'd not harm him.

"Kieran. His name is Kieran."

"And have you told him of me?"

Once more Meriel wet her lips, considering her reply. "He thinks Pelum is his father. I thought him too young to understand anything more."

"Did you ever plan to tell him about me?"

After how you so callously tossed me aside for my mother? Hardly.

"I hadn't given it much thought," she lied

instead. "There was no reason to dwell on it just now."

Gage gave a disbelieving snort. "Or ever, knowing you." He hefted Kieran more comfortably against him. "Well, no matter. What's important is that you meant to keep him from me."

Meriel paled. "I don't know what you—"

"The lad's a potential pawn between us," Gage interrupted coldly. "You kept him from me so I wouldn't be able to use him against you."

"And will you?"

A subtle sneer curled his lips. "But of course, sweet femina. I'm no fool. I use *everything* to my advantage."

"But he's hardly more than a baby!" Meriel cried. "I've already surrendered not only my planet but my body as well. What more is there to give?"

"Your utmost loyalty and complete cooperation." His mouth lifted in a contemptuous smile. "Those attributes are vital to the success of my mission here. The same attributes that are so sadly lacking in you. Or at least," he added, "until now."

"A-are you threatening to harm Kieran if I don't help you?" Meriel whispered, forcing the words past a constricted throat.

"Hardly. If anyone in this universe is innocent, it's this child. No, if I fail here thanks to you, I'll simply take him away with me and you'll never see him again." Gage cocked a speculative brow. "How much do you care for the lad? Enough to give me everything I ask?"

"Yes," she breathed, her arms reaching out to

her son. "I'll do *anything* for Kieran!"

"Indeed?" He turned away, refusing to allow her to take the boy. "Well, we'll have to see how deep a mother's love runs, won't we? I haven't been too impressed in the past with the strength of maternal feelings, but perhaps you'll prove me wrong. In the meanwhile, the lad stays with me."

"What?" Meriel couldn't hide the hysteria that threaded her voice. "I told you I'd cooperate. Please, I beg you, don't take Kieran from me! He's too young to be separated from his mother. He'll be terrified!"

Gage glanced down at his son, nestled so contentedly on his chest. "Ah yes, I noted that immediately."

"It-it's the lingering effects of the narcotic. But once he fully wakens—"

"You *drugged* my son?" Fury blazed in Gage's eyes. "You cared so little for his welfare that you'd drug a child just to best me? Why, you heartless she-devil! If you think I'd ever leave him with you now—"

Meriel grabbed his arm, unconsciously scoring his flesh with her nails. Gage wrenched away.

"Please, listen to me!" Meriel followed him as he backed toward the door. "After what you said in the Great Hall, I was uncertain what you might do. I only meant to protect Kieran. Wouldn't you have done the same?"

"What I think is that you'd use anyone and anything to your advantage—including your own son!" An expression of utter loathing twisted his face. "In the end, you're no different from *her*! But have no fear, *sweet* femina. I know how to deal with women of your ilk. Know very, very well."

"You don't know me at all, you stubborn son of a subterranean slime weevil!" Frantically, Meriel glanced around for a weapon, anything, to hit Gage with. He *wouldn't* take her son from her! She'd kill the breeder—or die trying—before she let that happen.

Gage saw the wild look in her eyes and recognized the intent. "I wouldn't try it if I were you, femina. It'll earn you nothing but a long visit in the holding cells."

"Curse you!" Meriel screamed in frustration. "I don't care what you do to me! Just give me Kieran!"

She lunged at him then, grasping for her son. The boy started, clinging tightly as Gage lithely sidestepped, then pivoted around behind Meriel to grab her by the hair. With one hand, he jerked her up against him.

"You try my patience, my beauteous Queen," he rasped in her ear. Kieran began to whimper. "And you're upsetting our son. You'd be wise to stop now."

"K-Kieran. J-just let me have Kieran," Meriel pleaded, tears flowing from her eyes. "I *beg* you! I won't fight you; I'll support you in every way. Just give me back my son!"

"You'll do all that and more, sweet femina," he whispered, his rock-hard body pressing cruelly, relentlessly into hers. "On the morrow, before an assemblage of this entire palace, you'll bow down before me and pledge your unswerving fealty to King Falkan and the Imperium. Then, one by one, each and every one of your servants and guardsmen will do the same. The famed Tenuan code of honor will guarantee your total loyalty and cooperation after that, won't it?"

Meriel twisted in his grip to face him. "You know it will!" she gasped. "And then you'll give Kieran back to me—after the ceremony?"

Gage released her and stepped away. "Perhaps. I haven't decided as yet. A lot will depend on how convincing you are on the morrow. And in my bed," he added, his glance sliding down her body, "when a more opportune moment presents itself."

With that, he turned on his heel and walked out of the room, Kieran clasped in his arms. He never once looked back, leaving Meriel standing in speechless horror.

For a fleeting moment, the numbness held the pain at bay. Then the tears welled anew. The grief burgeoned until it exploded in a despairing wail. Meriel sank to her knees, weeping her heart out in helpless, frustrated anguish.

She didn't know how long she knelt there before Meriel heard the door open and soft footsteps pad across the floor. She couldn't muster the strength to lift her head or identify her newest visitor. A soft murmur of concern and a gentle hand upon her shoulder told her that it was Dian.

"Meriel!" Panic tightened her friend's voice. Dian knelt beside her. "What happened? What did that animal do to you?"

Meriel turned into the comforting embrace of Dian's arms. "H-he took Kieran!" she sobbed. "He took my babe away from me!"

"Curse his soul to the depths of perdition! I was afraid of that. The breeder didn't seem the sort easily fooled." Dian stroked a tear-damp lock from Meriel's cheek. "What will he do with the lad?"

"I-I don't know," Meriel hiccuped. "He means to k-keep Kieran from me to ensure my c-cooperation. Ah, by all that is sacred, I hate him!"

"We'll beat him yet! It's only a matter of time!"

"Your search!" Meriel sat back and stared up at her friend. "Did you find Torman? Did he have the key controls?"

A grim look settled over Dian's features. "Yes, I found him. He's alive and well—and locked in the holding cells with all the other officers. I caught a glimpse of Torman while I was helping the cook deliver the guards' meals, but I wasn't able to get close enough to talk with him."

"Well, no matter. Torman will pledge his fealty on the morrow with all the others. Time enough for you to talk with him then." Meriel sighed. "I suppose Kieran can survive one night without me. The breeder was gentle with him. The lad will manage."

"Yes, that he will." Dian cocked a speculative brow. "But what of you? How did the breeder treat you?"

"He didn't ravish me, if that's what you're asking. Kieran awoke before he had the chance to bed me." At the memory of Gage's lips upon hers, his tongue in her mouth, his hand upon her breast, a rush of heated blood coursed through Meriel. Gods, she had almost let herself succumb, almost let herself want him again!

Shame flooded her. How could she ever want a crude, cruel man such as he? She shook the question—and the unsettling emotions—aside. There was too much still to be done to waste time worrying about what was past—and never more to be.

Meriel rose, took Dian by the arm, and pulled her to her feet. "You must stay near during the ceremony of fealty. Then, just as soon as the oaths are pledged and the people dispersed, seek out Torman. Get the key controls from him and directions for the passages. And," Meriel added, a thoughtful gleam in her eyes, "try to bring Torman to me as well. If the breeder truly keeps his word, our captain of the guard may well be free to help us smuggle out Pelum and Kieran."

"But you'll both have sworn fealty to the breeder by then," Dian protested. "You won't be able—"

"I have no intention of betraying the breeder," Meriel interrupted firmly. "I will stay and help him in every way I can to save our people. But I *won't* have Pelum and Kieran remain at his mercy. In the end, *I* owe the breeder unstinting loyalty. He owes me nothing. I can't risk the possibility that his unstable emotions may eventually turn against me. And the only power he has to do me harm is through my family."

"Something must be done, and soon, or the Bellatorians will ruin all our plans," the Volan lieutenant who inhabited the body of the Tenuan royal seneschal muttered. "We *must* find some way to enslave the two leaders!"

"And we will, Dirmat," his own leader soothed.

"The Bellatorian takeover was inevitable. No Imperial planet is powerful enough to withstand their military might for long. But we have a solid foothold on this planet, and will soon be firmly ensconced within the palace itself."

"But they're jamming our transmissions from the Mother Ship!" another Volan who was master of the palace head cook cried. "No more hive occupants can be transported down. We're cut off from communications, from our vital directives! How will we make decisions or know what to do next?"

"We are capable of independent thought when necessary," the leader snapped. "That ability is programmed into our collective consciousness just as thoroughly as obedience to the hive command. We serve as well by initiative as by following orders. You have only to obey me in the interim. That is all that is required."

"I say the best plan is to enslave the Lord Commander," the Volan/royal seneschal stated flatly. "With him under our command, the rest will be easy."

"And also far too obvious," his leader drawled in reply. "Bellator is well aware of our presence here. If Bardwin suddenly changed . . . Besides, I doubt he'd be easy to enslave. With his tracker's instincts and acute reflexes, he doesn't strike me as a man who'd sleep soundly enough for us to complete the transfer process." He shook his head. "No, better to see to his destruction. If his death occurred at the hands of someone who had motive and opportunity, no one could easily suspect us."

"You have a plan, then?" the Volan/royal seneschal inquired. "A murderer and a motive?"

A thin smile twisted the Volan leader's handsome mouth. "Indeed. The Tenuan Queen wishes Bardwin dead. It should be a simple thing to manipulate her to our needs."

"She is a female, weak and faint-hearted as are all of her sex," scoffed the Volan/head cook. "She'll never have the courage it takes to kill. One of us will have to enslave her to see the deed done."

"Queen Meriel is stronger than you think, especially when the welfare of her people is involved. But I agree. We will attempt to enslave her. If that fails, we'll use her beloved husband to 'convince' her. He is frail, though. I'm not certain how long his body could withstand the stress of an enslavement. We will try the Queen first."

The royal seneschal chuckled. "Who and when will one of us pay her a dream-visit?"

"You may, Dirmat, this very night. We've still a few biospheres available that contain females, don't we?"

Dirmat grinned broadly. "More than a few, Exalted Leader. But why a female? I'd be willing to inhabit the Queen's body, and as strong a personality as mine would be of more use than that of one of our simpering females."

Somehow the thought of another male inhabiting the little Queen's body repulsed the Volan leader. "There are plenty of females to choose from!" he snapped. "Choose one who possesses more of the aggressive qualities you so prize."

"May I presume to suggest Lavia then?" Dirmat

was quick to offer. "Her biosphere is the oldest and beginning to fail. She can easily turn the Tenuan Queen to our way of thinking. The threat of the Bellatorian Lord Commander will soon be no more."

"Lavia it will be then. See that it happens." The Volan leader rose from the table. "You all have your directives. Continue as instructed until I request otherwise. You are dismissed."

He watched his followers depart the room, then strode over to the intricately beveled, stone-cut window. For a long while he gazed out on the dawn-streaked horizon, searching in vain for the faint signal beacon emitted from the Mother Ship. The sky was empty of any artificial light.

Perhaps the jamming signals had confused the Mother Ship. Perhaps it had been recalled to the Abesse for further instructions. The Volan leader couldn't know, wouldn't know, until contact was resumed. In the end, it didn't really matter. The last directive was all the orders he needed. Take over Tenua. Destroy the Bellatorians. He'd been bred and born to obey, to follow the collective mind of the hive ship, as were all his kind before and after him. To ensure the survival of the Volan race, his mission was the unceasing traversal of the universe in search of fresh bodies to enslave. Endless travel, relentless searching, until his own span was over. In selfless service to his people, in unswerving, unthinking, unfeeling devotion.

That was all that mattered.

The Volan leader turned from the window and strode back across the room. Time to rest the body he inhabited, as strong and well-muscled

as it was. It was a good body, one of the best
he'd enslaved in a while. He wanted to conserve
it for as long as possible.

By tomorrow night they'd have another Tenuan
to use, in the body of Queen Meriel. Tomorrow they'd set the stage for the downfall of
the Bellatorian Lord Commander. Yes, tomorrow promised a far more productive day than
this one had been.

He paused at the door, resuming the well-
known, stern-faced expression of the stoic Torman. Then, cloaking his presence from the guards
who stalked the corridors, he made his stealthy,
silent way back to the holding cells.

"I pledge my undying fealty to King Falkan
of Bellator, and to the exalted union known as
the Imperium of Planets," Meriel intoned with
outstretched arms as she knelt at the Lord Commander's feet in the Great Hall.

Below them, the palace servants, richly garbed
nobility, and soldiers watched, all awaiting their
turn to climb the throne platform and swear
allegiance. But, for now, the room was silent,
the occupants frozen in watchful fascination as
their Queen and ruler was first to publicly bow
to Tenua's conqueror.

Crimson with shame, sick to the very marrow
of her bones, Meriel forced the required words
through clenched teeth, then rose to squarely meet
the gaze of the tall, blond man who towered over
her. She faced him neither with defiance, for that
would have been foolhardy, nor with subservience. In her heart she would never be slave to

him, no matter what he did to her. But help him she would in every way possible—until her people were safe at last.

Once that was accomplished, Meriel didn't know what she'd do, but the nebulous future was too distant to worry over just now. The present—and the horrendous task of evacuating Tenua—was enough to deal with. That, and the removal of her husband and son from the Lord Commander's evil clutches.

He stared down at Meriel for a long moment, his dark eyes slicing through to the depths of her soul. Then he smiled, a ceremonial gesture that quickly dissipated in the depths of his eyes, and extended a hand.

"Come, femina." Gage's voice lifted in volume to reach all assembled. "Sit beside me as I accept the fealty of your subjects. It is fitting that we do so together, as we are now sworn to a common goal—the salvation of your people."

As Meriel rose and accepted his hand—a hand rough and callused but warm and strangely stimulating at the same time—out of the corner of her eye she noted the presence of Teran Ardane, moving to position himself at the right of the Lord Commander's chair. It was *his* words that the breeder had mouthed, Meriel sensed, when he'd made the offer for her to join him on the throne platform. There'd been no softening, no forgiveness in his hard gaze when he'd looked down at her. And no shred of kindness or acceptance in his heart.

Misery engulfed her. She was so tired, so lost, so confused. She'd barely slept last night, tossing and turning, rethinking the past day and what had transpired. Was it over then, or was there something else she could do? Something, anything, to thwart the Bellatorian who now held her captive?

Then the memory of her newly spoken vow returned. She must obey him in all things, for he was now King Falkan's representative on Tenua. If only he weren't so cruel, so heartless! If only he were more the man she'd once imagined him to be!

Meriel forced her wayward thoughts back to the present. She climbed the platform steps and, without a sideways glance in his direction, took her seat on the Lord Commander's left. Lifting her head in a regal gesture, Meriel acknowledged the gathering with a small nod.

Gage glanced at Teran, his mouth quirking in amusement, then turned back to the assemblage. "Your Queen has sworn her loyalty. It is time for the rest to follow her example." He made a sweeping gesture that encompassed the room. "Let the ceremony of fealty continue."

One by one, Meriel watched her people mount the steps, kneel before the Bellatorian, and pledge their allegiance. Despair, mixed with a sense of failure, nearly overwhelmed her before she numbed herself to the cruel irony of it all. The irony that less than a month ago, in a small, private ceremony, their pledges had been for her as their new Queen.

Finally, Torman mounted the steps and stared up at them through a hooded gaze. His blue eyes were cold, hard, and for a moment Meriel feared he might leap for the Lord Commander's throat. Then he forced a tight smile and made his obeisance.

Meriel relaxed. She smiled back at her captain of the guards, the look bright and happy. Torman nodded in acknowledgment, then turned and descended the steps.

Gage noted the glance that Meriel had bestowed upon the powerfully built, darkly handsome man. Something stirred within him, an emotion he could only describe as suspicion. There was something between the two, but what he had yet to discern. Perhaps, just perhaps, the deceitful little Queen had managed to find a potent lover after all.

A half hour more and the ceremony was over. Gage lost little time in escorting Meriel from the hall and into an adjacent, more intimate receiving room. Lord Ardane followed, bolting the door behind them. From outside the chamber, Meriel heard several guards move into place.

Something of import would be spoken here, something the two Bellatorians didn't want overheard. Meriel's heart beat a staccato rhythm beneath her breast.

She turned, her glance scanning the room. A sleek couch, its armrests curled into tight knobs at both ends, sat before a small, marmor stone fireplace. Two overstuffed stools and a long, low table of deep red robur wood stood opposite the couch. On one wall alongside the hearth was a narrow table set with a bowl of fruit, an aureum wrought plate of sweet cakes, and a topaz-hued crystal flask of uva wine.

Meriel smiled. Even in times such as these, her servants could be trusted to see to the smallest details. She strode over to the side table, then turned, gesturing to the food and drink.

"Would either of you care for refreshment?" she asked, determined to maintain some semblance of graciousness and breeding, despite the Lord Commander's growing reputation for boorishness. "After such a long ceremony, surely you've a need for a cup of wine to ease your thirst."

With a weary sigh, Teran lowered himself to one of the stools. "I'd be grateful for a cup, Domina, and one of those sweet cakes." He shot Gage a questioning glance. "What about you? Care for anything to eat or drink before we settle down to business?"

"No," Gage growled. "This isn't some Cygnian tea ceremony. We're here to work!"

Teran cocked a brow. "Indeed?" He turned back to Meriel. "The sweet cake and wine, if you please. *I* work better with something in my belly."

Beneath the glowering gaze of the Lord Commander who moved to stand at the fireplace, Meriel served Teran, then took a seat on the couch with her own cup of wine. She sipped it, struggling to contain the trembling of her hands.

It wasn't that she was afraid of the breeder, she hastened to reassure herself. It was only that she feared the upcoming conversation. Somehow she sensed it would deal with the plight of Tenua— and what the Bellatorians would and wouldn't do for them. The silence grew, the tension building to unbearable proportions. Meriel thought she would scream.

In a frantic effort to regain control, she turned to a topic she hoped would be less threatening for both of them. "Kieran," she began, her violet gaze lifting to the man glaring down at her. "Did he sleep well, Lord Commander?"

"Gage," he snapped. "My name is Gage. I do have an identity besides Lord Commander—and breeder!"

Meriel started, puzzlement furrowing her brow. "I . . . I only meant to pay you proper respect. You didn't approve of my familiarity with my maid-servant, so I thought—"

"Well, you thought wrong, femina!"

Teran choked on his cup of wine and smothered a smile. Gage glared at him, then swung back to Meriel.

"Well, femina?"

She feigned an indifferent shrug. "As you command . . . Gage."

He gave a snort of disgust, then walked over to throw himself down on the couch beside her. "He slept well."

Meriel stiffened at the nearness of his powerful form, now so close that his broad shoulders brushed hers. "Wh-what?"

"The lad slept well. And when he awoke this morning, my presence beside him appeared quite acceptable." He eyed her intently. "Kieran isn't quite the babe you still think him to be."

Meriel swallowed hard and tried to unobtrusively place a few millimeters of space between them. It did little good. She was already nearly up against the arm of the couch. With a small, resigned sigh, she gave up the attempt.

"Kieran is just a little over two cycles old," she said, turning back to the topic at hand. "He's hardly ready to learn the ways of battle. He still needs his mother."

"And a father as well," Gage muttered.

"He has a father!" Meriel cried. "Pelum loves the lad!"

"Love isn't enough. A lad needs a strong role model, someone to teach him courage, honor, to toughen him to the harsh realities of life."

"And you're the man to do it, aren't you?" Meriel leaped to her feet and turned to confront Gage. "You, who haven't a shred of kindness, of mercy or gentleness in you! Well, I won't have it, do you hear me? My son will be raised in the Tenuan way, and grow to be a good, kind, honorable man!"

Gage grinned and lounged back on the couch. "Indeed? And when did you suddenly regain command? You pledged your loyalty and undying cooperation to me just a short while ago. *In all things.* And that includes the issue of our son."

Fury engulfed Meriel. If he thought she would *ever* allow him to influence her son, he was—

"Er, pardon, if you please," Teran interjected, his mouth twisted in amusement. "We are deviating from the true purpose of our meeting here, and it once again falls upon me to play the peacemaker. Surely two parents who both have the welfare of their child at heart can work out some satisfactory compromise. In the meanwhile, we have more pressing problems to discuss."

With a superhuman effort, Meriel regained her rapidly waning composure. Lord Ardane was right. It was pointless to argue with *him!*

It would only stir his suspicions regarding her commitment to her vows. And she didn't dare risk Kieran and Pelum's safety for some transient satisfaction in a war of words.

She forced her lips to form a conciliatory smile. "I beg pardon," she said, glancing at Teran. "You are correct, of course." Meriel paused, turning her attention back to Gage. "I meant no disloyalty. It was only a mother's concern for her child. What really matters is when can I have him back? I miss him so."

Gage eyed her, his expression sharpening to glittering awareness. He'd intended to return the boy to her after the fealty ceremony, realizing he hadn't the heart to separate his son from a mother who meant everything to him. But there was something in Meriel's tone, in the spark of defiance gleaming in her eyes, that gave him pause. She was up to something—and that something included his son.

"I haven't decided." Gage propped up his feet on the small robur wood table, then shot her an indolent look. "It might be best for the lad to stay with me a time longer."

He raised a silencing hand when Meriel opened her mouth to protest. "I will allow you a generous amount of time to visit with Kieran each day. He is still young and does need his mother."

Meriel clamped her mouth shut, knowing she should be grateful for at least that concession. But it would make Kieran's escape from the palace all that harder. Well, she consoled herself, the Lord Commander would only slow her plans, not thwart them.

"I thank you for that." Meriel hesitated. "There's one thing more."

Gage quirked a brow. "Indeed? And what is that?"

"Pelum. You didn't include him in the ceremony of fealty. Yet I know he'd be happy to pledge his loyalty to you as well."

"Would he now?" Gage made a sound of disgust. "And to what purpose? So he'd regain his freedom and skulk through the palace, plotting my death? I think not, femina. Your husband is where I want him, and there he will stay."

"But it's not fair!" Meriel protested. "He means you no harm. And he's frail. He needs special meals, special medical—"

"Enough!" Gage silenced her with an upraised hand. "He is well cared for, and you have my permission to arrange for his other 'special' needs. But your consort stays where he is." He motioned to the couch. "Now sit. We've more pressing problems to discuss."

She resumed her place beside Gage, then turned to Teran. "And what, Lord Ardane, were the 'more pressing problems' we needed to discuss?"

Teran grinned at Meriel's overt attempt to snub Gage, then glanced at his friend. "It's time we told the Queen about the Volans, don't you think, my friend?"

"The Volans?" Meriel's gaze swung to Gage. "What is he talking about? What do the Volans have to do with Tenua?"

Gage gave a snort of disbelief and turned to face her. "Are you telling me you don't know about the Volans' renewed attempts at infiltrating the Imperium? You were Queen. You should be aware of each and every threat to your planet's welfare."

"Curse you, Gage Bardwin!" Meriel cried in exasperation. "For the past month since I assumed the throne, I've been embroiled in a hopeless war! I've hardly had the time to worry about some threat from outside our galaxy! So, just tell me and be done with it!"

Surprise flickered in the depths of Gage's eyes. "You've only been Queen for a month? How did your mother die?"

"She collapsed one day, you ignorant sandwart, without reason or cause. It was impossible to revive her. And I became Queen in the midst of a terrible war, without any hint of what my mother had planned!"

"Indeed?" Gage challenged, regaining his icy composure. "Then you don't know, do you?"

"Know what?" Meriel demanded. "Curse you! Stop playing games!"

He leaned forward, a fierce-burning fire in his eyes. "I play no games, Meriel. It's the Volans who do that. They are even now on Tenua, in possession of many of your subjects—and, before her death, I'd wager they'd enslaved your mother as well."

Chapter Six

Meriel's eyes widened in horror. "You lie! It-it isn't possible! My mother would never allow—"

"She hardly had a choice," Gage bluntly interrupted her. "A Volan mindslaver doesn't stop to ask permission to take over a body. And it served their purposes well to inhabit your mother. We wondered for a long while why Kadra was so adamant about evacuating Tenua to the Abesse and sending her people straight into Volan hands. Her possible motives made no sense—unless she was also Volan-enslaved."

"I-I can't believe it!" Meriel inhaled a shuddering breath. "Mother . . . enslaved by a Volan."

"As horrible as it is to contemplate," Teran offered, "it must be considered. As well as the imminent reality that the Volans mean to take over your entire planet."

"How do you know this? What makes you so certain that Volans are attacking the Imperium?"

"Nothing concrete, to be sure. It's not as if we could physically see their entities, or as yet know how to detect their presence." Teran sighed. "But the signs are there nonetheless. The significant increase in sudden, unexplained deaths, attributable to no known disease, for one. The reports from other galaxies that the Volans are once again migrating this way, now that the Knowing Crystal is no more. The strange activities of certain groups of people on various planets. Yours, most especially."

Teran's eyes locked with hers. "Then there's the inescapable certainty that it was bound to happen, sooner or later. And the time is right for a Volan invasion. We are once again virtually helpless against them, as were all the other planets they eventually enslaved."

"How do they do it?" Meriel whispered. "Enslave a person?"

"All we've been able to discover so far is that they enter the body when the being is asleep," Gage offered. He paused to lean forward, pick up Meriel's cup from the table and hand it to her. She accepted it wordlessly, clasping both hands about it as if, by its feel alone, the cup would ground her in a rapidly disintegrating reality.

"Perhaps it's necessary for a person's guard to be down," Gage continued. "Perhaps Volans have no power over someone who's awake and unwilling." He sighed. "We really aren't certain. It's all supposition at this point."

"What can we do?" Meriel took a swallow of her wine and turned to Teran. "There's no fate more horrible than a Volan mind enslavement. The only escape is death!"

"So it would seem," Teran gravely agreed.

Cup in hand, Meriel rose to pace the hearth before them. "Do either of you know how many of my people might already be enslaved?"

"No," Gage replied. "But perhaps in time we'll be able to develop some mechanism to discern their presence in others. Until then, only the sharpest vigilance can help us. Any person discovered enslaved by a Volan must not be transported to Carcer. We must not unintentionally seed the rest of the Imperium with more of those foul beings."

Meriel halted, turning to face the hearth before venturing to ask the next question. She didn't dare let the two men see the fear, the desperation, in her eyes. And everything hinged on the Bellatorians' next answer.

"Then you'll continue plans to move my people? In spite of the Volan threat?"

"The Volan threat will be a serious problem for a long time to come," Gage muttered from behind her. "Our scientists are working on ways to identify their alien presence, remove them from other beings, as well as rig some form of protection against them. In the meanwhile, the Tenuan evacuation must begin. Firestar's destructive course won't wait for our convenience."

Meriel swung around to face the two men. "What do you wish of me? Ask, and it shall be done."

Gage and Teran exchanged glances.

"Your mother's former evacuation plan to the Abesse," Gage replied. "If it was well orchestrated, it might save time if we can adapt it to our needs. A planet-wide vidcom announcement of the change in destination would be helpful as well. As their former ruler, it would be best received if given by you."

"As you wish," Meriel said. "I will discuss my mother's evacuation plans with my council. Perhaps she shared them with some of her royal advisors."

"You don't know what her plans were?" Incredulity tightened Gage's voice.

Meriel clamped down on an exasperated retort. "I told you before. My mother never shared *anything* she planned with me. *She* was supreme ruler. I was never included."

"I find that difficult to believe."

Her hands fisted on her hips. "Well, it's the truth!"

Teran laughed and held up a hand. "Enough! You two can't maintain a civil conversation longer than a few seconds. A little trust and acceptance of the other—from the both of you—would aid our cause immensely."

Meriel tossed her head in a defiant gesture. "I'd be glad to, if *he'd* cease to doubt my words! How can anyone work with someone who calls you a liar at every turn?"

"Well, Gage?" Teran inquired mildly. "Do you think you can manage to dredge up even the tinest amount of trust in your heart?"

"You ask too much, when it comes to this woman!"

"But it has to begin somewhere," Teran prodded. "And she has pledged her fealty to you."

Gage raggedly shoved a hand through his hair. "I know. I know." He glanced up at Meriel. "I'm sorry I called you a liar."

"Your apology is accepted," came her stiff reply.

Teran rose. "Good. It's a start, albeit a bit shaky." He glanced over at Meriel. "When can you call a meeting of your council? Discover your mother's plans?"

"Immediately. If there's an answer, I'll have it within an hour or two."

"Good. Then we'll meet here again in two hours' time." Teran rendered her a half bow, then strode from the room.

Meriel turned to Gage. He slowly unwound himself from the couch and climbed to his feet. He stared down at her until uneasiness fluttered through her.

"After we settle this pressing business," his deep voice finally rumbled, "would you care to visit with Kieran?"

Joy flooded her. "Yes. I'd like that very much!"

At her eager response, his jaw tightened. "Don't delude yourself, femina. I do this only for the lad's sake."

"But of course," Meriel hastened to reply. "I never presumed otherwise."

"Good. Just as long as we understand each other." Gage extended a hand. "Come. Allow me to escort you to your council chambers. The day burns on even as we speak."

Late that night, Gage paced the confines of his bedchamber for long, lonely hours, battling with his need to go to Meriel. The frustration grew, no matter how he fought against it. He was a fool to want her, he told himself time and time again. He was fool enough to even work with her.

He had argued with Teran over the wisdom of revealing the Volan threat to Meriel. What if she was as crazed with revenge—or just plain crazed—as her mother?

But her response to Teran's shocking revelation had been an appropriate one, of horror and determination to join in the fight to remove the Volan presence from the Imperium. Though Gage still found it hard to believe that Meriel had known nothing of her mother's plans—plans, it appeared from the results of the council meeting earlier that day, which Queen Kadra had revealed to no one—it was evident that Meriel cared deeply for Tenua and would do anything to help her planet. He paused, grimacing at the recollection of Meriel standing before him, proudly naked, willing even to bed him for the sake of her people.

She'd looked so lovely, so tantalizing, so beguiling, her long black hair cascading around her shoulders and down her back, her womanly curves all shadow and softness. Even the memory was enough to stir anew his lust, send the blood pounding through his groin. Gods, she was a disease that permeated his being, a fever that threatened to consume him, body and soul!

There was only one solution to it all. He must seek Meriel out, join with her, and satisfy, once and for all, the debilitating, mind-drugging need. No matter that she might well be more innocent in this interplanetary war than he'd originally imagined, no matter that she truly seemed to love her people—and their son. No matter that her dignity and courage never wavered, despite all the intentional cruelties he'd heaped upon her. All that mattered was his need—and that her body was the sustenance for his raging hunger.

In a few quick strides Gage crossed the room and was out the door. The darkened corridors, dimly lit with perpetual torches, were traversed in a surprisingly short time. He soon found himself standing outside her bedchamber.

The guard stationed there started in surprise, then rendered a quick salute. Gage waved him aside. With a deep breath, he activated the hand imprint panel. The door slid open. He walked in.

The room was dark save for the moonlight streaming in from the long wall of gauzy curtained windows. The illumination ended in a pool of silvery light on Meriel's bed. Beneath a light cover, Gage could discern the outline of her body, an undulating landscape of slender shoulders, narrow waist, and womanly hips. He moved toward her.

She faced him, sound asleep, her hands pillowing a flawlessly smooth cheek. Her lips were full and innocent in her slumber, her long-lashed lids brushing the curve of her high cheekbones. The cover had fallen away while she slept, and the thin, low-cut sleeping gown did little to hide the swell of breasts that were accentuated by the pressure of her upraised arms. Her hair was tousled, wild, and a long lock curled down to nestle in the shadowed valley of her bosom.

Gage swallowed hard, his hand unconsciously reaching down to lift the offending strands that obstructed his full view of her enticing breasts. With the gentlest of touches, he swept the lock aside. Meriel stirred, murmuring softly in her sleep. A scent of sweetly fragrant woman, of flowers in summer, wafted to his nostrils.

The smell, the gentle sounds of her, all but sent Gage over the edge. Sweat broke out on his brow, his throat went dry, and his heart thundered in his chest. His fists clenched at his sides.

Gods, he wanted her, wanted to pull her into his arms, bury his face in the rounded sweetness of her breasts and feel her body mold to his, but knew it would be wrong. This night of moonlight and shadows was tinged with magic. A magic that beckoned him back three cycles, into the arms of a lovely innocent who had shared her first mating with him. A lovely innocent, gay and laughing, who, for a fleeting moment in time, had shown him a love that asked nothing save he open his heart and delight in the pure goodness of giving . . . one to the other.

Whatever happened between them, Gage knew he'd never be satisfied with anything less than that same generous response. He wanted the Meriel of that day long ago. But did any part of that girl still exist?

She'd said she was innocent of wrongdoing, yet dare he trust her? *No, never,* a small voice deep inside him cried. *Use her body if you must, but never, ever open your heart to her again. She's not to be trusted. No woman is.*

He should leave her, Gage thought. Walk from her room and never look back. Deal with her only in the most superficial, task-oriented of ways, until the time came to walk away forever. But the morrow was soon enough to do so. Though he'd not force his presence on Meriel tonight, nor demand the fulfillment of the vow she'd made him, Gage couldn't quite find the strength to leave her.

The two lounge chairs, their shadows looming in the darkness that shrouded the fireplace, beckoned to him. He strode over and threw himself in the closest one, turning the chair until he faced Meriel's bed. Then, from the darkness that mirrored the gloom that had settled about his heart, he watched her until he finally fell asleep.

Blackness engulfed her, heavy, thick, and smothering. Meriel struggled, her hands clawing through the dark mist—a mist that gained substance, texture, until it became a hot, oozing mass. It seeped into her nose, her mouth, choking her. It permeated her skin, scalding her.

She tried to scream, to call out for help, but the thick, sticky ooze slid down her throat, strangling her cries. She was dying, consumed by the slithering, black morass, and no one would hear, would know—until it was too late.

A vision of Kieran's chubby little face, of Dian, her dark eyes warm with love, filled her. Then another set of features—a ruggedly handsome man with thick, dark blond hair and piercing brown eyes, a firm, sensual mouth and battle-hardened body . . .

Gage.

Confusion flooded Meriel. He didn't matter to her, meant nothing! Nothing save danger to her and her people. To Pelum, Kieran . . .

Anger swept through her, banishing the swarming mists and choking slime. He *would not* win! She would not die and leave her family and people at his mercy. Leave, never knowing if what they'd once shared had been false, nothing more than a terrible parody of love.

A cry, strangled, gasping, clawed its way from Meriel's throat. Her eyes snapped open to a room of darkness. Out of the corner of her eye she saw a figure looming over her. A figure of evil, of malice, who grasped her head and pressed her face downward.

Meriel screamed again, flailing wildly. A sudden horrible realization filled her. Somehow, someway, the mysterious intruder had found a way to penetrate her brain, and was even now stealing her mind! And there was nothing, absolutely nothing, she could do to stop him!

Gage jerked awake, momentarily disoriented. Where, by the five moons, was he?

A cry of sheer terror pulled him to his feet. His gaze swung to Meriel's bed. There, bending over her, was a man. In his hands he held a small, luminescent green sphere that he pressed to the back of her head.

With a shout of rage, Gage flung himself across the room, straight toward the intruder. Suddenly the man was no more, dissolved into the blackness. Gage stood there beside Meriel's bed, poised for battle, listening. Though all his tracker's instincts were attuned to any sign of another's presence, they caught nothing. Whoever it was, he was gone.

"G-Gage!"

He turned to find Meriel sitting upright in bed, her eyes wide, tear-filled and questioning. He sighed, then lowered himself to sit beside her.

"The danger's over, femina. He's gone."

"But who was he?" Panic hovered on her words. "And what was he trying to do to me?"

"My bets would be on a Volan mind enslavement," Gage offered grimly. "Just before he disappeared, I saw a small, glowing sphere in his hand. I wonder if that's how the transfer process occurs—from the Volan entity to its host?"

"I-I don't know. I don't know how they do it . . ." Meriel paused, shuddering in remembrance. "But possibly. He, or something, was in my mind, trying to take me over!" She grasped Gage by the arm. "Why? Why would a Volan want me? I am now powerless. I couldn't send my people to the Abesse even if I wanted to."

Gage shrugged. "I don't know, femina. But you can be sure that I won't allow them to succeed. I won't let anyone harm you."

She bit back a sob. "But what can you do against them? They have powers we've yet to fathom fully, much less fight against. Oh, Gage, I'm so afraid! Help me!"

At her sweet, tear-choked entreaty, his guard against her momentarily softened. "It'll be all right, Meriel," he soothed, stroking away the tears that trickled down her face. "I swear it!"

"Don't leave me! I can't bear to be alone! Please, Gage, don't leave!"

He gathered her into his arms, a fierce protectiveness welling within. "Hush, Meriel. I won't leave you. You're safe. I won't let anything happen to you."

Her arms entwined about his neck; her slender body pressed against his. "Thank you," Meriel murmured. "I know I've been nothing but a problem for you, but I'll try to do better. We've got to help each other, or the Volans will enslave us all." She inhaled a tremulous breath, then relaxed in his arms. "Yes, work together, for the sake of the Imperium, for the sake of us all . . ."

Gage held her for a long while, until Meriel's breathing finally evened and she drifted off into a fitful slumber. Yet, even then, he didn't leave her, holding her close until the night grayed into a hot, mist-shrouded dawn. Held her close, considering all the possible reasons the Volans had chosen her for their next victim.

Meriel awoke to a sensation of warmth and safety. She snuggled closer, her head seeking and finding a pillow on the long expanse of muscle and bone that was her resting place. She mumbled sleepily, then grimaced as her hairy pillow suddenly tickled her nose. Her nostrils flared. She inhaled deeply of heady man-scent.

Her lids lifted. Her eyes gradually focused. For an instant, Meriel blinked in confusion. She was indeed lying on her bed, but the mattress beneath her was suddenly hard and unfamiliar. She turned slightly, raising her head.

At the sight of Gage Bardwin, sleeping soundly beneath her, Meriel gasped. How, by all that was sacred, had he gotten here?

The memory of last night, of the evil intruder—the Volan—returned. With it came her recollection of Gage, of her pleas for him not to leave her, of his taking her into his arms and holding her tightly.

Confusion flooded Meriel. He hated her, yet he'd been there when she needed him. He hated her, yet he'd stayed when she'd asked him, keeping her safe throughout the remainder of the night. Safe . . . in the powerful haven of his arms.

A sudden thought assailed her. How was it possible that Gage had been in her room just when the Volan attacked? And why had he been there?

Ever so carefully, Meriel lifted herself off him, then edged back until she was sitting on the bed. Gage's tunic had fallen open sometime during the night and his broad, hair-roughened chest rose and fell with each slow, deep breath. She watched him, a wild mix of emotions roiling within, and suddenly found she couldn't bear to be near him a moment longer.

Meriel scooted back until she stood beside the bed. She turned toward the door. Was the guard still there, or had Gage dismissed him after entering her room? If so, there was a chance—

"How fickle of you, sweet femina, to leave without a good morning kiss."

Meriel swung around. "Y-you're awake!"

"And have been for quite some time," Gage drawled as he levered himself to his elbows. "I was curious what your reaction would be when you woke to find me in your bed."

He leveled a pair of intense brown eyes on her. "You don't appear too upset over my presence. Shall I take that to mean you enjoyed sleeping with me?"

"Yes! I-I mean, n-no!" Meriel sputtered. "Oh, you confuse me so!"

"Over such a simple question?" Gage shook his head in pity. "Truly, Meriel, I expected more of a queen. A ruler should be quick, decisive, and never appear distraught or—"

"Oh, stop, you vile son of a Cerulean seaworm!"

Gage reared back, his initial expression of mock incredulity rapidly transforming into a broad grin. "Really, femina, such language isn't at all proper for one of your breeding. Have a care, or you'll soon sink to the depths where I'm certain you already imagine me to be."

She stamped her foot, opened her mouth to deliver a stinging retort, then hesitated. Her lips clamped shut and a calculating expression flared instead in her eyes.

"I can be as decisive as the situation calls for, Gage Bardwin. And I'd like to know what you were doing in my bedchamber last night when the Volan arrived."

It was Gage's turn to look uncomfortable. "Oh, that. Would you believe I was concerned for your safety, and had just slipped in to check on you?"

"Try again, Bardwin!"

He flushed, then sat up, swinging his long legs over the side of the bed. "I came because I was hot for you," he growled, his searing glance capturing hers. "I came to demand payment of your vow to me."

"But you didn't . . ."

"No, I didn't." Gage sighed and ran a hand through his hair. "Instead, I took a seat in one of those chairs"—he motioned to the fireplace—"and soon fell asleep. Your cries woke me."

An impulse to ask him why he'd decided against coming to her bed struck her, but Meriel quickly brushed it aside. It was unsettling enough to know he still wanted her. To discover why he'd chosen not to take what she'd promised was more than she could deal with just now.

It was far safer to change the course of the conversation. "Have you any further insights as to why the Volan attacked me last night?"

A wolfish, knowing grin twisted Gage's lips. Meriel was as uncomfortable with his admission as he had been. He was tempted to pursue the topic further, then thought better of it. There were more pressing issues at hand. He shook his head. "None, save the possibility they intended to use you in some way to subvert our plans for the evacuation."

"But how? No matter how I tried, you and Lord Ardane would never have allowed me to do that."

"I don't know *how*, Meriel," Gage patiently reiterated. "All I know is that, until we discover the details, you must be guarded constantly. You need a personal bodyguard. Any suggestions?"

"A bodyguard! You can't be serious! I've never required one before, and I certainly don't—" She paused, her mind racing. A bodyguard would be with her at all times. She'd have ready access to him, and he to her. And if on one of their journeys through the palace in the course of her duties, there was opportunity to seek out the tunnels . . .

She smiled. "There is one man in my palace guard who'd be perfect for the job. His name is Torman. There is none braver or more loyal than he."

"Torman, eh?" Gage frowned. "I cannot say I recall a man of that name in your guard."

"He was the tall, powerfully built man with blue eyes who was one of the last to pledge fealty to you. He is . . . was . . . the captain of my guard."

The memory of a well-muscled, darkly handsome man kneeling before him, and Meriel's delighted smile at his arrival, flooded Gage. A primitive instinct stirred. There was something amiss here. An impulse to deny her request filled him, but then his tracker's sixth sense kicked in. He was most successful in ferreting out his quarry when he was patient. And the relationship between Meriel and this Torman would bear careful watching.

He nodded his acquiescence. "I hope you have chosen well. Your life could depend on it."

Happy relief surged through Meriel. "I've trusted Torman with the safety and security of my entire palace. I certainly trust him with my life."

"And what of *my* abilities to protect you?" Gage inquired coolly. "Are they as impressive?"

Meriel frowned. "I don't know what you . . ." Tact, and a well-bred sense of diplomacy, forced her to change the course of her next words. "But, of course, you're just as impressive. You saved me last night."

"Good. And I want you to continue to be safe, to sleep well."

"I'm sure I will, with Torman nearby."

"Torman, sweet femina, will be your bodyguard only during the day. He, too, has a need for rest."

Meriel wet her lips, suddenly wary about where this conversation was leading. "Then who will guard me while I sleep? It seems the most dangerous time of all."

"At the risk of sounding arrogant," Gage drawled, "I have a great talent for waking at the slightest sound." He shrugged apologetically. "Comes from a strong need for survival after all those cycles of tracking."

The blood drained from Meriel's face. "Are you suggesting that you—"

"Plan to sleep with you in order to guard you each night?" Gage finished for her. "Yes, femina. That I do." He arched a challenging brow. "Any objections?"

Objections? Meriel thought glumly. What would be the point? She'd already agreed to mate with him whenever he wished. She exhaled a resigned breath. "No. No objections at all."

A pair of cold blue eyes followed Meriel and Gage later that morning as they made their way across the palace gardens to a meeting with Teran Ardane. In the midst of a large, painstakingly

sculpted arosa garden, they joined. Out of earshot of all, the trio talked for over two hours.

Torman watched and waited, his anger and
frustration growing to explosive proportions, and
could do nothing. Lavia's attempts to enslave
the Tenuan Queen last night had failed—fatal-
ly for her—when Gage Bardwin had intervened.
There might never be another opportunity, if the
protective way the Lord Commander now hovered over the Queen was any indication. They
would have to watch and wait, and hope at
some moment Queen Meriel would again fall
into their clutches.

In the meanwhile, it was best to put the second part of the plan into action. Dirmat would be
sent this very night to see to the enslavement of
Prince Pelum while he slept. The consort would
be manipulated to work his wife to perform their
ultimate decision—the murder of Gage Bardwin.
The only difficulty lay in finding some way to get
Meriel to Pelum without Bardwin finding out.
But Torman knew that sooner or later an opportunity would present itself. All things came to the
patient—and the Volans certainly had more time
to spare than the Tenuans.

A sound, a movement behind him set the fine
hairs on his neck to rise. He whirled around, ready
to leap at the intruder, and found Dian, Queen
Meriel's maidservant. Torman relaxed. There was
no danger from the shy, pretty maid. No danger
at all.

"What is it you wish, femina?" he asked, slipping easily into the Imperium common language
after cycles of intensive practice.

Dian blushed and lowered her eyes. "The Lord Commander sent me to fetch you. He wishes a meeting."

Once more Torman's hackles rose. Did Bardwin suspect? He quickly shoved that concern aside. It was impossible. He'd been too careful, as had his compatriots. And the remaining biospheres, still hooked to the life-support system, were hidden in the bowels of the palace, in a secret chamber known only to him.

"Shall I meet them now, in the garden?" Torman indicated the trio below him sitting among the arosa bushes.

"Yes, if you please."

Torman made a move to stride past her, but she stayed him with a gentle, hesitant hand. He halted, his brow quirking in inquiry.

"Yes, femina?"

Dian swallowed hard. "Are you well, Torman?"

"But of course. Why do you ask?"

"You suddenly seem so distant. And you've not once sought me out since the ceremony of fealty and the return of your freedom to once more roam the palace." She blushed crimson. "Is there something wrong? Are you angry with me?"

Torman frowned. Whatever was she talking about? He searched his slave's memory for any hint of enlightenment. There was something, a vague recollection of a growing affection for the little femina. And nothing his training had ever prepared him to deal with.

He shrugged her hand aside. "Nothing is wrong, femina. It's but the stress of the past several days. We'll talk more, when things calm."

Happiness flared in Dian's eyes. "I understand. I just didn't want you angry with me."

Torman stared down at her, patiently awaiting further discourse. When there was none, he cleared his throat. "I must not keep the Lord Commander waiting."

"Oh, no. Of course not." Dian stepped back.

He turned and strode away, banishing the confused jumble of thoughts and emotions the brown-haired maid had stirred in him. It was but his slave's memories rising to the forefront of his mind. He must assume tighter control.

As Torman approached, Gage and Teran rose from the stone bench. The captain of the guard halted before them and rendered the required military salute.

"My lords," Torman said. "What is it you wish?"

"Your Queen has need of your services," Gage immediately replied. "She is in danger and requires a bodyguard to stay with her at all times while she is awake. She has requested that I name you to that vital position."

Something flickered in Torman's eyes, but he quickly masked it by bowing his head in obeisance. "As you wish, Lord Commander." Triumph welled within him. "I will be honored to see to her safety."

Chapter Seven

"Play ball! Play ball!" Kieran cried as he ran across the large terraced balcony outside Meriel's bed-chamber. He halted before the captain of the guard and lifted his ball high. "Play ball."

"Domina," the big man protested.

Meriel glanced up from the serica thread tapesty she was telepathically weaving with a hand-held mindweaver. She smiled. "Play with him, Torman. Surely standing there at military attention for the past two hours must be wearing thin. Indulge yourself a little."

Indulge himself indeed, Torman thought morosely. Playing with that wild little animal?

He glanced at the setting sun and sighed. Only a few more hours and it would be time for that *child* and Queen Meriel to take their rest. Then, he would be free of his duties.

Not that guarding *her* had proven so very difficult. She was a quiet, self-effacing woman who

149

enjoyed her own company and didn't babble incessantly like some of the other palace woman. But that child of hers! He was constantly into things, constantly moving. And Torman didn't know anything about how to entertain or deal with the young.

All Volans were developed in hive pods from fertilized embryo to the young adult form. They were of no practical use to the collective until they reached an appropriate age and size, so there was never any point in foisting the raising of young upon the adults. After watching this humanoid child for the past two hours, he now understood—and appreciated—the wisdom of his kind. Children were nothing more than irritating pests!

"Play! Play!" Kieran prodded at him in his childish way.

Torman looked to Meriel. "I know nothing of this 'play' the lad demands."

She arched a slender brow, surprised. True, Torman's past duties as captain of her guard had precluded such intimate interactions with the royal family, but Meriel couldn't fathom his reluctance to play with Kieran. "It's the same as you did when you were little. Didn't you play with your brothers and sisters?"

"I have no brothers and sisters."

"Then your friends. Didn't you have friends to play with?"

He knew he was easing into danger-fraught waters. There wasn't any way to plausibly explain his upbringing without giving away his identity. It was better to acquiesce. Torman nodded.

"Yes, I had friends. But it's been so long ago.

Tell me how to 'play' with the lad, and I will attempt to do so."

Meriel laughed. "Well, don't make it sound so awful. All Kieran wants is for you to throw the ball back and forth with him."

"Oh," Torman mumbled. "I understand."

He put out his hands and Kieran tossed the ball to him. Torman tossed it back, a little too hard, and it bounced off the boy's outstretched hands and rolled away. Kieran toddled after it, then returned, a wide grin of anticipation on his face.

"More! Play ball more!" he cried gleefully, and threw the ball back at Torman.

With the infinite patience of his species, Torman resumed the game, this time with more control, until Kieran was successfully catching half the balls tossed at him. Meriel watched, pride welling at her son's excellent coordination and agility. He would be as strong and athletic as his father, she mused, her thoughts not imagining Pelum as she resumed her weaving.

A suppressed memory of Gage, magnificently naked, drifted across her mind. Yes, as strong and magnificent as his father . . . With a start, she jerked back her wandering imagination. Such thoughts were worse than pointless. They were dangerous!

No matter what her eventual fate at Gage Bardwin's hands, she must never surrender her heart again—a heart long ago promised to Pelum. What she had briefly felt for the handsome breeder had never been the issue. Even if the cruel vagaries of war forced her to break her life mating vows, she must do so only in the flesh, never the spirit.

Pelum, and only Pelum, would remain the love of her life.

"Torman," Meriel carefully began when it became evident that Kieran was beginning to tire of his strenuous game. "Fetch Dian and have her take Kieran to the kitchen for his supper. He's had a very active day and will need to take his rest soon."

A look of utter relief spread across Torman's face. Then he recognized the transparency of his response and quickly masked it with his characteristic stoic expression. "As you wish, Domina."

Torman bowed low, then turned to leave.

"One thing more, my loyal captain."

He glanced back.

"You needn't rush back, if you wish a short time to talk with Dian, or walk with her in the gardens." Meriel gestured to the scene of fragrant blossoms and riotous color that lay spread out below them. "Such a glorious, romantic evening deserves to be shared."

Confusion flickered in Torman's eyes, then sudden realization. "Ah, yes, but of course. You wish time with the Lord Commander. I'll return shortly."

"The Lord Commander?" Meriel stared up at him, stunned. Then she laughed. "No, you don't understand. I meant you and Dian."

At his blank look, she leaned forward, eyeing him with renewed curiosity. "Torman, aren't you interested in her anymore? I could have sworn you were actively courting Dian before—"

"There's no time for such things," he hastened to interject. "Perhaps later, but not now." He paused, a look of distress twisting his face. "Please, Domina. I don't care to discuss this further."

Meriel sat back and sighed. "As you wish. It wasn't my intent to pry."

He stood there a moment longer. "Domina, have I your leave to fetch the maidservant?"

She resumed her weaving. "Yes, Torman. You do."

A short while later, when Dian had retrieved the squirming Kieran from Torman's firm grip and carried him away, Meriel motioned the big man back over. She patted a spot beside her on the bench. He quirked a brow, then complied.

"There are things I wish to speak of," she began. "Things I desperately need your help with, if you feel it's within your power."

"Domina," Torman protested, "if it's about Dian . . ."

Meriel lay a gentle hand on his tautly muscled forearm. "No, it's not Dian. I'll respect your request and not interfere—for now. What I've to say deals with the plight of my family."

"What can I do to help you, Domina?"

She met his inquiring glance with a resolute one of her own. "You have knowledge of the palace's ancient passages. Does one, perhaps, lead to the holding cells?"

With the greatest effort, Torman contained his rising elation. His slave's memories, for all their aggravating overlay of emotions, were very useful at times. "Yes, Domina. They haven't been used in many cycles, but there are several passages, including one to the holding cells."

"Do any of them also lead outside the palace?"

Not only outside the palace, Torman thought wryly, *but to your bedchamber as well.* He nodded. "Yes, Domina."

She inhaled a fortifying breath and squared her shoulders. "Can you get me to the holding cells and Pelum without anyone's notice? I need to speak to him."

Excitement pounded through Torman with every quickened beat of his heart. This was the perfect opportunity for Pelum's new Volan to begin his manipulation of the Tenuan Queen, without arousing any suspicions on her part.

He nodded again. "Yes, that can be arranged. Late tonight would be best. There are fewer guards about then."

Meriel shook her head. "I doubt there'll be any chance of me slipping away from the Lord Commander on this or any night for a while to come. He insists on sharing my bed."

"You sleep with the Lord Commander? Why?"

Meriel flushed at the bluntness of his question. "He wishes to keep me safe."

"Does he now?"

"Yes! Someone—we suspect a Volan—slipped into my room last night and attacked me."

"A Volan?" Torman laughed. "And why would one of those aliens travel across galaxies to seek you out? It's far more plausible that the Lord Commander sent one of his men into your bedchamber last night. Truly, Domina, I fear he is playing you to his own purposes."

"And I say you overstep your bounds!" Anger tightened her voice.

He opened his mouth to reply, then thought

better of it. "I beg pardon, Domina. I did indeed overstep my bounds, but I fear the man. He is wily and cruel. I don't want you hurt."

"And *I* know what happened to me last night," she stated firmly, even as the doubts began to insinuate themselves into her mind. Perhaps Torman was right. Perhaps Gage *had* sent a man to attack her, with the hope of gaining her trust and gratitude with his subsequent rescue. It would certainly explain his timely presence in her bedchamber.

But why would he do such a thing? He had everything he wished from her at his mere command.

It was too much to comprehend—and nothing she wished to deal with just then. There were more important matters at hand. Like how to find a way to Pelum. Meriel brushed Torman's comments away with an airy wave of her hand.

"I thank you for your concern, but the issue here is not the Lord Commander, but how to get to my husband. We can visit him during the day as well, even if it's necessary to use more caution."

"Yes, Domina."

Meriel smiled. She had always been blessed with faithful followers, and, aside from Dian, Torman was the most loyal of all. "Good. We'll make further plans on the morrow. In the meanwhile, it draws near for the supper meal. This will be a special, farewell feast, as Lord Ardane must transport back to Bellator on the morrow for a meeting with King Falkan." She rose. "Would you escort me to the dining area?"

Torman stood, taking her proffered arm. "It will be my honor, Domina."

As he crossed the balcony, various plans and strategies raced through his mind. Ardane soon out of the way, Pelum set to manipulate his wife to kill Bardwin. There was much to be accomplished by the morrow to ensure an adequate amount of private time for Meriel to visit with her husband.

Torman smiled a secret smile. Things were rapidly falling into place.

Meriel was first to say her farewells the next morning as they stood with Teran in the transport chamber. Once those were given, she asked leave to depart with Torman, her bodyguard. Gage eyed her quizzically, then nodded his assent. He had work of his own to deal with once his friend had transported.

Both men watched Meriel leave, then turned to the other. They clasped arms in the Imperial tradition, their gazes locking in deep affection.

"Go gently with her, my friend," Teran finally said. "I begin to fear for your heart—and hers as well."

Gage frowned. "Teran, don't start . . ."

"When it comes to Meriel, you're treading in uncertain territory."

Dark brown eyes riveted on him. "Then tell me what to do. I've always known how to handle the feminas. But somehow, with Meriel, it's different."

"How?" Teran demanded. "How is it different?"

Gage sighed. "I don't know. It just is."

"What will you do? She *is* life-mated."

"She was mine first!" Gage snarled, anger and a fierce possessiveness flashing in his eyes. "And that marriage of hers is a travesty."

"In your eyes, perhaps."

"Then help me find a way to make it so in hers!"

Teran slowly shook his head. "Gage, are you sure you understand what you're setting into motion here? Meriel is devoted to her husband, no matter how weak he may be as a man. To turn her heart to you and against her mating vows, then use her solely to satisfy your needs before tossing her aside, might well destroy her. Are you prepared to risk that? Or do you even care?"

"I thought you were supposed to help, not make me feel even more like a heartless bastard!"

"And don't I help as well when I point out the problems, the pitfalls?" Teran sighed. "There is more here than just her marriage that complicates things, and you know it. Taking a Queen as spoils of battle is one thing. Hoping to eventually have her as mate is another. It cannot be, Gage."

"I know that," Gage growled bitterly. He released Teran's arm and stepped off the transport platform. "You've done your job well, my friend. I'm even more confused now than I was before."

Teran moved to the center of the platform and motioned for the transport technician to engage the shield. A transparent, semicircular barrier lowered around him. "Good. Then I've served you well."

Gage signaled the transport technician, who

immediately shoved the power lever forward. A buzzing filled the room. A moment later, Teran disappeared from view.

He led her through the ancient passages, past blanketing obstacles of delicately woven cobwebs that parted easily to then flutter back and cling tenaciously to hair and face and clothes. Through dark tunnels with walls slick with slime, with moisture that condensed and dripped from the ceiling in frigid, splattering plops that invariably found its exasperating way down necks to chill body and soul. The scent of putrefaction, of things long dead, hung on the stagnant air until it was difficult to take a breath that didn't make the head spin or the stomach roll.

If not for the faint but steady light from the perpetual torch Torman held high above his head, Meriel could have imagined she was entombed in a place rife with noise and smells and unearthly, spine-tingling sensations. If not for the sturdy, reassuring presence of her captain of the guard, for the solid feel of his strong arm beneath her hand, she felt certain she'd have fled back to the safety of the palace long ago. Surely no one had the courage to brave such tunnels alone.

But Pelum, her beloved husband, awaited her at the end of the terrifying journey, and Meriel no longer just wanted to see him—she *had* to see him. After the disturbing events of the past few days, Meriel desperately needed the reassurance that it was only the separation that had weakened her resolve—and had set into motion the doubts as to her true feelings for her husband.

Seeing Pelum again would put it all back into perspective.

Torman halted at an artfully concealed door, then shoved his key control into a slot in the wall. It had been difficult to obtain the valuable pass to the passages and dungeons, as the Bellatorians had confiscated them in the palace takeover, but Meriel's captain of the guard wasn't a man to be thwarted. Once he'd regained his freedom after giving his oath to the Lord Commander, Torman had systematically set himself to regaining possession of one of the coveted key controls.

With a groan of age-rusted gears, the panel slid open. A long corridor lined with cells led away from the portal which, once they passed through to the other side and it closed, appeared one with the stone wall. Meriel glanced expectantly up at her companion.

"Your prince is in the third cell down," he whispered. "I'll get you in, then stand guard. Keep your voices low, and knock once when you're ready to leave."

Meriel nodded, then followed Torman down the hall.

She was surprised to find, when she entered Pelum's cell, that it was quite comfortably furnished with bed, chair, a desk, and shelves to store a large supply of the books Pelum loved to read. If her ears weren't deceiving her, a small bathing room off to one side was even equipped with a hot mineral bath. Gratitude for Gage's kindness welled in her. He really was a good man, beneath his sometimes gruff, intimidating exterior.

With an effort, Meriel shook aside the warm surge of emotion those thoughts invoked. She directed her glance to Pelum, lying prone on his bed, his head buried in his hands. Meriel stepped inside. Immediately, the door closed behind her.

She hurried over to Pelum, knelt down, and laid a gentle hand upon his shoulder. He stiffened.

"Pelum, love. It is I, Meriel."

With a groan, he rolled over. Meriel gasped. His face was gaunt, his hair unkempt and filthy. His clothes looked as if they hadn't been changed in days.

Confusion filled her. Her husband had always been fastidious to a fault. What had happened to him? What was wrong?

"Meriel!" he wailed, then flung himself into her arms. "Ah, Meriel, I thought you'd never come. Thought I'd never see you again!"

"Hush, my sweet one." Meriel stroked his head, his back, in an effort to calm his terrified sobs, as all the while panic spiraled within her. "Tell me what's wrong. Tell me, and I'll do all within my power to see it righted."

"Th-the Bellatorians! The Lord Commander! He hates me, means to see me dead! He m-must be stopped!"

"What has he done?" Meriel paused to once more glance around the decently furnished room. "I see only that he has treated you kindly."

"K-kindly?" Pelum drew back in horror. "This room is only a façade. He has had me beaten, half-starved me, and threatened me with the most excruciating torment if I don't renounce my vows to you and give you over to him. And his ultimate plans for our people, once they are transported to Carcer . . . !" He grabbed her arms, pulling her to him. "The man *must* be stopped!"

Apprehension rose in Meriel. "What plans has he for our people? Tell me, Pelum!"

Her husband shivered. "Enslavement."

"Enslavement?"

Pelum nodded. "A rich vein of precious martenite was discovered about two cycles ago on Carcer. It runs throughout the planet. The Bellatorians want our people evacuated there for the purpose of mining the ore—as slave labor!"

"I don't believe it!" Indignation threaded her voice. "It's against Imperial law to purposely enslave any of its citizens!"

"And when, since the loss of the Knowing Crystal those hundreds of cycles ago, have we been considered Imperial citizens?" He paused, a fierce light gleaming in his eyes. "Why do you think your mother's choice was always for the Abesse, rather than Carcer?"

"How do you know this?" Meriel demanded. "Who told you?"

"Who else, my beloved? Your mother, of course." Pelum cocked his head. "Didn't you know?"

Frustration flooded Meriel, and a sense of being manipulated on all sides. "No," she muttered bitterly. "That was yet another detail my mother failed to share with me."

Pity flared in Pelum's eyes. He wiped away his tears and took Meriel's chin in his hand. "I'm sorry for that, beloved. Kadra had no right to keep such vital information from you. But, be that as it may, it changes nothing. We can't allow the Bellatorians to succeed!"

Meriel's mind raced. Was it possible? Had Gage and Lord Ardane always meant to save her people only to force them into the service of the Imperium? The rare martenite, a vital catalyst in the power unit of an interplanetary transporter, was a prize beyond comprehension. To possess such rich stores of the ore would make Bellator immensely wealthy—and powerful—for other galaxies required martenite just as desperately for their own transporters.

This newest revelation also directly contradicted Gage and Lord Ardane's reasons for her mother's choice of the Abesse over Carcer. Was there in fact no Volan threat? Had the intruder in her room the other night been planted for some other purpose, as Torman had hinted? One way or another, someone was lying.

She gazed into Pelum's eyes, eyes as guileless and loving as always, and knew, with an aching, desolate misery, that the liars were the Bellatorians. But how was that possible? Was she *that* poor a judge of people?

Confusion, then shame, then anger overwhelmed her. Tears filled her eyes and she wrenched her head from Pelum's gentle grasp.

"Meriel? Beloved? What's wrong?"

She heard her husband's voice through the steady thrum of blood rushing past her ears, saw him, his eyes wide with concern, through a haze of moisture. Gentle, loyal, loving Pelum.

Meriel squared her slender shoulders. "Nothing's wrong anymore, my love. I'll deal with the Bellatorians in my own time. In the meanwhile, I want to see you and Kieran safely away from here. Torman knows secret ways out of this palace. He'll help you both escape."

"And what will become of you?"

"It doesn't matter. But with you two free, whatever I do, I can do with an easy heart."

Pelum shook his head. "I won't leave you. I must stay near to aid in the fight!"

"No!"

He grabbed her by the arms and pulled her to him. "Meriel, listen to me. You can visit me easily now. I need to be here to help you in the overthrow of the invaders."

For a fleeting moment, she clutched him to her, seeking solace in the embrace. Then, with a shuddering sob, she pushed back. "I don't even know yet what I'll do to beat the Bellatorians at their own game."

"There's only one thing *to* do," her husband persisted eagerly, "and the time could never be better. With Ardane gone, Bardwin's the only obstacle to regaining power and resuming plans to transport our people to the Abesse."

"Pelum, we are defeated, an occupied planet!" Meriel protested. "Even with both Bellatorians out of the way—"

"Listen to me, Meriel!" A strange, savage light flared in his eyes. For the first time, she noted that his skin was hot, flushed, as if he were consumed by an inner fire.

"Listen and hear me well," Pelum continued. "Torman has been in contact with large portions of our army that went underground just before the Bellatorian forces closed in. They but await your command to march on the palace and retake it. With Bardwin out of the way, the Bellatorian forces will be temporarily without a leader. The timing is perfect!"

"Perfect?" A frustrated incredulity tightened her voice. "What in the heavens are you talking about? And how do you plan to get Bardwin 'out of the way'?"

Pelum smiled, then licked his lips in feral anticipation. At the action, a shiver ran through Meriel.

"*You* must get Bardwin out of the way, beloved," he rasped. "You are the only one he trusts who is close enough to see the deed done."

He grabbed Meriel's arm in a viselike grip, squeezing until she nearly cried out from the pain. "This very night," Pelum said, his voice lowering to a hoarse whisper, "lure him to your bed with the promise of a mating. Then, when he's overcome with passion and at his most vulnerable, kill him!"

Chapter Eight

"What will you do, Domina?" Torman asked a short while later once he'd escorted Meriel back to her room.

"I don't know," she mumbled, awash in heartsick misery. She lifted her gaze to the tall man who stood beside her. "Truly, I don't think I can kill him. I don't possess that sort of strength or ruthlessness." Meriel choked back a sob. "Ah, Torman! What am I to do? *What am I to do?*"

Something, an instinctive impulse to comfort, or perhaps his slave's natural tendencies momentarily overriding his tight control, moved Torman to take the weeping woman into his arms. He held her against him as she cried her heart out, awkwardly patting her back, and cursing his own weakness.

Fool! he mentally berated himself. This is not the time to ease her pain, but to strengthen her resolve! As unfortunate as it might be to coerce the little queen into such a horrendous act, it had to be done. Too much hinged on Bardwin's death.

The renegade army was indeed in hiding outside the city. What Meriel didn't know was that the leaders and ranking officers were all Volan slaves. Even now, they massed near the primary Bellatorian outposts, awaiting orders for a surprise attack and a swift, brutal massacre of their conquerors. Then, as soon as communications could be resumed with the Volan Mother Ship, the transport of additional hive occupants to Tenua would begin. The more enslavements that occurred between now and when Bellator was once again able to regain control would only aid their cause.

The plan to evacuate the Tenuans to the Abesse was no longer the best of options. For a brief moment this morning, the Bellatorians' jamming signals had faltered. Just before communications from the Mother Ship were once again cut off, he had learned that the decision had been made to allow the Bellatorians to transport the Volan slaves to Carcer and begin the seeding of the rest of the Imperium. All that was needed was to maximize the enslavements on Tenua for a short while longer.

First, however, the Bellatorians' jamming signal must be permanently halted to allow renewed Volan transport from the Mother Ship. That necessitated getting Bardwin out of the way. He was the obstacle to all their plans.

Later, once Tenua was empty of life, the planet

would still be a perfect way station for some time to come. There were shields even the Imperium would find impossible to penetrate to protect the Volan invaders, once there was no purpose in maintaining a secret of their presence on Tenua. And, though the bodies they enslaved to operate the way station couldn't withstand Firestar's increasing heat indefinitely, there were methods, for a time, to force their slaves beyond what they were normally capable of.

But everything depended on Bardwin's death.

"You must be strong, Domina," Torman forced himself to say, turning back to the task at hand. "A queen must be willing to sacrifice all for the sake of her people."

"Even m-murder?" Meriel sobbed, lifting her tear-streaked face to his. "Ah, Torman, it's crime enough to go back on my vow of fealty to him, much less attempt murder! And, even if I had the heart for such an undertaking, I've no idea how to go about it! Gage Bardwin is a trained warrior, a man skilled in anticipating the unexpected. I could never take him by surprise, even in the throes of passion."

"You underestimate the power of a female over a male," Torman chided her smilingly. "It surpasses all races, all cultures. There is nothing more powerful than the urge to procreate a species. And the weapon of his death can be both quick and lethal. The single scratch of a thorn from an Arborian nexus bush will kill him in the space of a few seconds. The neurotoxic effect is that fast. He'll not suffer."

"A small consolation, to be sure." Meriel sighed, then shook her head. "I can't do it, Torman. I just can't."

"Are you in love with the Bellatorian, then?" he prodded, realizing he must alter his attack if there was to be any hope of success. "Has your lust for him now taken precedent over your loyalty to your people and family? And what are your vows of fealty to an enemy, over those you gave to your husband, to Tenua when you accepted the crown?"

"Stop it!" Meriel jerked away. She stepped back, her body rigid, her fists clenched at her sides. "How *dare* you imply my carnal desires are of greater import than my royal duties? How *dare* you judge me?"

Torman shrugged. "I am a simple soldier. I see past the emotions to the end result—the salvation of our people. I am sorry if that seems cruel or heartless, but it's how I deal with things. In this case, at least, you'd do well to keep the emotions out of it. It only complicates the inevitable."

"The inevitable?"

He nodded. "Yes, Domina. You know as well as I that you but rail against something that must be done. There is no other recourse. If there were, I'd be the first to suggest it."

All the fight drained from Meriel. It was all too much to fathom, much less deal with just now. "Go," she whispered. "I need time alone, to think and decide."

"But I am ordered never to leave you."

She turned beseeching eyes on him. "Please.

Just for an hour or two. If there's truly no Volan threat, as both you and Pelum assure me, then I should be safe for a short while. And you can await me just outside my door."

"As you wish, Domina. I'll stand guard until you call for me."

He turned on his heel and strode away, leaving Meriel to her thoughts, knowing that it was but a matter of time until the Queen came to the decision all on her own. Already, he knew her heart as well as she. Meriel would never shirk her royal duties, no matter how difficult they seemed. She was too good, too honest, too self-sacrificing to do otherwise.

A twinge of some alien feeling, surprisingly akin to the humanoid emotion of guilt, plucked at Torman's heart. He quickly shoved it aside. It was a normal reaction, forced as he was to inhabit a human slave and work in such close proximity, to be compelled, time and again, to delve into their emotions so as to understand and pass for them. Sooner or later it was bound to happen. And now, with the influence of the Mother Ship all but nonexistent, he was essentially on his own.

Yes, a normal reaction indeed, Torman reassured himself. And, once recognized, easily controlled. For the sake of his own kind he must be as ruthless with himself as he was with the Tenuan Queen. There was no other choice, for any of them. . . .

Meriel watched Torman depart, his broad shoulders, his solid, powerful form dwarfing the doorway for a brief moment before disap-

pearing. She choked back a cry for him to stay,
clamping down on an impulse to run after him.
She needed his help desperately even as she knew
there was nothing more he could do. The decision
was hers, and hers alone, to make.

She turned and headed morosely across her
room and out onto the balcony. The sun blazed
down from its position high overhead, hot, energy-
draining and life-sapping. There was little green
left on the planet's surface save for the copious-
ly watered palace gardens. Even those plants
were wilting, their leaves beginning to shriv-
el and brown in Firestar's intense heat. If
not for the produce still grown in the vast
underground caves that wound through the
planet, famine would already be rampant. In
another cycle or two, even that food source
would be gone, the water was that quickly
dissipating.

The planet was literally burning up. Soon the
oceans would be too hot to swim in; the fish
would die. Soon Tenua would be little more
than a steaming land of vapors and rotting
things, as the lakes and oceans boiled away,
the planet's crust softened and melted. Eventually Tenua would become lost in the growing
outer layers of Firestar as the dying sun continued to expand, the planet swallowed up for
all eternity.

But that ultimate calamity was perhaps hundreds or thousands of cycles from now. The rising
heat would drive them from Tenua long before
then. The evacuation must begin immediately;
there were too many to be transported to waste

any more time. As it was, transporting an entire planet would take two cycles with the planet's transporters running constantly.

A decision—whether to send her people to Carcer or the Abesse—was the decision that over-shadowed all others. It had to be. She couldn't face the other, more horrible one of what to do about Gage just yet. And Pelum was right. The timing was perfect if they were to thwart the Bellatorians' evil plans.

The heat on the balcony became unbearable. Perspiration sheened Meriel's face and arms, the moisture trickling between her breasts and damp-ening the airy gown until it clung to her body. With a sigh, she left the balcony and reentered her room.

A mineral bath might be soothing. She would simply set the temperature down to cool her sun-fevered flesh in more tepid waters. Perhaps there, in the bath's surging waters, she'd find some peace, a fleeting respite from the terrible thoughts and a destiny not of her choosing. Per-haps there, she'd finally find the strength to do what must be done.

The bath felt heavenly. Meriel sank down in the churning, lightly floral-scented waters until her chin was partially submerged, then closed her eyes. The low, rhythmic rumble, the fine spray of the roiling bath, gradually beckoned her to another world, a world of simpler, far more pleasant memories. The recollection of a mist-shrouded pool in a dimly lit, underground grotto filled her mind. A vision of a ruggedly handsome face, of piercing brown eyes with golden flecks and a superbly muscled, battle-honed body overwhelmed Meriel.

Gage.

She'd fallen in love with him that day, with his gallant concern, his gentleness, his integrity, his courage. Though loath to admit it, she'd carried the deep feelings for him ever since, in her heart never fully believing he was as bad as her mother had said. And now, just when things were again finally warming between them, she found herself once more betrayed.

What counted, what had really mattered all along, was not the physical response to Gage Bardwin or romantic notions of a perfect love. What mattered was what she had committed to—her husband, her family, her people. There'd been no hesitation, no compromise intended when she'd made those vows. There could be none now.

Yet the thought of killing Gage sickened her. No matter how he'd betrayed or intended to betray her and her people, despite his treatment of Pelum and his selfish, seemingly obsessive desire to possess her, Meriel wasn't a murderer. Try as she might to stimulate the necessary emotions, the hurt and shock after Pelum's revelation had done nothing but drain the anger from her. She felt bitterness and regret, but little else.

Meriel wondered if such flat, empty emotions would be enough to empower her to kill. She hoped so. One way or another, she was going to have to do it.

With a heavy heart, Meriel rose from the mineral bath, its pleasures dissipated by the harshness of a reality she couldn't escape. She dried herself and donned her bedrobe, then padded from the room.

A child's laugh, followed by the rumble of a deep masculine voice, floated to her ears. Meriel halted. The laughter came again, delighted, excited, mingling with the agitated chirping of birds. The herbivorium. Kieran was in the herbivorium. But with whom?

She gathered her robe about her and crept over to the entry to the indoor, artificially maintained garden. Meriel peeked in. Her heart caught in her throat.

There, Kieran in his arms, stood Gage. His back was turned to her as he lifted the boy high toward a branch where sat a brightly colored cavea bird. The tiny, emerald green creature, its head adorned with two tufts of long, dark magenta feathers that spanned the length of its body, flitted from limb to limb, just out of Kieran's reach.

"Higher," he cried. "Lift higher!"

Gage chuckled. "Easy, lad. If you get much higher, I'll lose my grip on you. And your mother won't appreciate fishing you out of that little fountain just beneath us."

"Bird! I want bird!"

"And the bird you'll have," his father reassured him. "But perhaps a different strategy is required."

He lowered Kieran to a secure perch on his shoulder, then bent to pluck a sweetsuckle blossom from a nearby bush. Raising it above his head, Gage offered it to the little cavea bird.

The feathered creature eyed it with a wary tilt

of its head, then hopped closer. Its bejeweled eyes examined the flower for a long moment. The bird moved nearer. For the space of an inhaled breath, the cavea hesitated. Then, with a tiny chirp, it fluttered down onto Gage's hand and began to drink from the flower's nectar.

"Put out your hand, lad," Gage ordered quietly.

Kieran complied. In a gentle, ever so careful transfer, the cavea bird soon sat on Kieran's chubby little hand. He grinned.

"Bird. I have bird."

Gage nodded. "That you have, lad. Treat him kindly and he'll be your dearest friend. Never betray his trust and he'll always come to you. Just like people, lad. Their feelings are as delicate and as easily damaged as this small bird."

"My bird," Kieran murmured in a voice filled with wonder. "My friend."

Carefully Gage lowered the boy to the ground. The bird, still greedily imbibing of the succulent nectar, hardly seemed to notice. Gage motioned toward the small stone bench beside the fountain.

"Go, walk slowly and take a seat over there," his father instructed. "Hold the cavea steady, and when he empties the sweetsuckle, pluck another from that bush. Your little friend should remain with you for a time if you keep him busy eating."

Fascinated with his new pet, Kieran merely nodded. Gage smiled, and turned.

His gaze locked with Meriel's.

She started, horrified to be caught watching

him. It was bad enough to have to deal with the renewed emotions his fatherly interaction with Kieran had stirred, without also having to confront him so soon after having made her fateful decision. She clutched her bedrobe to her and turned to leave.

"Wait." Gage's low plea stopped her.

Like a woman going to her execution, Meriel turned.

He glanced back at Kieran, still delightedly engrossed in his little bird, then at Meriel. With a quick motion, Gage indicated for her to leave the herbivorium.

She halted as soon as they were out of earshot of their son. Summoning all the poise she possessed, Meriel turned to Gage.

"Did you wish something?" she inquired cooly. "If not, I desire a moment of privacy in which to dress."

His gaze dipped to the swell of her breasts beneath the fabric she clenched so tightly in her hand. He smiled. "Don't let me keep you from such a pleasant task. I can wait."

Meriel flushed. "This is not the proper time for your personal entertainment, not with Kieran nearby. If you wish for me to disrobe, I must obey. Only first send my son away."

"His place is with his mother."

A frown marred the smoothness of her brow. "I don't understand. You took him from me—"

"And I am now giving him back." Gage's mouth lifted in a crooked smile of apology. "I had no right to take him away, Meriel. It was my anger driving me, that and a need to exact an equal measure of pain from you. Can you forgive me?"

His words were like tiny daggers stabbing into her heart. Forgive him? By all that was sacred, his former actions against her were nothing in comparison to what she'd resolved to do to him!

But it didn't matter. She didn't dare let it matter or she'd never find the strength to carry through with her cruel plan. With a superhuman effort, Meriel steeled herself to the pangs of conscience. To the heartbreaking sight of Gage standing there, a shy, uncertain look gleaming in his beautiful eyes. To the sudden aching sensation that swelled in her throat.

Meriel nodded, the action wooden and mechanical. "There's nothing to forgive. We were both angry and hurting. But that is over. It is time to move on."

She licked her lips, as if considering her next words. "I thank you for the return of my son, but request one favor more."

"Ask, and it is yours if I can grant it."

"Allow him another night away from my room. . . .You and I need that time together."

Gage cocked his head. "Indeed? And why is that, Meriel?"

She clenched her hands into tight little fists until the nails scored her palms. "I owe you a debt, a fulfillment of a vow. I wish to repay both tonight."

Something dark and hungry flared in his eyes. "You wish to mate with me, do you?"

"Yes."

"And why this sudden change of heart? I thought you needed more time."

Meriel forced the words past a tightly constricted throat, her heart hammering beneath her breast. "I've had more than enough time."

"Enough time to begin to want me? Answer me that, Meriel."

As he spoke, Gage moved until he stood so close she could feel the heat emanating from his big body, smell his man-scent. Yet still he didn't touch her, as if he were holding himself back until he received the answer he sought. She swallowed hard and raised her eyes to his face.

A slight flush suffused his striking features. His nostrils flared, his throat worked erratically, and the pulse at the base of his neck throbbed with a wild beat. He was as excited as she, if for entirely different reasons. He imagined, hoped, she finally desired him.

That cruel, most bitter of ironies tore at her heart. Oh, she wanted him all right. Wanted to kill him.

Her gaze dropped. She couldn't bear to look Gage in the eye, to foster the deceit for a second longer. Tonight, her true motives cloaked in the anonymity of darkness, she'd face him again. But not now. It was too much to bear just now.

Meriel nodded, nearly choking on the lie that, on another plane, was closer to a truth she didn't dare face. "Yes, Gage. I want you."

"Care for another serving of roast domare steak?" Gage inquired from his seat across from Meriel at the small dining table set up in her bedchamber.

Reluctantly Meriel glanced up from her plate

where she was engrossed in rearranging an assortment of food that held no appeal. The hand in her lap clenched reflexively around the small, spring-loaded case that contained the Arborian nexus thorn.

"Wh-what did you say?"

"Would you like another piece of meat?" he repeated patiently. "You took very little the first time. Not that you've eaten much of what you did take," he muttered, observing the contents of her plate. Gage laid down his fork and knife and leaned back. He folded his arms across his chest. "What's wrong, Meriel?"

"Wrong?" She shook her head in a vehement, denying motion. "Nothing. I-I'm fine." At his raised brow, Meriel corrected herself slightly. "Well, I suppose I am a bit nervous about . . ." Her voice faded and she lowered her eyes.

"About our mating?" Gage finished for her gently. "Is that it, femina?"

She nodded.

"Meriel, look at me."

Violet eyes lifted.

Gage smiled. "We're not strangers to each other, sweet femina. And this time there'll be only pleasure. Just like I promised you that day long ago. The pain is gone, over—forever."

And I say you are wrong, Gage Bardwin, Meriel silently replied, the anguish twisting her heart into a tight, constricted knot. *All I've traded is a fleeting physical pain for one more terrible and eternal. There'll be no pleasure whatsoever in killing you. Only a torment that will remain with me for the rest of my life.*

But that wasn't the answer he sought or one she dared give. For her people, Meriel bitterly reminded herself, and managed a wan little smile. It was all for her people.

"Then perhaps it's best we not prolong the inevitable. My anxiety won't lessen with the waiting, no matter how you strive to allay my fears." Meriel shoved the thorn case in her pocket, then rose from the table and walked around to stand beside him. She offered Gage her hand. "Come. Come with me to bed."

He stood, drawing her hand through the crook of his arm, then covered it with his own strong fingers as if to infuse a little of his confidence into her. His head cocked briefly downward, indicating the crystal flask of uva wine and their two goblets.

"Should I bring them along? Perhaps another cup or two might ease your anxiety?"

And dampen my resolve as well, Meriel thought grimly, *not to mention my aim with the nexus thorn.*

She shook her head. "No. Only the act itself will ease my concerns. Please, just take me to bed."

He laughed then, a deep, rich sound that made his dark eyes dance with light. "You really must work on the subtleties of seductive behavior, femina. A man wants to believe a woman is moved by his virile presence, not by her need to get it over with."

It was too much—his concern, his gentle teasing. He was making this so hard! Hot tears rushed to her eyes.

"Please, Gage. Don't. I can't bear it!"

"Meriel . . . I didn't mean to upset you!" Regret mixed with confusion twisted his features. Gage drew a ragged breath, then pulled her to him. "If the thought of mating with me distresses you so, I release you from your vow."

She went still, her eyes wide and wary. "What is this? You suddenly don't want me anymore?"

He chuckled softly, wryly. "I doubt I'll ever cease to desire you, femina. But I also want you to come to me willingly, or not at all."

"But I *do* want you!" Meriel cried, belatedly realizing where this was leading—and that she must manipulate him to take her to bed or all was lost.

She grabbed his hand and pulled. It didn't matter that he was making her decision more and more difficult, first with his offer to return Kieran to her, then with his willingness to free her from any sexual obligation to him. But why now, when she fought to maintain her view of him as a heartless, manipulative liar who meant to use her and her people, did he have to be so . . . so kind?

"Wait, femina!" Gage dug in his heels, effectively halting Meriel's forward progress.

When she slid to a stop he jerked her against him, then swung her up in his arms and strode to the bed. Lowering Meriel to her feet, Gage stood there for a long moment, staring down at her. Then, imprisoning her against the hard wall of his body, he dipped his head.

She awaited him, rigid, all breath suspended. His kiss, when his lips met hers, was man-hungry and fiercely demanding. Meriel's hands rose to Gage's chest, balled into fists in preparation to push him away, but all strength suddenly ebbed from her body.

With a moan, she sank against him, her arms lifting to entwine about his neck. His tongue probed for entrance, then thrust in with masculine need and command. Her hands moved wildly, stroking his head, clutching at his massive shoulders.

"Gage," Meriel gasped when he finally drew back for breath. "I—I . . . ah, by all that is sacred!"

"It's all right, sweet femina," he soothed. "You are mine, have always been. Don't fight what is meant to be."

She shook her head to evade his marauding mouth. "Don't. It's not . . ."

At the memory of what she must soon do, nausea welled in her. "Please understand. I can't help it. I haven't any other choice!"

He moved then to capture her face in the clasp of his big hands. "You are right. You have no other choice," Gage said, the husky catch in his voice belying his outward calm. A sudden need assailed him. A need to tell her all, to test the depth of her commitment, her affection for him. And the truest test was to tell her of his mother—and, because of her, the kind of man he had become.

"Neither of us has a choice, no matter how hard we fight against it," he began, before his courage failed him. "In the end," Gage inhaled a shuddering breath and forced himself to continue, "neither your mother nor mine could keep us from finding each other—and the healing we both so desperately need."

She gazed up at him, confused. "*Your* mother? *My* mother? I don't understand. What have they to do with us?"

He eyed her intently. "Do you seriously think your mother didn't have a hand in separating us that first time? Did she tell you lies—like I now suspect she told me—of how I used you, then cast you aside?"

Meriel's heart began a wild beat. "What do you mean?"

"I hated you after that day we first mated," he whispered, a faraway look in his eyes. "I'd thought we'd shared something special, if only for a short time, and then you left without even a farewell to run to your beloved prince."

"But I didn't—" Meriel stopped short. It all fell into place now, Gage's anger, his mistrust, when she had done nothing to him. Had her mother manipulated them both?

It was indeed possible. Once Meriel had left for Pelum's lands, her mother could just as easily have turned to Gage with another story. But why? Why would her mother have been so intentionally cruel?

She wouldn't have thought of it as cruel, Meriel realized with a rush of insight. Kadra would have seen the act of emotionally as well as physically separating her and Gage as a brutal necessity. Further entanglement with an off-world breeder would only complicate things, hinder the evolution of Meriel's predestined fate. And, above all, Kadra had wanted to protect her daughter for as long as possible. Though Kadra had been misguided and self-serving at times, Meriel had always known that her mother loved her. Loved her enough to hurt her by turning her against Gage.

"She said you weren't attracted to me," Meriel hesitantly offered, "that you'd always wanted her instead. It broke my heart. I-I fled to Pelum for comfort." Her mouth curved in apology. "Please try to understand. I was so young, so naïve, so vulnerable then . . ."

Gage smiled. "I do understand. I was as wrong, as misled as you. Can you ever forgive me for how I treated you when I returned as Lord Commander?"

"It ceased to matter when I saw your compassion for my people, your kindness to Kieran." Meriel paused, a sudden thought wrinkling her brow. "You mentioned your mother as well. What has she to do with us?"

A dark, emotion-laden memory stabbed through Gage. Ah, yes, his mother. He girded himself for the disclosure to come, afraid yet determined to see it through. But, Gods, if she turned from him after hearing the truth . . .

"I've never told anyone this besides Teran. Not even King Falkan has any inkling of the real facts. But it's time you know." Gage's jaw clenched. His mouth went tight and grim. "My mother betrayed her husband, Prince Bardwin, then expected me to live the lie. All the cycles she encouraged me to excel at the Imperial Academy, she did so only to groom me for a position I had no right to claim."

"Perhaps she meant to assure your future. Meant to help you," Meriel ventured. An uneasy premonition, that this unsettling turn of conversation wasn't what she wanted to hear, twined about her heart.

"Help me? Be damned, Meriel!" Anger twisted his features. Gage released her and turned to grip one of the tall bedposts, his head pressing into the carved robur wood. He closed his eyes. "There was never one shred of concern for me in her actions," he gritted through clenched teeth. "She always meant to use me, use everyone! And I was so young, so trusting! It broke my heart."

Panic filled Meriel. She couldn't deal with this, couldn't bear to see him expose his pain and vulnerability like this. Not now. Gods, not ever!

Meriel took a quick step back from him. "Don't, Gage. I-I shouldn't have asked. I don't deserve to hear—"

"Yes, you do. You more than anyone else." He turned and pulled her against him. His hand cupped her chin, lifting her face to his. "You need to hear it all, know it all. And know as well everything I am. That I'm a bastard, even if of royal blood."

"A-a bastard?"

He nodded grimly. "My mother was a royal princess, to be sure, but my father was never who I thought him to be. I was raised in the Royal House Bardwin, and thought for all the cycles of my youth that I was heir to the High Prince's lands and throne. But my real sire was nothing more than a palace guard, one of many my faithless mother took a passing fancy to. And one she disposed of just as quickly when he threatened to reveal their affair to the Prince."

"Disposed of? She had your real father k-killed?" Disbelief snaked through Meriel.

"She cared only for herself and her own needs." His gaze captured and held hers, as if refusing to allow Meriel to evade the bitter truth any more than he could. "It was just before graduation at the Imperial Academy that I received word the High Prince had died of mysterious causes. I transported home and commenced an investigation—an investigation that uncovered more than I ever wanted to know. My mother's duplicity was revealed at last—and the truth of my real parentage."

"What did you do?" Compassion mixed with sick despair roiled within Meriel. Gage a bastard, betrayed by a heartless mother, confused and wounded and suspicious of everyone's motives from that day on. It revealed so much about the man he'd become . . . and the hard shell he'd built around his heart.

"My beloved mother," Gage rasped out the words, "wanted me to hide the truth. Wanted to place a bastard on the throne to protect her interests. Expected me to carry on the lies and deception. But I wouldn't do it." He crushed Meriel to him, his big body shuddering with the force of some horrible memory.

"Hush, hush," she crooned, stroking his head, frantically striving to find some way to stop him. "It's all right. It's over. Please, I don't want to hear any more! *Please* don't tell me any more!"

"I have to!" he cried, his voice trembling with emotion. "I have to. Only then will you know it all, see me for the man I really am. And then, if you still want me, knowing the truth . . ."

She sagged against him in defeat, terrified of the revelations she'd hear—and what havoc that knowledge would wreak with her heart—but helpless all the same to refuse him what he so needed to share. "Tell me then," Meriel choked out the words. "It won't change what is, what must be, but tell me."

"I walked away, but she still wasn't done," he said. "In her rage at being thwarted, she accused me of leading the plot to assassinate the High Prince. I was imprisoned, to await execution for treason."

Gage inhaled a ragged breath. He rubbed his hands up and down her arms as if to soothe himself, reassure himself she was still there. "But even that wasn't enough for my mother. I had an older sister, the High Prince's only legitimate child and rightful heir to the throne. A sister who had seen through our mother long ago and hated her. Hated her so deeply that our mother knew she could never hope to rule through her. My sister died as well, found dead in my prison cell, strangled."

"But how? How could that have happened?"

"I'm not sure. I slept through the murder, thanks to some drugged wine served me for the evening meal. But I awoke in time to find her dead, awoke in time to be also accused of her death."

Meriel's heart began to hammer beneath her breast. Somehow, whatever came next, she knew that Gage had been drawn into it against his will—and still dealt with the horrible consequences. Consequences that she must now face as well.

"What happened then?" she prodded, wanting the suspense over and done with.

"What else? My mother got what she wanted."

"How?"

"I escaped. My mother was left as sole ruler—until her past caught up with her. Her evil deeds, at least some of them, were finally discovered. She was tried and convicted of her husband's and daughter's murder."

Gage paused, the look he shot her one of anguished despair . . . and something else. A plea for understanding, forgiveness—acceptance.

There was still more to come, Meriel knew, and this last revelation would be the hardest of all for him to share. She sensed it would expose some facet of Gage he didn't like. Something he regretted, perhaps even despised. Yet, whatever he told her, Meriel was just as certain it wouldn't change her feelings for him, or her conviction that he was a good, brave man.

"Tell me," she murmured huskily, a tiny smile breaking through in spite of the pain and apprehension. "Though it doesn't really matter what you did in the past. What you are now is all that matters."

He clutched her to him in savage desperation. "But, once you know it all, will you still want me? That's what matters to me!"

"Tell me, Gage," Meriel whispered. "*You'll* never be certain until you do."

The light, the fire, died in his eyes. His mouth went grim. "No, I suppose I won't."

Gage studied her for a moment longer in thoughtful silence. "There's really not much more to tell. When I heard the news of my mother's impending execution, I was in a tavern on some planet I've long ago forgotten the name of. I did nothing more than shake my head and down another mug of ale. I didn't care, save that it seemed right that she die. My entire family was dead and I might as well have joined them, for what emotion or faith in humanity I had left."

Incredulous relief filled her. "And you thought I'd turn from you because you didn't care if your mother died? Because you didn't lift a hand to save her?"

"A man of honor might have tried. She *was* my mother, after all."

"A man of honor . . ." Meriel smiled sadly. "I think what haunts you most isn't that you turned from her. It's that you never forgave her."

Gage briefly considered that observation, then shrugged. "Perhaps. If the truth be known, I probably never will."

"Then how can you ever hope to be a true father to Kieran and mate to me?"

A thunderous expression formed in Gage's eyes. "What, by the five moons, does whether I forgive my mother or not have to do with us?"

"Everything. How can you totally commit to me and a life together, with that terrible bitterness still encompassing you?"

"It's not the same," Gage stubbornly replied. "I won't allow it to affect us."

"You watched your entire family destroyed, lived all these cycles with distrust and hatred in your heart, and all because of one woman's cruel machinations," Meriel persisted. "How can you say it won't affect us? Every time you get angry with me, you'll see your mother in me. Every time you think I've betrayed you . . ."

"Yes." Gage's shoulders slumped and he groaned his defeat. "Yes, I'm guilty of it all. But, as unworthy as I am, though I lack the courage to forgive my mother, I still need you, Meriel. I still need our son. You've given me hope, that day so long ago and now, that there's still a chance of happiness for me."

She met his expectant gaze, but didn't answer.

He went quiet then, his stance guarded, waiting. "Will you turn from me then, because of that one weakness?" Gage demanded raggedly. "Will you, Meriel?"

At his words, so full of soul-deep torment and aching need, Meriel's heart swelled with anguished love. She knew nothing, remembered nothing save the powerful, hurting man in her arms. A man who asked for nothing but that she give of herself, and promised the universe in return.

"No," she breathed. "I won't turn from you. I'm no more perfect than any other person and not fit to judge you. And, the truth of the matter is, I still love you."

Forgotten were her royal responsibilities, the plight of her family and people. Forgotten were Pelum's words of Gage's impending betrayal of them. She knew now, with a woman's sure, loving instinct, that they weren't true. All that Meriel could think of was Gage, and easing his torment in any way she could.

Her hands moved, stroking his head, his neck, his shoulders and chest. He groaned and buried his face in the curve of her neck, his own hands equally wild and fevered.

"Meriel. Gods, Meriel!"

She laughed softly, thrilled by his need, his trust that she'd not only accept him, but his past as well. Never had a man touched her as Gage did in humbling himself to reveal his innermost fears and failings—and the heartbreaking pain that had dogged him since the destruction of his family. It took the greatest courage to take a chance on happiness after what he'd experienced, yet he had been willing to risk it one more time—for her.

But, though her plan to kill Gage had disintegrated in the searing revelations and renewed admissions of love, she *was* still Pelum's wife. And those vows could not be severed. Before things went any further, she must remind Gage of that.

"A moment," Meriel said, taking his hands in hers to still the soul-stirring caresses he wrought on her body. "Please, you *must* listen to me!"

Gage stiffened, controlling his rising passion with the greatest of efforts. "What? Tell me and tell me quickly, femina! I want you. I need you. There's little more to be said or done than the fulfillment of that!"

"And I want you as well," she breathed. Gazing up into the sweet, dark depths of his eyes, Meriel lost the heart to tell him the truth of their relationship. The morrow was soon enough, though the pain of her admission would be all the more bitter because of it. She just couldn't bear to wound him further, not when he'd so recently bared his heart to her.

His penetrating brown eyes leveled on her. "That's not all you'd meant to tell me, is it?"

She couldn't bear to meet his gaze. "It doesn't matter just now."

"If it's Pelum you wish to remind me of, you're right. It doesn't matter—and never will. You are mine, Meriel. Were mine long before he wed you. It is my child you bore, my body that joined with yours—not his. He is husband in words only. I am yours in heart, and body, and soul!"

"Nonetheless," she countered, angered at his stubborn persistence regarding a topic she'd meant to at least temporarily spare him, "I am vowed to Pelum. It would destroy him for me to turn away. I can't do it, Gage. I won't!"

"It's because I told you I'm a bastard, isn't it? You know now I'm not worthy of you, a Queen and fine lady!"

"No!" Meriel cried, stung by the accusation. "I don't care about that! Perhaps I should but I don't. It's Pelum and only Pelum who comes between us."

Pain slashed across Gage's features. His grip tightened on her arm. "And what of me? What of my needs, my feelings?"

"I love you. I'll always be there for you. But in time you must give me up, allow me to return to my husband. I couldn't bear the guilt if you didn't."

"You make it sound as if we do something sordid."

"No," she denied hotly. "Not sordid, but wrong. I have no right to mate with another. I want you desperately, but I have no right."

"Then let the wrong be on my head." Gage pressed against her, his body hard, throbbing with a wild, primitive need. "Let it always be my fault, for I'll never, ever let you go!"

He bent, his arm slipping beneath Meriel's knees to lift her and lay her upon the bed. Then, in a quick movement of hands and clothes, Gage stood there naked. His powerful body trembled with passion, his huge, thick shaft unmistakable proof of his readiness.

Meriel gazed up at him, the sight of his magnificently nude body setting her on fire, filling her with a wet, aching, unbearable need. She closed her eyes against the sight of him, for one last fleeting moment fighting Gage in his unlawful desire for her. But it was already too late.

Though Meriel knew she could never completely be his, tonight she would give herself to him. To deny Gage after what he'd just revealed, to plunge the dagger of rejection into his heart, was more than she could bear. And in some tiny, hidden place within her, Meriel knew he had spoken true.

All sisterly affection aside, Pelum had never been more than a husband in words. Gage *was* the husband of her heart and body and soul.

"Come." She lifted her arms to him. "Come to me."

With a feral growl, Gage bent and ripped her

gown asunder. His hungry gaze raked her body, taking in her lush, full breasts, softly rounded belly, and dark triangle of curls at the apex of her thighs. He shoved his hand between her legs and spread them apart. The sight of her pink woman's flesh nearly drove him over the edge.

He lowered himself to kneel between Meriel's legs, his hand slipping through the dense curls guarding her femininity, his fingers parting the wet folds of her to slide into her deep, slick cleft. He thickened even more, his glans flaring, dark pink, its tip glistening with desire.

"Meriel," he groaned. "Forgive me, but I can't wait."

She smiled then and pulled him down to her. "Neither can I, my love. Neither can I."

One of his hands slid beneath her, closing over her buttocks and lifting her groin completely against his erection. He grasped himself with the other hand, guiding his shaft to her moist, secret place. He bent to capture a soft nipple with his mouth, sucking then nipping it until it puckered to taut arousal.

"G-Gage!" Meriel cried.

At her soft cry, the last of Gage's control shattered. He thrust abruptly into her, burying himself in her tight, hot sheath. She arched against him with a gasp that was both pain and pleasure. For a long, exquisite moment they pressed tightly, one to the other, savoring the deep, thick union of their bodies.

Then, with a savage sound, Gage withdrew, to plunge again and again, the tension building to unbearable heights. Building until nothing, nei-

ther life, nor family, nor honor, mattered more
than the fire rising, burgeoning, then exploding
between them.

The universe and its problems would wait.
Tonight was theirs, until the darkness grayed to
dawn . . . and reality intruded once more.

Chapter Nine

Gage woke to sunlight streaming through the long expanse of windows. The balcony door was open and the hot, dry breeze added nothing of relief save to ruffle the gauzy curtains in a sporadic, undulating dance of fabric. He lay there for a time, watching the play of sunlight and shadow on the tile floor, strangely content.

Beside him, Meriel slept on, her dark mane tousled and wild upon the pillow, her delicate features relaxed, her soft, moist lips parted slightly with her gentle breathing. Gage leaned over to stroke a flawless cheek, a fierce, loving possessiveness filling him. After last night she was indeed his. He would never give her or his son up, no matter the vows she had once made to that weak, simpering man she called husband, No matter the shame of his family . . . and birth.

His frowning gaze shifted back out the balcony window. The unfortunate circumstances of his birth be damned. He was the Lord Commander. If he must possess Meriel by right of the ancient Imperial law of spoils to the conqueror, so be it. Pelum was frail. He'd not live forever. Sooner or later, Meriel would be his in every way.

The thought of having Meriel's husband disposed of, either by execution or by accident, crossed his mind. As attractive as the idea was as a solution to his problems, Gage knew he couldn't do it. He wasn't a cold-blooded murderer, no matter how hard his mother had worked to make him so. And no woman, not even Meriel, would ever drive him to such depths of depravity. He wouldn't *ever* allow himself to become the kind of person his mother had been.

Not that Meriel would ever have asked it of him, Gage thought, turning his attention back to her. She was perfection in every way, from her glowing, radiant beauty to her pure heart and generous self-sacrifice in the service of her people. That was why he loved her.

The admission drew him up short. It was still so novel a realization—his love for Meriel—and Gage turned it over and over in his mind.

Love. Indeed, what did it entail? Commitment, trust, a wholehearted giving without expectation of anything in return. Was there truly a chance for such exalted concepts to grow and flourish between him and Meriel?

For the first time, Gage allowed himself to hope so. He'd been no fool those three cycles ago when he'd imagined Meriel a good, kind, and honest if naïve girl. In the interim the cruel vagaries of life had interfered, but that had been neither of their faults. And the future was at last theirs to control.

The hot breeze wafted over him. Gage stirred restlessly, suddenly aware of how stifling the room had become. He threw off the thin sheet and levered himself to one elbow, intent on rising and seeking out the refreshing coolness of the mineral bath. As he did, a small case lying on the bed beside Meriel's torn dress caught his eye.

He picked it up, turning it over in his hand. His brow furrowed in puzzlement. What in the heavens was it? His thumb found the small knob on the side of the case, unlocked its safety mechanism, and shoved the lever over. A lethal-looking thorn sprang out, its tip needle-sharp, a drop of amber fluid suspended from the end.

With a low curse Gage flipped the lever over, retracting the thorn back in its case, and climbed to his knees. He stared down at the instrument of death, his mind whirling. He'd seen the killing weapon many times in his tracking career. The Arborian nexus thorn, a tool of cowards and assassins.

What was Meriel doing with it?

The answer was impossible to ignore. She must have carried it with her in the pocket of her gown and knowingly brought it to their meeting last night. But had Meriel meant to use it on him, or was it a weapon she'd acquired long ago, for personal safety purposes?

Gage raked his hand through his hair, setting the thick, curling strands awry. Something, call it his well-honed tracker's instinct, told him that the only safety she'd meant to ensure was her safety from him.

As much as he fought to deny it, the niggling doubts grew, spiraling into a certainty that filled him with a sick horror. At some point last night, Meriel had intended to kill him.

His fist clenched about the thorn case. Pain stabbed through him with each beat of his heart. She had given herself to him, said she loved him, needed him. And then . . . then she had taken a killing nexus thorn to bed.

Gage swung off the bed, turning from the heart-rending scene of Meriel, all softness and delectable woman, sleeping in unguarded innocence before him. At that moment, he hated the sight of her, hated her guiltless repose while his heart was slowly being torn asunder by the doubts, the anger, piece by agonizing piece. He forced himself to stride across the room, not knowing where he was going or why.

It had all been a farce—the love, the tenderness, the honesty. Rage boiled up like a fiery acid, consuming his anguish and every other emotion that cried out for rational thought. Curse her. Damn her to perdition!

He returned to the bed and dressed quickly, then bent and grabbed Meriel by the shoulders. "Wake up, you heartless little she-devil!" He shook her roughly. "Wake up and face what you have wrought!"

Meriel jerked awake. She tossed her hair out of her eyes and blinked in confusion. Her vision cleared to find Gage looming over her, a twisted, enraged expression on his face.

What was going on?

"G-Gage?" she mumbled in a sleep-thickened voice. "What's wrong? Is something amiss in the palace?" She attempted to rise, but he kept her firmly imprisoned on the bed. Apprehension flooded her, then the first tendrils of fear. "Gage? Answer me. What's wrong?"

He released her with a motion of utter loathing. A small case appeared in his hand and, with a quick movement of his fingers, the nexus thorn sprang free. "You tell me, femina."

Her eyes widened and she swallowed convulsively. A myriad of explanations, all meant to hide the true purpose of her possession of the thorn, raced through Meriel's mind. She discarded them all. After last night, there could be nothing but honesty between them.

She licked her lips before replying. "I meant to kill you."

"Indeed? And was that to be before or after our mating? Or did you plan on waking before me this morning to complete the deed?"

Meriel shrugged, a sick, miserable feeling roiling in the pit of her stomach. "Does it matter? I didn't do it, did I?"

He grabbed her by the arm, pulling her up to him. "But there'll be other opportunities, won't there? Now that I'm so passion-besotted? It'll be a simple thing to take me unawares, won't it?"

"No!" Meriel tried to wrench her arm free, to put some distance between them, but his fingers only tightened the more, gouging cruelly into the soft flesh of her arm. She immediately ceased her struggles, knowing that to fight against him was futile.

Her head dipped. Her ebony hair cascaded around her face. "I came to our mating intending to kill you," she whispered, "but found I couldn't do it."

She lifted her head, her tear-filled eyes locking with his. "You must believe that, Gage, or else everything we said, everything we did last night was for naught."

"Words can serve more than one purpose," he growled, bitterness tightening his features. "And females are particularly adept at manipulating words to many uses."

"And you think I meant to use you, betray you like your mother did? Is that it?"

Anger and a grim resentment twined like metal bands about Meriel's heart, wringing a ragged, choking laugh from her. "I told you this would happen if you didn't exorcise her memory from your heart, find some way to forgive her. And I see now the depth of your love and trust in me. Nothing I say will change your mind, will it?"

A dark brow arched in ironic amusement. "How clever. The incontrovertible proof that you meant to murder me lies in my hand, yet you now attempt to turn it upon me and play upon my guilt at doubting you to divert suspicion." His jaw hardened. "Try again, Meriel."

An urge to slap Gage's face, demand he leave her room, filled Meriel, but something stayed her. Love should be able to bear the doubts, the pain that could at times arise. And she truly *was* the one at fault. The burden of proof lay with her.

She inhaled a tremulous breath. "I thought you meant to enslave my people, once we transported to Carcer, to mine the martenite ore. I couldn't allow that to happen."

Confusion clouded his eyes. "Martenite? On Carcer? What are you talking about, Meriel? There's no martenite on Carcer."

"I was told otherwise."

"Who? Who told you such lies?"

Meriel's lips tightened. Here it comes now. She shook her head. "I can't tell you, but my source was reliable."

"Who was it, Meriel?"

She quailed before the intensity of his anger, then forced herself to face him. She couldn't implicate Pelum in this. His position was precarious enough. She'd have to bear the brunt of Gage's anger—and its consequences—alone.

"Please, Gage, try to understand," Meriel pleaded. "It doesn't matter who told me. For a time I questioned your motives, but I know now that you would never allow my people to be enslaved or misused in any way. No one can ever make me doubt you again!"

"It was that worthless husband of yours, wasn't it?" he growled. "He's the only one who could turn you against me."

"No!" Meriel caught herself, terrified that the intensity of her response would give her away. She schooled her features into one of calm composure. "No. It wasn't any one person. It was a lot of things, combined with my confused feelings about you."

He eyed her with frank suspicion.

She sighed. "I know I ask a lot in this, to expect you to accept my assurance that my doubts about you are over, that I truly *had* decided against killing you, but there's nothing more I can do. I love you, Gage Bardwin, but my people will always come first. What I almost did, I did for them."

"You swore a vow of fealty to me!"

"Only because I thought you would help Tenua. When I began to doubt your intentions, I was ready to go back on that vow."

"So, you now admit to also being a liar and traitor!"

Meriel flinched, then nodded slowly. "Yes, I suppose I was willing to become even that. I am Queen. There's no honor for me, save in the assurance of my people's welfare."

She smiled then, a slow, sad movement of her lips. "And perhaps there's no place for the love of a man in my life, either. If the choice ever came to him over my people . . ." Tears filled her eyes but she fiercely blinked them away. "Let me go back to Pelum. He understands his place in my heart, knows where my duty truly lies. You, on the other hand, would never be happy sharing me with anyone. And I couldn't bear to hurt you."

He flung her away from him. "Fine words from a woman who is no longer interested in a man! Can't you ever be honest, Meriel? Can't you just say you had your curiosity sated last night, and have no further need for me? I'm strong. *I* can take the truth!"

"Fine then, you stubborn son of an elephas! I'll be honest with you, though I doubt you'll believe this any more than you have anything else I've said. I love you. I still want you. But it won't work between us for so very many reasons, only two of which are that I'm already wed and I must always put my people before you. So take that truth and . . . and . . ."

"And place it in some appropriately distant part of my anatomy?" Gage ventured wryly.

"Yes, curse you!" Meriel stormed, her fists rising at her sides. "Ah, but you're the most infuriating, opinionated, thick-skulled man!"

"I suppose so," he admitted gravely, "but one gets that way with bitter experience. And you've enjoyed unusual success in hurting me, time and again."

Tears hovered on the edge of spilling from Meriel's eyes. An impulse to wail like a babe overwhelmed her. Gods, she couldn't bear to think of hurting him, much less hear him say the words!

"I've never meant to hurt you," she finally choked out the admission. "Truly I haven't. But it seems we are fated to always be at odds with each other."

"I just wish I could trust you, once and for all."

"I wish you could, too," she whispered, a single tear escaping to trickle down her face. "But I don't know what else to do."

With an infinitely tender motion, he wiped her tear away. "You gave your oath of fealty to me. Yet you've broken it time and again."

"That I have," Meriel admitted, swallowing back the sobs that rose in her throat. "In my attempts to be a good ruler to my people, I find myself constantly torn between horrendous choices and untenable compromises. And I seem to make such poor decisions, time and again." She shook her head, her shoulders slumping in dejection. "I fear I'm not a very good queen."

"It takes time to learn to rule well. You must give yourself that time." Gage cradled her chin in his hand and lifted her gaze to his. "In the meanwhile, you can't listen to and try to please everyone. You must trust your heart, your instincts, and rely more on your own judgment. You may be inexperienced, Meriel, but you're not stupid."

She smiled then, a shy, hesitant upturning of soft lips. "Truly, Gage? You think I'm smart?"

A grin tugged at the corner of his mouth. "Truly. And I suppose I believe you didn't really want to kill me, either."

"Wh-what?"

"I believe everything you've said," he patiently reiterated. "Including the fact that you still love me."

She stared up at him through a haze of tears, struggling to comprehend what she'd just heard. Gage believed her?

He smiled back in gentle understanding.

Joy flooded Meriel. With a small cry, she flung herself into his arms. "Truly? Ah, Gage? Truly?"

He gathered her to him. "Truly, femina. There's an old saying that love can make a fool out of even the strongest, bravest of men. I think I finally understand what was meant."

Leaning back, Gage stared down at her. "I love you, Meriel. I understand the terrible responsibilities of your position as Queen. I accept that there may be times when I must come second to your people. But you're worth it, just as long as you always come back to me."

"Yes, oh yes!" She clasped his face between her hands and kissed him soundly on the lips, then drew back, flushing in embarrassment.

Gage grinned. "Keep that up and I may just have to undress again."

Meriel eyed his broad-shouldered form, his heavily muscled chest, trim waist, and narrow hips, her gaze trailing down his body until it alighted at his groin. Already his manhood was swelling, beginning to strain the fabric of his breeches. She smiled.

She knew she should keep to her earlier resolve and beg Gage to let her go back to Pelum, before this growing relationship broke both their hearts. But he'd admitted he loved her. And, for one more time, she intended on savoring the emotional as well as physical aspects of that love. Surely, she was entitled to just one more time . . .

"A wise idea, indeed," she purred seductively, "for I intend to kiss you long and hard for the next several hours."

And without further preliminaries, Meriel proceeded to do just that.

"Something must be done, and quickly!" Pelum's Volan stated emphatically as he lounged back in the comfortable chair in his well-furnished cell. "The bitch failed us, as I knew she would. Bardwin *must* be killed!"

"And he will," Torman assured him. "The question remains how to assure that his death cannot be traced to us."

He took a seat in the other plush chair and steepled his fingers beneath his chin. At the totally human action, Torman caught himself. With a grimace, he swung his hands to lie rigidly on his lap. Curse it all, but he was taking on too many of these people's gestures. It was becoming too natural, too easy.

"We need someone who is expendable," he growled, forcing himself back to the business at hand. "Someone we can afford to lose."

"Might I make a suggestion, Exalted Leader?"

Torman glanced up. He nodded.

"This body is weak, nearly useless," Pelum said, disdainfully indicating himself. "It won't last long. And he is of little political use if his wife won't even listen to him. He has adequate motive for wanting to kill Bardwin—a man who stole his wife."

His leader eyed him with a speculative look. "Your idea has merit. The extra energy required to fight and kill Bardwin, however, would most likely result in the consort's death. We'll have to plan this very carefully, or you could easily be without a body and no place to transfer."

Pelum grunted in agreement. "A fatal miscalculation indeed."

Torman nodded grimly. "Indeed. The best plan is to lure Bardwin down to your cell with a message that you wish to speak with him. Then, if we ensure that there are enough guards about who are Volan-enslaved, even if you fail they can 'assist' in his demise. He'll be trapped down here one way or another, away from his men and any hope of aid."

"There remains one small problem. How will we get Bardwin to fight me?"

His leader frowned in thought. "Two males fighting over a female is the easiest to orchestrate. You must manipulate Meriel to anger Bardwin over you. I'll bring her for another visit this very day."

Pelum grinned. "It's a foolproof plan, as is everything you do, Exalted Leader. The Mother Ship chose well in naming you to head this latest infiltration force. We *will* succeed."

Torman rose from his chair. "Was there ever a doubt?" he tossed over his shoulder as he headed across the cell.

Yet one question continued to nag at Torman as he made his way through the secret passages to his guard post outside Meriel's room. The little Queen was as much a stumbling block as Bardwin. She might be naïve in the ways of power, but she was learning fast. And it was quite evident that, as short a reign as she had heretofore enjoyed, her people were already fanatically loyal to her. No matter how carefully he tried to hide the growing Volan enslavements, sooner or later Meriel would discern what was happening to her people. Then she, too, would have to be disposed of.

That consideration greatly disturbed Torman.

Once more Meriel followed Torman through the dark, dank underground passages. At the thought of facing Pelum, her heart thundered beneath her breast. Surely he would know that she had lain with Gage. Surely the guilt would be written all over her face.

But there was nothing to be done about it. All feelings of love and desire aside, Gage had originally demanded that she mate with him to ensure his assistance in evacuating her people. Pelum would just have to understand. And he need never know how willingly, how eagerly she'd joined with Gage even after he'd freed her of her vow. That was her secret, guilt-ridden and wondrous as it was.

She paused to compose herself, then entered his cell, which was now dim and empty save for his bed. She glanced around, shocked at the change. What had happened? And why?

Pelum sat on the floor in the corner, his head bowed, his legs drawn up. At the sound of her entry, he glanced up. Meriel gasped.

His eyes were sunken, the fragile skin beneath them smudged with shadow. His hair was matted. A scraggly beard darkened his jaws. But, beneath it all, a feverish light gleamed in his eyes and a hectic flush washed his cheeks.

"Pelum!" Meriel hurried across the room and knelt before him. "You're ill! And what happened to your cell? The last time I was here, it was clean, warm and—"

"The Bellatorian took an urge to hasten my demise," her husband interjected bitterly. "He had my cell stripped." He flung back his head and groaned. "Now it's so cold here, so dark and lonely. Gods, Meriel, I can't go on much longer!"

Fresh guilt stabbed through her. While she lay upstairs in a clean, comfortable bed, locked in a passionate embrace with another man, her husband languished in this cold, damp cell! It didn't matter that Gage made her so deliriously happy. It didn't matter that he fulfilled her like Pelum never could. What mattered was her betrayal of her husband, that she'd virtually forgotten about him down here in this horrible little room—that he was all but dying because of her!

"Here, my love." Meriel grasped him beneath the arms and pulled him to his feet. Gods, he was so light, so weak! "Let me help you up to your bed. Torman's outside. I'll send him for some clean clothes, warm blankets, and water for you to bathe in. Then, while I get you washed, I'll have cook make you a nice hearty soup and some of that special Argullian puff bread you love."

"Ah, that would be wonderful, beloved," Pelum whispered as he staggered over to his bed. "I've missed you so. Can't you come visit more often?"

She made a quick decision. "Yes, every day if you'd like. I'll have Torman make me a copy of the key controls to the passages and your cell door. I think I can find my way through the tunnels by now."

With a huge sigh, Pelum lay back on his threadbare cot. "Thank you for that, beloved. I know there is little you can do with Bardwin watching your every move." He glanced up. "How go the plans to kill him? Did Torman find you a nexus thorn?"

Misery knotted in the pit of her stomach. "Yes, he did. But I tell you true, Pelum. I can't kill Gage."

Weakly he levered to one elbow, a fierce light gleaming in his eyes. "You must, Meriel! Everything depends on it!"

She shook her head. "I can't. I won't. Gage isn't a cruel man. He won't do anything to harm our people."

"But the martenite on Carcer! The Imperium will get what they want no matter what Bardwin says or does!"

"You could be wrong in your information, Pelum," she offered gently.

His eyes narrowed to glittering slits. "Perhaps. But I find it most strange how you suddenly choose to believe Bardwin over me. Has he perhaps won you over with the power and majesty of his big shaft? Has he perhaps already lain between your—"

"Pelum!" Meriel cried, horror-struck at the crudity of his words. Never, in all the cycles of their marriage, had he ever spoken to her like that. "Please, don't say such things!"

He lay back and closed his eyes. "And what else am I to think? I lie here in this hole and rot, helpless to do anything. I ask one task of you, not for myself but for the sake of our people, and you not only fail to carry it out, but come back and defend the enemy to me. You've changed, beloved, and I don't know what to do to win you back. I've lost you, haven't I?"

"You haven't lost me!" She sat on the edge of the cot and pulled him into her arms. "I still love you as before."

"Then ask Bardwin for permission for me to leave this cell. Everyone has the freedom to roam the palace now save me. I am no threat to him. I can no longer even influence my own wife to do my bidding. And he quite obviously has won your body now as well as your heart. I am a broken man; I have lost everything. There is nothing more I can do to him."

He shot her a glance from beneath slitted lids. "Nothing except perhaps die down here and free you, once and for all, for him."

At his words, horror slithered through Meriel. Gage would never do that, even to have her. Would he?

She shook the ugly doubts away. No matter how much he wanted her, Gage would never stoop to killing Pelum just to win his wife. He knew her well enough to know she'd never forgive him.

Meriel sighed, suddenly weary with it all—the conflict, the guilt, the confusion. "Pelum, don't say that. Gage isn't a murderer."

"But isn't neglect a form of murder? I'll be dead either way, if he doesn't free me soon."

Tears welled, then spilled down onto Meriel's cheeks. As bitter as it was to hear, what Pelum had just said was the cruel, indisputable truth.

"It will be as you ask, my love," she said, grim determination filling her. "One way or another, I *will* procure your freedom. I owe you that much."

"No, Meriel," Gage calmly replied after they'd retired to her bedchamber for the night. He settled back on a lounge chair. "I won't free Pelum. He stays where I put him."

"But why?" she demanded, pacing the floor before the hearth. "He's ill, Gage. He's no danger to you."

"And I say you're singularly ignorant of the political significance of a royal consort to request such a thing. I have enough to deal with without also having to keep an eye on him. Pelum is well cared for. He stays where he is."

"Well cared for?" Meriel wheeled around to confront Gage. "How can you say that? He huddles in the corner of a cold, damp cell. He hasn't had a bath or fresh change of clothes in days. He is barely fed. And he's growing weaker and weaker!"

"Barely fed? A cold, damp cell? Meriel, what are you talking about?" His face hardened with suspicion. "But, more importantly, how do you know all this? Your erroneous assessment of his living conditions aside, you sound as if you've seen him."

She paled. By all that was sacred! Well, though she refused to lie to him anymore, there was no need to reveal the secret of the passages.

"Yes, Gage, I have seen Pelum. I asked Torman to take me down for a visit."

"Without my permission?"

"I saw no harm in it."

His mouth drew into a ruthless, forbidding line. "You play games again, femina. You knew I didn't want you seeing him. You disobeyed me."

"Disobeyed you? Is that all that matters? Not that I still owe some loyalty to my husband, that I've a sacred duty to care for and about him?"

"Your loyalty is now sworn to me—"

"In the support of my people—"

"Curse it all, Meriel!" Gage rose and jerked her to him. "Don't fight me over this! It's all I can handle that you're still his wife! Don't push me any further!"

"Why, Gage?" she prodded, refusing to relent. "What will you do? Have him killed, whether by driving him to illness or by some fortuitous little accident?" She inhaled a shuddering breath. "I said I loved you. I won't betray you, but I will never shirk my responsibilities to my husband. Let him go. Please!"

"And if I let him go, what if he requires you to return to his bed, as your duties as wife demand? Then whose arms will you lie in each night?"

"You know he is incapable of mating with me."

Barely contained rage emanated from every millimeter of Gage's taut, powerful frame. "Do you think I care? I can't even bear the thought of him touching you! I *will not* allow him to have you— *in any way!*"

All fight fled in one despairing, defeated rush. "Then you won't free Pelum?" Meriel whispered. "No matter how desperately I desire it?"

"No!"

She swallowed hard and looked away, her spirit shattered. "I hate you for that, Gage Bardwin. For your selfish cruelty, your blind, unthinking lust. Keep my husband where you wish. I can't stop you. But hear me, and hear me well. I can't love a man who acts in such a way!"

Meriel squared her shoulders and stepped back as Gage's hands fell away. "I'm sorry to put you in such a position, but there's little choice on my part, either. I have to live with myself, and you've already made that difficult enough."

He looked down at her with cold, savage contempt. "Have I now? Well, perhaps it's time to pay your husband a little visit and settle the issue of whose woman you really are!"

"No!" Meriel grabbed at him as he turned to go. "Leave him alone! He's no match for you!"

With a look of distaste, Gage wrenched free. "It's too late, femina. You had a choice and refused to make it. Now it's time for me to settle this—once and for all!"

Before she could take a step after him, Gage was out the door. Meriel ran forward and slammed her hand on the imprint panel. She *had* to stop him. In his current frame of mind, she didn't know what he'd do.

The door didn't open. Gage had locked her in.

She ran down the narrow passages, the perpetual light torch held high in her hand. Eerie shadows leaped at her, unearthly forms that loomed from the darkness just beyond the reach of the torch's span of brightness. Not for the first time, Meriel shrank back, terrified of the subterranean tunnels' secrets. In the process, she slipped on a slime-covered stone and sank to her knees.

The torch sailed from her hand, landing several meters away. For a heart-stopping instant, Meriel was shrouded in darkness, save for the tiny glow up ahead. Sounds assailed her, of water plunking heavily in some hidden puddle, of nails—or was it claws?—scurrying over hard-packed earth. An errant breeze from some unknown source caressed her face, stirring the dank, fetid air around her.

Meriel dragged in a tremulous breath and crawled forward. It didn't matter that the floor was slippery with unseen things. It didn't matter that her hand glanced off something warm and furry that quickly scurried away.

What mattered was reaching Pelum before Gage got to him. What mattered was finding some way to sneak her husband out of the palace through the underground passages. His earlier protestations that he stay and aid her were no longer feasible. Two men desired her—and one had all the power.

Her hand closed around the torch and, with a sigh of relief, Meriel climbed to her feet. Once more the way was bright. She forced herself to hurry along.

Thank the heavens that Torman had promptly provided her with a duplicate of his key controls after their return from Pelum's cell. She didn't know what she would have done otherwise. The thought of sitting by and helplessly awaiting Gage's return after his visit to her husband would have been more than she could have borne. If she could just reach Pelum first . . .

After a while, Meriel lost track of the time. She made a few wrong turns, but quickly retraced her steps, blessing her nearly photographic memory for aiding her in maintaining a reasonably straightforward course to the cells. At last she reached the stone door and inserted the key control that hung from her neck.

The portal ground slowly open. Meriel extinguished the perpetual torch, shoved it into a nearby recess, then stepped through into the corridor. She drew up short. Two guards lay dead outside Pelum's cell. His door was wide open. From the shouts, grunts, and thud of bodies slamming against the walls, Meriel knew there was more than just Gage and Pelum in the room. She crept forward.

"Kill him!" an unfamiliar voice snarled. "We have our orders. Finish him off now!"

Apprehension constricted her chest and set her heart to pounding, but Meriel forced herself to look into the room. There, sprawled across the entryway was the contorted form of her husband, a dagger transecting his neck.

Meriel choked back a cry. Pelum! Gods, Pelum!

Instinctively she bent to touch him, when a shout of pure, animal rage reverberated throughout the cell. Her gaze jerked up, then swung across the room. Two guards struggled to hold a wounded and bleeding Gage, while a third, his back turned to her, raised another dagger over his head, its downward trajectory aimed straight for Gage's heart.

All thoughts of Pelum fled. There was no way of knowing what had transpired in the moments before her arrival, or who had killed her husband. All she knew was that Gage was in danger.

Summoning all the strength within her, Meriel grasped the dagger and wrenched it free of Pelum's neck. In a blur of thought and motion, she flung herself across the room and thrust the bloodied blade into the nearest guard's back.

He screamed, staggered backward into Meriel, then toppled over on her. The impact of striking hard earth with a heavy body atop her momentarily knocked the wind out of Meriel. A scattering of stars whirled before her. Sounds engulfed her. Frantic shouts. Scuffling noises. The thud of fists against flesh.

Gage. I must help Gage, she thought through the swirling haze that consumed her. She shoved the guard partially off her, then scooted out from under him. The room spun wildly for a few seconds, then righted.

She turned to find Gage in a vicious battle with one guard. The second was even then advancing on her. Meriel shoved at the dead man lying beside her, frantically searching beneath him for the dagger she'd used to kill him. Gods, where was it?

With a snarl, her attacker sprang. He knocked her over. His hands went for her neck. She slapped, then clawed at him with one hand, while the other grasped at the dead guard. The dagger. She had to have the dagger!

Her attacker's hands were like vises, clamping on her throat, squeezing the air from her body. Meriel fought desperately, wildly. Panic consumed her. She battled past it, knowing it would be her defeat. Cold, clear logic was what was needed.

The hand beneath the dead guard glanced off something hard. She clutched at the object. Her fingers curled around the dagger. Exultation surged through her.

Meriel wrenched the weapon free and pressed its tip against the guard's throat. He froze, then slowly released her neck.

"G-get off me," she gasped.

The guard rolled aside, climbed to his feet, and cautiously backed away. Meriel followed him with the dagger until she had him flattened against the wall. She kept him there, loath to kill again, while behind her she heard Gage finish off the other guard. Finally, he drew to her side and commandeered her dagger. Before she could guess his intent, much less protest, he shoved her aside and drove the dagger into the other man's chest.

Meriel cried out, then swung around to find the other guard similarly disposed of. She wheeled about, sick and dizzy, as the full implications of what had just transpired—and what she had done—struck her.

"Ah, Gods," she moaned. "How could this have happened? How could you do such—such a thing? There was no need to kill them all!"

Gage grabbed her by the arm and jerked her up against him. He was slashed several times on the arms and upper torso. One particularly vicious cut traversed his body from his shoulder to his opposite waist, slicing through his tunic to lay bare an oozing gash amid the muscled flesh.

"Volans," he ground out, his chest heaving. "They were all—to a man—enslaved by Volans! Even"—he swung her around to face the doorway and Pelum's body—"your beloved husband!"

Pelum, covered with blood, a gaping wound in his neck, lay sprawled where she had left him. Fresh anguish knifed through her. Meriel twisted free of Gage and ran to Pelum's side. With a piteous cry, she knelt and gathered him to her.

"Pelum! Ah, Pelum, my love!"

Gage watched her with hard, bitter eyes. "Don't waste your tears on him. He hasn't been your husband for at least the past several days. His essence was gone long before he died."

"No. Not Pelum," she moaned, shaking her head in denial as she rocked him to and fro. "He swore there was no Volan threat. He said you fabricated that only to influence me to your needs."

"And I say he lied, or, should I say, his Volan master did? It was all a ploy, constructed by him and his cohorts, to use you against me. Unless"— Gage paused, his gaze suddenly intense, assessing—"you were in league with them all the time?"

She stared up at him, struck momentarily speechless. "What do you mean? I told you before I'd never betray you."

"Indeed?" He gave a small snort of incredulity. "Then it seems quite a coincidence that Pelum and his men were ready for my little visit. Almost as if someone had told him I'd be coming."

Pained disbelief twisted Meriel's features. "Are you implying I deliberately picked a fight with you over Pelum? That I manipulated you into coming down here to confront him?"

He shrugged. "Does it really matter? Pelum is dead. You are now totally mine. And sooner or later I'll discover who the real traitor was."

His hands snaked down to unclasp her hands from Pelum's body. With a grimace of pain he tried unsuccessfully to mask, Gage pulled Meriel up and away from the dead man. "In the meanwhile," he rasped, "your worst fears have come to fruition. I only wonder what you'll do now."

A terrible premonition curled around Meriel's heart. Her throat went dry. "What are you talking about?"

"He attacked me as soon as I entered his cell.

For such a frail little man, your husband's strength was suddenly superhuman. I had to fight for my life. Fortunately for me, in our prolonged struggle, Pelum was the unfortunate recipient of his own dagger."

The blood drained from Meriel's face as Gage nodded in grim irony. "Yes, sweet femina. Like it or not, I have finally killed your husband."

Chapter Ten

Meriel swayed, her knees buckled. With a low oath, Gage grabbed her about the waist and pulled her close to the hard length of him. For a moment more she swam in the chaos of overwhelming shock and emotion, half-tempted to succumb to a beckoning unconsciousness.

It was too much—Pelum's death, Gage a cold-blooded murderer. For murderer he'd be if there was no Volan threat. His only motive would lie naked then, exposed for what it truly was. Gage had implied, in so many ways, that he resented Pelum's right to her. That he all but wished her husband gone, if not actually dead. But to consider Gage in such a cruel, vicious light was painful to contemplate. Loving, courageous, passionate Gage.

Anger, then frustrated hopelessness, surged through her. Curse Gage for confronting Pelum! There was no reason to have brought things to a head. No reason save Gage's stubborn pride and possessiveness. And there had never been a more unfair fight—Gage a battle-hardened warrior, Pelum frail and weakened by his imprisonment.

Pelum's death screamed for vengeance, but there was nothing Meriel could do. Killing Gage, if it were even possible, would not bring her husband back. And it was a luxury she could ill afford. She still needed Gage's help in evacuating her people.

Her people.

Meriel choked back a groan of despair. Would the plight of her people always stand in the way of fulfilling her own desires? Would her vow of fealty to Gage Bardwin always bind her to him, no matter how dear the cost, how deep the pain?

She should hate him for what he'd done. She should demand his death. But she had no heart for it. Better that she'd never known him, never chosen him to give her a child . . .

Her mother's words on that day they'd found him at the breeders' auction flitted through Meriel's mind.

"You'll regret it," Kadra had said. *"He's not the male for you . . . "*

Her mother's words had been prophetic. Kadra, at least, had seen Gage for what he was, known that Meriel and he were not meant for each other. Kadra, in her own way, had tried to protect her from him.

Grief and a deep sense of loss flooded Meriel. She had tried so hard to keep both men, to find some way to love them, each in his own unique way. But, thanks to her selfish, short-sighted needs, she had lost them both. Pelum was dead, and Meriel no longer knew what to think, what to believe about Gage. Both, it seemed, had tried to use her for their own purposes, whether to gain control of her kingdom or her heart. And perhaps, just perhaps, both men had ultimately sought the same thing—total power over her.

Her mind swam with confused thoughts, with possibilities she was no longer capable of confronting. All Meriel wanted was to return to her room, to hide away and tend her wounded, aching heart.

She glanced up, blinking back the tears. There was no point in further weeping. She would live with the consequences of what she had wrought for the rest of her life. But she was still Queen. A Queen who held the fate of her people in her next words.

"Yes, you killed my husband," Meriel forced out the admission. "But there is nothing I can do about it, just as there has never been anything I could do about anything since that first day I met you. I must accept that."

At the flat, defeated tone to her voice, Gage stiffened. Gods, but he'd never wanted this to happen. Didn't she know that? Did she truly think he was capable of murder, just to possess her?

He shook aside the surge of emotions that consideration stirred. As much as he feared the thought of losing Meriel, of allowing her to imagine even for a second longer that Pelum's death hadn't been justified self-defense, there was no time for the luxury of a tender reconciliation. They were still in the gravest danger—

not only from other potentially Volan-enslaved guards, but from the continued, insidious Volan plotting that was even now going on about them.

His grip about her waist tightened. "We need to get out of here. There are still guards posted in these holding cells—guards I can't be certain aren't Volans—and they could happen by at any time. Unfortunately, the only way out of here is back up—"

A sudden thought assailed him. "How did you get here? I left you locked in your room."

Should she tell him about the passages? Meriel stared up at Gage, struggling with the decision. If she didn't, the only plausible explanation for her escape from her room was that Torman had freed her. That act of disloyalty might well cost him his life. Yet, if she told Gage about the passages, they were of no further use to her.

Meriel decided for Torman. Not only could she not bear another death because of her, but she desperately needed Torman's assistance. She couldn't fight Gage, if it became necessary to do so, alone.

"There are tunnels that wind through the palace," she carefully began. "Tunnels long forgotten by most. I used them to reach the cells."

"And used them all along to visit secretly with your husband, didn't you?"

She nodded.

"Curse you, femina!" he snarled. "You've never ceased to betray me, have you?"

"Nothing I did was meant to cause you harm!" Meriel protested hotly. "I only meant to protect my husband and child from you, to ensure the safety of my people. Though none of them mattered to you, they were *everything* to me!"

The thud of heavy shod feet, the coarse rumble of male voices echoing down the corridors, reached their ears.

"Show me these passages!" Gage swung her around, then pulled her across the cell and out the door, his movements pain-stiffened and awkward. "Our son is safe with me, as are your people," he gritted through clenched teeth. "But if you don't help me, and help me now, there soon won't be anything either one of us can do to protect them!"

Meriel hesitated but an instant, weighing the potential value of awaiting the guards and begging them to imprison Gage, versus the long-term advantages of continuing to assist him. Short of demanding and gaining his immediate death—which, no matter what had happened, she could never bring herself to do—she knew he'd soon be freed by his own troops. Then, whatever influence she might still have over him would be permanently destroyed. It was wiser, for the time being, to cooperate with Gage—at least until she could sort through everything and determine the real truth.

"Come. This way." Meriel indicated the hallway that ended in a wall. "The passage lies on the other side."

His eyes narrowed in suspicion, but Gage followed obediently in her wake. Only when she pulled the key control from her gown and shoved it into an all but invisible slot in the rough-hewn wall did he relax his guarded posture. Momentarily, the grinding of gears drowned out the sound of the approaching guards.

The voices, however, rose loud and clear as Gage and Meriel stepped into the dark tunnel. Then they were once more muted as the door slid closed behind them.

Blackness enshrouded Meriel. The heavy, fetid air filled her nostrils, weighed heavily on her, body and soul. The now familiar plop of moisture echoed in the distance.

Meriel repressed a tiny shudder and moved forward, groping along the wall for the perpetual light torch she'd left in the recessed slot. The stone was slick and cold, but she forced herself to persevere. Her efforts were quickly rewarded. A few seconds later a feeble light flared from the torch's tip, then steadied into a bright glow.

A callused hand closed about her wrist. Meriel glanced back, to find Gage at her shoulder.

"Let me carry the torch," he commanded stiffly, his features in the flickering light taut with pain.

She bit back a retort that she'd managed quite adequately to get through the tunnels without him before, then decided it wasn't worth the potential argument. Gage seemed near the end of his endurance. With a sigh, Meriel surrendered the torch. She couldn't quite resist a small dig, however. "Would you like to lead the way as well, since you seem to want to take charge?"

He glowered at her, then gave her a gentle shove forward. "Hardly. I'll have to trust you to get us back safely."

She shrugged and turned away, stepping forward into the darkness. "Yes, I suppose you'll have to, if you still think that's possible. Who knows? Perhaps I've laid a trap up ahead. Or an ambush of twenty armed guards. What will you do then?"

Gage moved up to her side. He grasped her tightly about the waist as much to keep her near him as to gain support for his rapidly weakening body. "What will I do? Why, hold you hostage, sweet femina. As I've done in the past and intend to do for a long time to come. What other choice do either of us have?"

"None, it would seem," Meriel gritted. "None at all."

They made the rest of the circuitous journey through the passages in stumbling silence, each immersed in their own thoughts. A sense of loneliness, of death and entombment, engulfed Meriel. Her mind drifted back to the scene of Pelum lying dead in his cell. He had been so dear, so gentle and kind, a weak, hesitant man in many ways, but still her friend and confidant. He had looked up to her, depended on her. In the end, she had failed him.

All her hopes, all her plans, were crumbling about her. Pelum was dead. Kieran was still within Gage's vindictive clutches, if Gage chose to be so. And her people . . .

The love she'd felt for Gage seemed a thing of the past. Her heart was broken, shattered beyond any hope of restoration, by Pelum's savage death. Everything that transpired between her and Gage henceforth would be tainted with the specter of her husband's death—and the lingering doubts as to how he died. She owed Pelum that much at least. That, and the resolve not to throw herself back into the arms of his murderer.

Gage had said Volans were responsible. If that was so, why had she seen no sign of their presence? True, the memory of that night in her room and the effect the intruder had had on her mind were difficult to explain away, but dreams did affect one strangely at times. And the earlier meeting with Gage and Lord Ardane, when they'd first revealed the Volan threat, had occurred only hours before. Perhaps the horror of that revelation—a revelation that included intimations that her mother had been Volan-enslaved as well—had set the stage for her susceptibility to Gage's suggestions that her intruder had been a Volan.

Weary frustration filled her. By all that was sacred, it was possible to dissect both Gage's and Pelum's explanations until the motives and manipulations of both men were suspect! And she stood in the middle, torn by confused emotions, not knowing whom to believe.

But not much longer, Meriel vowed as she led Gage further and further into the tunnels. She must make a decision, and soon. A decision that was informed and free of personal needs or feelings. A decision for the good of her people.

But not tonight. All she wanted to do tonight was go to sleep and forget, for a brief time, the horrible events of this day.

She slipped the key control from her gown as they drew near the door that led to her bedchamber, then shoved it into the special slit in the wall. Once more the stone portal ground open. Meriel stepped through, then awaited Gage as he extinguished the perpetual torch and replaced it in its holder. Once he was back within her room, Meriel keyed the door to close.

Turning, she faced him, determined to have the future settled. "What is my fate, Lord Commander? As always, I am at your mercy."

At the barely veiled antagonism in her voice, a thunderous expression darkened Gage's handsome features. "Don't start with me, Meriel! I'm exhausted, my wounds burn like the fires of Inferni, and I'm at the limits of my control! All I want is a bath, something to ease the pain, and a good night's rest. A night," he added, his glance pointedly swinging to her bed, "I intend to spend with you. Will you assist me or not?"

And what of my pain? she silently flung at him as she hurried to prepare his mineral bath and gather bandages and a healing salve from the medicine box in the bathing room. *Who will see to that, or assist me in steeling myself to touch you, to sleep in the same room with you?* she thought, glancing back at Gage as he limped after her into the bathing room.

"I'll assist you in any way you desire," Meriel answered instead. "But know this, Gage Bardwin. Though you still possess me in body, you no longer possess my heart. After what happened to Pelum, I-I can't lie with you and respond like . . . like before."

He went rigid, every muscle in his body drawing taut. "You play one game too many with me, femina, if you think to give of yourself, then take it back. I know now what lies beneath that cool exterior of yours. And I know, as well, how to rouse you, how to stroke that beautiful body of yours like some fine instrument, until you reach and exceed the heights of ecstasy."

Despite his wounds, he swiftly covered the distance between them. Grasping her jaw, Gage forced Meriel to look at him. "Do you seriously think, once I get you into bed, that you can long resist me? Answer me, Meriel, and, for once in your life, answer me honestly."

She wrenched her face away, refusing to meet his gaze. "Though my body might betray me, my heart never will. I can't forgive you for your part in Pelum's death"—her voice broke on a choking sob—"and I can't forgive myself, either. I, even more than you, am guilty of the most foul duplicity and cowardice. I sought to find some way between the two of you, selfishly seeking to have both a pure, spiritual love with Pelum and a . . . carnal experience with you."

"Carnal, was it?" Gage drawled mockingly. "Was that all it meant to you, Meriel?"

Tear-glazed violet eyes jerked up to his. "Perhaps I didn't mean it quite that way." She threw up her hands. "In the end, what does it matter? This was all my fault. I was a fool to think it could have been otherwise. But I *won't* be party to further death and destruction. You'd be wise to separate from me before it's too late."

"Despite your assessment of what we shared, it's already too late," Gage whispered, his voice raw with emotion. "I am bound to you, heart and soul. I can't give you up. And I am the biggest fool of all, for you speak true in saying it may well be my death!"

"No," she moaned. "I couldn't bear that, not after all I have already wrought. Please, Gage, let me go. Please!"

His hands rose to clasp her arms, then, with a ragged, rasping breath, he shoved her away. "This isn't the time to make any kind of decisions—neither for you or for me. We'll talk later, when we've both had a chance to rest and think things through less emotionally. In the meanwhile, would you help me undress?" He shot her a lopsided, apologetic grin. "My wounds hurt, and perhaps it's a gross abuse of your royal services, but I'd appreciate your assistance."

Meriel eyed Gage with frank suspicion. "If you think this some ploy to arouse me . . ."

"And how is that possible, femina?" he asked, a wry chuckle rumbling from the depths of his powerful chest. "If I can only touch your body and not your heart, what further influence do I have over you? I told you before I won't force myself on you. The only way I could possibly seduce you is with your consent."

Her lips clamped in a thin, tight line. She began to unfasten his tunic. "As you say, there is no possible way then. I beg pardon for my doubts."

"Your apology is accepted, Meriel."

She ignored him and slipped the torn tunic from Gage's shoulders. With his upper torso exposed, the full extent of his injuries was now bared to Meriel's view. The dagger slash across his chest and abdomen was deep, exposing but not cutting through his muscles. It was also, Meriel guessed, exquisitely painful.

The other wounds were less serious—a jagged slice across his right upper arm, a gash down the length of his left forearm, wrist, and hand. He also sported a cut over his left brow and a swollen abrasion on his cheekbone. Gage was, for all practical purposes, a mess.

Meriel motioned to the small bench beside the bathing tub. "Sit and I'll pull off your boots. Any efforts on your part to remove them will only cause your wounds to break open and bleed further."

Gage complied without protest, lowering himself to the bench in an awkward movement of tortured muscles and bruised body. He extended one booted foot. "Have at it, femina. I don't think my belly could've borne the stress of struggling with these at any rate."

She squatted before him and grasped his foot. A few tugs and the boot was free. The second, however, proved more difficult, sending Meriel sailing backward onto her bottom with the final, successful tug.

"Well done." Gage struggled to hide his grin. He rose and began to unfasten his breeches.

Meriel sat there on the cool stone floor, transfixed, as he peeled his breeches down to mid-thigh. Then, with a grimace he couldn't quite mask, Gage glanced down at her. Pain darkened his eyes, deepened the lines about his mouth.

"My nakedness shouldn't offend you by now. Would you help me?"

High color tinged her face, but Meriel complied. Then, his breeches in her hands, she rose. "Do you need help with your bath as well, or am I dismissed?"

He frowned. "You're not my serving maid, Meriel. If this is so distasteful, I can handle things from here out."

Remorse flooded her. With his painful torso wound, Gage would be hard-pressed to bathe himself. And she hadn't meant to imply that she'd loathe touching him. Far from it. What Meriel really feared was the effect the feel of his powerful muscles, his hair-whorled flesh, would have on her.

But that was her problem, not his. Gage was hurting, in need of her continued ministrations. And she'd not turn from anyone injured, be he enemy or friend.

"Come, let me help you into the bathing tub." Meriel averted her eyes from the sight of his lower body as she moved to take his arm. "I-I didn't mean to imply that I find your care distasteful. I only thought—considering the problems between us—that you'd prefer some privacy to bathe."

"Indeed? And what man would refuse the services of such a lovely assistant to scrub his back? Not to mention"—he paused, hissing in pain as he swung over and into the tub—"help just getting in and out of this tub."

Gage tensed as he eased into the churning bath, his eyes clenching shut as the warm waters made contact with his gaping flesh. His head arched back, the cords of his neck went taut and straining, and he paled. For a moment, Meriel thought he'd lose consciousness. Considerations of how she'd keep his greater bulk from sinking beneath the water raced frantically through her mind.

"Gage!" she cried, nearly falling into the tub herself in an attempt to tug him up and out of the water. "Gods, don't you dare faint on me now!"

"Faint?" he whispered hoarsely. "I've never 'fainted' in my life and don't intend to start now. Your lack of faith in my endurance cuts to the quick. Nonetheless"—his eyes opened and locked with hers—"I'd greatly appreciate it if you'd stop jerking on my arm. A dislocation, on top of everything else right now, might be the last straw."

"Oh. Yes." Meriel released him and stepped back. A damp tendril of hair tumbled down into her eyes. She blew at it and, when that effort proved fruitless, shoved it behind her ear.

Gage's eyes raked over her. He managed a lopsided grin.

Meriel was instantly on the defensive. "And what's so amusing, Bardwin?"

"You, femina. Your little foray in trying to rescue me from my bath did nothing for your appearance. Or, should I say," he added, his glance more languidly caressing her body, this time with obvious enjoyment and clear carnal intent, "it did *everything* for it?"

"What in the heavens are you—?" Meriel glanced down and gasped. The result of the splashing water as she'd tried to pull Gage up and out of the bathing tub, combined with the moisture rising from the churning bath, had plastered her thin gown snugly to her body. Her nipples thrust against the fabric, taut little buds whose deep rose color could now be easily discerned through the water-soaked cloth. And the rest of the garment clung so tightly that nothing else about her body was left to the imagination, either.

Heat flooded her, but whether from mortification or the searing fire that coursed through her veins at Gage's hot, hungry look, Meriel didn't know. Either way, she didn't dare let him realize he'd shaken her. The man had enough weapons at his disposal as it was.

A sudden thought assailed her. Weapons could be turned against the wielder if one knew how to do so. She smiled. Gage had taught her well of her power over him. She wasn't without some skills in the battle of male versus female.

"Have a care," Meriel murmured, "or you'll strain more than just your wounds. And I wouldn't want *anything* bursting forth in this bathing tub."

A slow flush crept up Gage's neck and face. "Then perhaps it would be wiser to change the subject, or you will find yourself in this tub, too."

She turned, as much to retrieve the container of cleansing sand as to hide her smile of triumph. She had no intention of joining Gage in the bathing tub, but the time had passed when she'd blush like a maiden and shy away when he made some lusty comment or shot her a passionate look.

The realization filled Meriel with a curious sense of freedom. There was nothing more he could do to her. She knew now that she was safe from him. Whatever had happened between Gage and Pelum, it was something primal and male, and had no effect on his earlier promise to aid her people. He would keep that vow. She knew he would never hurt Kieran, no matter what came between them. And now that he could no longer use his intimidating, masculine ways upon her, he hadn't even that power over her.

The power was all hers, Meriel realized. Gage still wanted her, desired her with a ferocity that was both heady and frightening. If she was very careful, she could manipulate him to her desires—

She caught herself in mid-thought. Gods, she was becoming more and more like her mother—and Gage's mother as well. Shame flooded Meriel. Though Pelum's death screamed for revenge, vengeance was a luxury she could ill afford. She still needed Gage to help evacuate her people.

Guilt, so common of late, wound about her heart. She must use Gage for the sake of her people. Even if that required the continued offering of her body.

It changed nothing, however, of her earlier resolve to pull back from him. But at least she was emotionally free of his unique man-games. And soon she'd be free, as well, of the tug on her heart every time she saw or thought of him.

Meriel turned, placed the container of cleansing sand on the edge of the tub, then scooped up a handful of the granulated sand soap and lathered it in her hands. "Lean over," she commanded. "Let me wash your back while the mineral bath cleanses your wounds."

Gage obligingly bent forward and Meriel spread the soap over the broad expanse of his upper back. Then, with strong, sure fingers, she began to massage and work his tautly strung muscles. The mist from the churning waters slowly saturated the air, fogging the ornate viewing mirror, heating the room until Meriel began to perspire.

He was silent for a time, then shifted his position in the tub slightly and lifted his head. "Ah, that feels heavenly," he sighed. "But it could just as well be my death, to turn my back on you like this."

Meriel's hands paused in their kneading motions. She grabbed a bath cloth and swiped away the moisture trickling into her eyes. "*Whatever* are you talking about?"

"There are tales aplenty of males murdered in bathing tubs by treacherous females. Are you sure you want to pass up such a perfect opportunity, femina? The thought of avenging your beloved Pelum must be quite a tempting consideration, wouldn't you say?"

"If this is another of your tests of my loyalty, it has failed, Gage Bardwin!" Meriel scooped up two handfuls of water and dumped them on his head. The liquid sluiced through his hair, down his face and neck, to flush some of the soap from his back.

"Besides," she stormed as she continued to heap more and more water over his head until she'd completely rinsed the soap away, "I wouldn't sully my bathing tub with your blood!"

"Then p-perhaps another nexus thorn while I sleep?" Gage sputtered under the deluge of water. "That would definitely be less messy."

"You took my thorn away."

He half-turned to glance up at her, unexpectedly endearing with his sodden hair hanging in his eyes, the water dripping from his face. "Another could easily be procured."

Meriel choked back the surge of tenderness his appearance stirred and instead graced him with a look of withering scorn. "What do you hope to accomplish with this turn of conversation? If you don't believe me, what would my assurances that I won't kill you matter? I could be lying either way."

"You're right, of course." Gage turned back. "I suppose I'll just have to keep a closer watch on you."

"Sleeping with me could be dangerous." To distract herself, Meriel began to lather his arms.

"Yes, I suppose it could."

"But you mean to continue anyway, just to punish me." She rinsed one arm, then the other.

"No," Gage replied, dragging out the word. "As much as I have come to enjoy the presence of your voluptuous body next to mine, my original motive stands. You are in as much danger from the Volans as I. You need my protection."

"And I don't believe there are or ever were any Volans!"

Gage shrugged, the sleek muscles of his back and shoulders bunching and coiling as he did. "That's more than obvious. Nonetheless, our sleeping arrangements remain as they were." He glanced back again. "I think my wounds are more than cleansed by this bath. Would you help me rise?"

"As you wish, Lord Commander."

Irritation plucked at him. "Don't start, Meriel.

I haven't the patience to deal with your feminine barbs just now."

An impulse to release Gage's arm and let him fall back in the tub struck Meriel, but she clamped down on the hostile inclination and instead steadied him when he finally rose to his feet. "Can you stand on your own for a few moments while I wash your legs?"

"For a few seconds, no more," he gasped, fighting the fresh surge of pain his efforts to climb to his feet had stimulated.

Meriel quickly lathered his legs, ignoring the arousal she experienced as her hands slid over his soap-slick flesh, felt the rasp of his coarse body hair beneath her fingers as she washed her way up his legs to his thighs, then groin. For the space of an inhaled breath, Meriel hesitated over the core of his manhood, then boldly soaped and washed it as well.

He stiffened beneath her hands, thickening even as she finished and began to rinse the lather away. She averted her eyes, forcing her movements into brusque efficiency. Gods, but it was hot in here! Finally, Meriel lifted her gaze to his.

"Your bath is done. Let me help you from the . . ." At the look of undisguised yearning, of naked hunger stamped across his striking features and shining in his dark, beautiful eyes, her voice faded.

Meriel's heart faltered, skipped a beat, then commenced a wild pounding. A hot ache rose in her throat. Ah, how she wanted to soothe that new, most primitive of pains gleaming in his eyes, to trace the outline of his sensuously molded lips with her own, to feel him deep—

She recalled her rampaging emotions with the greatest difficulty. He was no longer for her, had never been if the truth be told. There was only one purpose, one love left in her life—her people. Even Kieran must be sacrificed if need be.

But at that moment, gazing up at her son's father, standing wide-legged in the churning bath, his fists clenched at his sides as he struggled to master his own conflicted emotions, Meriel felt as if her heart were being torn from her body. He was so big, so magnificent. And that look of vulnerability and searing need in his eyes!

But he was not for her. It was over. Done. She must remind herself of that until the telling became reality. Her mother had been right when she'd told her long ago that as large as a Queen's heart was, the love of her people must fill it completely. There was no room for anyone else.

Meriel's hand shot out to grasp Gage's. She tugged, first gently, then harder to catch his attention. He blinked, then focused the full intensity of his gaze upon her.

"Come," she repeated. "Let me tend your wounds. We are both exhausted. It's as you said before. The morrow is soon enough to deal with the future—when we've had a chance to rest and think things through less emotionally."

He allowed her to assist him out of the tub, gently towel him dry, and apply the healing salve and bandages. Never once did he speak until she was done. Then Gage turned, took her by the arms, and stared deep into her eyes until Meriel wondered if he weren't perhaps casting his own, special kind of spell.

"It won't change anything." The deep, rich timbre of his voice caressed her, soothing Meriel's jangled nerves. "Further rest and all the thinking in the world won't change our destiny. You are mine, Meriel. You've already given me your body, your heart, your love. It's only a matter of time before you give me your vows as well—as my wife, my life mate. It can be no other way."

He turned and led her from the room. "We aren't always permitted to choose our destiny, sweet femina. No matter how we fight against it, it sometimes chooses us. And our destiny was sealed that day you took me to father Kieran."

"No," Meriel moaned. "I can't . . . I won't . . ."

"Hush, sweet femina," Gage whispered. He halted, pulled her to him, his lips brushing the silky smooth skin of her temple, her cheek. "It doesn't matter what either of us thinks should be. Not anymore. We are bound, one to the other, until victory—or defeat—plays its final hand."

Chapter Eleven

She lay there for long hours, stiffly supine on one side of the bed, while Gage, who'd fallen asleep almost as soon as his head struck the pillow, slumbered beside her. Through the warm, silent night Meriel listened to the sound of his breathing, torn with guilt and need. Her hands clenched the bed sheets, twisting them into damp knots as she fought against the tears.

Despite the turmoil that raged in her heart, Gage slept on, naked beneath the light sheet. A stray beam of moonlight thrust between the curtains, glinting off the smooth, rippling expanse of his back, slanting off the chiseled planes of temple, cheek, and jaw.

He looked so relaxed, so at peace with himself. And why not? Meriel thought bitterly. He finally had what he wanted. His victory was total now. As was her defeat.

With an inarticulate rumble of sleep-driven

words, Gage rolled over onto his back. At the action, new, most fascinating anatomy presented itself. From the wide shoulders bulging with muscle and sinew, to the swell of his pectoral muscles and undulating ridges of his bandaged abdomen, down to the first hint of his groin before sheet met flesh, Gage's body was the epitome of virile, masculine power. A power that was both intimidating and beautiful.

Though she doubted he'd have been of much assistance, much less awakened rapidly enough to protect her from any supposed Volan intruder tonight, Meriel knew that Gage was a man among men. Knew that his fierce possessiveness encompassed an equally fierce protectiveness, and that she and Kieran would always be safe with him. And knew, as well, that no one would ever take them from him, not while he drew breath.

The realization should have offered her comfort. At long last she had a man who was her equal and more, who possessed not only the intelligence and experience to aid her in the governance of her people, but also the courage and strength of character to make difficult decisions and stand behind them. And then there was the effect he had upon her heart and body . . .

But it didn't matter. As painful as it was to accept, she couldn't allow him to take Pelum's place. Gage might be used to winning, but this was one battle he'd lose. She couldn't *allow* him to win. To do so would dishonor the memory of her husband, a husband she had betrayed enough as it was.

"Please understand, my love," she silently

mouthed the plea of forgiveness to her dead husband. "For the sake of our people, I could do no less."

A presence, a sense of a gentle, loving spirit, wafted over Meriel. Pelum, she thought. She smiled into the darkness, hesitant but hopeful, awaiting the answer to her prayers.

And in that time weighted by moonlight and shadows, a soothing sensation of compassion caressed her being, her soul. She smiled, at peace for the first time. Pelum *did* understand, *did* forgive her. Meriel sighed, shifted in bed, and finally fell asleep.

Blood.

There was so much blood.

Buckets of blood. Rivers of blood. And all spurting in an endless flow of red from the gaping wound in Pelum's neck.

Frantically Meriel tried to stanch the spewing hole, pressing her fingers, then the entire strength of her hand and arm to the task. Pelum's lifeblood continued to ooze forth, dripping between her fingers into a growing pool.

She glanced around, searching for help. There was none. Pelum's face went white. His eyes rolled in his head. The sound of death rattled in his throat.

"Pelum," Meriel moaned. "Ah, Gods, no. Don't die. Please don't die!"

"Help me!" she cried, her voice rising on a thread of hysteria. "Someone, help me! Help!"

"Meriel!" A deep voice penetrated the mists of her terror. "Meriel, wake up!"

She jerked awake, panting, gasping for breath, her sleeping gown soaked to her skin. Above her, in the dim light of dawn, loomed the form of a man.

"P-Pelum?" she whispered, her hand lifting to tentatively touch his face. "Thank the Holy Ones you're alive. I dreamt—"

"He's dead." Gage captured her hand in his. "All the dreaming in the universe won't return him to you, no matter how dearly you'd have preferred my death to his."

"Gage?" Meriel blinked, forcing her vision to clear. Reality flooded back with the sight of the blond man leaning over her. It was indeed he. Alive . . . and Pelum dead.

"Ah, Gods," she choked. "I-I'm sorry, Gage. I didn't mean . . . There was just so much blood, and I didn't know what to do. Please, don't be angry with me!"

With a low oath, he pulled her into the haven of his arms, clasping her tightly to the full length of him. Heat from his tautly strung body seared through her, sent her pulse to thrumming through her veins. Forbidden pleasure that it now was, Meriel clung even tighter, burying her face in the furred expanse of Gage's chest.

His body hardened. His shaft swelled to press against her belly. Meriel tensed, suddenly more frightened with this newest turn of events than the dream had ever evoked.

"No," she moaned, pushing against him. "No! I won't! I can't!"

He refused to let her go. "Don't be afraid, sweet femina. I can't help my body's response when

I'm near you. But I swear, all I want to do is hold you."

"*No!*" Panic engulfed her. Meriel fought back, her hand wildly, repeatedly striking his bandaged torso.

"Gods!" Gage sucked in an agonized breath. He fell back, releasing her. His hands clenched at his sides as he struggled with the pain of his freshly abused wounds. "Gods, Meriel!"

She scooted to the far side of the bed and watched him like some terror-stricken cerva facing a predator. Finally Gage regained control and weakly levered to an elbow. He stared at Meriel, taking in the tousled mane and pale face, the wild, haunted look in her eyes. Gage sighed and shook his head.

"It's all right, Meriel. I didn't mean to frighten you after such a bad dream." He held out his arms. "Come, I promise not to hold you against your will again."

"No." Meriel shook her head. "Please, just let it be." She motioned with her hand. "Just . . . just go back to sleep. I'm all right now. I'll be fine."

Gage glanced toward the windows where the sun's light was already peeking through to brighten the room. "It's almost time to rise. There's little point in further sleep."

Her lips tightened in a mutinous line. "Well, I don't want you touching me!"

He swung off the bed, then turned to face her, proud and magnificent in his nakedness. Frustrated anger gleamed in his eyes. "When will you cease this foolish charade? I tire of your games!"

"I play no games!"

"Don't you?"

She rolled over and curled into a tight ball, her back to him. "Leave me alone! I don't know anything right now except I'm so very tired. Please, just let me sleep a while longer. Then . . . then we can talk."

"As you wish, femina." Gage backed away from the bed. "Take all the sleep you need. But when you waken, be assured that we will indeed talk."

The solid thud of his footsteps, carrying him across her bedchamber to the bathing room, echoed in Meriel's head long after she could no longer hear them. She clenched the bed sheets up to her chin, burying her head in her pillow to drown out the pounding of her heart. But, over and over, Gage's words reverberated in her head, taunting her, haunting her.

"When will you cease . . . this foolish charade? . . . this foolish . . . charade . . ."

Later that day, far from rested, Meriel ambled morosely out to a lounging chair on her balcony. Kieran, followed closely by Dian, toddled after her, a ball clutched in his chubby hands.

"Play ball, Mama," he demanded. "Play ball!"

With little energy to fuel her efforts, Meriel tossed the ball back and forth with her son. After a time, she glanced imploringly at her friend.

"Dian, could you please take Kieran down to the garden for a while? I haven't the strength to play with him just now."

The little maidservant rose and hurried over to scoop up the energetic child. "Of course. Is there anything I could order sent up from the kitchen in the meantime? You haven't eaten a thing and it's already well past midday. A bit of sweet cake, or perhaps a bowl of domare stew?"

"No." Meriel firmly shook her head. "I have no appetite." She managed a wan little smile. "Perhaps later."

As Dian turned to go, a sudden thought struck Meriel. "Torman. How goes it with you and Torman?"

Dian clutched the wiggling Kieran to her and blushed. "I've hardly had the opportunity to speak with him the past several days. And whenever I see him, he finds some way to evade me." She sighed. "I think it's over, Meriel."

"Perhaps." Her friend rose from her chair. "But perhaps not. I'll send him down to the garden with you and Kieran."

"Meriel, please, no!" Dian protested. "He'd guess your ruse. Besides, he's sworn not to leave your side during the day."

"Then I'll accompany you both and sit nearby. Perhaps under the cerasa tree." Meriel nodded, warming to her plan. If she couldn't find any happiness with the men in her life, at least Dian deserved a chance. She took her friend by the arm. "Come, and not another word. You know you want another chance to speak with Torman."

They commandeered the big captain of the guard, then headed down to the garden. The garden was warm, but an overcast sky muted some of the extreme heat of Firestar's burgeoning orb. Meriel soon found a shady sanctuary and closed her eyes. Even the effort necessary to herd Dian, Kieran, and Torman down to the garden required more energy than she possessed. Exhaustion, fanned by the warm, soothing breeze blowing through the garden, finally overtook her. She dozed off.

From their perch on a stone wall that separated the rest of the garden from a small pond stocked with water fowl where Kieran happily splashed, Torman watched Meriel finally fall asleep. Then he turned to Dian. A small frown of concern puckered her brow.

"What's wrong, femina?" Torman inquired, uncomfortable in the maid's presence and alighting on the first question that popped into his head. By the collective consciousness, how much longer would it be necessary to masquerade as someone he wasn't?

He'd been too long without directives from the Mother Ship. He desperately needed new information, new orders! It was as if he existed in a vacuum, a vacuum that begged to be filled. And there were too many sensations, too many feelings and needs that increasingly bombarded him. He was weakening. Something must be done, and soon.

Well, Torman thought, attempting to distract himself from the disquieting admission, perhaps something of use could at least be gleaned from Meriel's friend. Since Pelum's death, everything had been in a state of turmoil. All his carefully laid plans had gone awry and he needed new data to base further plans upon. Data that would ultimately result in overcoming Bardwin—once and for all.

"Well, Dian?" Torman persisted when she didn't

reply, distracted with Kieran's activities. "What is bothering you?"

She turned. At his unexpected question, surprise widened her eyes. "What do you mean?"

He waved in the vague direction of Meriel, sound asleep beneath the cerasa tree. "You appear worried about our Queen."

"She is heartbroken over Pelum's death. She feels that she is responsible."

"But that is insane. What could she do against Bardwin?"

"Nothing, when the plight of all our people hangs in the balance." The maidservant swatted at a small apis bug as it buzzed too close to her head. With an angry whir of its translucent wings, the fat black-and-yellow insect flew off in the direction of the arosa hedges.

Dian turned her attention back to her companion. "She has vowed to mate with the Lord Commander whenever he asks."

"I know."

"And did you also know," she asked, determined to ruffle Torman's calm stoicism, "that he loves her? That he wants Meriel as his life mate?"

He shook his head. "No, I didn't know that. What will the Queen do?"

"I'm not certain. Meriel's so confused, so overwrought right now."

"Does she love him?"

Dian turned the full force of her soft, luminous brown eyes on Torman. "She won't say, but I wonder . . ."

"What can we do to help?"

She shrugged in helpless frustration. "I don't

know. Just be there for her and—"

Kieran ran up, his ball in his hands. "Play. Throw ball!"

The boy shoved his colorfully swirled ball into Torman's hands. The man shot Dian a look of entreaty.

"Toss it back in the pond. Kieran is just looking for an excuse to play in the water."

With a shout of glee, the child scrambled after the ball that Torman quickly threw over the wall. The big man managed a lopsided grin. "The little ones. I feel so awkward with them."

Dian laid a comforting hand on his. "Few men seem too skilled in the entertainment of the young. Surprisingly, though, the Lord Commander appears to possess such a talent. Or at least," she added as an afterthought, "when it comes to his son. He really appears taken with the lad."

A spark of interest flared, then flamed to life. "Indeed?" Torman inquired carefully. "Is there some affection between them?"

"Most definitely. The Lord Commander is as possessive of his son as he is of his son's mother. I doubt he'd willingly give Kieran up. Meriel may have a fight on her hands if the day ever dawns when she wishes to separate from the Lord Commander and take Kieran with her."

"He loves the lad, then?"

Dian shot him a quizzical glance. "Didn't I all but say that? Truly, Torman, you've changed so very much in the past several months. For all your excuses that the palace takeover and Bellatorian occupation have preoccupied you, now that I think back, you became so distant, so different long before. What's wrong?"

Torman rose to his feet, unwilling to allow Dian to delve any deeper into his psyche. "Nothing's wrong. I just have many things on my mind." He strode off.

"Where are you going?" Dian called after him.

"To play with Kieran!"

"Tomorrow, Meriel," Gage exclaimed triumphantly from his seat across from her. "We begin the evacuation tomorrow!"

"At long last," she murmured, glancing up from the papers spread out on the table. "I thank you for your assistance. I could have never done it without you."

A lazy grin flashed across his features. "Don't shortchange yourself, femina. You'd have worked out a viable plan soon enough."

Meriel tamped down the surge of pleasure his compliment stirred. It had been surprising how well they worked together for a common cause. Though the problems of the bedchamber had yet to be resolved, the past six days spent developing the evacuation plan had been both fruitful and reasonably pleasant.

She smiled. "No one, not even a Queen, is an entity unto herself. The greatest act of intelligence, to my thinking, is having the wisdom to appreciate good advice."

"Quite true," Gage agreed. "But the basic attributes must be there to begin with. For all your mother's lack of interest in preparing you for your future role, you're a quick study."

"She meant to protect me for as long as possible," Meriel murmured pensively. "Her intentions were well-meant though ill-conceived, but considering the horrible fate she thought awaited me as Queen . . ."

"Fate doesn't always have to be passively accepted," Gage offered, his words soft and deliberate. "A lot can be accomplished if one chooses to fight and is willing to see past the superficial to what lies beyond."

She knew he spoke of more than her responsibilities as Queen. There was so much that lay beneath his rich-toned voice—a plea for understanding, for forgiveness—but Meriel didn't dare confront the hidden meanings. The wounds were too fresh, too raw, and she still didn't know what to think—or believe.

"Well"—her brow wrinkled in feigned concentration as she scanned the computer printout that lay before her—"there is still a fight ahead to prepare Carcer to accept Tenua's billions of inhabitants. Do you think we can reclaim enough land to feed all my people in just two cycles?"

"With the aid of Bellator's advanced agricultural technology, yes, I think it's possible. And in the meanwhile, Agrica has had an especially productive output these past several cycles. Its storage granaries are full to overflowing, in addition to all the produce it has exported throughout the Imperium."

"Bless fertile Agrica," Meriel murmured, warm gratitude filling her for the big planet that was the chief source of produce for the Imperium. "Their success couldn't have come at a more opportune time."

"Better management, not to mention the removal of Bellator's oppressive hand, was what was responsible for the record crops. The Cat Man, Karic, is the best Lord Commander Agrica has ever had."

Meriel quirked a questioning brow. "You sound as if you know him. Is he a friend?"

"Not at first," Gage chuckled. "Indeed, far from it. He thought I was trying to steal his woman.

"And were you?"

He shrugged. "If she'd been willing, yes, most definitely. Liane is one of the loveliest women in the universe. But she was madly in love with her Cat Man."

A totally unexpected, irrational twinge of jealousy shot through Meriel. Angrily she brushed it away. This mysterious Liane could have Gage if she wanted him, which, of course, she didn't, as she was obviously in love with another. Yet, if the truth be told, even the thought of Gage desiring another woman unsettled her.

Meriel refused to examine that surprising revelation any closer. She had enough to deal with in the successful evacuation of her people to Carcer. That mattered far more than her confused emotions over Gage Bardwin.

She resumed her intent study of the computer printout. "The first 100,000 people transported will be farmers, agricultural experts, builders, and craftsmen. Are you certain," she asked, glancing up, "that Bellator will have all the criminals on Carcer apprehended by the time my workers arrive? Perhaps it would be wise to include a few soldiers, just in case."

"Teran has assured me that almost every criminal has been captured. The govern collars they wear also contain a homing device. It makes the criminals relatively easy to apprehend, if necessary."

He cocked his head, a speculative look in his eyes. "But perhaps it might be wise to send a small contingent of soldiers, nonetheless. I don't need an unexpected Volan takeover of unarmed laborers."

A bleak, haunted expression flickered in Meriel's eyes. "Back to that again, are you?" she muttered. "If you're still trying to change my mind—"

"A lost cause, to be sure," Gage drawled. "At least for the time being. Sooner or later, Meriel, you'll see the truth for what it is. In the meanwhile, I've better things to do with my time and energy."

At the patronizing tone in Gage's words, Meriel's temper flared. A hot flush stained her cheeks. "Don't talk down to me as if I'm some ignorant child who doesn't understand, Gage Bardwin!" she stormed. "I haven't seen one shred of proof of the Volans' presence on Tenua. All I've ever had is your word for everything that has occurred, linking the Volans with what has happened. And, considering that many of your motives are suspect, especially when they come to me, I tend to be very skeptical.

"I also," Meriel continued, deciding she might as well get it all off her chest, "am sick and tired of you constantly ordering me around. I am doing the best I can, but I'm not some . . . some cursed soldier of yours!"

"Fine." Gage shrugged his broad shoulders in a motion of dismissal. "Be skeptical. All I ask is that you keep the *possibility* in the back of your mind. A smart ruler is open to all contingencies until proven otherwise."

He rose from the table and walked around to stand beside her. To meet his gaze, Meriel was forced to tilt her head back at an uncomfortable angle. In compensation, she glared up at him.

A slight curl of his lips was Gage's only concession to a smile. "A smart ruler also listens carefully to a warning of danger. And you and your people are in the gravest of danger—the danger of losing your lives and bodies to alien mindslavers. So if you don't want me constantly ordering you around, use a bit more of that sharp little mind of yours and keep your eyes and ears open. If not, I'll continue to do it for you."

"Fine. That sounds fair to me!"

"Fine."

Their gazes locked in a fierce battle, neither combatant giving ground. Gradually, however, Gage's attention began to wander to more intriguing things—like the full, rosy swell of Meriel's lips, the beguiling flush to her cheeks, the challenging gleam in her eyes. Gods, he thought, she was so beautiful, so alluring, and as close to being his as a woman could and still not be.

Nonetheless, he meant to have her. Her, and their son. In the past, he had seen them as simply another form of possession—Meriel as an object to sate his physical needs, Kieran as proof of his virility. He'd not dared to think any further than that, not with the taint of his bastard birth hanging over him. Instead, he'd forced himself to view Meriel as he did all women. A pretty object to use, to take and give mutual pleasure, but with no expectations of anything more.

That cold-blooded outlook, however, had slowly disintegrated as he came to know both mother and child. Now, they represented something stable and solid and good, filling, deepening his life. A life that heretofore, Gage realized with piercing insight, had been empty of much purpose save survival and the acquisition of material things.

Staring down into the defiant depths of Meriel's eyes, Gage also realized the difficulty of the road ahead. She had a surprisingly stubborn streak that was the match of his. Meriel was growing, maturing before his very eyes, and some of the same attributes that would make her a fine ruler were also those that would make his wooing of her all the more difficult.

As far as he was concerned, some things were best left unawakened.

He shoved his hand through his hair, setting the dark blond waves awry. "It grows late, femina. The plans are made and the advance party notified. Tomorrow is time enough—"

A frantic pounding came from the door. Gage wheeled around. "Curse it, I gave orders not to be disturbed."

Cries, snatches of a woman's voice, rose above the rumbling replies of the guards outside the door. Meriel cocked her head. The voice was familiar—

She shoved back her chair and leaped to her feet, nearly slamming into Gage. "Dian! It's Dian!"

He frowned in annoyance. "She oversteps herself in intruding." Nonetheless, Gage turned and strode to the door.

It slid soundlessly open when he slapped the imprint panel. Dian stood there, struggling wildly in the grasp of two guards. At the thunderous look Gage sent her, she momentarily stilled, her mouth agape. Then the reason for her unprecedented temerity returned.

"Kieran!" she cried, straining toward Gage. "Kieran's gone!"

For an instant Gage stared down at her, stunned. Then he found his voice. "What, by the five moons, are you talking about?"

He motioned for the guards to release the maidservant and grabbed her arm, pulling her into the room. The door closed behind them.

Meriel rushed up, her face white. "What has happened to Kieran? I heard you say his name. Is Kieran all right?"

Dian's glance swung from one parent to the other. "I-I don't know, Meriel. I went to check on him an hour after I put him to bed, and he wasn't in his room. At first I wasn't too concerned as he's done that before. Usually I find him playing in the moonlight on the balcony, or floating one of his boats in the mineral bath. But he was nowhere to be found. This time, I don't know where he is."

Gage released her arm with a chuckle. "The lad's wandered off. I'll set the palace to searching for him. He'll be found soon enough."

"I don't think so, my lord," Dian slowly replied. "I doubt he's anywhere near the palace by now."

"What do you mean?" Meriel grabbed her friend

by the arms. "What are you saying, Dian?"

Gage's mouth drew into a ruthless, forbidding line. "Yes, what *are* you trying to say?"

Dian paled, swallowing convulsively. Her mouth worked in soundless spasms.

Finally Meriel could take the suspense no longer. She gave her friend a hard shake. "Dian, tell me! Now!"

The maidservant's eyes filled with tears. She lifted a hand that clenched a folded piece of paper. Meriel pried the note from her friend's fingers.

With trembling hands, she unfolded the paper and walked to the table where the light of the perpetual lamps was brighter. Like an automaton, she spread the letter out on the table, smoothing the folds over and over in a strange, repetitive manner.

"What does it say, Meriel?" Gage demanded, frozen with dread to his spot near the door. "Read it, curse you!"

She inhaled a shuddering breath. " 'We . . . we have y-your son,' " she intoned in a halting, unsteady voice. " 'T-tell no one or the lad is dead. All we want is Bardwin. Come alone.' "

Meriel glanced up, her eyes burning pools of agony.

"Is there anything else?" Gage rasped. "Any hint of where I'm to go?"

"A-a map," she replied shakily. "That's all. A map that shows the way to the Isle of Insula, deep in the Cerulean Sea."

With a growl of rage, Gage strode across the room and snatched the letter from beneath

Meriel's hand. He scanned the paper for a brief moment. Then he looked up, his gaze capturing and holding Meriel's with a mesmerizing look that was both tormented and enraged.

"Volans, Meriel," he muttered, his voice dangerously soft. "The Volans have our son. I warned you of their threat. And now, whether alive or dead, they mean to have me as well."

Chapter Twelve

"Th-the Volans have our son?" Meriel repeated the words. She paused to consider that, then firmly shook her head. "I don't believe it."

Gage's face went rigid with glacial anger. "It's past time you cease your stubborn refusal to believe me," he growled, his voice turning low, deliberate, with an undertone that brooked no argument. "It will only make my rescue of Kieran all the more difficult if I leave his mother behind to sabotage everything I've tried to do."

"Left behind?" Meriel stared up at him blankly as the meaning of his words filtered through her stunned mind. "I'm not staying here while my son's in danger! I'm going with you!"

"You? A soft, pampered little Queen, with no ability to endure the journey, much less successfully complete the mission?" Gage laughed disparagingly. "Forget it, femina. I go alone, as the letter requested."

"And I don't care what the letter said!" Meriel snapped, stung by his belittling comments. "It makes no sense for you to go alone. If it comes down to you exchanging yourself for Kieran, who will bring him back?"

His eyes narrowed and a muscle twitched in his jaw. "That would solve all your problems, wouldn't it? Is that what you want then, Meriel? That I surrender to them in exchange for our son?" He grabbed her and jerked her up against him. "Do you want me dead that badly?"

As she stared up into the hard, brittle depths of Gage's eyes, Meriel's mind raced. It wasn't Volans, she thought. The men who held Kieran had to be part of the rebel army Torman had told her about. They were well-intentioned in trying to lure Gage to them, thinking all would be righted once they had the new Lord Commander in their grasp. But they were wrong. And only she, as their Queen, could convince them of that.

"No, I don't want you dead," Meriel ground out. She squirmed in his tight clasp, attempting to free herself. It didn't work. Meriel gave up the futile effort. "I need your help too badly to wish you dead, no matter how that would solve my problems or ease my guilt. Besides, I just plain don't want you dead."

She steadily met his gaze. "Yet, as convinced as you are that Volans have Kieran, I'm equally as certain his captors are some of my rebel army, in hiding since the palace was captured. You need me to convince them to surrender, and to explain that you are now helping us."

"How do you know there are troops hiding out

there? My spies haven't heard or seen any hint of a rebel army."

"My sources are my own." Meriel's chin tilted in a stubborn manner that Gage was beginning to find very irritating. "Just believe me when I assure you the information came from a very reliable source."

"Curse you, femina!" Gage gave her a shake. "You've proven time and again to be singularly naïve when it comes to your 'reliable' sources. You believed your husband when he told you he was being mistreated down in his cell. Yet was his cell ill-furnished, or did he lack for blankets or clean clothes? As bloody as Pelum was after I killed him, his clothing was the best, his hair freshly washed. And he was quite well-nourished and strong when I last had the misfortune to do battle with him."

He gave her another shake for good measure. "I want, no, I *demand*, to know your sources this time!"

Meriel's mind raced, harking back to the cell where she'd found Pelum dead and Gage fighting for his life. Once more, the room she'd found him lying in had been clean and well-furnished. And Pelum's clothes were definitely not the same filthy rags he'd worn before. It didn't make sense.

Awash in confusion, she lifted her gaze. "Give me your word you won't punish him," Meriel whispered, "and I'll tell you my informant's name."

"By all that is sacred!" Gage roared. "I'll do no such thing! If the information was come by innocently, there'll be no punishment. But if there was malice or manipulation intended . . ."

"I trust this man! He would never—"

"Tell me his name! Kieran's life may depend on it!"

Kieran, Meriel thought. *Gods, my son.* Her head slumped like a flower wilting on its stem.

"Torman. Torman told me."

Behind them, Dian gasped. "Torman! Ah, Gods, not Torman!"

Gage wheeled around, dragging Meriel with him. "And what is he to you?"

He studied the blushing servant, his acute intuition telling him what the brown-haired woman would not. "Your lover, perhaps?"

"No! We are not . . . have never been . . ." Dian shot Meriel a beseeching look. "Tell him, Meriel. But just don't let him hurt Torman!"

"Yes, please do tell me, femina," Gage demanded in a dangerously soft voice.

High color swept Meriel's cheekbones. "There's not much to tell, aside from what I've already revealed. Dian loves Torman, that's all. That's why she's so concerned."

"And why you're trying so hard to protect him? Because of Dian?"

"He's a good man, loyal, hard-working, and a brave and devoted soldier!" Meriel cried. "I care for his welfare as I would any of my people."

"Do you now?" Gage pulled her over to the door and struck the imprint panel. As the door slid open, the two guards jerked to attention.

"The Tenuan named Torman," Gage ordered one of his soldiers. "Send a party of our men to apprehend him and bring him to me. Now!"

The man saluted, then raced off down the hall.

Gage turned back to Meriel. "We'll get to the bottom of this soon enough."

Fifteen minutes later, Torman, his arms in shackles, was led into the room. Gage eyed him closely, noting that no signs of a struggle marred the big man's body. Good, he thought, the man had come without a fight. That was one thing in his favor. He dismissed the guards and motioned for Torman to sit.

The captain of the guard squared his shoulders and shook his head. "I'd prefer to stand."

Gage shrugged. "As you wish." He took Meriel by the arm and led her over to the table, indicating she should take a seat. She stiffly complied, then watched as Gage lowered himself to sit beside her.

He leaned back in his chair, steepling his fingers beneath his chin. Slowly, thoroughly, he examined the man standing across the room. "Meriel says there are rebels, an army big enough to be a threat," Gage began without preliminary. "Is that true?"

Torman's blue eyes swung to Meriel's. She managed a wan little smile and nodded. Torman swung his gaze back to Gage's.

"That is true."

"And what is your involvement with these men?"

"I've taken a vow of fealty to you, Lord Commander," Torman staunchly replied. "I have nothing to do with them."

"Spoken like a man of honor," Gage drawled with biting sarcasm. "If only I dared believe you."

"He is totally loyal to me!" Meriel cried, half

rising from her chair. "I swear it!"

"How convenient." Gage motioned for her to regain her seat. "You are totally loyal to me, and he to you. If I believe one, then it goes without saying that I can believe the other."

His glance moved to Dian, who was seated at the far end of the table. "And what about you, femina? How do you feel about me?"

"I think you're a foul, ill-tempered beast!" the little maidservant snapped. "You've never ceased to treat Meriel abominably. But I, too, gave my oath and will stand by it—as long as it doesn't hurt Meriel."

Gage's mouth twisted wryly. "Well, at least someone here is inclined to honesty. I think I begin to like you, femina."

"A singular honor, to be sure!"

"To be sure." At Meriel's gasp of horror, he shot her an inquiring glance. "She's as fiery-tongued as you. Did you teach her or did she teach you?"

Meriel bit back an angry retort. "Our manners, or lack of them, is not the issue here. Kieran is what matters. Will you permit me to accompany you or not?"

Gage swung to Torman. There had to be some way to penetrate that stolid mask of his, get to the real man who lay beneath. "What do you think, Captain of the Guard? Is it wise to allow your Queen to accompany me on a quest to rescue her son? And who, for that matter, do you think has the lad?"

Surprise flashed in Torman's eyes. "Someone has taken Kieran? That's impossible! I'm responsible for the security of this palace. How could an outsider get in, much less kidnap the Queen's son?" He paused, anger darkening his face. "When did this happen?"

"Tonight. And they left a note demanding I surrender myself in exchange for the lad." Gage arched a questioning brow. "I ask again. Who do you think has Kieran?"

Torman eyed the other man, his sharp mind weighing, calculating, sifting through the evidence and all possible options. Did Bardwin suspect his complicity in Kieran's kidnapping? Did he even suspect the Volan-enslavement of his captain of the guard?

There was no way to know, Torman realized, scrutinizing him. Bardwin's face was hard, implacable as stone, and just as difficult to penetrate. He was a crafty, dangerous opponent—and as close a match for him as he'd yet to encounter. He'd have to tread carefully here.

Bardwin now knew about the rebel army. Meriel must have insisted that the soldiers had taken her son. The ruse was the perfect opportunity to lead Bardwin into a trap—and make his eventual capture all the easier. If he could be lulled into expecting the usual humanoid means of vigilance, means for which Bardwin's superior tracking abilities were more than a match, his guard would be down. It would be a simple enough matter to capture him with Volan techniques.

The issue of Meriel was another matter. Bardwin would be a fool to endanger her by permitting her to accompany him, but that, too, would play right into his hands—and plans.

He didn't need directives from the Mother Ship to tell him it was past time to enslave her as well. By the collective consciousness, though, he'd hate to do that to the little Queen. She was so good, so kind, so fiery and brave. Everything one could ask for in a mate . . .

With an angry grunt, Torman flung that surprisingly stimulating consideration aside. Emotions had no place in his plans—and neither did a mating urge. That had been genetically programmed out of the Volan race thousands of cycles ago as too burdensome and divisive for a hive concept.

Or had it?

He focused his attention back on Bardwin. "I think it's as the Queen has said. The rebels have taken the child. Who else would know the palace, have friends within to help them? And"—Torman glanced briefly at Meriel—"I also think her plan to accompany you is wise. The rebels will listen to her."

"Your words have merit," Gage agreed half to himself. "But the evacuation begins tomorrow. Who will carry it on in our absence?"

"I could assist," Torman ventured. "I need but the master plan and a brief time of explanation."

"No," Gage said after a few seconds of consideration. "Meriel will need a bodyguard on the journey. Someone to protect her as well as get her back safely if something happens to me. You'll accompany us, Torman."

The big man bowed. "As you wish, Lord Commander."

* * *

"Teran, I need you back here," Gage stated without the usual conversational preliminaries. "Immediately."

From the vidcom screen, a dark brow arched over steel gray eyes. "Your timing leaves a little to be desired. What's wrong?"

"I'm not at liberty to say, save that it's a matter of life and death. I need you, Teran, desperately. The evacuation begins tomorrow and I've another mission that calls me. Can you come?"

Teran sighed. "No, not just yet. We're embroiled in a High Council meeting of Imperium magnitude. It's past time we shared our knowledge of the Volan threat with the other planets. If you weren't so busy on Tenua, I would've summoned you as well to add your special insights. As it is, we've all the Lord Commanders of every Imperial planet here."

Gage grinned wryly. "Please convey my regrets to them."

Teran chuckled. "To be sure." He paused. "How goes it with the Tenuan Queen?"

A grimace twisted Gage's face. "Poorly. Very poorly. But my mind is made up. Meriel will wed me. I don't intend to give up my son."

"Wed, is it now?" Teran frowned. "And what about her husband?"

"Pelum is dead."

The dark-haired man arched a brow. "Of natural causes, I presume?"

"He was Volan-enslaved. I assisted him into a fatal meeting with his own dagger."

"And how does the Queen feel about that?"

Gage sighed. "How do you think?"

Teran rolled his eyes and shook his head. "And how goes the Volan issue? Hopefully better than your interactions with Queen Meriel."

"Not much better, I'm sorry to say." Gage ran a hand through his hair in a ragged, frustrated motion. "Has any progress been made on identifying their presence, or eliminating them from their enslaved bodies?"

Teran shook his head. "We're no closer to discovering how to identify them than we were before. Research on the other matter is progressing, though. In another month or two, I think half our problem will be solved."

"Good."

"Now, about your original request . . ."

"What about Brace?" Gage offered. "Next to you or Karic, there's no other man for the job."

"I was thinking the same thing," Teran agreed, nodding. "Marissa won't be too happy being left behind, but now, with two sets of twin girls . . ."

"Brace should be eager for this assignment then."

"No, on the contrary. You've never seen a more doting father." Teran's expression turned serious. "Gage, is there anything else I can do to help? I don't like the feel of this secret mission of yours. It smacks of danger."

"And when have I ever had a safe mission?" Gage drawled, clamping down on the urge to reveal the true implications—and risks—of the undertaking. "My thanks for your concern, though. If I could enlist your aid, you know I would. But it's enough that you lend me Brace. That's a big burden off my shoulders."

Gage's hand moved to the disengage button on the vidcom panel. "I'll send word when I return."

Teran smiled. "Be sure that you do. I may have a new mission for you by then."

"No doubt," Gage muttered as he terminated the communication. Teran's image flickered, then disintegrated. "No doubt," he repeated, a heavy wave of foreboding washing over him as he rose and left the room.

They departed Eremita the next night under heavy cover of darkness, after Gage and Meriel had spent a good part of the day walking Brace through the intricacies of the evacuation plan. Later, in a private meeting, Gage filled the younger man in on the Volan threat and what had transpired so far. For his part, Gage left that night with great misgivings but, in the end, Brace was as well informed as any of them. Which was hardly at all.

As they sped along in the skim crafts, he and Meriel in one, Torman in the other, Gage glanced over at the woman beside him. Her thick, ebony hair was tied back in a high, braided ponytail and she was dressed in tan-colored, lightweight breeches, tunic, and soft, ankle-high boots. A dagger was strapped to one thigh, a stunner attached to a waist belt, and a blaster lay propped at her feet.

There'd been little opportunity to instruct Meriel in the functional intricacies of the weapons, but he'd make the time in the next two days of travel. One way or another, she would have to overcome any remaining squeamishness she might have at the thought of doing battle and killing. There was no other way if they were to have any hope of rescuing Kieran.

Somehow, Gage knew that Meriel was up to the task. She had proven her mettle over and over, even to the point of killing that guard to save him. She'd risk even more for her child.

Contentment, and a sense of proud possession, washed over Gage. Meriel was everything he could ever hope to find in a woman and a mate. Gently reared, kind and good-hearted, she also possessed an inner strength and determination that was up to anything life could toss her way. In that sense, at least, she was more than able to endure what lay ahead.

He hoped the mission wouldn't require too much physical stamina or athletic ability, however. Therein lay his greatest misgivings. Even Meriel's stubborn spirit could motivate an untrained body only so far.

Time and again, Gage regretted allowing her to come along. But there *was* the remote chance that some rebels held Kieran. And if that was so, he might well need her presence as Queen to rescue their son. On the other hand, if Volans were involved in the kidnapping—which Gage still strongly suspected—there was no safe way at all. In that case, however, he'd leave Meriel with Torman to protect her and go in after Kieran alone.

That part of the plan he intended to keep from Meriel until the very last second. There was no need to cause unnecessary or premature dissension between them. There were enough other issues to deal with in the meanwhile.

Gage hated the need to go in secretly, with only Torman's help to protect Meriel. It was a dangerous, foolhardy plan. But the message had said come alone and he risked enough in even bringing Meriel and her bodyguard along, much less leading a larger force. There was just something strange about the whole thing . . .

Fleetingly he wondered about the man who followed behind them. Was Torman to be trusted? Was his loyalty to Meriel really total and unswerving?

Meriel had assured him that it was. Gage had to trust that her assessment was correct. But so much hung on her belief in her captain of the guard. *Her* life, at the very least . . .

"Will the skim crafts make it across the Cerulean Sea?" Meriel's voice rose from the darkness that surrounded them. The faint blue glow from the craft's instrument panel was the only illumination, outlining her face but throwing its details into shadow.

Gage inhaled a deep, considering breath. "They've the power to make it to the isle of Insula and the return trip home. Fuel isn't the problem; it's the weather. If we're unfortunate enough to encounter a sea storm, that's another situation entirely. Between the fierce winds and heat lightning, not to mention the magnetic currents stimulated by the friction of the wind over the gelatinous surface of the sea, I've serious doubts if the skim crafts' electronic systems could function."

"What will we do then?"

"Sit out the storm. What other choice is there? As thick as it is, we could probably walk across the sea's surface, but that would take at least half a day . . . half a day," Gage added, "that would place us at the mercy of any Tergum that slithered by."

At the mention of the dreaded Tergum, a huge, voracious, amoebalike creature that engulfed any life form it came upon, Meriel shuddered. Several were known to inhabit the Cerulean Sea, a unique, membranous-surfaced, almost gelatinous soup teeming with cellular life forms. There was so much danger, not only in the rescue of Kieran when they finally reached the mysterious, eternally cloud-shrouded isle, but even in the journey to Insula. So much danger, so much uncertainty, and now she had begun to doubt even Torman's motivations . . .

Meriel had said her farewells to Dian a few moments before they departed, clasping her friend to her in the privacy of her bedchamber. The little maidservant had fought bravely against the sobs that wracked her slender frame, then finally given into them.

"It's time to go," Meriel at last informed her friend as she slung her pack over her shoulder.

With a small cry, Dian grabbed her arm, halting her. "A moment more," she said, forcing the words through a tear-choked voice. "There's something I must tell you . . . about Torman."

"Yes?" Meriel had prodded.

A flush slowly stained Dian's cheeks. "H-he's

not the same man anymore. He's not Torman."

"What do you mean? Of course he's Torman. Who else would he be?"

There was a dead silence.

Meriel remembered well the rising sense of horror that had curled within her then. "No," she whispered, shaking her head in fierce denial. "I can't believe it! Are you finally beginning to side with Gage in his conviction that Volans are everywhere, plotting to enslave us?"

"I-I don't know what to think anymore. All I know is Torman isn't the same man I once knew and loved. He's now so cold, so distant, so unemotional. He isn't Torman!"

He isn't Torman.

Her friend's words echoed in Meriel's mind even now, as she sped along in the skim craft, the blackness of the night engulfing her, the blue light from the console a dim, eerie link to a rapidly disintegrating reality. What would she do if Dian's suspicions were correct? If the man following closely behind in the second skim craft was Volan?

Meriel's mouth tightened in a grim line. There was only one choice. Kieran's life was at stake. If Torman was a Volan, he'd be dealt with as any Volan must. He'd be eliminated.

Chapter Thirteen

Dawn rose over a barren waste of brown, parched grass and deep crevices. Crevices that slashed across the terrain, their dried-up beds a tragic reminder of the mighty rivers that had once supplied vast amounts of irrigation water to a land dotted with fertile farms.

A land that would soon be no more.

The day would be clear, Meriel thought as they flew along, without even the wispy shade of clouds to block any of Firestar's blazing heat. Even now, before the sun had barely peeked above the horizon, the air was still, warm . . . stifling.

A herd of prong-horned Dorcas stampeded below, their small water-storing humpbacks flopping with each pounding stride, spooked by the unexpected appearance of the skim crafts. They were well adapted to life in the desert, but nonetheless Meriel marveled that the swift-footed creatures had survived so long in the wild. Everyone—

and everything—needed water sooner or later.

She blessed the foresight of her mother, who had directed that a representative sampling of the planet's flora and fauna be gathered where they could be carefully maintained in preparation for evacuation. Otherwise, there'd have been few left to salvage by the time they prepared to leave Tenua.

In the distance a dark line indicated the outlying foothills of rougher terrain, a small chain of low mesas, then a virtual forest of tall, jagged outcroppings of volcanic rocks. The Outlands they'd been called since the beginning of recorded time, a place of blowing sand that swirled and shifted lazily over the flat-topped mesas before picking up velocity to whistle eerily through the volcanic forest, a prehistoric testimony to a time of seething lava jetting into the air and unstable, shifting land plates.

Luckily, Gage possessed the foresight to have acquired the military form of skim crafts which were equipped not only with a burrowing mechanism if the need arose to hide the craft, but a force field bubble as well. With the bubble's relative wind-breaking abilities to contain the air within, they'd be protected from being virtually sand-blasted alive as they flew through the huge stone monoliths. It would also be possible, with the bubble up, to utilize the craft's cooling system. There wasn't much to be done for the sun's rays, but at least there'd be some chill air blowing on them.

They'd make camp within the volcanic forest tonight, Gage had informed her earlier. Once light faded, it would be too difficult, not to mention dangerous, to attempt to weave a path through the tall stones.

Tenua, Meriel mused as her loving gaze scanned the land, was a planet of wide contrasts, of wild, untamed terrain that only the bravest dared venture into, and gentle, fertile grasslands, verdant forests, mighty mountains, and powerful, pounding seas. Or at least it had been, she reminded herself with a sharp pang. In spite of all it had become and would continue to become as Firestar slowly consumed it, it was her home. She loved this planet and would do anything to save it. Anything . . . if there was anything anyone could do.

"We're making good time," Gage observed, intruding on her bleak thoughts. He shot her a quick glance. "We'll stop early for the night so I can give you some blaster and knife-wielding lessons."

Meriel managed a halfhearted little smile. "I look forward to that."

"You'd better, and make the most of the lessons, as well," Gage muttered grimly. "We'll reach the Cerulean Sea by sunset tomorrow. If the conditions are right, I plan on continuing on to the Isle of Insula under cover of darkness. No sense in advertising our arrival by flying over in full sun."

"What then, Gage? What are your plans after that?"

His eyes remained riveted straight ahead. "We'll make camp, then I'll go out and see what I can find."

"I don't understand."

"Meriel," he sighed, "it's quite simple. I'd prefer to discover who our opponents truly are before they discover us. Rebels are one thing—and easily dealt with. Volans are an entirely different matter."

She bit her lip against the surge of stark terror that engulfed her. "What will you do . . . if they truly are Volans? How will you get Kieran away from them?"

Surprise jolted him, then a surge of relief. At last. At last Meriel was beginning to believe.

"I don't know," he admitted with painful honesty. "I've never done battle with a Volan, save for my brief skirmish in Pelum's cell, much less tried to take them by surprise. I don't even know if it can be done."

"Then why are we doing this?" Meriel cried. "If you think it's so hopeless—"

"There's a chance Kieran's abductors could be your rebels. We won't know unless we follow the letter's instructions. And even if they're Volans, we have to begin to poke and prod a little at them. How else are we to discover their weaknesses as well as strengths?"

"This sounds more and more like a foolhardy, fatal experiment," she muttered. "I don't like it. Don't like it at all!"

"Losing heart for the quest so soon, femina?"

At the mocking lilt to his words, Meriel twisted in her seat to face him. "I've as much heart as you, Gage Bardwin! I just don't like the implications that you consider this a suicide mission."

"You'll be safe, Meriel," he softly replied. "That's why I brought Torman along. If it truly is Volans we're dealing with, there's nothing you can do. I either bring Kieran out, or I don't. And if I don't, you're to head back to Eremita as fast as you can and enlist Brace and Teran's aid. If they can't help you, there's no one in the Imperium who can."

"B-but what about you?"

The sound of her tremulous voice sent a strange, sweet pain rocketing through Gage. Gods, she almost sounded as if she cared what happened to him! He could die happy, even if he failed, knowing that.

He bit back the impulse to ask her, knowing it would only complicate things. It would be hard enough to go against the Volans. Though Gage wouldn't admit it to Meriel, he didn't have much hope of making it out alive—or avoiding Volan enslavement if he did. But he had to try. It was Kieran's life if he didn't.

That thought sent an icy chill prickling through him. He was a man who lived for control—control over his life, his environment, others. It had been hard enough learning to adjust to Meriel, to compromise and accede. And he loved her like no other.

But to lose possession of his mind, his body, his actions, was more than Gage could endure. It smacked of the control his mother had once had over him, before he'd finally seen her for what she was. Even the remotest consideration of ever being manipulated in such a way again sickened him.

He would never allow it to happen.

He would *die* before it happened.

"Have a care, sweet femina," Gage replied instead, forcing his attention from the misery of old memories and haunting fears. "If you persist, you'll have me beginning to think you're worried about me. And that could lead to expectations I'm sure you've no desire to fulfill."

"And how do you know what I do or don't desire?" Meriel snapped, irked by the sly look Gage sent her way. "You're far too thick-skulled and insensitive ever to have the remotest chance of understanding what goes on in my—"

"I yield, I yield," Gage interrupted laughingly. "You're right, of course." He shot her a hot, intense look. "You're always right, especially when you open that honeyed mouth of yours to my kisses, when you spread your legs and beg me to take you—"

"Gage!" Meriel could feel the heat steal into her face. "That was totally uncalled for and totally . . . inappropriate."

"But not vile? Not disgusting?"

Her gaze lifted to his, her thoughts guilty, uncertain, nervous. "Please, Gage, let's not talk about this anymore."

An aching gentleness flared in his compelling eyes. "And if we don't talk soon, we may never have the chance. Do you wish to risk that? I don't."

Meriel didn't either, but at that moment she was confused, torn between her rapidly disintegrating resolve to maintain her loyalty to Pelum and her burgeoning need to make peace with Gage. Finally she managed a despairing sigh. "There isn't anything to say. There can never

be anything more between us, save as Lord
Commander and Queen. Too much stands in
the way."

Frustration welled within Gage, followed closely by anger. Curse her, would she never listen?
Never understand?

"Then you refuse to forgive me? Is that it?"

"It's not a matter of forgiveness!" she cried in
exasperation. "If it were, I'd have granted you
that long ago. It . . . it's an issue of who deserves
my first and greatest loyalty."

"And forgiving me would be disloyal to Pelum."

There was no mistaking the bitterness hovering
on the edge of Gage's words. It only fanned
the flames of anguish searing Meriel's heart.
She ached to tell him how much she still
wanted him, loved him, but didn't dare. All
she had to offer was her thanks and undying
gratitude for what he risked in attempting to rescue Kieran.

"Yes," she nodded reluctantly. "I'm sorry if that
hurts, but it can be no other way."

"We'll see about that," he gritted through
clenched teeth. "You're mine, Meriel. I'll make
you admit that if it takes the rest of my life!"

The first faint rays of sunlight crested the hills
of the dying, shriveled lands, washing Gage's
handsome features in strokes of lavender and
rose. Meriel's heart twisted beneath her breast.
Gods, how she loved him, wanted to soothe the
pain from his deep, dark eyes! But it could not
be. No matter how hard she tried to tear it
down, there was one final barrier that refused
to fall.

She blinked back the tears and turned to face the dawn—a dawn of fresh hope, new beginnings . . . for everyone save her and Gage.

The ride through the volcanic forest was both terrifying and exhilarating. Only the battle-honed reflexes of both men saved them several times from sideswiping a huge monolith and crashing to the ground below. As it was, the journey came to an abrupt halt when the setting sun's rays failed to pierce deep enough into the maze of stone obstacles.

They set up camp beneath an enormous volcanic rock whose base, hewn by thousands of cycles of driving wind and rain, provided a small alcove that could serve as shelter for the night. A quick supper of journey bread, meat sticks, and dried fruit, washed down by a generous draught of unfermented uva juice, was soon completed. Then, as Torman prepared their beds, Gage took Meriel a short walk away to teach her the rudiments of the blaster gun.

Much to his surprise, she proved a quick study. Meriel was soon hitting every target Gage pointed out. Finally he called a halt.

"You're lethal enough with the blaster," he muttered dryly. "Am I to presume this keen aim is just another one of your heretofore hidden talents?"

Meriel shrugged and slung the blaster over her shoulder with liquid grace. "But of course." She withdrew the huge knife strapped to her thigh. "Let's see if my aim carries over as readily with this."

Wielding the heavy knife proved far more difficult, however. Meriel was only passably competent by the end of her first lesson.

"You've some real potential with the knife as well," Gage observed as he led her back to camp. "But, for the time being, I advise saving it for close combat. The blaster's your best bet overall."

"I tend to agree," Meriel chuckled, rubbing her right arm. "By the morrow, I'm afraid I'll be too stiff to even withdraw my knife from its sheath, much less throw it very far."

"I could give you a massage," he offered. "Rub the knots out of your shoulders and neck as well. It would alleviate some of the soreness and keep your muscles supple."

She considered his offer, both attracted and wary at the prospect of Gage's hands upon her. Practicality won out. Torman's presence would dampen any untoward overtures that might arise, and she needed to be at her best for the morrow. Stiff, sore muscles would only hamper her when she might need a quick response the most.

"I'd like that." Meriel eyed him solemnly. "This massage will be confined to my arms and shoulders, won't it?"

Gage expelled a melodramatic sigh. "Most definitely. I'm a man of my word, after all."

Meriel smiled. "Indeed."

They rejoined Torman, who had ignited a perpetual flame box for light in the deepening shadows of twilight. After Meriel unbound and combed through her hair in preparation for sleep, Gage positioned himself behind her and began to knead the tightly strung muscles and tendons of her shoulders, gradually working his way down to her arms. After the initial tenderness passed, the rhythmic touch of Gage's big hands began to relax Meriel.

Her lids drifted closed. She sighed in pleasure. "Ah, that feels heavenly!"

"Just one of my many hidden talents," he softly replied.

"Yes, I can see that," Meriel murmured, her voice low, husky with pleasure. "Whatever you do, just don't stop."

Her head tilted back, her thick mane cascaded to cover Gage's hands and arms in a lush fall of ebony. The scent of her hair wafted up to him, of flowers and rain-washed land. He inhaled deeply, savoring the smell, the feel of her, imprinting it upon his memory to last for a lifetime.

A lifetime that might well be over in another day or two. In spite of himself, desire pounded through Gage, swirling through his body to pool in his groin. He hardened.

It was a natural enough response, he assured himself, even as he cursed the easy effect she always had upon him. For all practical purposes, he was girding himself for battle, and the night before combat always turned his mind to the potentially final opportunity to ease his lust.

Not that all he felt for Meriel was lust. A mating with her would have been more than just a physical release. He desperately needed the healing of wounds that still burned raw within him. He wanted to hear, just once more, Meriel's words of love. He wanted to know, if he failed in this quest, that he left behind a mate who mourned his passing, and a child who would be raised with proud memories of his sire.

But that was not to be. Not tonight at least. Even if Meriel would have accepted him, Torman's curious gaze would have been more than enough to quench the fires simmering within him. So Gage contented himself with the silken brush of Meriel's hair against his hands and bare forearms, the delicate scent of her, and the feel of her soft body beneath his touch. It was far less than what he craved and so desperately needed, but it was all he had.

After a time, Meriel began to doze beneath Gage's soothing ministrations. Her head lolled from side to side, dipped forward to rest upon her chest before she once more jerked awake. Gage finally ceased his massage and lowered her to her bed.

Meriel's eyes fluttered open when he pulled off her boots and covered her with a light blanket. For an instant, confusion glimmered there, then she recognized him. With a gentle, sleepy little smile, Meriel closed her eyes, turned on her side, and went back to sleep.

Gage lingered for a tender, heart-stopping moment, that now familiar sense of fierce protectiveness and possession flooding him. As committed as Meriel was to participating in the quest to rescue her son, he knew she depended on him to make certain they succeeded. As willing as she was to learn the skills of a warrior, he knew as well that it was his abilities that she so desperately needed.

He must not fail her, no matter the cost, even to the sacrifice of his life. Meriel and their son were what mattered. Without them there was no hope, no purpose, no future.

A lock of precariously perched hair eased its way down Meriel's forehead to dangle in her eye. With an infinitely tender movement, Gage swept it away. He glanced up then, and his gaze slammed into Torman's.

The other man had been watching them, an intent, strangely tormented look in his eyes. At Gage's piercing glare, he quickly turned away. Scooting down, Torman climbed into his own bed, then glanced back up at Gage. He managed a tentative smile.

Gage stared back stony-faced, then reached over and extinguished the perpetual flame box. Darkness enshrouded them, the silence complete save for the wind whistling high above, a bleak, haunted lament for a dying land.

The rays of dawn came late, penetrating the flinty forest with tediously slow increments of light. Gage was up before the others and had everything packed by the time the sun's rays roused Meriel and Torman. After a quick meal, they broke camp and were on their way.

It was a silent ride for Gage and Meriel. Both dealt with emotions drawn taut as bowstrings after the past several days, compounded now by the anticipation of the second, and most dangerous part, of their mission. By midday they'd cleared the last of the volcanic forest and set their course for the distant horizon. As they skimmed over the undulating terrain that gradually flattened to a tiny, intricate patchwork of parched, cracked earth, clouds began to gather in the distance.

Uneasiness coiled within Meriel, twisting ever tighter the closer they drew to the first sight of the Cerulean Sea. Their worst fears had come to fruition. A storm churned over the gelatinous wastes, awaiting just the proper moisture content absorbed from the sea's vast depths to combine with just the right temperature and wind velocity to unleash its fury.

Frustration filled her. Awaiting a storm to run its course could take all night. And, since Gage was adamant about not crossing the sea in full view of any observers stationed on Insula's coastline, they'd be forced to sit through another whole day before daring to approach the isle.

"Our luck isn't running too good, is it?" Meriel inquired morosely.

"We're not beaten yet. Those storm clouds could be a bluff. I've seen those kinds of weather formations boil around for hours, then slowly dissipate. Let's just see how conditions are when we get there."

Fresh hope surged through Meriel. She nodded, a fierce, determined movement of her head. "Yes. Let's just see."

Sunset deepened the evening to shades of gold and red before the skim craft circled for a landing in a thick stand of dead trees and boulders at the edge of the Cerulean Sea. Before them, the mass of life-sustaining gelatin undulated rhythmically, its wavelike motion magnified by the winds already swirling about them.

They climbed out of the skim craft and walked up to the edge of the sea. On closer inspection, Meriel noted millions of tiny, luminous creatures flitting beneath the thick, membranous surface. Cerulean sea worms, Meriel thought. Larger jellylike organisms occasionally passed by, bloating and then contracting to convey themselves through the viscous morass. Further out in the rolling sea, several huge, lurking forms slithered past. Meriel shivered and turned to Gage.

He quirked a questioning brow. "See any Tergum skulking about?"

"They don't need to skulk. They can cover ground—or should I say sea?—so rapidly that no creature could escape. Their great speed and stealth put the odds entirely in their favor, and by the time they emit their kill cry, it's too late. But, in answer to your question," Meriel replied, "no, there aren't any Tergum nearby."

"My thanks for your enlightening and totally depressing lecture," he muttered. Gage glanced over his shoulder at Torman. "What do you think? The storm doesn't look to be growing any worse. Is it worth the risk?"

Torman glanced up at the lowering sky. Though time was on his side, he preferred getting this increasingly difficult task over with. He cared nothing for Bardwin and his ultimate fate, but every time Meriel smiled at him or inquired about his comfort, the pang of guilt grew stronger. And he couldn't even begin to comprehend, much less deal with, the surprising surge of desire he felt every time he looked at her.

When the barrier of his current slave's body was eliminated, she wasn't even his kind of life form. Yet, for just one chance to feel her, taste her, touch her, Torman would have willingly relegated the span of his existence to a humanoid body, with all its frustrating limitations.

That was one thing to be said for humans, he admitted wryly. They were oversaturated with sensitive nerve endings that heightened every sensation, every need. And that, perhaps more than anything else, was what had led him to this distressing state of affairs. That, and the prolonged loss of contact with the Mother Ship.

Torman knew, with a certainty innate to his species, that he could not long continue on the course of his current programming. Too much had happened in the past month to distort his perceptions, twist his resolve, pluck at a conscience buried under hundreds of thousands of cycles of deliberate, collective brainwashing. That there was anything left to stir into any semblance of honor and morality was a total surprise in itself.

But, be that as it might, it changed nothing. Torman's perseverance was slipping; his Volan training was dissolving. Prolonged contact with these most unique and troublesome of all species was gradually transforming him. He was beginning to think and feel for himself.

That realization terrified him. His identity had always been that of the hive. All decisions, all choices, had always been made for him. It was a safe, sane, well-reasoned approach.

Not like this free-floating, sometimes impulsive, and never wisely sanctioned human way of doing things. Each was on his own. Each was responsible for his decisions—and its consequences. Did any of them ever agonize over whether they'd made the right choice or not?

Yet the lure of total freedom, of the wealth of experiences that spread before one courageous enough to take such a chance, was heady indeed. Heady . . . and nearly impossible to resist.

He forced himself to pause and intently scan the sky before giving the only reply his desperation demanded. "Yes, I think it's worth the risk. But only if we depart immediately. Otherwise, we may end up walking across the sea, a difficult, not to mention extremely dangerous, undertaking."

Gage's mouth quirked in grudging admiration. "A man after my own heart. There's no sweetness in victory without the risk, is there?"

"No, most definitely not," Torman muttered as he turned and headed back to his skim craft.

With a muted roar of powerful engines, the two skim craft rose in the deepening twilight and sped off over the sea. The wind howled overhead, blowing hard, buffeting the little crafts. Occasional flashes of heat lightning danced about them, causing hair to rise with the static electricity.

Meriel clung to the handholds inset in the door and control panel, certain that any moment a bolt of lightning would strike them and send the craft careening down to crash on the sea. She refused to close her eyes and shut out the horror building above and around them. She had made a choice to join Gage on this quest. She'd face it all as unstintingly as he.

Meriel inhaled a shuddering breath, swallowed hard, and shot Gage a quick, surreptitious glance. His features were carved in stone, his lips tight, an almost feral grin of pleasure on his face.

A sudden revelation struck her. Gage saw the storm as nothing more than a challenge to overcome. He was exhilarated by the danger and conflict.

Envy twined within her. If only she had the courage to see beyond the danger, to find some cause powerful enough to contain the fear before it paralyzed her. But though her mother's love would see her through it all, Meriel doubted she could have come this far without Gage to sustain her.

She was a coward, had always been. She wasn't fit to rule, much less be a mother to Kieran. If she'd been more of the woman that both Pelum and Gage deserved, perhaps she could have found some way to save them both.

What fear could not do, shame did. Meriel's eyes squeezed shut against the tears. She'd been a fool, a silly girl, a faithless wife. But she'd not fail her son. Not now, not ever!

Her lids snapped open and her features hardened with resolve. Her fingers clenched, knuckles white, about the skim craft's handholds, but she forced herself to face it all. Around her the storm raged on, taunting and teasing the crafts with a barely leashed fury that hovered on the brink of breaking forth into its full-fledged might.

Insula, its peaks and uplands girdled by thick, churning clouds only sporadically illuminated by bursts of lightning, drew nearer and nearer. Finally Gage programmed in a landing sequence that would settle the craft behind a massive outcropping of rocks that jutted from the sandy beach. They circled lower and lower, not utilizing their landing lights until they came within meters of the stones' dark, looming shadows. Gage skillfully maneuvered the skim craft downward until they touched ground with a soft bump. A few seconds later, Torman landed beside them.

Slinging his blaster over his shoulder and into firing position, Gage immediately slipped off into the darkness. Meriel sat there, the tension building with the uncertainty, until a hand settled on her shoulder. She jumped, bit back a startled gasp, and turned.

It was Torman. "Come, let's get these skim crafts buried. One way or another, we'll be easy prey out here on the beach once the sun rises."

Grateful for something to do to keep her mind occupied, Meriel climbed out, retrieved the two supply packs, and placed them at the base of the stone barriers. She made a move to return to Torman, hesitated, then went back for her blaster.

He eyed her when she drew up before him. "Getting to be a real warrior woman, aren't you?"

Meriel shrugged. "I don't intend to let either you or Gage down. Now," she gestured toward the skim craft, "show me how to bury these things."

"Stand back."

As Meriel moved away from the first craft, Torman leaned over, punched at the control panel, then jumped aside. With a high-pitched whine the craft began to vibrate, then sink slowly beneath the sand. The second craft was soon dispensed with in a similar fashion. With nothing better to do, Meriel and Torman sat down to await Gage's return.

Above them, the storm finally discharged its pent-up fury. The wind howled, the rain poured, and jagged, blue-white bolts of lightning slashed across the sky. Meriel huddled close to Torman's solid form, enduring the lash of the elements, thanking a kind fate that had held back the storm until after they'd arrived. Sheets of water pelted them, the isle, and the Cerulean Sea.

With the rising sun, she well knew, the rain would soon evaporate back into the air above Insula, setting the stage for yet another storm. A waste of desperately needed water, to her way of thinking, this constant recycling over a sea that was incapable of absorbing the moisture, and falling on an isle that was usually uninhabited.

All too soon, even that water would permanently evaporate in Firestar's searing heat. The Cerulean Sea would shrink and its sea creatures die, as the delicate gelatinous soup became too hot to sustain life. There was nothing on Tenua, no matter how hardy, how self-sustaining, Meriel thought as she sat there in the pouring rain, that could survive a sun's fiery death process for long.

An hour later Gage suddenly reappeared, without sound or warning. Meriel leaped to her feet, her blaster ready, before she recognized his shadowy form.

Gage grinned. "A little trigger-happy, aren't you? Have a care with that gun. I'd at least like to make it through tonight." He glanced down at Torman, who was leisurely rising. "I assume you heard me coming."

"Of course," the big man replied. "You're very good, but battle has honed my hearing."

"Far better than most," Gage muttered, suspicion thickening his voice. "I can normally stalk wild cerva without them hearing me, and there are few animals with better ears than they. And then"—he glanced up at the rain—"if my usual stealth wasn't enough, there was the additional cover of the storm to cover my approach."

"And should I apologize for my talents?" Torman stiffened, ready to strike if Gage should make a move toward his weapons. "I'd think you'd be grateful, rather than resent it. I'm sorry if your pride has been damaged, but I can't change what is."

"Gage, Torman's right," Meriel hurried to offer, puzzled over the sudden current of hostility that arced between the two men. "Besides, there's no time to waste. What did you find and what shall we do next?"

Gage wrenched his attention from Torman, only temporarily quashing the uneasiness that had filled him at the discovery of the other man's extraordinary auditory abilities. It could well be as Torman said. He might possess special, sensitive hearing. But the odds of that were slim. Gage was just too good a tracker. And, with the added cacophony of the storm, a herd of equs could have approached without notice.

Volans, however, among their other documented talents, were known to have highly acute hearing. Was Torman perhaps not all he seemed?

The consideration sent a chill prickling down Gage's spine. Gods, if he'd brought a Volan along to protect Meriel, he had placed her—and their quest—in the gravest danger! Yet, how was he to discern the truth, if Torman was truly a Volan? And, more importantly, how was he to extricate himself—and Meriel—without risking both their lives?

The simplest solution was to take the other man by surprise and blast him where he stood. That would be cold-blooded murder, yet an act he'd perform in a heartbeat if he was certain Torman was a Volan.

The morality of attempting to kill a Volan, however, was a moot point. The odds were stacked against a fair fight even if Gage tried a surprise attack. The only murder would be if Torman truly *was* Torman.

There was no time to delve further into this issue right now. His initial plan was to get Meriel to a less vulnerable spot on the isle. If he managed to find an adequate hiding place for her, he might even consider taking Torman along to scout the interior of Insula further. Time enough then to plumb the true depths of the man.

He ran a hand through his rain-soaked hair, shoving the dripping strands up out of his eyes. "There's nothing of significance in the interior of the isle for about an hour's walk. Whoever has Kieran is probably holed up within one of those two volcanic mountains further inland. We'll head toward them."

"Good." Meriel could hardly contain her excitement as she strode over to him. "Let's get going."

Gage paused to wipe a drop of water suspended from the tip of her nose, a surprisingly tender smile on his lips. "Then let's gather up the supplies. I want to cover as much ground as possible before sunrise."

He paused to retrieve a pack and sling it over his shoulder. "It's pretty much open terrain for the next hour or so, before the tree line at the base of the mountains begins. The rain will cover our tracks off this beach, as well as the site where the skim crafts are buried. As uncomfortable as this storm may be, it has turned out to be a blessing in many ways."

"To be sure," Meriel muttered as she gathered her gear and headed out after Gage. "If we don't die of a chill or get struck by lightning in the meantime."

Torman followed in brooding silence, slogging through the rain and heavy courses of water that ran downhill to the sea, his tension building as he impatiently awaited the right moment to act on his own plans.

That opportunity came sooner than he expected.

Chapter Fourteen

A half hour from the beach and distracted by the storm, Meriel lost her footing on some unstable ground. She fell, sliding down a steep slope that dropped into a muddy, rain-swollen ravine. Though the water was not deep enough to drown in, its force, churning down the narrow passage, was strong enough to repeatedly knock her over. Each fall pulled Meriel farther and farther downstream before she was able to climb to her feet, only to be knocked over again.

The roar of a waterfall not far away warned of the ultimate destination of the coursing water. Gage swung to Torman. There was little time to rescue Meriel, and he desperately needed the other man's help.

The captain of the guard was already slipping out of the coil of rope he'd worn slung across his chest. "What's your plan?"

Gage grabbed one end of the rope that Torman

had unfurled and knotted it firmly about his waist. "Let's head downstream from Meriel. Then I'll jump in and catch her as she goes by. You can haul us out."

Torman nodded. "It seems the best plan."

For the span of an inhaled breath, Gage hesitated, then handed the big man his blaster. He knew he took a chance entrusting his weapon to someone he was no longer sure of, but there wasn't time to mull over the wisdom of the act. Meriel's life was in danger, and Torman's greater strength would be needed to pull them both out of the river.

They took off at a dead run, following the edge of the ravine. The rumble of the falls grew louder. Up ahead, Gage could see the mist rising just beyond the point where the river ended to cascade hundreds of meters down onto the deadly rocks below.

The water flowed deeper now. Meriel could barely touch bottom. Her progress downstream picked up speed. She floundered, was dragged under, then rose to the surface, gasping and choking. She heard the falls. Terror engulfed her.

Gods, no! Gage! Help me!

She twisted in the water, searching frantically for sight of him. A movement up on the edge of the ravine caught her eye. Was it Gage?

Before she could identify the object, the water pulled her under. She slammed into a tree branch half-lodged in the river bed. Meriel grabbed at it, hoping to halt her forward progress. For a fleeting instant, it seemed to work. Then, with a sickening crack, the branch broke free. Once more, Meriel was caught by the surging water and dragged downstream.

She was going to die, her mind screamed, carried over the falls to smash on the rocks below. She would never see Kieran again. She would never see Dian. She would never be able to tell Gage she still loved him . . .

Anger flared, fueling her resolve. Meriel fought her way across the churning water to claw desperately at the river bank. For a time, she found a hold. Gage would come, she told herself, fighting to control her rising panic, if only she could maintain her grasp long enough. If only—

A loud splash just a few meters downstream caught Meriel's attention. She glanced over her shoulder, even as she felt her grip beginning to slip. A sleek, dark blond head broke the water's surface, then a familiar, oh so welcome, face.

Gage.

"Let go!" he shouted above the fall's roar. "Float down to me! Torman will pull us out!"

Her perspective shifted. Her glance moved from Gage to ten meters past him, where the river ended in a union with the clear blue sky. There was one—and only one—chance. If the river pushed her past Gage, or he couldn't hold onto her, it was over.

Meriel clamped her eyes shut, fighting a sickening surge of terror. Ah, Gods, she couldn't let go, yet she must. Torman couldn't hold Gage forever. And she couldn't hold on forever, either.

With a small cry, Meriel released her grip and shoved off from the river bank. Her aim was true, but the force of the water's current was difficult to compensate for. She was carried past Gage, their fingertips brushing.

"No!" he roared and, with a superhuman effort, lunged across the water. His fingers grasped cloth, and tugged. The sturdy fabric of Meriel's tunic held. She felt herself hauled backward. Then an arm curled about her waist, pulling her against a hard body. She swallowed a waterlogged sob.

Slowly, ever so painfully, they were pulled across the raging river as Torman drew in the rope. Once they reached the river bank and Gage was able to secure a footing, he swung Meriel behind him and onto his back.

"Hold on," he ordered. "Torman can't do all the work. I'm going to try and help by climbing as well."

Meriel nodded, too exhausted to do more. The trek up the shifting, unstable side of the ravine was difficult, even with Torman pulling from above. They slipped and slid back down as frequently as they made upward progress.

The last several meters were sheer torture for Gage. Meriel could see his muscles quivering with the strain, feel the effort it took for him to drag them up. At last they topped the edge and, aided by Torman, climbed over.

Meriel was the first to recover from her exertions, awkwardly shoving herself to her knees. Gage lay beside her, his chest still heaving.

She glanced up at Torman and smiled. "My thanks for your great strength and loyalty. We could have never made it without—"

"Move away from him, Meriel." As he spoke, Torman used the end of his blaster to emphasize his order. "Now."

She frowned. "Torman, I don't understand. Let me first help Gage—"

"Get away from him or I'll blast him where he lies!"

Her eyes widened. Ever so cautiously, Meriel climbed to her feet and stepped away from Gage.

Gage shoved to one elbow and glared up at the captain of the guard. "My misgivings were well-founded. I only wonder why you didn't let us both die down there in the river."

A grim smile quirked the corner of Torman's mouth. "You're both too valuable to waste. Or at least," he added savagely, "your living bodies are."

Horror shivered through Meriel. "No!" she cried. "Gods, no, not you, Torman! You're not a Volan! Please, tell me you're not!"

"And would my lie change what is?"

"But y-you guarded me all those days, you played with Kieran, you helped me visit Pelum. . . . Pelum," she whispered on an agonized thread of sound. "Was he, too, a . . . a Volan?"

He hardened his heart to her. "Yes, your husband was a Volan."

Meriel's mind raced. She must have a plan; she must do something! She glanced about her, finding their blasters lying well out of reach. No hope of getting to them before Torman could easily kill both Gage and her.

And her stunner, though by some miracle still fastened to her belt, might not even work after its dousing in the river. She didn't dare count on it. Perhaps if she enticed Torman to talk, she could buy Gage time to figure out a better plan. A weak or cajoling approach with Torman wouldn't work, however. The Volan would most likely see through it immediately.

Her chin lifted a defiant notch. "And what do you plan to do with us?"

"Isn't that obvious? We've wanted Bardwin for a time now. When the ploy with Pelum failed, we turned to the child to lure him to us." Torman withdrew his stunner and flipped the setting to maximum, all the while maintaining his blaster's aim on Gage. "The enslavement of his body will grant us access to all the royal houses of the Imperium and, most especially, the royal house of Ardane."

Anger flashed in Meriel's eyes. "You won't stop, will you, until you've—"

A sound, guttural, enraged, erupted from deep within Gage as he flung himself at Torman. It was a wild, desperate gesture and gained him nothing. With a reflexive motion, the Volan took aim and fired.

Gage plummeted to the ground, instantly unconscious. Meriel's hand went to her own stunner, then froze when Torman swung his weapon toward her.

"Care to chance it, little Queen? All you'll get for your efforts is a throbbing, post-stun headache."

Meriel's hand fell from her waist. "What do you want from me?"

He extracted a pair of beryllium shackles from the pouch at his belt and tossed them to her. "Bind him, hands behind his back."

When the task was completed, Torman withdrew another set of shackles and motioned toward her. "Turn around and sit on the ground with your back to me. Don't move or try anything. Do you understand?"

She nodded and did as ordered. Cold bands were clasped about her wrists, then clamped shut. The tiny sound reverberated through Meriel's brain, growing in volume until it reminded her of a door slamming shut. A door to her and Gage's freedom, to their minds, their memories, and all their hopes and dreams. Despair engulfed her.

"This is Rand, leader of the palace force," Torman's deep voice rose from behind her. "I have Bardwin and the Queen. Send immediate transport to the location of my homing beacon."

Torman. A Volan.

The realization pounded through Meriel's skull with each beat of her frightened heart. Torman. Good, gentle, kind Torman. Gone forever.

A memory of Dian tugged at Meriel. She had promised to take care of Torman for her. To bring him back to her. But Dian's lover was no more. In his place stood a hard-eyed, scowling Volan named Rand. A Volan who held her and Gage captive, pawns whose only purpose now was to help destroy the Imperium.

It was too much to deal with. She couldn't face any more. Meriel closed her eyes and willed herself to flee deep within her mind.

"They'll get to us sooner or later, you know," Gage muttered through clenched teeth that did little to compensate for his painfully pounding headache. "We've scoured every millimeter of this cell and there's no way out. All they have to do is wait until we finally fall asleep . . ."

Meriel snuggled closer to the warmth of his hard-muscled body. The underground cell the Volans had thrown them in was not only cool, thanks to its position deep within a volcanic mountain, but damp as well, with its underground spring bubbling up from a far corner of the large chamber. But at least it provided a source of fresh, if cold, water, she tried to console herself. They'd not go thirsty.

"We could take turns sleeping," Meriel ventured, lifting her gaze to his. "If one of us always stood watch over the other . . ."

Gage smiled, then bent to kiss her forehead. "A clever plan indeed, femina. It might well hold them off for a time. But they still have Kieran."

"My poor little one." She sighed and stroked the broad, flat planes of Gage's chest. "What will they do with him?"

"I don't know, Meriel. I hope they only took Kieran to draw us here. But if there's some way for them to continue to use him against us, be assured they will."

"Torman—I mean, Rand—said that enslaving you would grant them access to all the Imperial royal houses, and especially the Ardanes'. They mean to infiltrate at the highest levels, don't they?"

"Yes," Gage hissed savagely. "Think how easily they can use me to get to King Falkan and Teran. My best friend, and he won't suspect a thing—until it's too late."

Her hands clenched in the cloth of his tunic. "We can't let that happen, Gage! But what can we do? There's no way out of this cell save the door, and it's locked and made of solid metal." She laughed, a hollow, hopeless sound. "As if we had anything to cut our way out with."

"There's nothing to do but wait until the Volans show their hand."

Meriel didn't like the quiet despair that roughened Gage's voice. "When will that be?"

"The Volan Rand said something about the morrow." Gage frowned. "He's a strange one, even for a Volan. And when he looks at you . . ."

"What?" Meriel prodded. "What do you see?"

"Regret, concern . . . I don't know. But he doesn't look at you the way the others do."

Hope flared in Meriel's breast. "Is there some way I can use that to our benefit?"

Gently Gage pushed Meriel back from him. He quirked a brow. "What exactly did you have in mind? Seducing a Volan?"

She blushed. "I didn't exactly plan on a seduction. But if there's something, anything, I can do to influence him into helping us . . ."

Gage pulled her back to lie against him. "I don't know if there's any hope of help from him. Remember, Volan minds and lives aren't their own. They're driven by continual directives from their hive. They have no freedom of choice."

"How very, very sad," Meriel murmured. "No choice of where to live, who to mate with, what to do with their lives."

"Curse it all, Meriel! Save your pity!" Gage choked back the savage fury that flooded him.

"They're nothing more than animals, animals who made their choice long ago! When they found their bodies in danger of extinction from their own highly evolved minds and destructively accelerated metabolic rates, they could've sought some other course than the enslavement of other species. Only fiends would decide their survival was more important than hundreds of other life forms. Yet, do they ever stop and ponder the morality of that for a moment? No!"

"Gage . . ." Meriel began.

"I hate them," he went on, seeming not to hear her. "They threaten everything I hold dear, even my woman and son! I want to slaughter them all, with my bare hands if necessary, yet there's nothing—absolutely nothing—I can do!" His head lowered to the soft, sweet hollow of her neck. "Gods, Meriel, I love you and Kieran, and I can't do anything to protect you!"

"Ah, Gage, don't torment yourself over me," Meriel whispered, stroking his head. "I don't deserve your love. I fought you, betrayed your trust, turned from you time and again. And I'm such a coward, so weak. I've never been worthy of you."

"Little fool." Gage moved her more squarely onto his lap, then turned her face to his. "You're the bravest, most loyal woman I know. Yes, you fought me, but only when you thought me wrong, and only for the sake of others. And yes, you did go against me at times, but only because your conscience dictated otherwise. Pelum was unworthy of you, a weak, helpless little man, but that doesn't lessen the value of your loyalty and devotion to him.

"On the contrary," he added, bending to brush his lips across hers. "I find that I desperately want that same loyalty and devotion—and love—for myself. Can you ever find it in your heart to share that with me, as well?"

"Yes," Meriel breathed. "Oh, yes! I've wanted to since that first day I met you. Perhaps that seems like a foolish, romantic girl's dreaming, but even then I loved you. Even then I knew you were special, a man among men."

His teeth flashed white in a lazy grin. "Tell me more. I find the turn of this conversation most gratifying."

She smiled, the movement of her lips slow and unconsciously provocative. "There's little more to tell. I only wonder how I can prove it to you?"

"Here? Now?" Gage's lips twitched with laughter. "Truly, femina, your ardor flares at the strangest of times and places."

Reality—their utterly dismal situation, the unpleasant, uncomfortable lodgings—suddenly returned with disconcerting force. Yet it only intensified Meriel's need for Gage. The morrow might be the end. This might be the last night they'd ever spend together. Somehow, someway, they must find a strength from it to sustain them for what was to come.

Her hands slid up his thick chest muscles to entwine about his neck. "I want you, Gage Bardwin. The Volans may soon take everything from us, but I don't want them to have it all. What we share here tonight must bind us—across time, space, and life itself. No matter what happens, our minds must always retain the memories of what we had—and remember."

"It seems the only weapon we have left against them," Gage sighed. "Our love, our commitment to each other. I only hope it's enough."

"Believe it, my love. Bury it deep within your mind where no one but you can ever go. And I will do the same."

She paused to grasp Gage's face and lower his head until his lips were but a warm breath from hers. A wild conviction spiraled within her, some knowledge, ancient and sure, arising entirely from outside herself. "Then, if one of us survives," Meriel said, "that one will seek out the other and call forth our love."

It was but a woman's romantic, idealistic dreamings, Gage told himself, this belief of Meriel's that their love was strong enough to overcome a Volan mind enslavement. There was no force in the universe strong enough to do that. And yet, the strength of his feelings for her *was* a powerful thing. It had carried him through three long, lonely, vengeance-driven cycles to find Meriel again, had shown him, with a painful, haunting clarity, how empty his life had been before her. It had created a child, whom he treasured and fiercely wanted to nurture, teach, and love.

He *wanted* to believe with Meriel's pure, stunning conviction. But he knew what he was, just a man of sinew, muscle, and bone. His body was strong, his mind clear, but he had no special powers. He was just . . . a man.

Doubts curled within him. Perhaps that had always been the fundamental problem. He was too ordinary, too common to be worthy of a woman like Meriel.

The doubts grew, assuming substance, comprehension. He'd been mad to presume to take a Queen. Mad to think she could life mate with him. Her people, if not tradition, would never permit it. And, though he'd spoken of such a goal many times, Meriel had never done the same. Even now, when she proclaimed the miraculous powers of their love.

Gage knew she loved him, but knew as well that it didn't blind her to the reality of her position. Perhaps that was why, even as her heart and body had begun to respond to him, she'd still clung so tenaciously to her marriage to Pelum. He was a man sanctioned in the ways that ultimately mattered. He was royal and gave their union credence and legitimacy. Pelum was no bastard.

"Gage," Meriel whispered, intruding on his self-deprecating thoughts, "what's wrong? Don't you believe me? Don't you want to mate with me?"

He covered her hands with his, gently removing them from his face. "Yes, sweet femina. I believe you're convinced of the power of our love. And I do want to mate with you. Very, very much."

"But you don't believe our love is enough to overcome the Volans."

"No."

She pulled him to her, pressing her soft breasts into his chest. He went very still. Meriel smiled.

"Then perhaps it's time I convinced you. Showed you how it really is between us."

Her hand slid down his chest, over his rigid, rippling abdomen, to slip between his legs and grasp him. At her intimate touch, Gage sucked in a breath.

"You like that, don't you?" she purred. "You want that and more."

"Yes," he growled, the sound animal, warning. "But you're treading in dangerous waters. If you're not careful, you may rouse more than you can handle."

"Like this?" As she spoke, Meriel glanced up archly, then down again at the bulge already straining against his breeches. "But that's exactly what I meant to rouse. That, and every other exciting, beautiful millimeter of your body."

"Then you've been fairly warned, femina." Gage jerked her more closely to him. "And it won't be gentle. I've wanted you too long, too painfully, to hold anything back now." He dipped his forehead to press against hers. "If you can't deal with it, with me that way, tell me now. Now, before it's too late."

Her answer was her hands unfastening the front of his tunic, spreading it apart to slip it from his shoulders. Her fingers tugging free the opening of the belt that circled his trim waist, then the opening of his breeches. Her ragged breathing and overbright eyes as she finally stripped him naked.

Meriel leaned back, her hungry gaze raking him. He was so magnificently virile, the bulge of his hair-roughened flesh merging from broad shoulders and chest to a long, smooth line of torso and narrow hips, before flaring out into hard, whipcord-muscled legs. But it was the primal thrust of his hot, swollen shaft that fascinated her most. That, and the anticipation of how he would feel inside her . . . and the wild, savage, uncompromising love they'd share.

"I can deal with you any way you wish to come to me," she breathed, her voice husky with barely repressed desire. "Just as long as you always want me, always love me. What other way could there be between a man and a woman?"

"No other way," Gage admitted, pulling Meriel down to him. His hands tugged at her clothes until she thought he'd rip them in his eagerness. She laughed, pushed his hands away, and finished the job for him. Then, with a smile, she returned to his side.

Her hand moved back toward the stiff object of her fascination, but Gage halted her. "No. If you touch me now, I swear I'll lose control. And," he rasped as he rolled her over onto a soft cushion of moss flowers growing near the underground spring, "I don't intend to do that until I'm deep inside you."

He rose on hands and knees, poised over her. "Spread yourself for me. Let me see you. Pleasure you."

Meriel did as Gage requested, unsure of his intent as he moved down between her legs, his dark blond head dipping nearing the sweet, secret core of her. His hands grasped her, spreading her wide. At the first touch of his tongue gently flicking her highly sensitized nub, she gasped, flushed crimson and tried to clamp her legs shut.

"G-Gage!" Meriel struggled to rise to her elbows. "What are you d-doing? I don't want . . . it isn't right—"

"Hush, sweet one," he huskily commanded. "It's what you want and have always wanted. You just don't know it yet. Trust me. Lie back, open your legs, and trust."

With a breathless sigh, Meriel did as he asked. She was acutely embarrassed, but if Gage wished it of her, she'd bare even that most private of places to him. She'd already given him her heart, her soul. Her continued hesitance with the more mysterious aspects of their lovemaking seemed so insignificant, even foolish, in comparison. And she did trust him, trust that he'd never do anything to hurt or shame her in their matings. If Gage insisted this was something she wanted, then it must be so.

She watched his head lower between her legs, felt his cheek brush against the dark thatch that shielded her woman's secrets. Then, once again, his tongue touched her, lightly flicking, then circling the satin nub. Silken fire shot through Meriel. She choked back a strangled cry, arching toward him.

Gage captured her thighs, pinning her to the ground. "That's it, little one. Surrender to it. Enjoy it."

His tongue laved her again and again, then he paused to eye her with hot, hungry eyes. "Gods, but you're so sweet!"

Meriel's only reply was to writhe in his grasp, overcome by the exquisite shards of sensation each touch of Gage's tongue sent stabbing through her. It was piercing agony, then exquisite pleasure, all mixed into one mind-boggling, rising, unbearable tension. She moaned. Her fingers clutched in Gage's hair.

At her unbridled response he made a low sound of satisfaction, stroking, squeezing the soft flesh of her inner thighs, urging her, luring her to the brink of ecstasy. He ran his teeth over her sensitized nub, eliciting a startled, strangled cry.

Then her whole body tightened, arching upward in shuddering spasms of delight. A moan of anguished pleasure tore from her lips. She called out Gage's name.

Before Meriel had plumbed the depths of her climax, Gage had released her and was moving back up over her. She lifted passion-weighted lids to find him poised above her. Meriel smiled. Grasping his swollen organ, she pulled him down to her.

With an anguished groan, Gage followed the course of his tautly straining shaft, gritting hard against the control that threatened to shred right there in the clasp of Meriel's hand. She guided him into her, lifting her hips to ease the passage, then, with a contented sigh, lowered them both to the ground.

Gage trembled above Meriel, his head thrown back, his eyes clenched shut, his rock-hard sex thrust deep within her. If she would only lie still for a moment, he thought through the passion-heated mist that swirled through his brain, he might regain control, might still be able—

A slender body arched beneath him, sheathing moist, hot silk around him. Back and forth, the rhythmic, feminine thrusting sent Gage spiraling over the edge. With a guttural cry, he hauled her up against him, plunging into Meriel with a mindless, savage need. The pressure built to agonized proportions, finally erupting in deep, shuddering pulses of release. With a low sound, Gage gave himself over to surrender, to pleasure, and to love for the beautiful, passionate woman lying in his arms.

When both could breathe once more, Gage rolled off Meriel and pulled her back to lie against him, pillowing her head on his chest. He covered her with their discarded clothing, then tenderly kissed her cheek.

"Go to sleep, little one. I'll stand guard."

"Wake me in a few hours," Meriel murmured drowsily. "I'll take my turn then."

She drifted off almost immediately, her gentle breathing filling the damp, hollow chamber of stone. And slept through the remainder of the night, for Gage didn't have the heart to wake her. He knew he wouldn't sleep at any rate. Too much uncertainty awaited on the morrow. Uncertainty and a growing fear of what lay ahead. The Volans wanted him, meant to have him. And they had Meriel and Kieran as well.

If it came to their lives, their welfare, Gage's choices were few. The Volans knew that. They held every advantage. And there seemed nothing, absolutely nothing, he could do about it.

They arrived about mid morning, if it were possible to accurately estimate time in a cell without outside light. Gage was once more bound, then dragged down the long, winding stone corridor between two guards, Meriel led close behind. The tunnel slanted gradually upward, past various chambers, some filled with small, translucent, glowing balls hooked to a large machine that resembled both a computer and a life-support system, then through a huge, high-ceilinged room that held what looked to be an exotic form of transport chamber.

Finally they came to another large room, this one occupied by a small group gathered before a dais on which sat an imposing, scowling man. Behind him and to his right stood Torman.

Or rather the Volan Rand who inhabited Torman's body, Meriel hastened to correct herself. She must stop thinking of Torman as a human being, or even as alive, anymore. The real Torman, her loyal captain of the guard, was gone. Forever. All that remained was his outer shell—and a vile, heartless alien who dwelled within.

A side door opened and another Volan carried in a squirming Kieran. With a small cry, Meriel twisted free of her guard and ran to her son. In impassive silence, the Volans, to a man, watched as she took the lad and hugged him to her.

"Kieran. My darling son," Meriel murmured. "Are you all right? Mama missed you so!"

"Mama, Mama!" the child chortled and hugged her in return. "Want down. Want to play!"

"No," she informed him firmly. "You'll stay with me for now."

Kieran took one look at the stern expression on his mother's face and quietly acquiesced. "Okay, Mama." He snuggled up against her, laying his head upon her breast. "Kieran stay with Mama."

Meriel turned and would have made her way back across the room to Gage's side, but the scowling leader motioned two guards to waylay her. "Bring the female and young one to me," he ordered, a cold, flat look in his eyes.

The two guards led her and Kieran to stand on the dais before the Volan leader. For an instant, Meriel's gaze met that of his compatriot. Scorn and utter loathing filled her. She glanced quickly away.

"I did what I had to do," Torman's Volan said, stepping forward. "I followed orders to ensure the survival of my species, just as you would for—"

"Enough!" his leader snapped. "No explanations are necessary. The decision was never yours to make."

Torman's Volan bowed low and stepped back. The Volan leader, a heavyset, hirsute man of medium height, turned to Meriel. Sweat trickled down his flushed face as his pale, dilated eyes surveyed her. "You look strong and healthy enough. Your body should sustain one of ours for the maximum time."

Pelum, Meriel thought. Pelum had looked much like the Volan leader the last time she'd seen him. As had her mother shortly before she died.

"And yours won't last much longer for you, will it?" she inquired, beginning to collate and interpret all the signs she'd unconsciously noted in the past several months. "Even now, the strain on your slave is showing. How long will it be before you need a new body?"

"Soon enough," the Volan admitted grudgingly. His glance swerved to scan Gage. "His would have suited admirably, if we didn't need his body for a more strategic purpose. But, most unfortunately for me, we do."

With an imperious motion, the leader signaled Gage forward. When he wasn't prompt in responding, his two guards dragged him along. They halted at the base of the dais.

"This is your mate, your child." The Volan leader grabbed Meriel by the arm to jerk her to him. "I am told such possessions are of inestimable value to the males of your species."

Gage eyed him.

"So, you don't care to corroborate our data?" The leader shrugged. "No matter. We've studied your kind long enough to know it is true. You will allow yourself to be enslaved, or we will kill them both."

"And why is my permission suddenly so vital?" Gage demanded. "You've only to wait until I finally sleep and you can easily enslave me."

"Perhaps. But we've no time to spare, and I'd imagine you'd be a difficult enslavement at any rate. I'd prefer you willingly allowed the process—and allowed it immediately."

"Be damned!" Gage fought against his captors, savagely twisting to be free, but the guards' Volan-induced strength was too great for him. He finally slumped in their clasp, gasping for breath, furious with his rising sense of helplessness.

"Calling down curses won't change their fate, only hasten it." The alien leader indicated Kieran. "Bring me the young one."

"No!" wailed Meriel as one guard imprisoned her arms and the other wrenched Kieran away.

A bewildered look spread across the boy's face, his lower lip began to wobble, and he, too, broke out into a loud wail. "Mama! I want Mama!"

As Gage watched in impotent despair, his son was carried up onto the dais and placed in the Volan leader's hands. Shifting the child, the alien withdrew a small case. With a flick of his thumb, he released an evil-looking thorn.

"No! Oh, Gods, no!" Meriel screamed as she recognized the deadly nexus thorn. "Don't hurt my son! Take me instead!"

The leader's face twisted in a wolfish smile. "But then who would be left to plead for the young one's life?"

"Take my body instead," she pleaded, the tears coursing down her face. "I am the Queen of Tenua. I can go wherever you meant to send Gage. I already said I was strong enough to sustain one of you for the maximum time!"

"But I already have other plans for you. It's the male we need help convincing."

He grasped Kieran's head and bent it to bare his neck. The little boy squirmed, but could do nothing to free himself. Ever so slowly, his alien captor lowered the nexus thorn until it was only millimeters from pricking the child's neck.

Meriel's gaze swung to Gage's, an anguished entreaty gleaming in her eyes.

It met and intensified his own sense of defeat. He had known it would come to something like this. Known and dreaded it throughout the long night. But to now finally face the inevitable, to allow such a desecration and degradation, to surrender to enslavement!

If it had been only his life at stake, he'd have died before yielding to such a fate. But that option had never been his. The Volans had planned too well, studied him and his kind too thoroughly, to ever permit such an occurrence.

Gage swallowed hard, choking back the surge of sheer terror that engulfed him. There was nothing to be done but submit. Nothing for either him *or* Meriel. He had seen the look in too many killers' eyes to doubt the intent burning in the Volan leader's. The alien would kill his son without a second's hesitation.

"Have done with it then," Gage rasped, his voice raw, rough with despair. "But only swear that you'll send my son back as he came, to his own people."

The alien leader's eyes gleamed with triumph. "You humans are all too easily led by your emotions. It will be your ultimate downfall in the end." He motioned to a Volan who stood to the left of the dais, holding one of the strange-looking globes in his hands.

"Come, the time is upon us. Bring me the Volan who will assume the body of this male."

Chapter Fifteen

The Volan bearing the globe stepped forward, placing the container in his leader's hands. The alien took it, eyed it for an instant, then smiled. He held it out for Gage's view.

"A most efficient life-support system, wouldn't you say? This biosphere can maintain one of our entities for almost ten of your cycles."

"How?" Gage demanded hoarsely. "How does the enslavement work?"

The leader studied him, a faint gleam in his eyes. "And if I told you that, you'd know our secrets, our vulnerabilities. It would be a poor tactical maneuver to reveal that to an enemy."

"Then you must doubt the strength of your techniques, to hesitate to tell me anything." Gage cocked a speculative brow. "There *are* ways, then, to overcome a Volan mind enslavement."

His captor's eyes narrowed. "Think that if you will. In all the hundreds of cycles since we began this process, no one has escaped our hold."

"Then why the hesitation in revealing the process? I'd think you'd gain a perverse satisfaction in sharing your superior technology. Besides, in our culture, it is customary to grant the last wishes of a dying man."

The Volan gave a snort of disdain. "Is it now? And your last wish is to know more of us? Truly, you humanoids have the strangest beliefs."

Gage didn't reply.

A grin spread across the alien's face. "Well, I suppose it would do no harm since, in a sense, *you* really are dying." He lifted the globe again and shook it gently. A bioluminescent glow filled the thin outer layer that, until now, had been invisible.

"Those are the life forms known as temeritas." The Volan lifted his gaze briefly to Gage. "They maintain our spirit entities through a biochemical process similar to that in the neural network we feed on in our hosts. When the time comes, the temeritas also prepare the route into a slave's nervous system, easing our transfer from the biosphere into a life form."

It was all too clever, too perfect, Gage thought with a rising sense of despair. Nausea roiled in his gut, but he forced himself to go on. Perhaps something, some small bit of this information, might aid them at a later date.

"How? How does the transfer occur?"

"Warmth, either from friction as when I shook the globe, or the heat of a slave's body when the biosphere is pressed to its neck, stirs the temeritas to gravitate toward that warmth. The outer shell of the sphere is semipermeable. The temeritas migrate through it, penetrating the slave's body and its neural network. Once the way to the brain is prepared, the Volan entity follows."

"How efficient," Gage muttered.

"And successful," the Volan leader agreed. He rose from his chair. "But enough of the science lesson. It is past time we commence the enslavement."

He motioned the guards to lead Gage forward, then handed the globe back to the Volan who had originally produced it. As the alien strode over to Gage, Gage's guards forced him to his knees, then shoved his head down, baring the back of his neck.

Numbed by the horror of it all, Meriel had watched and listened in a stunned silence. But in that moment as Gage was pushed to the ground and prepared for enslavement, she finally came alive. With a wild cry, she twisted free and ran to him. Throwing herself down, Meriel flung her arms about him and buried her face against his neck.

"Ah, by all that is sacred!" she sobbed brokenly. "I can't bear any more! What will I do, what will any of us do, when you are gone? I don't have the strength to watch this happen and not go out of my mind! Ah, Gage, I love you. I need you! I can't bear this!"

He lifted his head. The aching gentleness gleaming in eyes face took Meriel's breath away.

"You *must* bear it. There is no other choice for you, little one. When I am gone, you must go on. For yourself, for Kieran, for us all. What

I have left unfinished, you must finish. Our love can allow no less."

"I-I can't, Gage," she choked. "I haven't your strength, your courage. And I'm s-so afraid!"

"Then it was all a waste."

"Wh-what?" She paused in stunned incredulity. "What was a waste?"

"Our love. It accomplished nothing, and will leave nothing of value behind."

Meriel eyed him for a moment more, then comprehension, followed swiftly by a wrathful glare flared in her eyes. "Don't ever say that about what we had! Our love is a beautiful thing, strong and true and of the greatest value."

"Then fight for it, Meriel!" Gage cried, struggling to find some way, any way, to bolster her courage. And bolster his as well for the horror to come. "Carry it with you until we meet again. Then call it forth from me, as you promised you would. But until then, don't give up. Don't fail me!"

Confusion darkened her eyes. "But how can I . . . ? I, too, will soon be enslaved—"

"Enough!" an irate voice pierced the misty world that, for a brief moment in eternity, had been only theirs.

Meriel started, lifted her gaze to the Volan leader glowering down at them, then turned back to Gage. A tremulous smile lifted the corners of her mouth. She gently stroked his forehead, brows, nose, and lips, as if memorizing them for the long days and nights ahead.

"I'll come for you if I can," she whispered, then rose and stepped back from him. "I promise it," her lips mouthed silently.

Her guards moved forward, pulling her around to stand several meters behind Gage.

He followed her progress for as long as he could, forcing one last smile through the anguish that twisted his face into a tortured mask. Then, with a deep, shuddering sigh, Gage turned his gaze up to the alien leader.

"You still owe me an oath." His eyes slammed into the Volan's.

The alien cocked a brow. "Indeed? And what might that be?"

"My son. Swear, by whatever is of consequence to your kind, that you'll spare his life and send him back to his people untouched by your foul influences. I must hear that promise from your lips before I'll submit to this . . . this vile, loathsome act."

"Vile and loathsome is it?" The Volan laughed, the sound hollow, bitter. "As it is for us as well, you can be sure. But what choice do any of us really have?"

He retracted the nexus thorn into its case and handed Kieran to Torman. "The oath is sworn, before us all. I've no need for the child once I have you. Besides, it's not worth our time or effort to enslave the young. Their bodies aren't mature enough to withstand our entities. Far better to allow them to grow to suit our needs later.

"Now, enough of this." The leader motioned once more to the guards who held Gage. "Prepare him."

The two guards shoved Gage's head down. One grasped his hair to anchor him firmly in place. The

Volan who held the biosphere stepped around the dais and walked over to Gage. For an instant suspended in time, he held the globe motionless, then swirled it to stimulate the temeritas. A scattering of green luminescence instantly flared in the container.

Meriel's horrified gaze swung to Gage on his knees, his big body shaking with the effort to remain still and allow the impending enslavement to occur. In a flash of insight, she comprehended the full extent of his sacrifice. A sense of his abject fear, his rising nausea, his frustrated helplessness—and the superhuman will that kept it all in check—overwhelmed her.

Her fists clenched at her side. Her breathing came in ragged gasps. But, all the while, Meriel's gaze never left Gage. It was so very little compared to what he would suffer, but she'd be with him to the end. She could do no less. He was everything to her.

Ever so slowly, the glowing biosphere was lowered toward Gage's neck, then touched it. The outer shell appeared to soften, mold into the contours at the base of his spine. The glow brightened. The light within began to swirl and churn wildly.

Suddenly Gage cried out. He stiffened, then arched backward, his face contorted in agony. His mouth opened. A choking sound rattled in his throat. And, all the while, the biosphere remained attached to his spine, joined as much from the contact with its now membranous exterior as from the Volan's hold.

The luminescent glow slowly dissipated, as if

the globe's contents were diffusing through the membrane into Gage. Gradually his spasms eased. His powerful frame went slack. A strange stillness came over his body.

When the biosphere was empty, the Volan pulled it away. He stepped back and glanced up at his leader. "The enslavement is complete, Exalted One."

The Volan leader smiled, then turned to glance down at Gage. "Rise, Mardant. Welcome to your new body and new life. Rise, and hear your mission."

With a slight movement of his shoulders, Gage's Volan shrugged off the hold of the two guards and lithely climbed to his feet. He bowed low. "I am at your command, Exalted One."

"As it should be," his alien compatriot replied. "Your directive is of the utmost importance if we are to expeditiously complete the overthrow of the Imperium. You will leave here immediately and transport to the planet Bellator. Once there, you will seek out King Falkan's emissary, Teran Ardane."

He signaled another Volan, who stepped forward with yet another softly glowing biosphere. The alien handed the globe to Gage's Volan.

"That is for Teran Ardane," the leader said, indicating the biosphere. "Either enslave him or kill him. One way or another, he will no longer hinder our ultimate mission."

Gage bowed again. "It will be as you command."

"Then go, and don't fail the hive."

Turning, Gage strode from the room, but not

before his gaze slammed into Meriel's who stood directly behind him. As his glance met hers, her blood turned to ice; her breath solidified in her body.

Flat and hard, his eyes looked straight through her.

"Mama. C-cold."

Kieran's childish cry wrenched Meriel from her anguished thoughts. She pulled him more snugly to her, wrapping her arms about his chubby little body to pull him into a more compact, warmth-conserving ball.

"It'll be all right soon, sweet lad," Meriel murmured, tenderly kissing his tousled head of hair. "Cuddle close to Mama and you'll soon be warm."

"Mama. S-scared."

The quaver in Kieran's voice plucked at Meriel's heart. These might be the last few moments they'd have together as mother and son. The last few, most precious of moments . . . before the Volans came to enslave her. Somehow in that time she must comfort him for all the cycles of his life. She must instill in him the memories of her as she now was, so he would never doubt her love or wonder if she'd left him of her own volition.

"There's nothing to be afraid of." Meriel pushed Kieran back and tilted his small face up to hers. "Mama loves you and always will. But if somehow we're separated, or if Mama seems to change, it doesn't mean she doesn't love you any less. I'll always love you, no matter what happens. Do you believe that?"

Kieran nodded. "Yes, Mama."

"Good." Footsteps echoed down the corridor. Dread congealed the blood in Meriel's veins. They were coming for her.

She pulled her son back to her, savoring the warmth, the softness, the sweet essence of him. Never, Meriel vowed, no matter what they did to her, would she forget the love she had for her son, or for his father. They would never take that from her. The memory, the emotions, were embedded in every cell of her body, would course through her with every beat of her heart.

A metallic key control clinked as it was slid into its slot. The door ground open. There was the sound of soft footfalls—a single visitor— moving forward, then halting beside her, but Meriel refused to acknowledge the Volan's presence. She wanted to block out the awful reality of her impending fate for as long as possible, to absorb every last nuance of this moment and her child. It was all that was left, all she'd ever—

Kieran squirmed in her grasp. "Torman. Play with Torman!"

Meriel's heart faltered, then commenced a wild pounding. She glanced up.

Torman stood there, and for a crazy moment hope flared. Then the dim green glow of the biosphere he carried caught her eye.

It was Rand, not Torman, Meriel reminded herself. All hope died. Dark despair engulfed her.

"Come to see the task done to completion, have you?" she taunted, determined to defy him until the end. Whatever happened, she would not cry, nor shame herself by begging. "It would have been a kinder act to have sent someone other than you, but then, when has a Volan ever been known to be kind or compassionate?"

"A curse on kindness and compassion!" Rand spat out the words with savage vehemence. "You humans allow too much besides clear, cold logic to rule you. It only confuses things, clouds the truth, and lessens the importance of what really matters."

"And what is that?" Meriel demanded. "The survival of a species that should have died long ago, when they first tossed aside concern not only for themselves but for others? But survival ceases to have value once love and self-respect are gone. Perhaps that's why your people turned to the collective consciousness and hive mentality. You couldn't face the agony of living at the expense of others. And now there's no individual conscience left to torment, is there?"

Rand squatted beside her and pulled her up to him. "There shouldn't be, curse you! It's indeed agony. But the Mother Ship has lost contact with me long enough to allow me to think, to feel on my own. And I don't like what I am anymore."

He gave her a hard shake and held up the biosphere. "This is your new Volan, woman. I've decided that the only way to rid myself of the guilt and sense of betrayal I've been feeling for my own kind, ever since I met you and yours, was to be the one to enslave you."

The biosphere trembled in his hand, the movement once again stimulating the temeritas to glow. He shoved it almost into her face. Sensitized to the relative warmth emanating from her in the chill room, the globe flared into brilliant luminescence. Meriel stared at it, mesmerized by the light . . . and the sense of impending doom.

"Kieran," Meriel whispered. "Promise me you'll be the one to take him home. He knows you, trusts you. I don't want a stranger to take him home!"

"Is that all you care about? What happens to your son?" Rand's face contorted in rage. "Rather, what about you? Why aren't you begging me for mercy? Begging me not to enslave you?"

He pulled her up until they were face-to-face, his warm breath a whisper of air upon her skin. "We almost had you enslaved that night in your room. If Bardwin hadn't been nearby, we would have succeeded, too. The temeritas had already entered your body, were preparing the way, when you wakened. Because of it, the Volan awaiting you in her biosphere died."

"And the temeritas inside me?"

"Isn't that obvious?" he sneered. "It's a symbiotic relationship. One needs the other."

"Just like any other being. None of us can survive alone." She stared up into his tormented blue eyes. "How have you done it for so long? Haven't you ever been lonely, or wondered if there were more?"

"Never!" he ground out the word. "Never, until I met you!"

Meriel blinked in surprise. "Me? What have I to do with this?"

Rand glowered back at her. "Everything, and nothing. I'd never have become sensitized to your appeal if the cursed Bellatorians hadn't jam-

med communications from the Mother Ship."
He released Meriel with a jerk and rose to his
feet. "But they did, and nothing has ever been
the same."

She stared up at him, clutching Kieran to her.
Gazing down at Meriel, Rand was flooded with
the most compelling urge to pull her to him, to
taste, for the first time in his existence, the feel
of a woman upon his lips. He was totally joined
with the nervous system of his slave. He'd feel
everything, even if his upper neuron interpreta-
tions might be slightly different.

Somehow, though, Rand sensed that the experience would be pleasurable. That was a surprising
revelation. He quickly attributed it to one of those
erratic memory breakthroughs of his slave. There
was no other plausible explanation—at least not
one he dared accept.

Suddenly there were just too many revelations
about himself he didn't want to accept. But one
thing he was certain of, and would accept. He
couldn't enslave Meriel, or allow anyone else to
do so. And the only way to ensure that was to
help her escape, then, once she was safely back
in her palace, guard her from other Volan entan-
glements.

Rand picked up a sharp-edged stone from the
ground and punctured the biosphere. The low
whistle of air rushing from the globe's interior
filled the room. The container slowly collapsed.

"Wh-what are you doing?" Meriel cried. Disbelief shot through her, then a wondering, cautious
joy.

"Eliminating the Volan entity that should have

been yours. You *have* been enslaved, however. Act accordingly in the presence of the others here."

"My . . . my thanks," Meriel stammered. "I never dared hope—"

"Stand up." He flipped open a small case and motioned for her to rise.

When Meriel did so, Rand turned her away from him, brushed the hair from her neck, and began to rub some cream from the container over the base of her spine.

"Ouch, that burns!" Meriel tried to squirm out of his clasp. "Stop it, Rand!"

"Hold still. I'm almost done," he commanded. "The absorption of the temeritas creates a temporary allergic response at the entry site. It is a telltale sign that you'll be checked for to verify enslavement. This cream contains an irritant that will create the same appearance as the rash."

Meriel bore the discomfort in silence, elated that all her fears of what the Volans would do to her were no more. She still couldn't quite believe that Rand had decided to help her, or that they would soon escape. Now, if there were still time to reach Gage . . .

Doubts assailed Meriel. What would she do once she found him? Though she'd gleaned vital information about Volans in the past several hours, none of it would aid her in freeing Gage of his Volan. Perhaps Rand knew.

She flipped back her hair and turned to him when he finally seemed satisfied that he'd irritated her skin sufficiently. The questions hovered on the edge of expression before Meriel thought better of it. Rand had made no mention of helping Gage, and his motives in assisting her were still unclear.

Meriel made a quick decision to withhold her plan to go after Gage until she and Rand were back in Eremita. Then, if Rand refused to accompany her, he could be detained while she went on to Bellator.

"When can we leave?" She carefully chose her words. "The longer I remain, the greater the chance they'll discover I'm not enslaved. And the greater the danger you are in."

"Arrangements are being made even now to transport us to where our skim crafts are hidden. Our leader wants you back in your palace as soon as possible. You were to corroborate Bardwin's story if there were any questions about his unexpected arrival on Bellator."

"And is that where you still plan to take me? Back to Eremita?"

He shot her an enigmatic look. "It seems the best plan. I-I'm not certain what I'll do after that. This decision to betray my own kind is not an easy one. I'm not sure how far past sparing you I want to go."

Compassion flooded her. Rand was risking everything. His newly accepted emotions that allowed for the humane act of rescuing her were still too fresh, too unfamiliar, for him to deal with comfortably, much less utilize consistently in making decisions. She must not press him too hard just yet. He must be permitted to work all this through in his own time.

Meriel laid a hand on his arm. "I understand. Please, if I make some demand upon you that

you cannot agree to, tell me. The formation of
a conscience is a difficult process, but one we
humans have had all the cycles of our youth to
develop. I know you will need time. I will try to
give it to you."

Piercing blue eyes captured hers, holding her
in a gentle prison of wonderment and warmth.
Meriel's breath caught in her throat. She had never experienced such a sensation of bonding, of
total understanding of another. It startled, yet
gladdened her all the same. She was sharing in
the birth of a person, a soul, within a fully formed
body.

A body that was not his to possess.

With a quick mental shrug, Meriel flung that
thought aside. For the time being she needed
Rand's help, and to help her he needed a body.
The morality of his enslavement of Torman would
have to wait.

He disengaged from her clasp. "I'll return for
you in a half hour. Prepare yourself. From the
moment I next enter this room, you must act the
Volan. Do you think you can do it?"

"Act cold and distant? Emotionless?" Meriel
nodded. "Yes. Even we humans have our heartless moments. You could ask Gage about that."

At the wistful note in Meriel's voice, a strange,
angry pain plucked at Rand's heart. He shoved it
away. In time, Meriel would have to accept that
Bardwin, as she knew him, was gone. There was
no way safely to rid a slave of its Volan unless the
Volan wished to leave. And Mardant would never
leave Bardwin willingly.

"Good," he growled. "It's of the greatest importance that you fool the others. All our lives may depend on it."

He turned then and strode from the room, the heavy door once more grinding shut behind him. Meriel stood there for a time, stunned into immobility by the sudden turn of events—and her great good fortune. She had escaped enslavement . . . Rand would help . . .

A fierce resolve filled her. There was much yet to be done to rid the Imperium of the Volan threat, but the first steps had been taken. There was hope in the revelation that the evil aliens possessed the rudiments of a conscience, that beneath the constant bombardment of mind-numbing directives there were beings still capable of compassion and independent thought. There was hope in the possibility that another way might yet be found to prevent the total annihilation of either the Imperium or the Volans. And now there was renewed hope for a life with the man she loved.

If only she could reach him in time. If only she could find some way to free him from his Volan. But those, most unfortunately, were both very big ifs.

"No." Rand vehemently shook his head. "It's hopeless. There's no way to free Bardwin from his Volan master."

Meriel glanced up from the report Brace Ardane had prepared on the status of the ongoing evacuation. She closed the embossed domare-hide folder that held the papers, shot Brace an exasperated look, then tried again.

"I won't accept that without further proof," she

persisted patiently, "but, be that as it may, the Volan inside Gage must be stopped. Will or won't you accompany me to Bellator?"

Rand chewed his lower lip in indecision, then caught himself. By the collective consciousness, he was taking on human mannerisms at an astounding rate!

He grimaced at his own eagerness to assimilate every nuance of these beings. "I didn't rescue you from one set of Volans to allow you to fall victim to others. Bardwin isn't the only slave at the royal court."

"Teran needs to be warned!" Brace leaned forward on the table. "He needs to know about Gage as well. There's too much at stake to waste another—"

"No." Rand's calm command cut the Bellatorian short. "There's no way of knowing if the message would be intercepted. And our one advantage is in taking Mardant by surprise. If he suspects a betrayal, he'll immediately kill your brother. Not to mention"—he glanced at Meriel—"that we'll lose the additional advantage inherent in the Volan hierarchy's ignorance of your lack of enslavement."

"Fine," she agreed, struggling to maintain a semblance of calm. "We'll not warn Teran until we can talk with him in private, and we'll not let Gage see us until we've a foolproof plan to take him. But, one way or another, the Volan within him needs to be dealt with before he succeeds in his mission."

She paused to eye Rand intently. "Are you with me or not? I'm leaving for Bellator within the hour."

He should have known it would come to this, Rand thought in rising frustration. Once he took the step that placed him on the side of the Imperium, he could only become more and more involved. And there was no way to convince Meriel that her hope of regaining the mind of her Bellatorian lover was futile, save allowing her to see it for herself.

"It's as I said before," Rand sighed. "I didn't rescue you to lose you again. Besides, you'll need me if you wish to take Mardant alive. Few of your species are powerful enough to overcome a Volan."

Meriel smiled. "Thank you. I'll admit, I didn't know what I'd do if you wouldn't come with me."

"But you would have gone anyway, wouldn't you?"

A haunted expression glimmered in her eyes. "I have to. I promised Gage. And I won't desert him when he needs me most."

"Have it your way. Not that it'll do you, or him, any good."

"Perhaps not, but I have to try." She turned to Brace. "We'll send word as soon as it's safe. In the meanwhile, continue with the evacuation as planned. It appears to be going very well. I thank you for that."

He scowled. "I'd rather be transporting with you. I don't like the fact that my brother's in danger and I can't be there for him. It's obvious why Teran wouldn't believe this Volan, with or without his disguise, but he'd believe me just as readily as you. Why not stay behind and take over the evacuation? I can go in your stead. This could get very violent, and no place for a Queen to be."

"Gage needs me." Meriel's chin lifted in stubborn resolve. "I *have* to go, Brace. There's no one who can do what I can do for Gage."

He eyed her skeptically. "Truly, Meriel, I have the deepest faith in the power of love, but to take on a Volan . . ."

Meriel rose from the table. "I *will* succeed. I have to."

"A day, Domina," he warned, a grim light in his eyes. "You have a day before I transport to Bellator myself. We can spare no more time in developing a plan to combat the Volans, now that we possess such valuable information about them."

"A day is fair enough." She stepped forward to offer him her hand. "Farewell, Brace Ardane. It's past time that I depart. Your brother is in too much danger for me to tarry longer."

His large hand engulfed hers. "Farewell, Domina." His glance moved, locking with Rand's. "Take care of her. Help her."

The Volan nodded. "She's the only reason I go. Turning against my own doesn't sit well with me, but I'll do what I can for Meriel."

Brace's mouth quirked wryly. "Then you help us in the bargain. And, I think, ultimately help your own kind as well."

Rand gave a bitter, disparaging laugh. He rose from the table as Meriel began to walk toward the door, intent on following her. "There's no help for us. Our continued survival is your destruction. And our destruction," he grimly shot over his shoulder, "is your only hope of survival."

*   *   *

"T-Torman's a V-Volan?" Dian breathed, her words tremulous, disbelieving. "Ah, no, Meriel! Tell me it's not so!"

Meriel took her friend by the arm and led her over to the chairs placed before her bedchamber hearth. She motioned for her to sit, then took the opposite chair.

"It's true enough," Meriel admitted, "but the Volan who inhabits Torman is different from the rest. His name is Rand and—"

"I don't want to know his name!" the other woman snapped. "He took my beloved away from me! I hate him! That's all that matters."

"I know, I know," Meriel soothed, leaning forward to take Dian's hand. "There will never be any acceptable justification for taking over another's life and body. I didn't mean to condone what he did—even if to the Volan way of thinking it meant survival of their species. I'm just trying to explain how valuable an ally he's become. We need Rand's help, desperately so, if we're ever to defeat the Volans."

"What does it matter?" Tears welled in the maidservant's eyes and streamed down her cheeks. "Torman is gone. There's no way to get a Volan out of a body once it's enslaved."

Meriel returned her gaze, silent.

A wild hope flickered in Dian's breast. She leaned forward. "Well, is there?"

Her friend inhaled a deep breath. "Rand claims there isn't, unless the Volan wishes voluntarily to leave."

"Then it *is* possible?" Excitement gleamed in

Dian's eyes. "I *can* have my Torman back?"

"Dian, you must try to understand." Meriel shifted uncomfortably in her chair. "I can't ask that of Rand, not now, not when we need him so."

"Need him more than you need Torman, is that it?" The brown-haired woman jerked back, anger twisting her pretty features. "It doesn't matter what he did, only that he's found some ploy to worm his way into your affections! Gods, Meriel, I didn't think I'd ever live to see you turn your back on right and wrong for the sake of expediency!" Dian's lips curled in disdain. "You've finally learned, and learned well, how to rule, haven't you?"

Pain lanced through Meriel. "I know you don't mean that." She stood. "He's outside, Dian. I'll give you a short time to speak together before we depart. Perhaps if you talk with—"

"Never! Do you hear me? Never!" Her friend leaped to her feet. "If you truly love me, Meriel, don't ask it of me."

"No, I won't, if that's what you want." Tears filled Meriel's eyes. "You've suffered enough."

She hesitated, then touched Dian's face with a gentle hand. "It's farewell, then. I must go."

"Go safely, my friend." Her maidservant wiped the tears away with the back of her hand. "I wish you fortune in rescuing Gage. The tragedy would be too great if we both lost the men we loved."

Yes, too great a tragedy indeed, Meriel thought as she departed her bedchamber and joined Rand in the corridor. Her glance momentarily met that of the man-alien she was forced to depend upon—

for her own life as well as Gage's. He smiled, a tentative upturning of firm, sensitive lips.

Compassion and a bittersweet pain flooded her. Wasn't Rand's fate equally as tragic as Gage's and Torman's? All too unwillingly, he had been awakened to an existence he'd never known yet now desired with every fiber of his being. An existence he deserved as much a chance at as the rest of them. Yet an existence he had no right to take from another in order to possess for himself.

It was all so very tragic.

Meriel shoved the consideration firmly aside and turned her thoughts to the task ahead.

Chapter Sixteen

They arrived on Bellator a little past midday, transporting to the capital of Rector. Meriel was dressed as a lad, her hair tucked up in a loose cap, an oversized brown tunic shoved into dark green breeches, and soft, ankle-high boots on her feet. Rand wore an eye patch, false mustache, and similar nondescript clothing. More than anything else, they'd no wish to attract attention.

The journey to the palace was tedious, the city walkways jammed with shoppers on market day. Mouthwatering scents of fresh-baked bread and smoked meats hanging on display mingled with the more delicate fragrances of flower bouquets and spice and perfume booths. Happy shouts and good-natured arguments filled the air as people pushed and jostled each other to gain a closer look or better bargaining position. At any other time Meriel would have joined in, reveling in the anonymity that permitted freer access to a way of life she'd only seen from afar.

But not this day, she grimly reminded herself. There was business of far graver import afoot than a carefree wish to pretend to be someone she wasn't. Gage was here, intent on a deadly mission, and must be stopped. Somehow the Volan in him must be eliminated as well. Somehow, someway, she *must* find a way to save the man she loved.

Rand didn't think it possible, and neither did Brace. At the recollection of their meeting several hours ago, Meriel choked back a surge of despair. She didn't dare let herself lose hope. Without hope, there was only one fate left for Gage. And she wasn't ready to accept it.

"The palace can't be too far ahead," Rand muttered, drawing her into an alley. "Keep your head down and eyes averted when we arrive. There's no telling where Mardant is. If he recognizes either one of us, we lose our advantage. Once inside, I'll find a place for you to await me while I search out Teran Ardane."

"But Ga—Mardant could just as easily recognize you," Meriel protested. "Your disguise isn't *that* good."

Rand grinned. "I have no intention of roaming the palace in full view of everyone. There's yet another power we Volans have that your kind doesn't know about."

"Oh? And what is that?"

"We can cloak our presence from view and go anywhere we wish without notice."

"How convenient for you," Meriel muttered dryly. "But then so can Mardant, and any other Volans that may be in the palace. And won't they be able to see you even if the rest of us can't?"

"Yes," Rand admitted. "That's a risk, but I do have some skill in stealth. And even a Volan can't see through walls or around pillars. I'll be fine, Meriel."

She forced a wan smile. "I know you will. But I'll worry nonetheless."

"For a Volan?" Rand forced down a surge of warmth and a corresponding impulse to take Meriel into his arms. He chuckled instead and shot her a teasing grin. "Really, femina, if you're not careful, your concern will go to my head."

"And if you're not careful," she teased back, "you'll soon be so human you'll actually begin to expect it."

His grin faded. "I fear you're right, but I'm not so sure I like my rapid integration of your species' mannerisms and outlook. It's rather frightening at times. I'm afraid I'm losing my Volan identity."

"And what have you lost but someone else's predetermined concept of what you should be?" Meriel laid a comforting hand on his arm. "I'd say, instead, that you are only beginning to discover your true self."

"Perhaps," Rand muttered, "but the process is damned uncomfortable. Suddenly there are too many choices. I can now make the wrong decision."

"Free will can be a big responsibility. But I wouldn't have it any other way."

Rand pulled back from the clasp on his arm that was suddenly too uncomfortable, too stirring. And pulled back, as well, from the violet eyes gazing up at him, luminous and beguiling. No matter how much he assumed the outward appearance and mannerisms of these people, he'd never be one of them. Never be permitted to assimilate so thoroughly that he'd be accepted by a female of the species.

No, as much as he found himself desiring it to the contrary, Meriel—or any other woman—was not for him. He must remind himself of that inescapable fact over and over. He could help these humans, but he'd never truly be one of them.

"Come," he growled, his voice harsh with anger and frustration. "The sooner we get into the palace, the sooner we find Mardant and thwart his plans."

Startled by the sudden change in Rand, Meriel shot him a puzzled glance, then obediently followed as he turned and strode back into the surging mass of humanity. Through the narrow, twisting thoroughfare they went. Finally they caught the first glimpse of gray walls and turreted buildings stacked one atop the other. Each spire was adorned with a colorful flag that flapped wildly in the stiff breeze gusting overhead.

A long, broad expanse of steps led to the first pillared doorway of the main building. The entrance was crowded with people awaiting their turn to pass inspection of the soldiers standing guard. Rand and Meriel took their place in line.

"Our first obstacle to overcome," he muttered under his breath.

Meriel smiled and jangled the coins in the pouch that hung from her waist. "Guards are the same the Imperium over. A few coins will improve their disposition toward us as no amount of eloquence ever could."

"And one fine example of how free will can be turned to less than admirable purposes."

She graced him with a grudging nod. "Your point is well taken. But, in this case, it serves us well."

"That it does, little Queen." Rand took her elbow and guided her forward. "That it does."

Not long thereafter, a recompensed guard happily motioned them through the huge outer doors and into the stone-tiled receiving hall. Rand scanned the big, high-ceilinged room, found no sign of Mardant, then moved on to search out some alcove where he could temporarily deposit Meriel. A small side room that also served as a waiting area was the eventual choice.

"Await me here." He motioned to a chair positioned before a wall lined with books. "It's best if I search out Lord Ardane alone and bring him to you. The risk of Mardant finding us out is considerably less if you're not along to hamper me."

She knew he was right, though the thought of passively awaiting his return gnawed at her pride. "How long?" Meriel demanded. "I can't stay here forever."

Rand's gaze narrowed. "Your roaming the palace on your own will only increase the chances of alerting Mardant. You *must* await me here!"

She sighed her acquiescence. "As you wish. But I'll only wait until sunset, no longer. There's no way for me to know if something happens to you. If you're hurt or killed, I must carry on."

"Fair enough." Rand turned to go. "All I ask is that you give me a chance. I don't want you endangered unnecessarily."

"Get out of here," she laughed. "Your time is already racing away."

He grinned and strode from the room.

Time passed with lumbering slowness. For the first few hours, Meriel found it impossible to sit still. She paced the confines of the small room, took down several volumes from a bookshelf, and then couldn't read a word.

Through it all, she cursed her sense of impotence. Doubts assailed her. What if Gage's Volan discovered Rand? What if Teran refused to believe Rand and had him imprisoned? And if Gage had already managed to enslave Teran, what would Rand do then?

Worse still, what if, even if Rand returned with Gage, she was unable to reach him and drive the Volan out? What if, despite all her grandiose claims to the contrary, love *wasn't* enough? Or, horror of horrors, *her* love wasn't enough?

Fear wafted through Meriel, feeding her self-doubts and weakening her resolve. She rose once again to restlessly pace the room, as if the movement would empower her and set it all back into perspective. But still the questions rose, relentlessly pounding against the back door of her mind.

Who was she to think her strength was equal to the task ahead? All she'd ever possessed was an arrogance and callous indifference for the safety of others. Already she'd endangered Rand, and probably Teran as well.

But what other choice was there? Desert Gage without a fight? Allow Rand to kill him, and live the rest of her days wondering if she could have made a difference?

No, Meriel decided for the hundredth time as she finally flung herself down in a chair. As terrifying as the confrontation was to come, she must face it. She couldn't let Gage down.

Yet, as the day burned away, the tension grew to almost unbearable proportions. More times than she dared count, Meriel strode to the door, intent on taking matters into her own hands, before reason—and Rand's parting words—halted her. Then, with a frustrated sigh, she'd force herself to turn and take her seat again.

The ancient tower bells chimed the passing hours. Finally, at the fifth hour past midday, the hollow sound of footsteps echoing off the stone floors drew near. Meriel leaped to her feet, dragged damp palms down her cloth-covered thighs, and anxiously glanced toward the doorway. What if it were Teran and Gage instead of Rand? What if they were now the enemy? What would she do?

She grabbed the stunner off her belt and set it to high stun, then covered it with the back of her hand and lowered it to her side. It was meager defense against the potential threat, but it gave her comfort. She'd at least go down fighting.

Rand entered first, followed by Teran. Meriel eyed them both for the span of an inhaled breath, her gaze swinging from one man to the other.

Then Teran smiled and she knew it was all right. Gage hadn't gotten to him yet.

The tall Bellatorian held out his arms and Meriel ran to him.

"Welcome to House Ardane," his deep voice rumbled beneath the face she pressed to his chest. "I'll admit to some surprise at finding the Queen of Tenua dressed as a lad, hiding in one of our antechambers, but considering the purpose of your visit . . ."

"Gage." Blushingly, Meriel disengaged from Teran's comforting clasp. "Have you had a chance to talk with him yet?"

He nodded. "Yes. He seemed quite himself, if the truth be told. Is Torman's tale true?"

"That Gage is enslaved by a Volan? That Torman is really Rand, a Volan himself? Yes, it's all true."

Teran's eyes narrowed. He shot Rand a considering glance. "He didn't volunteer that particular bit of information about himself. A Volan, is he?"

"A Volan who made the decision to aid our cause," Meriel hastened to add. "He saved me from enslavement and transported willingly to Bellator to help Gage as well."

"Indeed?" Teran's brow lifted as he turned the full force of his attention on Rand. "And how do you propose extricating the Volan from Gage? I wasn't aware that was possible."

Rand shrugged. "There's no way to free a person from his Volan master unless the Volan wishes to leave. I've already explained that to Meriel, but she refuses to listen. I came only to foil Mardant's directive, which was to enslave or kill you."

"Mardant?" Teran frowned. "Is that the name of the Volan who inhabits my friend?"

The other man nodded.

"What do you suggest, if we can't get the Volan out of Gage?"

"Kill them both. It's the only way. And it needs to be swift and unexpected, or Mardant will notify the Mother Ship and your advantage will be lost."

"No!" Meriel stepped forward. "I don't believe that's the only way. Gage is still there, beneath the hold the Volan has on him. Capture him, Teran, then let me have a time to speak with him. I made a vow . . . to try to reach Gage. I *must* try."

"Try what, Meriel?" the voice of the man they were all talking about intruded unexpectedly. "And why are you here, for that matter? We agreed you were to remain on Tenua and oversee the evacuation."

The room's three occupants swung around to find Gage Bardwin standing in the doorway, a wary look glittering in his eyes. Teran was the first to recover. He motioned his friend in.

"Come, sit and we'll talk. Meriel and her captain of the guard just now arrived. They've some very interesting news."

Gage's glance met that of Rand's and his face hardened. "That man is Volan-enslaved. He's not to be trusted."

"Strange," Teran drawled, "but he says the same about you. Are you enslaved as well, my friend?"

"Of course not!" Gage snapped, meeting Teran's questioning gaze. "Ask me anything about the times we've been together. See if I'm not still the man I've always been."

"A clever ploy." Rand stepped forward to place himself between Gage and Meriel. "But you and I both know it's possible to draw from our slave's memories anytime we wish. Show Teran instead the rash at the base of your neck and the small wound made when the temeritas entered Bardwin to prepare the way for you."

"I-I have no rash . . ."

"Then show him, Mardant," Rand snarled, "and keep your hands away from the com-device in your pocket!"

With a savage curse, Gage whipped out a small, palm-sized box and flipped it open. Before he could activate it, Rand's stunner was in his hand and fired. Gage gave a strangled cry, staggered backward, then braced himself as he fought against the stunner's neurological impact.

"Grab him!" Rand shouted. "Get the com-device away before he overcomes the stunner's effects!"

Even as he gave the command, Rand flung himself across the room at Gage. Both men toppled over and fell to the floor. Teran quickly joined the fray, shouting at Meriel over his shoulder.

"Get the guards! Hurry, Meriel!"

She hesitated but a moment, then turned and ran. The great receiving hall was empty. Where was everyone? she thought, her panic rising. Then she remembered the guards at the front doors.

Meriel wheeled about and raced to the front of the building. Four guards stood at their positions outside. She grabbed the nearest one by the arm.

"Lord Ardane!" she cried. "He needs you! Immediately!"

The man eyed her with frank skepticism. She pulled off her cap and her long hair tumbled down about her shoulders. Meriel tugged at him. "Now, you fool! Lock me up later if you find I've lied, but I tell you, a man is trying to kill Lord Ardane!"

They followed her then, their blasters slung into firing position. Terror pounded through Meriel as she sped back across the hall to the small antechamber. Would she reach Teran and Rand in time? Volan-enslaved bodies were superhuman in their strength. Thank the heavens Rand was there or Teran might have already been dead!

But what about Gage? What if the guards fired on him? She must find some way to prevent that from happening!

The sight that greeted her when she reached the room was one of deadly strife. Teran lay unconscious on the floor, blood trickling from a gash in his forehead. Gage and Rand struggled nearby, each fighting viciously for the advantage.

Meriel halted, mesmerized by the ferocity of their battle—and by the sheer, animal power emanating from both men. The guards drew up beside her and, though they aimed their blasters at the two combatants, didn't fire. She turned to them.

"Whatever you do, don't shoot." Meriel motioned to where Teran lay sprawled on the floor. "Two of you get Lord Ardane out of here. You," she said, motioning to the third man, "go for additional help. If Gage Bardwin wins this fight, we'll need more than a few men to overcome him."

The fourth guard remained as Teran was quickly carried from the room and the other guard ran off for reinforcements. All the while, Gage and Rand fought on, neither giving quarter as they wrestled with and viciously pummeled each other.

Meriel considered stunning them both to end the fight, but that would have defeated her purpose in having Gage awake for the attempt to drive out his Volan. It might come to a stunning if the battle turned against Rand, but for the moment she decided to wait. Wait and hope that Rand could subdue Gage long enough for her to touch and talk to him.

Both men began to tire with the strain of meeting and matching the awesome power of the other. Movements became sluggish, breathing rough, labored. Sweat sheened their faces and dampened the clothes to their bodies. But still they fought on until Meriel thought their hearts would burst from the exertion.

At last Rand was able to slip an arm about Gage's throat and, flipping him over, hold his opponent in an arm lock. "N-now, Meriel!" he gasped. "T-talk to him. Convince yourself o-once and for all that the Bellatorian is gone—f-forever!"

She hesitated, suddenly terrified. The moment had come and she didn't know what to say, what to do. She glanced around, her look wild, hoping, praying the guards would arrive.

"Meriel!" Rand cried. "Now! Help me!"

His cry stirred her to action. She ran to them then, flinging herself down to kneel beside Gage. He continued to struggle wildly, his face purpling with lack of air, his features twisted in a grimace of pain and anger. She reached out, touching him, stroking his sweat-slick cheek and jaw.

"Gage?" Meriel whispered, choking back a sob. "Gage, it's Meriel. I have come as I promised I would. Listen to me. Fight past your Volan. Remember our vow—that we would seek out the other and call forth our love. Remember that, Gage!"

Dark eyes, blazing with hatred, swung to hers. "Get away from me, bitch!"

Meriel drew back, momentarily shaken. Then anger and fierce resolve flooded her. Curse the Volan! He *would not* take the man she loved away from her! If his determination to continue to inhabit Gage's body was strong, hers was even stronger! She would fight him until the breath left her body and her heart ceased to beat. But she would never give up!

She grasped Gage by the hair and forced his head to turn, to look up at her. "Never, do you hear me? You get away, get out of him! He's mine! We are vowed, one to the other. I'll *never* let him go!"

As she held him, Meriel willed all the power of her love into the man before her. She clamped her eyes shut to block out the vision of the contorted features that glared up at her, filled with a murderous rage. Instead, she imagined Gage as he last was. From somewhere deep within her a force flickered, then flared to life. It swirled, grew, gaining power and impetus, then flowed forth, down her arms and into Gage.

The Volan within him screamed. "Get out! Get away. No! No! Damn you . . ."

He gagged. He choked. He writhed, then moaned, the sounds turning weak and piteous. Meriel heard it all from afar, for something else beckoned from the darkness. A voice, beloved and familiar.

Gage.

She intensified her efforts, calling forth every bit of strength she possessed. The voice grew, became louder. Then an image flickered to life. Gage, smiling, his dark eyes shining with love and understanding . . . calling to her.

The black morass that encompassed Gage grayed, shrunk. Meriel watched it ebb to the back of his mind. A sense of another spirit, one of strong, pure, loving intent, filled her. The Volan presence was no more, she realized with a rush of utter joy and relief, relegated to a secure prison of will-induced captivity. Present still, yet powerless.

"M-Meriel?"

At the hesitant words spoken in her beloved's voice, Meriel's eyes slowly opened. Gage stared up at her. Eyes that were now lucid, gleaming with a loving wonder, met hers.

"Gage?" She uttered the single word, aching to know if he had truly returned. "Is it really you?"

He shifted restlessly in Rand's clasp, but made no move to free himself. "Yes, it's me. How did you manage to free me? I didn't think it possible to drive a Volan out of a body."

"It isn't," Rand growled from beneath him. "At least not permanently. Though Meriel summoned forth your own powers to overcome the enslavement, the Volan is still a part of you. It's only a matter of time before he regains power. You'll never drive him out."

Panic rocketed through Gage. Frantically he searched the furthest reaches of his mind and found the Volan, contained but far from defeated. He paled. He swallowed hard against the surge of bile that rose in his throat.

Gods, it was horror enough to give oneself over to enslavement, yet at least once it was done, there was no further awareness of the shame. But to regain his mind and memory only to find his enemy still there . . .

For the rest of his days he'd carry the knowledge that an evil presence lurked within him, awaiting only the right moment to flare forth again. *You'll never drive him out . . . still a part of you . . .*

Rand's words reverberated in his mind, setting his head to pounding, his gut to roiling. Despair flooded him.

He met Meriel's gaze, his eyes bleak and tormented. "You should have never called me back. You didn't save me. Instead, you've condemned me to an existence worse than a living death. And if the Volan within me doesn't eventually kill me, the shame will!"

*   *   *

"Gage, stop that incessant pacing!" Teran grumbled from his chair in the royal library. "It's past time you accept what is and face what must be done. You're back in control. Make the most of it. I need you too badly in this battle against the Volans—and so does Meriel."

The tracker wheeled about to glare down at the three people seated at the huge table. Teran steadily returned his stare. Rand's mouth twisted and he shook his head. Meriel blinked back tears.

"And I say *you* don't understand!" Gage cried, his voice harsh, raw. "None of you. You can never begin to understand what it's like to have another being inside you, a being who constantly fights to break free, to resume control. The longer I remain here, the greater a threat I become!"

"But you've contained your Volan," Meriel protested, quiet desperation gleaming in her eyes. "And I'll be close to help whenever—"

"That's just my point!" He ran his hand through his hair in exasperation. "Don't you see? You can't be with me all the time. Is that what my life is to become, a pitiful existence constantly tied to you, dependent on another person for my continued survival? Gods, Meriel, you'll sicken of it before I do!"

"I don't care!" She rose to her feet and strode over to stand before him. "I love you, Gage. I'll do it if I must, for as long as it's necessary. And some day we'll find the answer, discover a way to free you permanently of your Volan."

He stared down at her, his jaw set with implacable determination. "Well, as hard as this is to hear, love is poor compensation for a man's pride. I'll not become another Pelum."

"A-another Pelum? Poor compensation?" Shock momentarily took Meriel's breath away. She barely contained the impulse to slap that obstinate look off his face. "Curse you, Gage Bardwin, but I've never heard two more ridiculous statements in my life! The only thing you need to avoid is becoming an arrogant, narrow-minded, lonely fool!"

He glowered down at her, a dangerous look in his eyes. "I warn you, Meriel. I don't like being called a fool."

"Then accept help from others, for once in that thick-skulled life of yours, including," she bit out the words, "help from me. You insult me with your implication that I'm incapable of supporting you in your time of need, or that the depth of my love is insufficient for the task."

A flush suffused his rugged features. "I didn't mean to imply—"

"Oh, I know what you did and didn't mean to imply! And I also know you just didn't think! But the time has come to change that, my handsome tracker. If, that is, you hope to maintain any kind of relationship with me."

"Not to mention," Teran added gravely, "assist in this battle against the Volans."

Gage knew when he was beaten, at least verbally, at least for now. He had no intention, however, of deviating from his predetermined course, but this wasn't the time to fight that battle. For all their sakes, though, he must eventually leave them. A man's honor couldn't suffer such shame as an alien presence within him, and the threat it would always present to those around him.

Meriel must go on with her life, search for another mate. He'd been a fool to think he'd ever had any right to her, even before the Volan. His enslavement had just brought it all to the forefront.

Not that the shame of his lineage could ever become a point of dissension now. The continuing danger to Meriel and his friends because of the Volan lurking within him overshadowed all other difficulties. The problem was convincing Meriel of that, of sparing her heart.

There was nothing to be done for *his* heart, Gage thought glumly. He'd love Meriel for the length and breadth of his days. And whatever pain came of that was a well-deserved punishment for what he had so stubbornly and blindly wrought. But Meriel didn't deserve to be hurt. She had been manipulated from the start into a situation her naïve young heart had no experience dealing with. She was innocent of any wrongdoing, while he, far older and wiser in such things, was guilty. Arrogantly, selfishly guilty.

In the meanwhile, he did intend to tie up the loose ends—like ridding Tenua of the Volans and finishing the evacuation to Carcer. He owed Meriel that much—if he could just control his Volan long enough to see the tasks to completion.

"Fine," Gage sighed his assent. "I never had any intention of backing away from the Volan threat."

Teran smiled and leaned back in his chair. "Good." He motioned to the two empty chairs across from him. "Sit, both of you. I've received some very interesting information. We've plans to make."

Gage scowled, eyed the chairs, then strode around the table and sat down. Meriel pointedly ignored the empty chair beside him and instead took a seat on Rand's other side.

With a long-suffering shake of his head, Teran picked up a stack of computer printouts and sorted through them until he found the page he wanted. He scanned it briefly as if to refresh his memory, then lifted his gaze to his three compatriots.

"This report confirms the growing concern that our jamming signals on Tenua are no longer effective. It seems the Volan Mother Ship has found a way to circumvent our transmissions and is once again bombarding the planet."

"It was only a matter of time," Rand muttered.

Teran shot him a quick glance. "Yes, I agree. And I also begin to wonder if those transmissions weren't the primary means of control the Volan High Command had upon its own kind. Perhaps part of the reason for your change of heart was because we managed to block your ship's signals for so long."

All eyes turned to Rand. He met each gaze directed at him, then nodded slowly. "I suspected as much myself. In the end, I think, we've never been all that different from you. True, our physical forms are dissimilar, but our inherent beliefs and sensibilities, our moral decision-making abilities, just may have evolved along parallel lines."

"Then there may be more Volans on Tenua who are experiencing the same conflicts as you," Meriel ventured, struggling to keep the rising excitement from her voice. "Volans who, even now, are following their hearts and beginning to subvert the Volan directives!"

"It's quite possible," Rand agreed, "though there are some who would choose to follow the guidance of the Mother Ship even if they had free choice." He shot Gage a narrow glance. "Mardant is one of those, I can assure you."

"How do you know that?" Meriel demanded.

Rand shrugged. "How does anyone know for sure? I was reared in the same hive cocoon as he. While in other bodies, I attended our form of military indoctrination training with him. I served with Mardant on all the same assignments. We are as close to brothers as we can be in a society that refuses to recognize family or bonding. And I tell you true, Mardant will never change, no matter how weak or ineffectual the Mother Ship's transmissions become."

"It wouldn't matter anyway," Gage growled. "I won't tolerate *any* Volan within me. This is my body, my mind, and I don't intend to share it with any slime-ridden alien!"

"Gage!" Meriel cried. "That's cruel and unfair. Rand has been a friend and ally. If it weren't for him, I would've never had the chance to reach you and call you back."

"He has no right to the body he inhabits!" Barely contained rage smoldered in Gage's eyes. "He took what wasn't his, and a human being has been sacrificed because of that. The essence of Torman is gone; he is dead to those who love him. Call him a friend if you will, Meriel, but I call him a thief, a murderer, and an inhuman devil!"

He took my beloved away from me . . .

Dian's plaintive cry reverberated in Meriel's mind, echoing in union with the words Gage had so bitterly uttered. Frustration warred with a sense of rising futility. There *was* no way to defend Rand's original motives in enslaving Torman's body. And the deed once done could not be later justified by a change of heart. Not when it required the continued use of another being's mind and body.

She turned anguished eyes to Rand and knew, from the sudden flare of understanding in his, that he sensed her dilemma—sensed, accepted, and agreed. Her eyes widened. She shook her head.

"No, Rand," Meriel whispered. "You can't. Not now."

He smiled, and she was struck by the aching sadness in his gaze.

"No, not now, little Queen. But the time will come . . ."

"Er, excuse me." Teran loudly cleared his throat. "The issue, if I recall correctly, was the resumption of the Volan Mother Ship's transmissions to Tenua." He extracted another sheet of paper from the pile before him. "Our galactic surveillance systems have located their receiving station on the isle of Insula. One that appears to be the source of all communications from the Mother Ship."

"It also serves as a transport site for the receipt of our biospheres," Rand informed them, "as well as for the removal of enslaved bodies to be sent to subvert other Imperial planets. The station on the isle of Insula is currently the prime location for the infiltration of the rest of the Imperium."

Teran frowned, set down his paper, then leaned forward. "Then it must be destroyed. The elimination of the station will solve several of our problems, not to mention slowing the Volan advance." His glance locked with Gage's. "Will you lead the force to Insula?"

The blond tracker hesitated, then nodded. "Yes. There may be more at that station than stores of biospheres to be destroyed. I intend to search as well for information that can aid us in permanently eliminating the Volan threat from the universe. And how to rid myself of my own mindslaver in the bargain."

"Those biospheres contain life. I won't cooperate in a plan to annihilate my people!" Rand rose. "If that's your ultimate goal, I withdraw my assistance."

Gage glared over at him. "What did you think our intent would be, Volan? Ask your people to kindly leave us alone and move onto some other galaxy?"

"We have as much right to survive as you do!" Rand snarled.

"I think the only moral solution is to assist the Volans in finding some way out of their dilemma," Meriel offered quickly. Her glance moved nervously from one man to the other. Both were battle-taut and appeared ready to leap across the table at each other. "It's as Rand said. The Volans have just as much right to survive as a species as we do."

"Noble words without a shred of practical advice to back them up with," Gage growled, rounding on her. "And how do you propose to do that? They need physical forms to house their entities in. Where do you propose to find uninhabited bodies to serve that purpose?"

"I don't know, or at least not yet," Meriel snapped, stung by his angry sarcasm. "That's what we have scientists for. Perhaps we can clone them bodies, or develop some suitable androidlike forms. First things first, Gage Bardwin. The main thing is that you not alienate a source of valuable aid. We need Rand."

"But can we trust him?" Gage demanded. "He could well be leading us into a trap."

"Just as you could be, Bardwin," Rand interjected. Once again, all eyes swung to him.

Teran arched a dark brow. "And how so, Volan?"

Rand shrugged. "Who's to say which of us is potentially more dangerous—I, or the Volan within Bardwin? I have total control over my slave. But Bardwin walks a precarious line in containing his Volan, an entity far more powerful than the human I hold in check. Who would be more likely to turn traitor?"

"Gage won't betray us." Meriel's chin lifted defiantly as she scanned the three men sitting around the table. "As long as I am near, we can work together to control his Volan."

She inhaled a steadying breath in the heavy silence that settled over the room, then forged on. "The solution to our problem is simple. Dispatch a secret army to Insula, infiltrate and collect all the Volan biospheres for safekeeping, then destroy the receiving station.

"And," she continued with grim determination, "to ensure Gage's loyalty during the undertaking, I will accompany the invasion force."

Chapter Seventeen

"You'll do nothing of the kind!" Gage exploded, leaping to his feet. He strode over to stand beside Meriel's chair, his jaw taut with rage. "This is a dangerous mission that must be executed carefully. I'll not have you endangered, or endanger the rest of us, with your inexperience."

"I am Queen of Tenua," she calmly replied, refusing to quail before him despite his intimidating bulk towering over her. "The success of this mission is vital to the safety of my people. I have every right not only to accompany you, but"—she paused to add further emphasis to her next words—"even to determine if you go or not."

He gave a start of surprise, then his lips twisted in cynical amusement. "You forget yourself, femina. I'm still Tenua's Lord Commander. You rule only by my leave."

"Indeed?" Meriel eyed him coolly. "And pray, *Lord Commander*, do I rule or not?"

Gage clamped down on a savage curse. Be damned, but the woman had maneuvered him into a no-win position. If he humiliated her before Teran and the Volan, and ultimately before her people, she'd never forgive him. And, as hard as it was to admit, much less accept, he sensed her words were true. Without Meriel at his side, his hold over his Volan presence was tenuous at best.

But if he acquiesced to her demands, he all but formally rescinded his control as Lord Commander—not to mention agreed to risk the woman he still loved, even if he could no longer have her. The loss of his position as absolute ruler of Tenua didn't disturb him, Gage realized with a small twinge of surprise. He'd always been a loner at heart and had little patience for all the pomp and circumstance, even in the days of his youth when he still thought he was rightful heir to the Bardwin throne. He'd never wanted the job as Lord Commander to begin with. Teran had all but forced it on him.

There was no doubt of Meriel's fitness to rule. That assessment had only grown with each passing day. She was smart, fearless, and totally devoted to the welfare of her people. She had learned and adapted to the takeover of her planet, surrendered when she couldn't win, then resiliently reappraised the situation and tried again. She *was* the Queen of Tenua. To claim anything else would be a lie—and a travesty of justice.

• Gage shoved a hand through his hair and scowled. "Yes, you rule. But I ask you to reconsider your demand to accompany me to Insula, for Kieran's sake if not your own. I am already dead, whether I die fighting the Volans or not. I would at least like our son to have one surviving parent."

"And I'd like him to have both." Meriel shook her head. "No, I won't reconsider, Gage. We made each other vows, and mine won't be fulfilled until you're free of your Volan."

Pain slashed across Gage's features, and he shuddered with the force of the effort it required not to take Meriel into his arms. Gods, he needed her so badly, the feel of her soft woman's body pressed into his, the solid comfort of holding her in his arms, the tactile reassurance that he was alive and real and still the man he remembered himself to be. But, in the end, it wouldn't help either of them. He must distance himself from Meriel to ease the pain of the eventual separation, and it was past time to begin.

"Then at least give me your word you'll obey me on this mission and keep yourself out of dangerous situations," he demanded, irritation threading his voice. "For all your courage, you're no warrior queen."

"Not yet," Meriel grinned in relief, "but I already wield a mean blaster, and with a few more lessons, I'd wager I could become proficient with a dagger." She paused to glance out the window to where the single, yellow sun of Bellator was slowly easing its way toward the distant horizon. "In fact, if we hurry, we could get at least an hour's practice in before nightfall. Are you game, Bardwin?"

Gage caught Teran's glance and rolled his eyes. "It'll take more than an hour to get a soft little Queen like you in fighting condition."

"Yes," Meriel agreed, "but even the rudiments are better than nothing at all." She turned to Teran. "Is there anything else we need to discuss just now?"

"We must have a battle plan, as well as decide on the best way to coordinate a surprise attack," the dark-haired man replied, "but it can wait a time. We'll meet here again after the evening meal to work out the final details. In the meanwhile, I'd wager we could all use a brief respite. Go, practice your knife-throwing. I can't think of a more intimate way for two lovers to spend time together."

"Can't you now?" Gage muttered sarcastically. He glanced down at Meriel. "Well, what are you waiting for?"

She arched a brow at his brusque demand. "Nothing, Lord Commander. Nothing at all." And, without another glance in his direction, Meriel rose and strode from the room.

Teran watched until both had departed, then turned to Rand. "What's your interest in the Queen?"

Rand's mouth quirked at the other man's abrupt change of subject. "I'm not certain what you're really asking."

"Do you want Meriel for yourself?"

In spite of himself, a flush crept up Rand's neck and face. Damn the human response to an embarrassing situation! He looked down for a long moment to recover from the stab of pain that

Teran's question had stirred. Then Rand glanced up.

"What does it matter what I want?" Piercing blue eyes met those of gray. "I know my place in the scheme of things. And I'm astute enough to recognize that she'll never want me as I want her. Your friend is in no danger from me. I won't turn on him to get his woman." Rand arched a mocking brow. "That *is* what really concerned you, isn't it?"

"Partially."

"And the other part? Is it perhaps that you and your kind barely trust me? That you can't help but despise my enslavement of this man called Torman, and tolerate me only because you temporarily need my services?" He gave a bitter laugh. "Don't delude yourself. I'm well aware of what will happen when I'm no longer of use."

"Are you now?" Teran drawled. "And how did you arrive at that conclusion?"

Rand shrugged. "I symbolize a danger that will never disappear until all Volans are gone—and that danger is our ability to mindslave. No matter what happens, what we promise, how can you be certain we won't turn on you again?"

"We can't," Teran agreed. "But there are many other species, even in our own galaxy, who will always possess similar potential to turn on us. Why, we risk that even from our own kind." He shook his head. "No, it isn't the future possibilities that concern me. It's your continued enslavement of Torman. How long do you plan to keep him? Until you burn out his body and destroy him?"

Rand's jaw tightened. "I don't want to return to a biosphere. I spent over five cycles in one the last time, until I received this body. Before that, there was a period of another two cycles, and before that, seven. After what I've experienced this time, the next relegation to a formless entity trapped within the constraints of a small globe will be unbearable."

"Yet the time will come . . ." Teran softly reminded Rand.

Rand's features twisted in a mask of anguish. "Yes, the time will come. Just as Bardwin's will as well. The Queen cannot sustain him forever."

"No, she can't." Teran rose from the table. "For both your sakes, I hope we can find an answer to your dilemmas—before it's too late."

Meriel rose from the bathing pool and wrapped a long warmed bath cloth about her, tucking it snugly into the valley between her breasts. She blotted her hair dry with a smaller cloth, then combed through the damp tangles until they hung smoothly down her back. With a small sigh, Meriel turned and reentered the room she and Gage would share for the night.

It certainly wasn't the appointments of their quarters that distressed her. Teran had obviously given them one of the finest rooms in the palace. The bedchamber was a soothing, romantic haven, from the huge fireplace blazing with logs to warm the winter-chilled air, to the thick, white Argulan furs strewn before the hearth and the large inviting bed strewn with plump pillows. No, the heavy sense of despair was due exclusively to the scowling man standing before the fire.

He had shut her out, from his life as well as heart. Though Gage was still in control of his Volan, the other's presence permeated him, influencing everything Gage thought and felt and did.

A sense of the sad irony of it all flooded Meriel. She had rescued him, yet so much of the man she had known and loved was indeed gone. Gage had returned to her a stranger.

Yet, there was still hope. Meriel refused to think otherwise. Though Gage had changed in many ways, she was determined to regain his love. Somehow she knew that beneath his disturbing new veneer there remained the essence of the man she loved. The courageous warrior, the tender lover, the proud father. He had just withdrawn to protect her from his Volan.

A fierce resolve filled Meriel. She had achieved her first goal, the defeat of the Volan's control over Gage. The war wasn't over, but a decisive battle had been won. Other, equally difficult battles lay ahead before total victory was hers. But she meant to win. And that goal included the use of every weapon at her disposal, every advantage that was hers.

As soon as they returned to Tenua, she'd enlist Kieran's aid in seducing his father's heart back to them. She would step up her own campaign in a woman's way as well. In the meanwhile, her scientists would be called upon to achieve the greatest discovery of their careers—the means to removing the Volan from Gage.

Yes, Meriel thought as she glided across the room to the fireplace, her plan was sound. It was all just a matter of time.

He heard her approach with his tracker's-honed ears. His body went taut, sensing her intent, her aura of feminine sensuality and desire a palpable, heated thing.

Gage choked back a tormented groan. Gods, he was so weary, so confused and disheartened! He didn't know how he'd refuse Meriel if she touched him, much less attempted to seduce him. Yet he must. To give her any sign of encouragement or hope would be cruel and pointless.

His hands clenched into white-knuckle fists and he lowered his head on the arm that rested upon the mantel. Gods, he hated himself! And hated what he must do. But turn Meriel away he would, just as quickly and painlessly as possible.

"Gage?"

A small hand touched him on the shoulder. The sensation sent a jolt of anguished awareness coursing through his body. Gage shuddered, then forced himself to straighten and turn.

The sight of Meriel standing there bathed in firelight and shadow took his breath away. His heart thundered in his chest, his mouth went dry, and the hands that longed to touch her, to pull her to him, dampened. With only the most super-human of efforts, Gage controlled the impulse to narrow the space between them.

Instead, he shot her a cool, distancing look. "What do you want, Meriel? I'm exhausted and in no mood for talk."

She swallowed hard, the hopeful, hesitant light in her eyes fading. Then her chin lifted and she stared back, regal in her renewed determination. "But talk we will. You owe me that much, Gage Bardwin."

He arched a dark brow and his mouth quirked briefly. Gods, she was all but irresistible when her eyes sparked with anger like that.

"Do I now?" Gage silkily inquired. "Can't this wait until our return to Tenua on the morrow?"

"No. We must start somewhere, and there'll be little time for us once we're back home. You know as well as I that we've only a few days to gather our invasion force and set out. Time is our only advantage if we're to successfully overthrow the transport station on Insula."

Gage eyed her with an intent, assessing look, then gestured to the two chairs before the hearth. "As you wish, Domina. But let's try to make it brief. Even with your assistance, the effort required to keep my Volan contained is quite draining."

Meriel quickly took a seat. "I understand."

No, you don't, Gage thought as he lowered himself into the other chair across from her. *You don't understand how desperately I need your help, the nearness of your physical presence, to maintain control. Even when you were but a few meters away in another room bathing, I felt a definite rise in my Volan's power. If you hadn't finished your bath when you did, I'd have had to come in after you.*

But he'd never admit that to Meriel—how truly tenuous was his own hold over his Volan entity. How deeply he needed her.

Frustration, mixed with an uncomfortable surge of fear, lanced through him. It was one thing to need a woman to ease his physical cravings or fulfill an emotional component, but to become subservient to even that person's comings and goings was a bitter revelation. It foreshadowed eventualities his proud spirit could never accept. Eventualities like dependence, helplessness.

The admission filled Gage with anger, an anger that found a release in his voice and words. "Fine," he gritted. "Then if you understand, get on with it."

Annoyance tightened Meriel's lips. "Your behavior ever since I helped free you from your Volan's control, as well as your attitude right now, is the first of several things I'd like to talk about. I'm tired of being made to feel as if I committed some crime because of what I did. You're acting like a spoiled, petulant child!"

"And you're refusing to accept my feelings!" he shot back, stung by her scathing if painfully accurate assessment. "I have the right to choose how to live my life and—"

"You asked me to find you, to try to free you!" Meriel burst out in exasperation. "What was I to do? Turn my back and walk away?"

"If you'd been smart, that's exactly what you should have done."

"Smart?" For a moment, Meriel couldn't believe her ears. How dare he insult her, belittle her efforts, her concern?

Her nails dug into the chair's padded arms. "There was nothing smart about it," she corrected him furiously. "You have a responsibility to me, to our son, to your friend Teran Ardane, and, most of all, to the Imperium that gave you a home and its protection. And you're the one who agreed to become Tenua's Lord Commander, with all the burdens of responsibility that entails in light of Firestar's eventual destruction. So don't whine to me about how unfair life has suddenly become. You're a man; act like one!"

"Fine. Then quit your harping and allow me to do just that!"

With the greatest of efforts, Gage controlled the impulse to throttle Meriel. He didn't need her taunts on top of everything else. He hated what he'd become as it was, without her adding further to his rapidly worsening self-concept. A self-concept that was still honest enough to admit that her words had struck far too close to the truth.

Gage inhaled a deep breath. "I'm trying, Meriel," he said, gentling the tone of his voice. "But this is all so difficult. I truly don't need any more pressure right now—and especially not from you."

She smiled, relaxing a bit. "I suppose I *was* a little hard on you a few seconds ago. I didn't mean to call you a whiner."

He shoved an unsteady hand through his hair and grinned. "Even if I really was one?"

"Yes."

A weary smile twitched the corners of Gage's mouth. "I'll do what I can for you, Kieran, Teran, and the universe, but I must tell you one thing more. As painful as this may be to hear, it's over between us, Meriel. It can never be the same again. Do us both a favor and accept it."

Shock warred with disbelief in Meriel's breast, a battle royal until both were vanquished by the onset of yet another element—her fierce, unquenchable love. "I'll never accept that," she cried, "no matter what you do or say to me. I know you too well, Gage Bardwin. It's your stubborn pride talking, pride and that inability to ask for, much less accept, help."

She rose and came to kneel before him, her hands settling upon his knees. "You want me. You'll always want me. I can see it even now, burning in your eyes, trembling through your body. At least allow me to ease that need tonight, to give you solace, release. The other problems won't be solved anytime soon. We both know that. But, in the meanwhile . . ."

As she spoke, Meriel ran her hands up Gage's legs, pausing at his groin before traveling back downward again, this time to stroke the sensitive skin of his inner thighs. He went rigid, his sex swelling, hardening. He bit back a savage curse.

"Meriel, don't," Gage groaned, capturing her hands before they could reach and discover his arousal. "If you truly love me, don't do this."

She leaned back, a provocative smile on her lips. "Oh, never doubt that I love you, my handsome tracker. And never doubt, as well, that I know what you need even before you know it." Meriel freed one hand and loosened her bath cloth. It fell to the floor.

Gage's heart leaped in his chest, faltered a beat, then commenced a wild pounding. His hungry gaze raked her body, the firm, jutting breasts, the soft, rose-colored nipples, the graceful indentation of waist and gentle flare of womanly hips, the dark triangle of hair at the juncture of her thighs. He groaned again.

"No, Meriel. I've made my decision when it comes to us. I won't mate with you ever again. It's over."

With that, Gage shoved her back. He rose and stalked away, leaving Meriel kneeling on the floor. Making his way to the bed, Gage sat and pulled off his tunic and boots, then grabbed a quilted throw at the foot of the bed. Wrapping himself in it, he lay down and turned his back to her.

"Come to bed, Meriel," he growled over his shoulder. "I need your physical presence to ward off my evil Volan, but that's all I need. The sooner you accept that, the better."

She stared at him from her place on the floor, a myriad of emotions whirling through her head. Anger warred with hurt, determination with frustration. By all that was sacred, what was she to do with the man? How was she to win him back? Ah, if only she had the finesse, the experience, of her mother!

But she didn't, and never would. Unlike her mother, she would only know and love one man. It was the only way for her, Meriel mused sadly, but one that, conversely, ill prepared her for the obstacles that were now thrown in her path. Gods, would they never end?

Perhaps their love was never meant to be. Perhaps it *had* been doomed from the start. Perhaps it was time to admit defeat and turn her energies to more productive things. She couldn't salvage their love all by herself, and Gage refused to meet her even halfway.

The future seemed to stretch before Meriel, a bleak scenario of endless pain, rejection, and despair. Only a fool would submit oneself to further anguish over a hopeless situation. Only a fool would have tried so hard from the start. And only a fool would fight on.

But she loved Gage to the point of foolishness and beyond. Because of that, she would never give up. Though the journey was fraught with uncertainty and pain, it promised wondrous things as well—if only she had the courage to walk the path.

With a small sigh, Meriel gathered her bath cloth back around her and headed over to the bed.

Two days later, the secret invasion force of fifty hand-picked men stood ready in the royal palace in Eremita. As Gage completed the final inspection and briefing under heavy security precautions, Meriel stood nearby, Kieran in her arms. Dian waited quietly at her side. Though pride swelled in Meriel's breast as she watched Gage, the consummate warrior and leader of men, a sad despair slowly entwined through it all.

All her efforts had come to naught. Though Gage had stolen a few moments out of the chaotic past few days to find time with his son, and his love for Kieran had been more than evident, even those interactions had failed to thaw the icy determination that now drove him. He was cold, distant, and disinterested whenever he spoke to her in public. The nights spent together, sleeping so close that Meriel could feel the heat emanating from his big body, had not lured Gage any closer, either. He came to bed very late, curled up as far away from her as he could, and then promptly fell asleep.

There was little more Meriel could do. She had slammed up against the rock-hard wall of Gage's resolve, and this time could find no chink through which to slip in. There was only one consolation in it all. Gage's Volan had yet to regain control. A small consolation, in light of what she'd hoped for, but all there was.

At last the final meeting was over. The heavily armed soldiers dispersed, using the palace's ancient tunnels to reach the gathering site outside the city where their skim crafts waited. In less than an hour, once the sun set and darkness fell, the journey would begin.

Gage watched his men file out, then turned to where Meriel waited. The sight of her dressed in dark tunic, breeches and boots, beryllium-impregnated chest armor, wide pouch belt that held her stunner, knife, short-range com-device and emergency rations cinched about her waist, her blaster propped against one leg, filled him with a mixture of admiration and anguish. Meriel had transformed before his eyes from a gentle, hesitant young woman reluctantly thrust into the forefront of life, into a brave, resourceful Queen willing to do battle to save her people. A battle she would not only help lead, but physically engage in if necessary.

That consideration worried Gage more than anything else. It was torment enough to give her up, but to allow Meriel, the mother of his only child, to risk her life ate at him. Somehow, someway, he must assure her safe return to Eremita. He would protect what was his, though he must eventually turn his back and walk away. There was no other choice.

He squared his shoulders and strode over to where the two women and his son waited. Drawing up before Meriel, Gage reached out for Kieran. The boy came to him without hesitation, entwined his arms about his father's neck, and planted a loud, wet kiss on his cheek.

Gage flushed in pleasure and returned the gesture with a tender kiss on the boy's forehead. Then his gaze met Meriel's over the top of Kieran's head. The look he saw gleaming in her eyes almost brought him to his knees.

Love, deep and enduring, burned there. He knew, with a sudden stab of realization, that he'd never be able to turn her away, to ease the pain of his leaving, to kill the love she had for him. No matter how unworthy he felt, Meriel loved him, wanted him, and would never give him up.

The admission angered Gage. His one and only consolation had been to spare her pain. Even that was now an impossibility. There would be nothing of honor allowed him in this whole sad, sordid mess. He had control over nothing—not his life, his happiness, not even the outcome of his decisions and their impact on others.

At long last the final humiliation, the secret, innermost terror that had dogged him all his adult life, had found him. Once again he was at the beck and call of another, intrinsically evil force, and this time he couldn't even walk away. He was all but impotent, manipulated by the untenable situation his Volan had put him in. He couldn't control anything, least of all events that might spare his loved ones pain. He was helpless where it mattered most.

With a silent, savage curse, Gage handed Kieran back to Meriel. "He'll be told about me when he's older, won't he? No matter what I become, I won't have you hiding the fact that I was his father from him."

At the barely restrained anger in his voice, a puzzled expression flitted across Meriel's face. "He knows already. Ask him what your name is."

He shot her a wary glance. "My name, lad." Gage cradled Kieran's chin in the curve of his big hand and turned his face to his. "What's my name?"

The boy blinked in momentary confusion, then grinned. "Papa. My papa."

A haunted, anguished look twisted Gage's face and was gone. Then he smiled. For an instant, Meriel saw his guard lower. An aching gentleness gleamed in his compelling eyes. His smile widened into a boyishly devastating grin.

Meriel's heart swelled with happiness and relief. Once again, Gage was the man she knew and loved. And if he could respond so warmly to his son, there was still a heart capable of loving her beating beneath his breast. She placed a hand upon his arm.

He turned. At the warm glow in Meriel's eyes, Gage remembered himself. His jaw hardened and a closed, shuttered expression settled over his features. He arched a cynical brow.

"Yes, femina?"

"Are you reassured now? That Kieran will know about his true father?"

"It's a start." His words were abrupt, clipped. His gaze turned to scan the now empty room. Through the large window across the chamber, the setting sun illuminated the horizon in an explosion of ever-deepening shades of rose, lavender, and blue.

His gaze swung back to hers, distant, devoid of emotion once more. "It's time we depart. Kiss Kieran good-bye and come with me."

Without another word, Gage grabbed Meriel's blaster and strode away, his long, pantherlike strides quickly carrying him across the room toward the tiny alcove where the passage stood open. Meriel turned to Dian.

Her friend stared back, deep concern gleaming in her eyes. "I wish you fortune in liberating your man from the Volan horror. My prayers are with you, my dearest friend."

"And mine, with you," Meriel murmured through a tear-choked voice. She kissed Kieran, then stroked back a lock of hair that had tumbled down onto his forehead. For a moment more Meriel hesitated, then handed her son to her friend.

"Tell him of me as well," she whispered, "if I fail to return. Tell him of the love I had for him and that I died fighting for his birthright—and to save his father."

"There's nothing more honorable or c-cour-ageous," Dian quavered, her own tears coursing unchecked down her cheeks. "You are truly Queen, just as I knew you would be."

Meriel managed a wobbly grin. "Thank you for that, my friend. It seems so long ago that I worried over it."

"Yes," Dian agreed, smiling through her tears. "You've accomplished so much in such a short time. You've borne a child, known love, been a brave and good ruler. I'm happy for that."

"As am I." Meriel stepped back. "No matter what happens, I wouldn't have missed such a glorious experience." She smiled once more in farewell, then turned and went to join Gage.

He eyed her, noting the single tear trickling down her face. Wordlessly and with the gentlest of touches, he wiped it away, then handed Meriel her blaster. She shouldered it, glanced back one last time at the scene of Dian cradling a chubby, squirming Kieran in her arms, then strode past Gage into the blackened opening that led to the ancient passages.

Chapter Eighteen

Two days later they reached the Cerulean Sea. For a change, it was calm, though the clouds overhead had begun to color a little, hinting of the bad weather to come. Meriel hoped that whatever brewed wouldn't linger into the night, when the surprise attack was planned. The task before them was difficult enough without the chaos and danger of another storm.

They made camp in the large stand of dead trees near the shore and awaited the fall of darkness. Though the barren trunks and branches provided little cover from the air, the shelter from the ground was more than adequate, thanks to the large boulders and fallen trunks strewn here and there among the still-upright trees. And the cloaking device Rand devised prior to their departure had, so far, managed to prevent the skim crafts' electronic presence from being detected.

Cook fires were prohibited, so all ate a cold supper. Meriel, along with Gage and Rand, sat apart from the rest, reviewing the battle strategy one last time.

"We must stay together at all costs," Gage began, pouring himself a cup of faba from a thermal cylinder. Cup in hand, his glance swung to Rand. "I want a chance at the data banks and will need your assistance. I also want to know you're there to help get Meriel out if something happens to me."

"There's *nothing* to help you in our data banks," Rand reiterated patiently. "Even if there were some way involuntarily to remove a Volan from its slave, that information would be safely stored in the Mother Ship. It wouldn't be common knowledge for the rank and file of us, much less accessible. And as far as Meriel goes," he continued, shooting her an assessing glance, "I plan to keep a *very* close eye on her. I have no intention of allowing her to fall into Volan hands again."

"Unless they're *your* Volan hands," Gage muttered beneath his breath.

"What does it matter anymore?" Meriel demanded, brought to the edge of her tolerance by his snide remark as well as the past days of fighting back her frustration and despair. "Whether you or Rand, it seems I'm increasingly at the mercy of their species. So save your biting sarcasm for someone else, Gage Bardwin. It's past time you begin to trust Rand and—"

"Never. Do you hear me? Never." Gage swallowed his cup of faba in one angry gulp, then wiped his mouth with the back of his hand. "I, more than anyone else, know intimately of their true intent. And I tell you, Meriel, they will destroy us any way they can."

"And *I* say they are no different than us," she protested hotly. "Some are good, some evil. *Just like us!*"

"Stop it, Meriel." Rand leaned forward to place a restraining hand on her arm. "There are more important things to deal with right now. Besides, I don't care what he thinks. I am here to protect you and ensure your success with this mission."

Gage gave a snort of disgust.

"And what do *you* care?" Meriel threw her half-chewed piece of journey bread aside and climbed to her feet. She gazed down at Gage through a haze of wrathful tears. "You've already closed your heart, shut yourself off from me. What does it matter what another wants? Or is it just that you don't want anyone else to have me, either?"

He scowled up at her. "You don't understand. I don't want any Volan near you, that's all. Aside from them, however, take up with any man you like. I'm sure anyone will be a decided improvement over me."

"Yes," Meriel bit out the word, "I'm sure any of them would." With that, she turned on her heel and stomped away.

Gage snarled a savage curse, threw his cup aside, and stood. After one more furious glare at Rand, he wheeled about and headed off in the opposite direction.

The Volan sat there for a long while, his own cup of faba untouched in his hand, marveling at the extremes to which love drove humans. Marveling and doubting, for the first time, whether he wished to allow such insanity to ever rule him.

The invasion was made in the dismal hour before midnight. The storm had intensified overhead, the clouds churned before a sliver of moon, and the winds howled in mournful anticipation. A shiver rippled down Meriel's spine as they crept up to the twin volcanic mountains. Had their approach truly been undetected, or did the Volans stand ready, prepared to annihilate them as they entered?

Their soldiers had their orders. Half were to take out the Volan sentries and other troops garrisoned within the mountain fortress. The other half were to find the transporter and destroy it. Gage, Rand, and Meriel would slip through to the data base computer and retrieve all its information for later study back on Bellator. Then, once the transport station was overthrown, the biospheres would be gathered up and taken back to the skim crafts. Despite Gage's and Rand's diametrically opposed opinions about what should be done with the Volan entities, for the time being Meriel had demanded that they be treated with care.

Though she knew that Gage would have vastly preferred to lead the first party in, he held back, fearing the risk to her. Only after the initial infiltration was safely and successfully carried out, and the signal given for the main force to enter, did Gage move forward with Meriel and Rand.

Up ahead, the sounds of battle began to reverberate through the mountain. Blaster fire, shouts and screams, the rhythmic thud of running feet. Meriel's heart began a wild staccato beneath her breast. As they entered the main tunnel, she swung her own blaster from her shoulder, shoved the safety mechanism off and the gun into firing position. On either side of her, Gage and Rand did the same.

The fortress's interior was just as she remembered—long, winding stone corridors slanting downward into the earth until they finally leveled at the chambers filled with biospheres and the huge room that held the Volan transport chamber. The soldiers ahead of them split up then, some to flush out Volan snipers, others to plant explosives around the transport chamber and its control panel. The rest of the force surged ahead to meet and take on the remainder of the Volan garrison.

Rand pointed to a side tunnel. "Down there," he shouted above the tumult of battle. "The data base computer is located through that passage."

Gage signaled Rand to lead the way, then motioned for Meriel to follow down a narrow, twisting tunnel. If not for the light beam Rand held high before him, she would have imagined she'd been buried alive. But she wasn't alone. Gage was behind her, Rand was before her, both men's presences reassuringly strong and solid. There was no way to turn around and go back if she wanted to.

The sounds of battle faded. A light gleamed faintly up ahead, growing steadily stronger. About a hundred meters from the next turn in the tunnel, which appeared to open into a room, Rand paused. Signaling for Gage and Meriel to halt, he moved stealthily forward. As he did, he disappeared from view.

Meriel choked back a gasp of surprise at Rand's unexpected use of his cloaking powers, marshaling her already finely strung emotions back into control. She listened past the blood pounding through her skull and heard nothing save the whir of various mechanical devices, soft footfalls, and the low murmur of voices. Then the sharp, harsh report of a blaster filled the air.

Again and again the weapon fired, followed by cries of pain. Finally, all was silent. Gage pushed her forward.

"Come on," he rasped close to her ear. "The Volan may have taken out his compatriots, but I don't want to leave him with the data files too long. Even now, he could be erasing some of the information we need."

Meriel bit back a stinging retort and stepped out, Gage's hand in the small of her back impelling her forward. The contact was both stimulating and sad for the same reason—it was one of the few times he'd touched her in the past several days. And now, when he did, it was only for the sake of necessity.

Rand was checking bodies when they reached the entrance to the room. At the sound of their arrival, he wheeled around, blaster at the ready. He immediately relaxed when he saw Meriel halt in the doorway.

"Come on in." Rand glanced about him. "It's

quite safe for the time being. We can't linger here long, though. This is a vital area, and once my people realize the tide has turned against them, they'll be down here to destroy the data files."

"Fine. Then let's get on with it." Gage shouldered his blaster and strode over to the main computer unit. He punched in a series of commands. His efforts were rewarded with nothing but a low beep. Frowning, Gage turned to Rand. "There's an access code, isn't there?"

Rand moved to stand beside him and began a two-handed manipulation of the computer panel. "But of course. The Mother Ship thinks of everything."

With a hum, the data files opened. Rand glanced up at Gage. "What exactly did you want to know?"

"Since you assure me there's no answer on how to free us of our Volan slavers," Gage growled, "I'd like a disk, instead, that contains all species Volans have successfully enslaved, all species they've tried and been unable to enslave and, if available, the reasons for the choices."

"There's no way to access the information save through the computer screen or a printout. There are no disks lying around to be pilfered." The Volan cocked a quizzical brow. "An interesting question, whether there are any species immune to Volan enslavement, one I think there might possibly be answers to. You surprise me, Bardwin. I wouldn't have thought a man of your more physical skills would also possess such a scientific mind."

Meriel stepped up beside Gage. "Why are you

so interested in knowing—"

The sound of footsteps echoing down the tunnel toward them drew her up short. She swung her blaster around, but before she could take a step toward the entryway, Gage halted her.

"Is there another way out?" he asked, glancing at Rand over his shoulder.

"Yes," Rand replied as the computer began its printout of their data file request. He pointed across the room to an opening behind two consoles. "Through that passage."

"Good." Gage cocked his blaster. "Take Meriel and the information and head out. I'll cover until you're safely away, so get a good start or I may end up running over you once there's a horde of Volans on my tail."

"No!" Meriel cried. "Let's stay and fight. I won't leave you behind to take them on alone!"

"Get her out of here. Now!" Gage shouted. Without a backward glance, he ran to take cover behind a metal console and aimed his blaster at the doorway.

Rand ripped off the computer printout, shoved the papers inside his tunic and grabbed Meriel's hand. "Come on!" he cried. "You only slow Bardwin's retreat the longer you linger here!"

As Rand dragged her across the room toward the other exit, Meriel shot an anguished glance back at Gage. Gods, if he should die there she'd never have the chance to say good-bye or tell him, for one last time, how much she loved him. And never have the chance, as well, to know if he still loved her.

But there was no time left for tender farewells.

Rand wouldn't allow it, and neither would the approaching Volans. Even as they raced out of the room and down the dimly lit corridors, Meriel heard the first blasts fired, the cries, the screams.

Let it not be Gage, she prayed, barely keeping up with Rand who all but dragged her along. *Let him come through this safely.*

The journey through the tunnels seemed to drag on endlessly. Even the sounds of battle behind them soon faded. All she heard in the long, endless tomb of stone was their own pounding footsteps, ragged, rasping breaths, hammering hearts. And finally silence when Rand pulled her to a halt.

"Wh-why did you st-stop?" Meriel gasped, laboring for air.

Rand put a finger to her lips. "Shhh-hhh. I want to hear if someone follows."

He listened for a few seconds. "It's as I thought. There is someone coming up behind us. He's quiet and very good, but he hasn't reckoned with my auditory skills."

Meriel found herself shoved into a small alcove, then the light beam was extinguished. She waited in utter blackness, her ears straining for the sound of approaching footsteps, and heard nothing. The tension grew. Was it Gage or Volans? And would Rand fire before he knew one way or another?

There was no love lost between the two warriors. Meriel knew this was Rand's best opportunity to kill Gage. And there was nothing she could do to prevent it. By the time she heard anything, it would be too late. Rand would have already fired.

An impulse struck her to beg Rand to shoot with care, but Meriel knew it was not only futile but dangerous. She didn't dare distract him at a moment like this. There was nothing she could do but stand helplessly by and hope he'd make the right choice.

In the next moment, Gage drew up, breathing heavily. His light beam found Rand, then glanced away to avoid blinding him.

"Where's Meriel?" the tracker demanded.

"Here, Gage." She stepped from the alcove. "I'm here."

"Good," his deep voice rose from the darkness. A powerful hand grasped her arm. "Then let's go. You lead off, Volan."

On and on they went, through the mountain to the other side, until at last a faint light glimmered up ahead. The light increased in intensity at times, then faded to near blackness. The answer to the strange illumination became apparent the closer they drew to the end of the tunnel. A storm raged outside.

Thunder boomed overhead. Lightning flashed, jagged stabs of brilliance that pierced the clouds. The wind howled, whipping clothes close to bodies, hair into eyes. And the rain fell in torrents, drenching them to the skin as they left the shelter of the mountain and ran for cover in the nearby forest.

Behind them the mountain shook, shuddered. Large boulders vibrated loose to tumble down its steep sides. A sound, momentarily louder than the thunder exploding overhead, reverberated across the isle. Gage glanced at Meriel and Rand.

"The explosives have detonated." He shoved his rain-soaked hair out of his eyes. "The transporter is destroyed."

The volcanic mountain vibrated again, then again and again. Larger chunks of stone rumbled down its sides. Before their eyes, the cone began to crumble.

And still the explosions continued, until the earth they stood on trembled. A crack rent the mountain fortress, extending downward until it joined with the ground. The ground separated, the crevice following in an ever-widening course as it raced to the sea.

Meriel lost her balance. Gage grabbed her, pulling her to him.

"What's happening?" she cried.

"Must be some sort of chain reaction," he shouted over the din. "I think the isle is coming apart." He turned to Rand. "Let's go! Let's get to the skim crafts!"

They ran then, weaving through trees that quaked with every explosion. Leaves fell, then branches, until the trio were dodging entire limbs as they sped along. Overhead a mighty robur tree groaned and bent in a grotesque parody of a more human action. The unnaturally strained wood screamed, then, with a sickening, cracking sound, split asunder.

The top half of the ancient tree fell, plummeting straight for them. With a hoarse cry, Gage pulled Meriel to him and leaped out of the way. They fell. Gage twisted to take the brunt of the fall and landed with painful impact.

Stars whirled before Meriel's eyes. For an ag-

onizing moment, she couldn't find her breath.
Then it returned, and the effort to inhale was
more painful than the lack of breath had ever
been. Beneath her, Gage groaned and shifted
awkwardly.

She rolled off and turned to face him. He lay
there, his face ashen, his features constricted in
pain. His left leg was twisted beneath him.

To steady him, Meriel grasped Gage by the hip,
then began to pull his leg free.

"N-no!" he gasped. "Don't! It's br-broken."

Meriel glanced around, searching frantically for
Rand. He limped over, rubbing muscles bruised
in his own leap to safety.

"Rand! Thank the heavens you're safe!" Meriel
gestured to Gage. "Help me. He thinks he's broken his leg. Help me get it out from beneath him
so I can examine it."

The Volan eyed the other man briefly, then
knelt before him and rolled Gage over onto his
side. Gage shot him a furious, anguished look,
but Meriel wasted no time in grasping his leg
and pulling it straight. She carefully removed his
boot. The leg was indeed broken, just above the
ankle. Luckily, the skin hadn't been punctured
by the fractured bone, but, one way or another, Gage's leg would have to be splinted before
he could travel further. Meriel pulled her tunic
from her breeches and began tearing strips of
cloth from her hem.

"Fetch me two relatively straight sticks," she
ordered Rand, "and be quick about it! This isle
isn't going to wait on us before it sinks beneath
the sea!"

Even as she spoke, the ground shuddered ferociously. Several other aging trees crashed nearby.

Rand returned with the sticks. "You do know what you're doing, don't you? This isn't one of my particular talents."

Meriel shot him a grim smile. "They taught me many things at the royal nunnery besides the art of ruling. The care of injuries was one of them.

"This is going to hurt for a moment," she informed Gage. Taking his foot, she placed it in Rand's hands. The two men's gazes met, narrowed, but neither protested.

"When I say pull, pull, but gently, steadily until I tell you to stop," she instructed the Volan. "Then maintain your hold until I tell you to let go. Understand?"

He nodded.

In a quick flurry of movements, Meriel readied the splint and cloth strips, placing them on either side of Gage's broken leg. Then she looked up at Rand.

"Pull."

He did as requested. Gage sucked in a sharp breath. His eyes clenched shut, but he didn't struggle or make another sound.

"That's enough," Meriel said when she felt the ends of the bone fall into place. "Now, just maintain that steady pressure until I tell you to let go."

She worked swiftly, expertly, and soon had Gage's leg splinted. She finished tying off the bandages, then glanced over at Rand.

"You can let go of him now."

He started from his intense concentration, then did as she said.

Her gaze turned to Gage. He was pale, clammy-skinned, and breathing heavily. She watched him for a few seconds, then glanced back at Rand.

"Can you carry him if need be? He may be a little faint for a while and we dare not stay in this forest a moment longer."

As if to add emphasis to her statement, another tree crashed nearby. The ground heaved. Gently Meriel wiped Gage's brow with a small wad of leftover cloth. Then she met his intent stare.

"Are you up to a little walk?" She managed a wan smile, his quite evident pain tugging at her heart. "It's getting a bit dangerous here and we really should be going."

"Help me up," Gage whispered. "There are few other options. I'll make it."

With Rand's assistance on his good side, they got Gage to his feet. He swayed for a moment before righting himself, then leaned heavily on Meriel.

"Gods," he murmured. "I didn't realize . . ." With a superhuman effort Gage straightened, a fierce light gleaming in his eyes. "Lead on. Let's get out of here!"

She eyed him, then motioned to Rand. "I'll lead out. I can see the way through the trees to the sea now. You're far stronger, and Gage will need your support."

The tracker scowled. "I don't need any Volan's help, I can assure—"

"Enough!" Meriel cut him short. "This isn't the

time to turn your nose up at *any* offer of help. You endanger us all by your stubbornness. Besides, you know you need assistance."

"Fine," he growled, his protest fading before the truth of her words. "Just lead on, will you?"

Meriel wheeled about and set off at a slow trot, the fastest speed she dared submit Gage to, as if the shaking ground and frequent explosions rocking the isle would have allowed for anything faster. After several more harrowing escapes from falling branches, they cleared the forest.

The storm raged on above them, one of the fiercest Meriel had ever seen. Once out of the relative protection of the trees, they were again exposed to the full force of wind and rain. Meriel squinted down the sea coast, trying to orient herself as to which direction lay the skim crafts. Skim crafts which she now doubted would even fly in the electricity-charged sky.

Rand and Gage drew up beside her. She turned, totally bewildered.

"Which way?" Meriel glanced from one man to the other. "I can't identify any landmarks in the darkness to tell me which way the skim crafts are."

Before either could answer, another explosion, this time followed by a high-pitched hissing sound, filled the air. The trio wheeled around. There, outlined by the lightning-illuminated clouds, was the top of the second volcano, glowing red, spewing jets of molten lava.

"Gods, haven't we enough trouble," Gage groaned, "without adding an erupting volcano?" He turned back to Meriel and Rand. "We'd better get off this isle and fast. I don't think there'll be much left of it soon."

Rand grabbed Meriel by the arm. "Come on. This way." He shoved her in the direction he'd indicated.

Meriel followed Rand and Gage. Gusts of wind and sheets of pelting rain buffeted them as they ran headlong into the storm. The top of the volcano in the isle's center began to spew copious amounts of lava, which coursed down the mountain at a distressingly fast rate. Periodically the ground shuddered and shook as the explosions within the other volcano that housed the Volan's former fortress blew themselves out.

But it didn't matter anymore if the isle rent itself asunder. The lava was now an even more potent threat. One way or another, they *must* escape the isle.

On and on they ran, stumbling and slipping in the driving rain and shaking ground, making slow but inexorable progress to the site of the hidden skim craft. They found a few men still about when they arrived, climbing into crafts loaded with biospheres, warming up engines, then flying off into the storm-tossed night. Men who preferred to take their chances with the weather than brave the oncoming lava.

Gage quickly consulted with the highest-ranking man available and found that the majority of the invasion force had already departed in skim crafts. The same choice was theirs. Meriel looked to Gage.

"I'll do as you choose," she said, lifting eyes full of trust and love. "As you said before, I'm no warrior queen. I haven't the experience to make such a decision. What should we do?"

As he gazed down into the depths of her luminous eyes, something twisted within Gage. Gods, why now, at a time like this, did she put such responsibility on him? Her life hung on the choice he made, and he was only a man. A man, he mused glumly, who was all but useless with his broken leg.

But no matter what it took, he wouldn't fail her. Gage dragged in a shuddering breath. "Don't sell yourself short, femina. You're warrior enough to please any man. But in answer to your question, I think our best chances lie off this isle. We'll try the skim crafts. At worst we might get halfway across the sea before the storm interferes. And there are far more terrible fates than crashing on a bed of soft, forgiving gelatin."

"But the Tergum," Meriel protested. "There's not much chance of surviving its attack."

Gage motioned to Rand to help him to the skim crafts. "Let's hope it doesn't like the storm any more than we do," he shouted over his shoulder. "There's little choice at any rate."

Glancing back at the lava flow, Meriel knew there really wasn't. The isle was small. The lava would reach the beach in a very short time—in less than a half hour at the speed it was progressing. There was no point in lingering in the hope that the storm would end in the meanwhile, Meriel thought as she glanced up at the dark, churning clouds and lightning-streaked sky. The foul weather offered no hope of blowing itself out anytime soon.

With a small, resigned sigh, Meriel climbed into the skim craft and waited as Gage programmed in the takeoff commands. Rand took his place in another craft and quickly did the same.

The crafts' engines were barely audible as they revved to life, the din of the storm, the roll of thunder and crack of lightning continuing unabated overhead. At long last Gage guided their craft up into the air and directed it away from the isle. As they flew off into the wind-tossed sky, Meriel glanced back at the isle of Insula.

The twin volcanic peaks still pierced the night, one's silhouette jagged, irregular, gutted by the chain reaction of explosions that had destroyed the Volan transport station. The other peak glowed eerily in the darkness, a red-gold light shrouding the entire mountain as the lava's inexorable progress consumed everything in its path. Already, the molten rock had reached the forest edge. Trees began to catch fire, their trunks and straining branches soon little more than fiery limbs clawing at the blackened night until extinguished by the rain.

Meriel shuddered and turned from the horrible scene of death and destruction. It was time to face what lay ahead.

The crafts flew through the darkness, buffeted unmercifully by vicious blasts of turbulent air. Lightning stabbed the clouds, sometimes so close the hair rose on their heads and their skin crackled with static electricity. Even with the force field bubble up, Meriel knew they'd never survive a direct hit.

Sheer, stark terror rippled down her spine.

They'd never make it through this alive! She glanced over at Gage. He sat there, an intent, narrow-eyed expression on his face.

An impulse to touch him, to absorb just a little of his courage and resolve, filled her. But she dared not distract him. Meriel consoled herself with the realization that they were together, even if it might well be the end for both of them. Gage wouldn't die alone, without someone close by who loved him. And that love would follow them both to the other side, for all eternity . . .

The winds grew stronger. The skim craft labored against the surging gusts of air, its engine beginning to strain. The instrument panel lights flickered, went awry.

Gage shot her an anguished look. "The electronics are starting to go," he shouted above the din of the storm. "I'm going to take the craft lower and see if that helps."

Her throat went dry and her heart thundered in her chest, but all Meriel did was nod. The skim craft's trajectory changed, angling downward. Yet as they lost altitude, the colorful chaos of the instrument panel only worsened.

"Be damned!" Gage pounded on the panel in frustration. "The craft isn't responding at all. We're going to crash!"

There was nothing to be done after that, and little time to prepare. Meriel managed to glance back to see how Rand was doing. He appeared to be having similar problems with his own machine. She flung him a mental prayer for his safe landing, then turned back to Gage, who was fighting to regain even the smallest amount of control as they plummeted downward. At the last moment, the best he could achieve was to level off the skim craft.

With a resounding, bone-jarring smack, the craft struck the sea, bounced high off its thick membrane, then struck again and again in ever-decreasing impacts until it slid the last ten or twenty meters. Finally the machine skidded to a halt.

Gage glanced over. "Are you all right, Meriel?"

She exhaled a deep breath, swiped a water-logged mass of hair out of her eyes, and nodded. "Quite a dramatic landing." She managed an unsteady grin. "What do you plan for an encore?"

He arched a dark brow. "Your tastes for excitement have certainly grown. Would getting us safely to land meet your needs?"

Meriel released her belt restraint and climbed out. "Yes, most definitely." She glanced around to see what had become of Rand. He had crashed, nose down, several hundred meters away.

By the time Meriel had helped Gage climb out, retrieved their blasters and supply packs, Rand had arrived. He eyed Meriel closely. "Are you unharmed?"

She flushed at the glower Gage shot her, then Rand. "Yes, I'm fine." She glanced around. "Which way is the shore?"

"Better yet," Rand muttered, glancing uneasily around, "which way is the Tergum?"

"Is one near?" Meriel heart leaped to her throat. "How can you know? They're said to be swift, silent killers."

"Even Tergum have life sounds, sounds my

auditory senses are attuned to." Rand's blue eyes met hers. "And I tell you true, there's one nearby."

"Then it will find us!" Meriel cried. "The Tergum can smell its prey thousands of meters away. We must go. Now!"

Gage gripped her arm and pulled her about to face him. "Which direction, Meriel? There's no way to know where the creature is. We could as easily run right into it as away from it. We must have a plan or we'll all die. Tell me, is there anything that attracts it more to one victim than another?"

She stilled, her mind racing. "I-I don't remember . . ." A light flared in her eyes. "Yes, there is one thing. A Tergum is said to be particularly attracted to wounded prey. I suppose the scent of blood . . ."

Her voice faded as she watched Gage whip out his dagger. In a nearly reflexive move, Meriel grabbed his knife hand. "What do you mean to do?" she demanded even as the sickening inkling of his intent filled her.

His dark eyes met hers for a long, emotion-laden moment, then he glanced over her shoulder at Rand. "Take Meriel, Volan. Pull her away from me and hold her tightly."

Rand immediately stepped forward. His powerful arms encircled Meriel. With an easy use of his superior strength, he disengaged her clasp on Gage's wrist and dragged her back. Meriel struggled briefly, then gave it up as futile.

A cold knot formed in her stomach, then grew, spreading swiftly through her body on frigid fingers of dread. "What do you mean to do?" she heard herself whisper even as, this time, she was already certain of the answer.

"It's the only way, Meriel," Gage replied, his voice low and hoarse. "Try to understand. One of us must lure the Tergum off so the other two can escape. And, reality being what it is, I'm the most expendable. I can't run with a broken leg. I'd only hold you back."

With that, he raised his dagger and slashed himself several times across the chest.

"No!" Meriel screamed even as she saw his blood well and begin to stain his rent tunic. She lifted her gaze to his, anguished, pleading, horrified.

Gage stared back, a grim smile on his lips that never quite reached his eyes. "It has to be, Meriel. I am doomed—if not now, then soon enough. Let me do this for you. It's the only honor left me."

"No," Meriel sobbed, the tears pouring from her eyes. "Don't do this. Don't leave me. I love you. We'll find a way to free you from your Volan. Don't sacrifice yourself while there's still hope. Please, Gage. Please!"

A mask of hard resolve tightened his face. He motioned to Rand with the blade of his dagger. "Take her. Now, before it's too late! Take her to safety. The shore lies behind you."

Even as Rand began to drag her away, Meriel fought him like an enraged she-cat. It did little good, one way or another. A helpless fury filled her, at Rand, but even more at Gage.

"Curse you, Gage Bardwin!" she screamed even as the darkness and wind and rain swallowed his tall, powerful form. "Curse you, I say! You're a coward, nothing more. A coward, afraid to face life, to fight for what matters. Even now you run away. Run away as I always knew you would . . . from me, our love . . ."

Chapter Nineteen

Meriel's cries haunted Gage long after she disappeared into the night. The parting had been more painful than he'd ever imagined. He hadn't meant for her to think he had been seeking an excuse to sever their relationship because he wanted to shirk his responsibilities to her. He'd just wanted her to understand that the Volan enslavement had changed everything.

He'd been used once before for evil means. He never intended to be used again. Yet the potential was too great that that would happen. Even now, with Meriel gone but a short time, he could feel his Volan entity stir to life, begin to reexert its power.

Not that it mattered. Volan-enslaved or no, the Tergum would find him. And even a Volan couldn't overcome that dreaded creature. That was the only other consolation, aside from ensuring Meriel's life. The Volan would die when he did. A Tergum wasn't particular about what life form it engulfed.

The rain fell, slanting from the swollen, turbulent sky in sheets of water. Huge puddles formed on the surface of the sea. The wind blew, chilling Gage through his rain-soaked clothes, drenching his hair until a steady trickle of water coursed into his eyes. He clasped his arms tightly about him and shivered. Gods, if the Tergum didn't hurry, he might first succumb to the cold!

He listened, straining his tracker's ears to catch the first sound of the creature's presence. Though he'd volunteered to sacrifice himself out in the middle of an alien sea, Gage had no intention of going meekly to his death. He was still a warrior. He'd fight with all the strength and prowess he possessed. His life, when he finally fell, would have been dearly bought—and for as much time as he could win for Meriel.

His Volan presence swelled, grew stronger. Anger burgeoned in Gage. Damn, he wanted to die awake, aware, laughing in the face of danger one last time! He wanted to be . . . himself.

The wind whipped by, snatching at his clothes, penetrating, then blowing through them. Gage's shivering turned to wracking shudders. Already his hands and feet were turning numb, his muscles knotting with spasms. He rubbed his arms and chest in an attempt to stimulate his circulation. It helped for as long as his efforts continued.

After a time, he thought he heard a sound—a rasp of something rough sliding over the surface of the sea. Awkwardly he hopped about, his dagger in one hand, his blaster immediately swung into firing position with the other. Sunrise was just tingeing the horizon with a faint wash of pink. His last sunrise, Gage thought dimly.

Something moved in the corner of his vision. He swung around. There, looming above him, was an eerie, nearly transparent, giant blob. The Tergum.

Its eyes were tiny, almost useless, its primitive nervous system glinting a silvery mauve as it wound its way through a shapeless body up to what must be its head. The creature formed, then re-formed again, shrinking to a tight little ball, then flowing out and expanding to twice its original size.

Gage watched, transfixed at the Tergum's amazing abilities. Then the creature paused in its amoebalike gyrations, emitting a piercing cry. Its mouth, suddenly huge and open, moved toward him, ready to consume its newfound prey.

Six long, agonizing days, Meriel thought bleakly from her seat on her bedchamber balcony overlooking the garden. Six days and her search parties had still found no sign of Gage, dead or alive. It was past time to accept reality. There was no sign because the Tergum had found and consumed Gage. He was gone. Forever.

Still the hope, however faint, remained that he wasn't dead. Perhaps it was the remnants of her love for him, Meriel mused forlornly. Or the lingering pain at the memory of their parting.

She had been so cruel in those last moments, cursing Gage in her fear and anger, calling him a coward. It wasn't the kind of farewell that sat well with her in recollection. She had called him a coward, then left him to face the Tergum alone in the darkness and wind and rain, all but helpless with his broken leg. Left him thinking she hated him.

"Meriel?" A gentle hand touched her arm.

Meriel started, then turned and sadly eyed her friend. "Yes, what is it, Dian?"

Dian's heart twisted in her chest. Meriel was so drawn, so pale, and that look in her eyes . . .

She shuddered. Ever since her return from the invasion of Insula, Meriel barely ate and slept even less. If she didn't begin to take care of herself, Dian thought, she'd soon drive herself into illness. But nothing Dian or anyone else said made any impact. Meriel would have to work through her loss herself. Some things were best handled alone.

"The Volan." Dian's lips curled in disgust. "He's here and wishes to speak with you."

"Rand?"

Meriel's expression brightened momentarily. It was all Dian could do not to chide her for still being so accepting of the alien who had stolen her beloved Torman. But he *had* helped them and brought Meriel home safely, Dian admitted reluctantly. If he just hadn't taken Torman's body she might have been more willing—

She caught herself. No matter whose body he stole, it was still wrong. She must not forget that. And, deep in her heart, she knew Meriel hadn't, either.

"Do you want me to bring him to you?" Dian prodded when Meriel remained silent. She was like that a lot lately, the maidservant thought. So distant, so easily distracted.

"What?" Meriel nodded. "Yes, please, Dian. I'm coming in anyway. It's far too hot to stay outside very long."

She followed her friend inside and took a seat in one of the hearth chairs. Dian strode to the door and ushered Rand in, her body stiff, her lips tight with her barely contained disapproval.

Meriel noticed and sighed. She'd so wished that Dian would come to accept Rand and see beneath his surface form to the being he truly was. But that was probably an unrealistic dream. Unrealistic and unfair.

The Volan, carrying a bag at his side, came to stand before Meriel. He rendered her a small bow.

She smiled and waved him over to the opposite chair. "The formalities aren't necessary here, my friend. Come, take a seat."

Meriel glanced up at Dian who stood nearby. "I'm so thirsty. Could you bring us a cool drink and perhaps some chilled fruit ice?"

"As you wish, mistress." Dian hurried away.

The Queen turned to Rand. "And what brings you to my quarters in the middle of the day? I thought you and Brace were busy developing the next part of the evacuation plan for my approval."

"We both decided it was time for a break." Rand set his bag beside his chair and sat down. "Besides, it's done. Brace will present it to you after the supper meal. I think you'll like it."

He paused. "I also discussed the problem of the rebel army with Brace. They must be dealt with carefully, as the leadership, almost to a man, is Volan-enslaved. I suggest you send the leaders a message asking for a secret meeting to discuss the overthrow of the Bellatorians. Then, when they comply, capture them."

"A wise suggestion. I'll see to it immediately."

Rand's brows knitted as he scanned her face. "You look awful, Meriel. You've got to stop your mourning and get on with your life. Bardwin's gone, and it's for the best."

"How can you say that?" Meriel leaped to her feet. "You, of all people, have no right to judge Gage or determine what is best for him!"

"On the contrary. I, of all people, do have that right." Something painful flickered in his eyes. "We shared similar dilemmas. Bardwin's was whether his life was more important than the lives of others. And mine is, and has always been, whether I have the right to steal another's body, even if for ultimately good purposes. So you see, Meriel, we both were forced to admit our arrogance in placing greater value on our own lives than on that of others."

"Gage didn't value his life, not in the way it truly mattered," Meriel muttered bitterly. "Deep down, he never thought himself worthy or deserving of happiness. And, to protect himself, he never allowed anything or anyone to really matter. It protected him from pain at least."

"He gave up his life for us, Meriel."

She shot Rand a puzzled look. "You defend him now? That's a strange turn for you."

"I've had a lot of time to think since our return. Though a great amount of what you say about

Bardwin might be true—his self-doubts, his reluctance to allow himself to truly achieve happiness— at least he had the right to pursue it. It was his body to do with as he wished and still he willingly sacrificed it. I, on the other hand, have no such right to do anything with my body."

Her eyes closed for a brief moment, then opened to lock with Rand's. "No, in truth, you never had such a right. But if you hadn't taken it, however unjustly, I wouldn't be here now."

He smiled. "I thank you for that, and for the friendship you've offered. It has been deeply cherished."

Rand leaned forward and took Meriel's hands in his. She looked down, marveling at how he engulfed her, his fingers long and blunt, his callused palms rasping across the flesh of her hands and wrist. She had always felt safe with him, even when he had first Volan-enslaved Torman. There was just something inherently good about him.

"The time has come, Meriel."

She jerked her gaze back to his, her eyes widening. "Wh-what time? I don't know what you mean."

"Yes, you do." He reached into the bag he had brought with him and withdrew a biosphere. "This biosphere is filled with temeritas but empty of a Volan. I want you to help me transfer into it."

Meriel stared at him in horror. Across the bedchamber, a door slid open and Dian walked in carrying a tray laden with a covered container, cups, and a crystal decanter of juice. She moved to the small table that stood between Meriel and Gage and lowered the tray. One glance at her friend, however, interrupted the maidservant's intent to serve her.

"Meriel? What's wrong?" she cried as she noted Meriel's ashen expression. "What did he say to you? What did he do?" Dian wheeled about to confront Rand. "I swear, if you've hurt her in any way—"

Rand held up a silencing hand, a thin smile on his lips. "It is nothing Meriel didn't expect. My departure is just occurring a little earlier than planned. Isn't it, Meriel?" he prodded gently.

"Yes," she breathed. "Oh, Rand, is it . . . must it be . . . ?" Meriel inhaled a ragged breath and looked up at Dian. "He intends to leave Torman."

The maidservant paled, then turned back to Rand. "You mean this? You won't change your mind?"

"No." Piercing blue eyes gleamed with resolve. "It is time you had your man back. His has been a fine body, but he deserves the opportunity to enjoy it for himself. And," he added, "the chance to be with the woman he loves."

"He l-loves me?" Dian's voice went breathless with joy. "Do you truly know that? He had never spoken the words before you . . . you took him."

"Yes, he loves you. From time to time his emotions force their way to my consciousness, and especially when you're around."

Dian lifted a trembling hand to her heart. Her eyes, filled with tears, swung to her friend's. "Oh, Meriel . . ."

"I could use your help as well, Dian," Rand said, deciding it was time to get the deed done before he lost the courage for it. The decision, difficult enough to make, had nearly disintegrated once he was again in Meriel's presence.

Meriel, he belatedly realized, was the catalyst to his initial change of heart. She would always be the elusive symbol of everything he desired and could never have. And only she could help him see this final, agonizing process to its bitter if justifiable end.

"How?" the maidservant asked. "How can I help you?"

Rand handed her the biosphere. "When I tell you the moment is right, press this to the base of my neck and hold it there until I lose consciousness. The transfer of my entity will be complete once that happens."

She accepted the globe gingerly and cradled it between her two hands. "Yes, I'll do what you ask."

He moved the table aside and came to kneel before Meriel. Once more, he took her hands in his. "I would like you to hold me, be with me until it is over."

His eyes locked with hers, and Rand's heart twisted at the shattered expression burning there. "Please, Meriel," he whispered. "I need to do this, but I don't think I can if you don't help me."

"Oh, Rand!" Meriel leaned forward until her forehead touched his. "I-I can't bear it! First Gage, now you. I haven't the strength, the courage!"

"You're the bravest woman I have ever known," he breathed, his voice so soft it reached only her ears. "I will never forget you, even there within my biosphere. We continue to remember and experience, you know. Our existence goes on, however incomplete it may be. And some day, if I'm fortunate enough to be granted another physical form, I'll come back. Friends do that."

Meriel's head lifted and she stared straight into his eyes. "Yes, friends do." She paused to gird herself for what was to come. "Are you ready? If you must do this thing, do it now or I don't know if I can see it through."

Rand nodded. "I'm ready. It's for the best. You know that, don't you?"

"Yes." The tears spilled down her cheeks. "It's the right thing to do."

He smiled then, a slow, gentle movement of his lips. Then he closed his eyes.

Meriel waited, but aside from a tightening of his grip on her hands, nothing happened. Then a nearly imperceptible change came over Rand. His breathing began to accelerate, his expression assumed a strained appearance. Tiny tremors began to shake him.

"Now," he gasped at last, lowering his head to rest upon his chest. "Press the biosphere to my neck!"

Dian quickly did as instructed. For a long moment nothing happened, then a swirling green luminescence suddenly flared within the container. Rand gave a hoarse cry and slumped forward into Meriel's arms, his body limp, lifeless.

Meriel clasped him to her, stroking his head, murmuring soft words of comfort as a mother would to her child. After a time, she glanced up at Dian.

"Remove the biosphere. The transfer is complete. Rand is gone from Torman's body."

With the greatest of care, the maidservant rose and went to place the globe back in the bag. Then she returned to sit silently across from Meriel, who still clutched the last remnant of the special friend she had found and lost, rocking him endlessly back and forth.

Brace programmed in the last of the commands that would encode the comvid transmissions to Bellator and glanced up. "Are you ready, Meriel?"

She nodded. "Yes. Initiate the link with Lord Ardane. I'm curious what he thought so urgent to communicate with us about."

"So am I." Brace punched in the appropriate command and sat down beside Meriel. The comvid screen crackled with static, then flickered to life. A moment later, Teran's handsome, bearded face came into view.

"Greetings, Lord Ardane," Meriel murmured. "And what is the purpose of your summons? The secret transmission you sent requesting to speak with us was most intriguing."

Teran smiled. "The Volan data sheets you brought back from Insula have been most informative. Our scientists have been analyzing them almost nonstop since their delivery to Bellator."

"And what have you found?"

"For one, some very interesting theories on Volan choices of hosts. They exclusively take only warm-blooded species. It seems they aren't partial to cold."

Meriel's brow furrowed in thought. "That would make sense. Volans originally came from a *very* warm planet. But how will that knowledge help us? We can't change our innate makeup."

"No," Teran admitted, "but we might very handily use it to drive a Volan from its host."

A surge of excitement coursed through Meriel. The information might have come too late for Gage, but if it would help in the battle against the Volan empire . . .

"How?" she demanded. "Have your scientists already developed a technique? And is it safe? We don't want to kill the host as well."

Teran chuckled and held up his hands. "One question at a time, femina. The technique is called 'icing' and it's a very sophisticated form of hypothermia. If it works like it should, the super cold will drive the Volan from its host. Then the host can be rewarmed back to life. The only question is how much cold is needed to remove the Volan. At this point, all we know is what parameters must not be exceeded if we are to safely bring the host back to life."

"There's no way to be certain what it will take without trying out the technique," Meriel observed thoughtfully. "And for that you need some preliminary subjects."

"Yes. We're in the process of attempting to capture a few newly enslaved hosts, utilizing the telltale clues you've provided. It's only a matter of time. I think we've finally made significant—"

A loud pounding on Meriel's door interrupted Teran. "What's going on there, Domina?" he inquired, his features tightening in irritation.

"I don't know." Meriel rose from her chair to go to the door, but Brace was already on his feet, striding across the room. The door slid open at his imprint and he faced Meriel's captain of the guard.

"What is it?" Brace demanded. "We are in the midst of a meeting, and orders were given not to be disturbed."

Torman bowed low. "I've news of vital interest to our Queen. I thought she'd desire immediate notification."

"Indeed?" Brace turned to Meriel. "Do you wish to speak with him now, Domina?"

She nodded. "Grant Torman entry. I trust his judgment. If he says it's important, it is."

Brace motioned the big man in, then imprinted the door closed behind them. Torman strode across the room and knelt before her.

Meriel smiled, though a bittersweet memory of Rand still lanced through her each time she saw him. She touched Torman on the head. "Rise. Tell me your news."

"A man was found not far from Eremita, skulking in the forest. I thought it wise to apprehend him for questioning. That intent, however, proved far more difficult than I imagined."

Torman paused for breath. Impatience filled Meriel. "Yes, go on," she urged. "Did you capture this man, and what was his purpose here?"

"Oh, we captured him, Domina," her captain muttered wryly. "He was extremely powerful and it took five men to subdue him, even with his broken leg, but we have him—"

"Powerful? Broken leg?" Meriel's hands clenched into tight little fists as she fought to contain the wild swell of hope within her.

It couldn't be. It just couldn't.

"The man," she forced the words past a tightly constricted throat. "What does he look like?"

Torman grinned. "Tall, blond and, according to the Bellatorians who know him, definitely enslaved by a Volan, Domina. And definitely our Lord Commander."

It took all of Meriel's considerable control to nod and smile at the news. "You've done well. Where do you currently have our Lord Commander housed?"

"In our most secure holding cell, Domina," he replied. "He's still quite dangerous."

"A wise decision." She made a motion for him to leave. "Await me outside and I will join you shortly. Then you may escort me down to visit our Lord Commander."

Torman bowed, then turned and left the room. Once the door closed behind him, Meriel turned back to the vidcom screen. "You heard it all?" she asked Teran.

A wide grin split his face. "Yes. As soon as you assist Gage in regaining control of his Volan, I wish to speak with him."

Meriel laughed wryly. "You have such confidence that I can free him again. Myself, I'm not that certain."

"You still love him, don't you?"

A soft light flared in the depths of Meriel's eyes. "Of course. To the end of my days."

"Then that Volan hasn't a chance." Teran paused, his brow furrowing in thought. "And I think, as well, that we may have found our first subject for our icing technique."

* * *

"Ah, this feels wonderful," Gage murmured blissfully two hours later as he sank into the churning mineral bath in Meriel's bathing chamber. "Obviously Volans have no problems with tolerating six days of filth, but I definitely do."

He glanced up at Meriel, who sat on the edge of the huge stone tub, a quiet smile on her lips. "Would you consider scrubbing my back? I know you're still angry with me—and rightfully so—but since Teran wishes to speak with me and the sooner I make myself presentable . . ."

She grabbed the container of cleansing sand and moved to position herself behind him. "Let's get a few things settled first," Meriel began as she moistened some sand in her palms and rubbed it into a lather. "I'm no longer angry with you. In fact, I regret my harsh words back there on the Cerulean Sea.

"I was terrified for you," she continued, spreading the lather along his shoulders and upper back, "not to mention so incredibly frustrated at my helplessness in the whole matter. Do you know what it did to me to be dragged away and leave you standing there, awaiting your death?

"And for that matter," she hastened to interject, "how *did* you escape the Tergum? You were crippled, virtually defenseless, and alone out there in the dark. What happened?"

Gage shrugged, immensely enjoying the feel of Meriel's hands on his body. "The chill weather, though I cursed it at the time, helped keep my Volan at bay. Even without realizing why at the time, I was able to remain in control. And I wasn't as defenseless as you may have imagined. The sun had begun to rise just enough for me to see the Tergum as it attacked. When I caught a glimpse of its neural system within its all but transparent body, I thought of my stunner. Luckily for me, the stunner worked. Then, while it lay there I finished it off with my blaster."

"Very clever," Meriel observed. "If you'd just used your blaster on it to defend yourself, it would've done little but anger the creature and hastened your end. But who would've thought a stunner . . . ?"

She moved down to wash one arm, then the other. "And now we know the defense against a Tergum. Not that it will matter much longer. In another few cycles we'll all be gone from Tenua. I see no point in transporting any Tergum along with the other flora and fauna of the planet."

Gage shot her a quick glance. "How goes the evacuation, by the way?"

Meriel smiled. "Very well. Brace has done admirably in keeping things flowing smoothly. I don't know what I would have done without him. Especially after Rand decided to return Torman's body."

"The Volan gave up Torman?" Gage grabbed Meriel by the arm and pulled her around to face him. "When did this happen? And why?"

"Three days ago." She inhaled a deep breath, struggling past the painful recollection, still so fresh, so poignant. "Rand finally came to a decision I knew he'd been struggling with for a long time. Just as you hated and despised the part of you that wasn't you, Rand hated and despised his actions in stealing someone else's body. He always knew it wasn't right."

Tears filled her eyes at the memory of those last moments before Rand transferred back to the biosphere. "I wish you could have been there, Gage. I think you'd have finally understood him, and seen him for the good being he truly was. It was so *very* hard for him to give up his body. He wanted to experience all the things he'd just recently discovered, to savor a life he'd always been denied."

"What will happen to him, now that's he's back in a biosphere?"

"He left instructions on how to fashion a life-support system to hook his biosphere to. We'll keep him on that until my scientists come up with a more viable alternative." She met his gaze squarely. "We may not be able to solve the entire Volan race's problem quickly, but I at least mean to find a way to devise some kind of special body to house Rand's entity in."

"Have a care, Meriel," Gage warned. "You could well end up with an enemy even more powerful than before."

"Perhaps," she conceded. "But I'm not afraid of what Rand will do or become with the new, stronger body he'll need to support his entity for a normal life span. I trust him implicitly. All he ever wanted was to have the same chance at happiness as the rest of us. Surely you can see that."

"Yes, I can . . . now. And I think I even begin to understand him a little, however late it may be," Gage remarked thoughtfully. "His courage in making such a painfully difficult decision shames me in comparison. I *am* running away, Meriel. I *am* a coward. It's always been easier than risking betrayal. And then, coupled with the certainty that I'm not worthy of you—"

"How can you say that, after all you've done?" she demanded. "We all have our personal obstacles to overcome in the pursuit of lasting happiness. And if you think, after what you've put me through in the past days, I'll ever let you go—"

"I'm a bastard, sweet femina," Gage reminded her. "Even if this icing technique works and I'm permanently freed of my Volan, I'll never be worthy to be your life mate. You're a Queen. You deserve better."

"Do I now? And thank you very much for making all the decisions for me once again, Gage Bardwin. That reprehensible tendency is, I think, your greatest flaw. If you truly mean to begin trusting me, you could start there. A little respect for my judgment, that I know what's best for me, would be deeply appreciated."

He leaned back against her, a devilish smile on his lips. "Have no fear, femina. I totally respect your judgment as Queen. You've proven your ability to rule time and again. It's your judgment as a woman I have a few misgivings about. You always were a little too soft-hearted when it came to me, even from the beginning."

"Was I now?"

"Yes, you were . . . and still are."

With that, Gage pulled Meriel into his arms to join him in the tub. She gave a startled shriek, then laughed, coming to him with all the eager abandon of a woman in love. And Gage kissed her soundly, thoroughly, willing away, at least for a time, the memory of the ordeal that lay ahead.

An ordeal that he might not survive. In his rock-solid determination to rid himself of his Volan once and for all, Gage knew he might well die in this last, most desperate of attempts.

Chapter Twenty

"I don't like it, Gage," Meriel murmured worried-ly a day later as they stood in a very utilitarian Bellatorian laboratory.

The lab was spotless, from the shiny metal tables and stone counters and cabinets lining the walls to the irradiated air, floors, and sterile instruments. But even the room's cleanliness, combined with the well-respected credentials of the group of white-robed scientists standing a discreet distance away in low-voiced discussion with Teran, didn't reassure Meriel. The icing technique was just too new, too untried, for her liking.

The inescapable fact was that Gage was to be the first humanoid subject to endure the severe hypothermia. And too much could go wrong—the lowering of his body temperature might drop past the point of safe resuscitation, the stress of driving out the Volan might be too severe a strain for his heart, or, worst of all, the experiment would fail and the Volan remain.

That, Meriel knew, was Gage's secret fear—to awaken with the Volan still within him, still lurking there awaiting the next opportunity to regain control. She could accept that and go on fighting. *Her* greatest fear was of losing Gage entirely.

"I know, sweet femina. The first time for anything is always the hardest." Gage took her hand in his. "But you must support me in this. It's what I want, with all my heart. Be brave for me. Stand by me."

She smiled, a tremulous upturning of soft, full lips, and glanced down at him lying there on one of those cold, metallic tables. He wore only breeches and boots, his chest and arms bared for the multiple puncture sites necessary to flood his body with the icing solution. Her heart twisted within her chest.

He looked so beautiful, even lying on a table awaiting the manipulations of others, so vulnerable, so trusting, so hopeful. Yet, even now, Gage still emanated the restrained power and unyielding authority she had come to know and need. Her eyes traveled down his body, imprinting the memory of his thick, curling blond hair, his ruggedly hewn features, his masculine form, all whipcord and sinew and muscle.

By all that was sacred, she loved him! Loved him and had lost him so many times now, only to win him back again and again. This time would be the last, though, Meriel vowed. Once she had Gage back, free of his Volan, she'd never give him up again. *Never* again . . . if only her love was equal to this last and most danger-fraught of tests.

"You know I will, my love," she whispered, squeezing his hand. "I'll always be there for you."

Teran walked over. "Are you ready?" He smiled down at Gage.

The tracker shrugged. "Why not? There's no point in prolonging the inevitable."

"I agree." Teran motioned the scientists over, then pulled Meriel back so they could prepare Gage for the icing.

In a surprisingly short time, Gage was ready. Several tubes ran from his arms, some to instill the icing solution, some to drain it off in a constant recirculation of the hypothermic solution. Finally they allowed Meriel to return to Gage's side.

He smiled up at her, already drowsy from the sedative that would take the edge off his discomfort as he slowly chilled to the point of unconsciousness. Ever so carefully, Meriel took his hand back in hers.

"It's good to have you here," Gage said. "I want your face to be the last I see and the first when I reawaken."

"Always, my love," she replied, her throat constricting with emotion. "Now, and every day for the rest of our lives."

One of the scientists programmed the instillation machine to begin. With a low whir and a sudden flare of power, the pump began. Meriel's grip tightened on Gage's hand.

"I've always loved you, you know," he mumbled sleepily. "Always. And . . . Kieran. I love . . . him, too."

"I know," Meriel breathed softly, but even then his lids were growing heavy, lowering, closing.

Soon the rasp of Gage's deep, even breathing was the only sound that filled the room.

Meriel watched the monitor that measured Gage's core body temperature and saw it fall . . . and fall . . . and fall. Finally she turned to Teran. "How low must it go? And how will we know when the Volan leaves Gage? How will we know when it's time to rewarm him?"

Teran shook his head. "None of us are certain, Meriel. Hopefully, the Volan will give us some sign when he leaves. Otherwise we have to continue to drop Gage's body temperature. He didn't want to be revived, you know, if we weren't convinced the Volan wasn't gone."

Her eyes widened with the effort not to protest, or demand differently. Instead, Meriel nodded. "I suspected as much."

Time dragged on. As each centigrade lost from Gage's body ticked off on the monitor's digital readout, the tension grew. At thirty-five degrees centigrade, Gage began to shiver violently. At thirty degrees, his heart rate and respirations began to decline. By twenty-six degrees, his pulse and respirations were undetectable. Cardiac irregularities began to occur.

Meriel couldn't take it any longer. "Gods, stop it!" she cried. "It's not working! You're killing him!"

Teran stepped around the table and put his arms around her. He pulled her back against him.

"We have to cool him further, Meriel. We must be sure."

"B-but you're killing him!" she sobbed.

"Not yet, femina. He's strong. He can bear it."

Twenty degrees centigrade, fifteen, then twelve, ten, eight. At five degrees centigrade, Gage twitched, then jerked, his facial muscles spasming in a grotesque mask of agony. His mouth opened, then his eyes. A strangled scream ripped from his throat.

"No! Curse you! *No!*"

Gage arched up from the table and, if not for the restraining straps across his upper chest and thighs, would have thrown himself from the table. He twisted, he turned, screaming, over and over and over. And still the pump forced the icing solution into him, and his core temperature dropped. Three degrees centigrade. Two.

Suddenly a green luminescence enshrouded Gage, then flowed away from him along the table in an uncontrolled manner, chaotic, mindless, as if seeking escape from the now frigid, inhospitable body it had once inhabited. Seeking some new haven. Seeking . . . and finding nothing.

The luminescence wavered, faded, shrinking until it was no more. And still the core temperature monitor ticked off the dropping figures. One, zero, minus one degree centigrade.

"Stop it!" Meriel screamed when all stood there as if transfixed at what they'd seen. "Turn the machine off. Warm him. Now, before it's too late!"

The men around the table sprang into action. The icing solution was slowly replaced with warmed solutions. Heated, inhaled gases were pumped into Gage's lungs. His body was swathed in a thermal blanket.

And, little by little, they gradually brought his temperature back up. The heart irregularities continued, however. Cardiac stimulants were employed, electric shock, and still Gage's heart wouldn't respond. Time passed, a quarter of an hour, than a half, and still the scientists labored.

In vain.

Finally their shoulders slumped in defeat. They stepped back from the table. Unable to meet Meriel's horrified gaze, they moved away. Her eyes swung to Gage.

He lay there, ashen, rigid, the tubes still attached to his body, his face surprisingly peaceful for what he'd endured. A small, choking voice filled the room, and it took a second or two before Meriel recognized it as her own. She twisted in Teran's arms.

"Let me go," she whispered. "Let me at least go to him now."

With a shuddering sigh, Teran released her. She ran straight to Gage's side, her eyes swimming with tears, her hands unsure of what to do, where to touch him. Then it didn't matter anymore. There was nothing more that anyone could do to hurt him.

With a broken cry, Meriel gathered Gage's lifeless body into her arms. Pressing his head to her breast, she rocked him to and fro, stroking his back, crooning his name.

"Don't leave me," she pleaded. "I love you. I

need you. Ah, Gods, don't leave me, Gage!"

He lay against her, limp, cold, sagging where she didn't support him. He didn't breathe; she couldn't feel his heart beat. Pain stabbed through her. Once again Gage was gone, and this time she hadn't even been given a chance to stop him.

Anger flooded her, a rage both hot and motivating. Be damned, but she'd not lose him again! Meriel clutched Gage to her, clinging to him so tightly his body's chill seeped into her. She clamped shut her eyes and willed all the strength of her heart, her soul, to him. Once more she imagined Gage as he last had been; re-forming him in her mind's eye, bit by agonizing bit.

And the vision held, took form, substance. From that being a warmth flared to life, flickered, then grew—into a heated, living light. The aura engulfed Gage, sustaining him, fueling the tiny flame that had all but died. A conflagration burst around him, surged high and strong. From it a man stepped forth, whole, reborn. He smiled, and Meriel knew he had come back to her.

A heart thudded against her breast. A chest heaved for air. A body stirred in her arms. Meriel smiled a secret smile and kissed Gage's clammy forehead.

"M-Meriel," she heard a deep voice groan. "Ah, Gods, Meriel."

Something wet and warm trickled down onto the hand that cradled a beard-stubbled cheek. Her lids slowly lifted. Gage stared up at her, his compelling eyes moisture-bright and wondering.

"You came back to me," she breathed. "Came back, as I knew you would."

"Yes," he rasped. Gage shuddered and clutched her to him. "I came back."

"I warned you this would happen."

Gage Bardwin glanced up at his friend as he packed his gear in preparation for transport off Tenua. His mouth quirked in wry remembrance. "Yes, you did. And I was a fool not to listen."

"You'll break her heart," Teran persisted. "After all she's gone through for you, it isn't fair."

With a sigh, Gage turned from the task at hand. "Nothing about this is fair. I should have left long ago, yet responsibilities and events I had no control over kept pulling me back. But now the evacuation is going smoothly, the Volan influence on Tenua will soon be contained, and Meriel's abilities to rule are quite sufficient to her planet's needs. I'll continue to help fight the Volan threat, but not here. You and Brace will have to assist Meriel in my stead."

"So you're not needed on Tenua anymore."

"Exactly."

Teran's eyes narrowed in speculation. "I've never seen you run away from a challenge. Why now?"

Gage tensed, fighting to contain his rising irritation. "I'm not running away. I'm freeing Meriel from a painfully difficult decision."

"And that is?"

"Curse you, Ardane!" Brown eyes flashed in anger. "Nothing that really matters has changed. I'm still a bastard. I can't life mate with her and you know it!"

"In reward for your services to the Imperium,

Falkan has offered you the Bardwin lands and throne. There is some standing in that."

"No." Gage shook his head in fierce denial. "House Bardwin deserves to go to those of the High Prince's blood. I've not a drop of it in my veins, even if I still carry his name."

"Then your mother's ancestral lands. You do carry her blood."

"No."

Teran moved to stand beside his friend. "Do you still hate her then? Your mother, I mean?"

Gage met Teran's questioning gaze. "I'll never understand nor accept what she did. It was wrong. But there's nothing to gain by continuing to hate her. Knowing Meriel, coming to love her, has finally taught me that."

"Yet it hasn't taught you quite enough, has it, my friend?"

Gage scowled. "What, by the five moons, are you talking about?"

"It's all quite simple," Meriel interjected from her unexpected arrival in the doorway. "You still judge everyone and everything—yourself included—in light of what your mother did to you. Because of that, *everyone* comes up lacking—and most especially you."

Gage shot Teran a pained look.

His friend grinned. "I think it's past time I excused myself. There's a matter I need to discuss with Brace . . ."

He graced Meriel with a small bow as he paused before her, then scooted past her through the doorway. She stepped into the room, and the door slid silently closed behind her.

"Were you even planning on saying good-bye?"

Gage flushed. "Of course. I'm not afraid to face you."

"But you are afraid to stay with me, to take a chance on a life together."

"That was never an option."

"Never an option?" Meriel's eyes widened in incredulity. "That's not the impression I got when you first arrived here and all but threatened to rape me. I was automatically yours by right of spoils of battle. How has anything changed?"

"You're Queen again," Gage snapped. "I've returned full power to you. You're no longer anyone's spoils of battle."

Meriel's hands rose to a position of fisted defiance on her hips. "Then I ask you, as Queen of Tenua, to become my consort. We can be life mated on the morrow. I'll invite Dian and Torman to wed as well. It's past time he ask her and—"

"No, Meriel." Gage shoved an exasperated hand through his hair. "You know that's not the reason. I'm a bastard. I can't life mate a Queen."

"But you said before that only Teran and I know of that. Even King Falkan thinks you're Prince Bardwin's son. And that's royalty enough to please—"

"*I won't live a lie!*" he fiercely spat out. "For all purposes, you ask the same thing my mother did. And I won't do that, not for you or anyone. I have little honor left as it is. I won't compromise on that."

Hot color stole into Meriel's cheeks. "You're right, of course. I beg pardon for even suggesting such a thing. I-I just can't bear to lose you. I'll do almost anything to keep you with me." Her voice broke. Her head lowered.

Pain slashed through Gage. Ah, Gods, he couldn't bear to hurt her! Yet what other choice was there?

He covered the short distance between them. Pausing before her, Gage captured Meriel's face, cradling it between his two large hands.

"Meriel, look at me."

She lifted a tear-bright gaze. Bitter regret was carved into his handsome features. An aching gentleness gleamed in his compelling eyes. But, despite it all, there was no glimmer of a weakening in his resolve to leave.

Despair filled her. There was nothing more she could do. Nothing. She had fought so hard to win him, but in the end it had all been in vain. She was beaten at last.

The door slid open behind them. Meriel whirled around. It was Dian, with Kieran in her arms. At sight of his father, the little boy squirmed, fighting to get down.

"Papa. Want Papa!"

Meriel nodded at the question in Dian's eyes. The maidservant lowered Kieran to the floor, then quietly left the room.

With a joyful cry, the boy ran to his father. Gage hesitated but an instant, then bent and lifted his son up to him. "What do you want, lad?" his deep voice rumbled.

Kieran flung his two chubby little arms about Gage's neck. "Love you. Love my papa!"

Gage went still. His features twisted in a mask of anguish. He met Meriel's gaze.

"Don't leave us," she whispered. "Don't condemn Kieran to the same fate you had as a child. Let him grow up knowing his real father."

"Meriel, don't do this," Gage groaned.

"And why not?" A renewed, ruthless determination welled in her. If not for herself, she'd fight him for her son . . . *with every weapon at her disposal.* "We need you. We love you. The rest of the universe and what they think doesn't matter. *We* matter."

At her plea, something shattered inside Gage. All the pain, all the anger, all the barriers he'd built around his heart came tumbling down. It no longer mattered that he still wasn't worthy of her. The look of love, of unwavering confidence and trust shining in Meriel's deep violet eyes, was all the reassurance he needed.

He had finally come home.

As much as Gage still doubted his ability to be the man for her, if she truly needed him as husband and father, he'd be it no matter the consequences. It was an awesome, frightening responsibility, but, for the first time, Gage realized he was willing to face it. Not for himself, but for Meriel and Kieran. He just wasn't sure he knew how . . .

"Help me," Gage rasped in a voice harsh with pain. "I know only fighting, how to use people for what I can get from them. I don't . . . know how to trust . . . how to commit my heart and life to others. I need you to help me, teach me that, if you will."

Wild, exultant joy swelled in Meriel. "I'll always be there for you, whenever you need me. But never sell yourself short. You *do* know more than fighting. I couldn't have fallen in love with you otherwise. You know how to love, how to trust when you choose to. You know how to be tender and gentle. You're everything I've ever wanted in a man."

"Just as you are everything I've ever wanted in a woman, even when I didn't even know I wanted a woman like you," Gage whispered, his voice raw, trembling with emotion. "You are gentleness, compassion, and all things female, yet you've the heart and courage of a warrior as well."

"Have I now?" Meriel asked archly. "Well, that revelation, along with many others, was certainly a long time in coming." She took Kieran from his father and sent him toddling off in the direction of his toys on the balcony. Then she turned back to the tall blond man who awaited her. Fierce pride and longing filled her.

She strode over to once more stand before him. "We'll begin a new life, a new reign on Carcer. New laws, new customs will be necessary to ensure our adaptation to that harsh planet. And the first will be my right to wed the man I wish, no matter his bloodlines. My people will understand the need for a strong leader and mate over title and wealth. And since you're already the true father of my son and heir . . ."

Gage grinned. "You've got it all figured out, have you?"

Meriel smiled. "But of course. A Queen must be prepared for all eventualities. You know, quick, decisive, and never distraught or—"

"Enough," Gage chuckled, holding up a hand

to silence her reminder of his long-ago comment. "You've certainly changed from the shy, uncertain girl I first met—in every way."

"Not in every way," Meriel murmured, stepping close until they stood but a hairsbreadth apart. "I *always* wanted you, from the first moment I saw you."

He gathered her to him, pressing her against his full, hardened length. "Then have me you will, until you finally beg for mercy."

"And the stars will burn from the skies before that day rises," she exclaimed with gleeful satisfaction. "We Corba women are quite insatiable, you know."

"Indeed?" Gage drawled.

"Indeed," Meriel purred. Then, entwining her arms about his neck, she lifted on tiptoe to kiss her handsome tracker firmly and most possessively on the lips.

Dear Reader:

I hope you enjoyed *Firestar* and Gage Bardwin's story, which begins another futuristic trilogy. My next book in the new *Love Spell* line is *Demon Prince*, an April 1994 release. Set in a land of knights and ladies, magic and superstition, it is the tale of Aidan, firstborn son of the queen of Anacreon, and Breanne, a beautiful peasant girl. Conceived in an unholy union between his mother and, unbeknownst to Aidan, the necromancer Morloch, the young prince has grown up shunned by all due to his birthing curse of the evil eye. Renouncing his right to the throne, Aidan roams distant lands as a mercenary until the eve of his thirtieth birthday, when the queen requires he return home. His kindness in rescuing Breanne from a pack of outlaws sets them on an inevitable course that not only binds their lives, but their hearts, in a desperate battle to save Anacreon from the evil Morloch. But in the end will love be enough to free the tormented Aidan from the curse of the *Demon Prince?*

Please feel free to write me about any and all of my books at P.O. Box 62365, Colorado Springs, CO 80962. I truly enjoy hearing from you. For a reply and autographed, excerpted flyer of Demon Prince, please include a self-addressed, stamped, long or legal-size envelope. In the meanwhile— Happy Reading!

Kathleen Morgan

LOVE SPELL

THE MAGIC OF ROMANCE
PAST, PRESENT, AND FUTURE....

Dorchester Publishing Co., Inc., the leader in romantic fiction, is pleased to unveil its newest line— Love Spell. Every month, beginning in August 1993, Love Spell will publish one book in each of four categories:

1) *Timeswept Romance*—Modern-day heroines travel to the past to find the men who fulfill their hearts' desires.

2) *Futuristic Romance*—Love on distant worlds where passion is the lifeblood of every man and woman.

3) *Historical Romance*—Full of desire, adventure and intrigue, these stories will thrill readers everywhere.

4) *Contemporary Romance*—With novels by Lori Copeland, Heather Graham, and Jayne Ann Krentz, Love Spell's line of contemporary romance is first-rate.

Exploding with soaring passion and fiery sensuality, Love Spell romances are destined to take you to dazzling new heights of ecstasy.

Futuristic Romance

Journey to the distant future where love rules and passion is the lifeblood of every man and woman.

Heart's Lair by Kathleen Morgan. Although Karic is the finest male specimen Liane has ever seen, her job is not to admire his nude body, but to discover the lair where his rebellious followers hide. Never does Liane imagine that when the Cat Man escapes he will take her as his hostage— or that she will fulfill her wildest desires in his arms.

_3549-9 $4.50 US/$5.50 CAN

The Knowing Crystal by Kathleen Morgan. On a seemingly hopeless search for the Knowing Crystal, sheltered Alia has desperate need of help. Teran, with his warrior skills and raw strength, seems to be the answer to her prayers, but his rugged masculinity threatens Alia. Even though Teran is only a slave, Alia will learn in his powerful arms that love can break all bonds.

_3548-0 $4.50 US/$5.50 CAN